S ... d's m ... ere ac ... vi- de ... 973 cer- tai ... prosecuted for framing their victims, and some were found guilty.

Among those acquitted was Detective Constable Adam Acworth.

This is Adam's tale. The tale of an ex-public schoolboy who mingled with the aristocracy at the weekends and engaged in under-cover work disguised as a bulk buyer of drugs during the week. Who entered the world of the hippie and found himself forced to rethink his initial idealism about police-work. Working closely with Adam, Gordon Honeycombe has written a rivetting documentary novel which is one of the most challenging and readable books of the 1970's.

Also in Arrow by Gordon Honeycombe

Dragon Under the Hill

Gordon Honeycombe

ADAM'S TALE

ARROW BOOKS

ARROW BOOKS LTD
3 Fitzroy Square, London W1

An imprint of the Hutchinson Publishing Group

London Melbourne Sydney Auckland
Wellington Johannesburg Cape Town
and agencies throughout the world

First published by
Hutchinson & Co (Publishers) Ltd 1974
Arrow edition 1975

Made and printed in Great Britain
by The Anchor Press Ltd
Tiptree, Essex

ISBN 0 09 911120 9

This book is for all those who were there:
in Courts 1 and 8 at the Old Bailey
17 September–14 November 1973

CONTENTS

FOREWORD

by Gordon Honeycombe

I first heard about some of the matters revealed in this book soon after Adam was summonsed and suspended from police duties. We were having a meal in an Indian restaurant in Chelsea. At the time Adam was a neighbour of mine in Battersea and I'd known him for nine months.

'What a story,' I said. 'Why don't you write it down?'

'I can't,' he answered, saying he didn't have the ability.

'Do you want *me* to write it?' I asked.

'Yes. If you like,' he said.

His account of himself and his experiences, as contained in this book, is naturally subjective. It is also limited, as there were some things he could not tell me and other things I was not able to report. Nor have I ventured to deal in unsupported detail with scenes and matters in which he was not directly concerned.

Everything he told me has been checked and verified as far as possible with contemporary newspaper reports, diaries, transcripts, court papers and other documents.

The Salah trial, so called throughout the book, is properly speaking that of *Regina* v. *Salah and Others*, which took place at the Old Bailey, 7 September–13 October 1971. The Perjury trial, also referred to, is *Regina* v. *Kelaher and Others*, held at the Old Bailey, 17 September–14 November 1973.

Accounts of Adam's dealings with the Salahs are in general taken from the evidence that he and other members of the Drug Squad gave in the Salah trial. It should at all times be remembered that the Court of Appeal was later to quash the convictions of the Salah family, and the book should be read with that in mind.

The transcripts of the alleged taped telephone conversations (the intercepts), though not produced at the Salah trial, were given in evidence in court in the Perjury trial, and put before the jury, and the extracts printed in the book and the information obtained from them have been taken from the evidence in those proceedings. The extracts, which will be recognizable by the change to italics in the text, and the information, have been placed early on in the book rather than in the body of the Perjury trial at the end, so that a chronological account of events as Adam saw them may be given.

Some conversations involving Adam are necessarily imagined, though based on the characters concerned and on the occasion. All of the characters are real, though a few have been given fictional names.

Although this is a true story, it is not the whole truth. Several factors, mainly legal ones, prevented that from being told; and the story has inevitably been somewhat limited in that it gives only one man's view of events. There are other stories that would be worth the telling – Kelaher's, for instance, and that of the Salahs. But this is Adam's tale. Perhaps I should add that the views and opinions expressed in it are his and not necessarily mine. Like him, however, I still have a great admiration for the average policeman, whose battle is not only against the law-breakers, but also sometimes against the system of law itself.

Permission to quote from the song 'Woodstock', by Siquomb Publishing Corporation, has been given by Warner Bros Music Ltd.

Permission to quote from a radio bulletin has been given by the BBC.

The extracts from Adam's evidence and that of Nick Prichard are taken from the original shorthand notes of and are printed by the courtesy of Messrs. George Walpole and Co., Official Shorthand Writers to the Central Criminal Court.

Permission to quote extracts has been given by the following newspapers: the *Sunday Times*, the *Daily Telegraph*, the *Guardian* and Associated Newspapers (the *Daily Mail*).

The quotations at the head of each Part are all from Shakespeare's *Measure for Measure*.

ADAM'S TALE

PART ONE

They say best men are moulded out of faults,
And, for the most, become much more the better
For being a little bad.

I

I was sitting in Nick's Mini-Cooper S, parked in Bryanston Street, just before its junction with Great Cumberland Place, which led on my right past one side of the Cumberland Hotel into the vehicular free-for-all around Marble Arch. It was Wednesday, 14 October, 1970 – an unusually warm day, dry and hazily overcast. The trees in Hyde Park were beginning to shed their leaves.

From where I sat I could see the rear of the hotel, which backed onto the continuation of Bryanston Street. Its main entrance was out of sight around the corner. Another entrance opened onto Oxford Street itself.

Inside the hotel, in a restaurant called the Carvery, Francis Morland, a well-known sculptor, was having lunch with a young American, Robert Palacios. The previous week, on Monday the 5th, they had also lunched at the Cumberland, after which Nick Prichard and I had followed Morland, who rode about on a scooter, back to his house south of the River Thames in Barnes, in a road called Castelnau. Palacios had been tailed into the Marble Arch underground station and had slipped away in a tube on the Central Line going eastwards. This time Nick and I were going after *him*. Another car would tail Morland when he left the hotel.

We had reason to believe that Palacios was the one who was going to deliver the goods – a conclusion reached through information supplied by informants, through our own observations and investigations, and through the services of the intercept, the phone-tapping arrangement with the GPO that we found very useful. In this case Morland had never made any untoward telephone calls – but he had arranged to have lunch with Palacios again. On this second occasion Palacios brought a bird along with him. We never found out who she was, and she can't have been too attractive, for all I can remember now is that she was a blonde.

They little knew, as the two men and the girl chomped away in the Cumberland Carvery, that every mouthful was being observed from a table nearby by a cheery couple who were in fact police officers of the Drug Squad – namely, Detective Sergeant Bassett and Woman Detective Constable Morag McGibbon – while in the foyer, at the hotel entrances and in the streets, were eight other members of the Drug Squad, all suitably and more or less unobtrusively costumed, waiting for that lunch to come to an end.

There were in fact eleven of us in all on the job that day – about half the operational Drug Squad at that time.

It was the climax of many months of watching and waiting, mostly involving Morland, whose house at the time of our investigations would later be alleged by the prosecution at the Palacios trial to be the main distribution centre for an international drug-smuggling ring. In such a set-up, a dealer would arrange for drugs in bulk to be purchased abroad, brought into this country, and then split up and sold to various buyers. These buyers would re-sell their purchases to small-time buyers and pushers, who passed the stuff on at a fairly high price to pot-smoking customers in cafés, clubs, pubs, parks, on public transport and in public conveniences. Everyone involved in the movement of the merchandise made a profit, though I'm not sure that the customer did. A ton of hashish, for instance, could be bought in Kabul in Afghanistan for about £8,000. In Britain, sold by the ounce, it would fetch eventually over £800,000. That was just one consignment. In fact about fifty tons of hashish were brought into Britain every year and the annual turnover of this business in drugs was probably £50 million.

Morland must have been after a slice of that easy money.

He was one of the so-called idle rich, educated at a public school, well-placed in society, with a large house and a lovely wife, and celebrated friends. He was even acquainted with royalty. He was thirty-six, and as I've said a sculptor by profession. Perhaps his funds were running low. Anyway, he knew how to make himself idly richer. All that was required was some ready cash, some careful planning and a bit of schoolboy daring. Where he came across Palacios, I don't for certain know – it may have been in Morocco. But Palacios was apparently game for any adventure. He was a young American, quite wealthy. He was a fairly stocky chap, 5 feet 9 inches or so, with dark hair which was thinning, and about the same age as me – that is, twenty-seven. You would never have thought, just looking at them, that as he and Morland enjoyed their lunch in the Cumberland Hotel they were very probably finalizing arrangements to bring what would turn out to be the largest consignment of cannabis at that time into England.

I wondered what they were eating.

Feeling somewhat peckish myself – we had been hanging about for nearly two hours, since 12.30 – I thought of getting a sandwich from an Italian-type restaurant across the street. But I might be required at any moment, and I was on active duty, when you just didn't eat or drink.

I had filled in the time by watching the cars and the people go by, thinking of Sam and thinking that she wouldn't like to see me smoking (which I was doing) and listening to the car radio. As I could never be happy just sitting, I also wandered around outside the car for a bit, and strolled to the corner of the street to have a word with the DC (Detective Constable) on duty there. He had spent nearly all his time studying the travel posters in the windows of Thomas Cook.

From his position I could see the hotel entrance, where Nick was, dressed in his swinging gold-brown velvet suit, with dark glasses on his forehead, smoking and fidgeting, as if he had been stood up by a bird.

I was using *his* car and not mine, a beige Volkswagen, because his Mini was faster and more manœuvrable. And he wasn't driving it himself as, I think, he fancied the cloak-and-dagger bit of hovering in disguise in expensive hotels, keeping a close eye on the suspect. He was also, though only a DC like myself, in charge of the tailing of Palacios that day.

I was in the car, biting my nails, reading through the entries in my notebook and making them fit a song from *Die Fledermaus* which was now going strong on the car radio, when I glanced up and saw the DC on the corner blow his nose.

That was the signal. Palacios was leaving the hotel.

I got the car going and shot off around the corner into Great Cumberland Place, as a soprano on the radio sang in German: 'What a curious – Ha! Ha! Ha! – situation – Ha! Ha! Ha!'

I switched her off.

Nick had already disappeared in the crowds of shoppers.

I zipped in and out of the taxis outside the hotel and turned left into Oxford Street.

There was no sign of Morland or Palacios. But Nobby Pilcher, our DS (Detective Sergeant), was standing by a newspaper vendor near the hotel's other entrance, and as if he were brushing away a fly from his face pointed to his left along Oxford Street.

I couldn't follow. The traffic had jammed to a halt at some red lights. I swore and thumped the steering-wheel.

We were using signals because the use of our portable radios would have been too conspicuous in the street. But someone was able to broadcast: 'Palacios and the girl have crossed to the south side of Oxford Street. Passing C&A's. Proceeding east.'

The lights turned to green, and were again at red at the next intersection by the time I had extricated myself from a mass of London buses and into the right-hand lane.

We had no idea where they were going of course, and whether anything useful would result from our surveillance. If they had chosen to travel by the Underground, as Palacios had done before, my presence in the car would have been rendered pointless. Fortunately, they had gone for a walk.

I was held up again at the next intersection, where the traffic from Baker Street on my left poured into Oxford Street. This was lucky, as I caught a glimpse of Palacios and his bird entering Barclays Bank on the opposite corner. I had pulled over and stopped beside Selfridge's when the message confirming their whereabouts buzzed on the radio.

They were not in the bank for very long. When they came out they turned into North Audley Street, going south. This was not so lucky, as I was now on the wrong side of Oxford Street and had to do an illegal U-turn through six lanes of traffic before I could go after them.

So it went on. It was no simple matter following two people on foot through the prime shopping-district of London. I *couldn't* follow in fact. I was forced in other directions by One-Way signs and No Entry signs, by signs indicating No Right Turn, No Left Turn, or Turn Right or Go Straight On, and there were always adverse traffic-lights to contend with, not to mention bloody-minded taxi-drivers and pedestrians with a death-wish. As it was I didn't actually *see* Palacios and the girl again until they got to Haymarket – though I heard about them on my radio.

They walked down North Audley Street to Grosvenor Square; then along Brook Street, past Claridge's, to Bond Street; then, via Conduit Street, into Savile Row, where to everyone's amazement and some mirth, they went inside West End Central police station.

'They're complaining about being followed,' someone said.

We found out later that Palacios had gone there to report the loss of a passport. In fact he hadn't lost one, but was trying to get another.

I had parked in Savile Row, and when they left the police station and cut across into Regent Street, I had a job fighting my way out of and around one-way systems and into Regent Street after them.

I knew London fairly well. I had been with the Metropolitan Police for over six years, though mainly in the East End. But you could never keep up with the ever-changing traffic system or avoid its attendant congestion.

There was a bad moment when at the bottom of Regent Street Palacios and the bird disappeared into Piccadilly Circus Underground.

I thought I was out of the game now, and it seemed for some minutes that we had lost them altogether. That's it, I thought, by now nearing the Circus myself.

Then my radio crackled with glee: 'Got them. Now in Haymarket. On west side . . . Now crossing road.'

They had merely avoided all the pedestrian crossings around the Circus by going through the Underground concourse and emerging on the other side.

All eager again, I revved the Mini and stormed after them, about the Circus and into Haymarket. I was stopped at the next lights, went on, and then saw them ahead of me, on my left. I slowed down. They walked past the Haymarket Theatre, and vanished into the offices of American Express. One of the DCs on foot emerged from the crowd and followed them in.

This side of the street was lined with bus-stops, so I pulled across to the other side and parked by Her Majesty's Theatre. *Fiddler on the Roof* was showing there – 'Over 1500 performances', it said.

Nick came by me, wearing his glasses properly now. He strolled on down to the foot of the street, to the lights by New Zealand House.

Before long the happy couple reappeared – Palacios was laughing – and taking their lives in their hands, nipped across the road through the one-way torrent of traffic, and ran straight towards me.

Strewth! I said to myself as they went behind the Mini-Cooper, so close that Palacios bumped against it. I watched them in the driving-mirror, feeling pretty shifty, while they giggled together on the pavement. Then they moved off into a side street by the theatre – a No Entry for me. Again I was facing the wrong way.

For a moment I was nonplussed, then shot off down to the lights, which were against me, and as soon as I could roared right into Pall Mall, and right again into Lower Regent Street. And who should be walking towards me but the American dream-boy and his mate!

I had to go past them, then stopped. Where were they off to now? In a moment I knew. They headed over Pall Mall towards the Waterloo Steps which led down into The Mall.

They're off to Buckingham Palace, I thought. Whatever bloody next! And that's what other drivers must have thought as I reversed against the one-way flow of traffic, backing into Pall Mall, and spun off to my left, finding time to remark to an uncouth taxi-driver: 'Bollocks to you, you rude bastard!' before I steamed off down Pall Mall.

A smart left turn between Marlborough House and St James's Palace brought me, after another left, into The Mall.

Everything seemed to happen at once. Palacios and Company crossed the road in front of me and hailed a flounder (taxi-cab) going in the other direction towards Buckingham Palace. Nick came leaping down the steps, followed by another DC, and a third ran towards me along the pavement. They hammered on the passenger door, which I'd forgotten to unlock, and piled into the car. The DCs crushed into the back seat, swearing and blinding, and Nick fell into the seat beside me.

'Follow that cab!' he yelled.

'Tally-ho!' I responded as I did a massive U-turn in The Mall before zooming off in pursuit.

For some minutes after that, it was a straightforward tail – along Buckingham Palace Road, then across Belgravia by way of Eaton Square to Sloane Square. In between mystified exclamations from the back as to what was going on, and where we were heading, Nick was putting out messages on his radio about our route.

We hadn't gone all that far when the taxi swung out of Sloane Square into Holbein Place, and stopped outside a car-sales yard and office called Frank Dale & Stepsons, a very swish firm. Palacios and Miss X dismounted. He paid off the taxi, and the two of them went into the yard.

'What's he want in there?' Nick inquired.

'He's going to buy a Bentley,' I said. 'And use it to pick up the stuff.'

'Oh, yeah?'

We cruised past in the Mini-Cooper, and I pulled into a left turning, where the other three got out. I turned the car about, ready for a quick off, and waited.

Nearby were piles of rubbish, the result of the council workers' strike, which was now in its third week. On my left was a Church of England secondary school. Poor sods, I thought. What's all that education for? It never did much for me as such. All I had to show for it when I left Gordonstoun, aged eighteen and a half, were three O-Levels: geography, maths and woodwork. I left in March 1962, a month before Prince Charles came to Gordonstoun, and so missed him. However, I was to meet him later.

My two sisters, who are older than me, were at Benenden, where Princess Anne was at school.

Isn't it odd? I thought. Here am I, still a DC after six years with the police and nine months in the Drug Squad, with nothing achieved, and worse off than the suspect being tailed.

When he reappeared he did so in style. I could hardly believe it. He and the bird suddenly drove straight past me, down Holbein Place, in a magnificent maroon Rolls-Royce.

For a moment I sat and goggled. Then I rammed the car into gear and set off furiously after them.

At the street corner Nick and one of the DCs scrambled in. We lost the other one. Either he didn't notice who was driving the Rolls-Royce or was too far up the road. But we couldn't hang about, and shot off out into Royal Hospital Road and so down to the River and Chelsea Embankment.

The Rolls proceeded on its lordly way, unaware of the plebbish Mini pursuing it and of the noisy guessing-games that were going on inside it, alternating with exclamations of envy from Nick and entreaties to be sodomized from the DC. We worked out that the Rolls was a 1960 model, or thereabouts, and noted down its registration number – VBK 2.

Before long we had tailed it up to Earls Court, where the traffic was thick on the ground – this being the opening day of the Motor Show.

'He's going to Philbeach Gardens,' said Nick.

This was a street beyond the Exhibition Hall, on our left. We had both seen Palacios enter a hotel there the Monday before last.

'He's going to have it off with the bird.'

But he didn't. Instead of turning left, the Rolls-Royce swung right and into Nevern Square, where the girl got out. So did the DC in the back. Someone had to follow her. We learned later that she had merely walked into a block of flats there. Meanwhile the Rolls had returned to the main stream of traffic in Warwick Road, and almost immediately, at the intersection of Warwick and Cromwell Roads, turned left into the A4, the road to the west.

'Where the hell is he going?' Nick was getting fed up with all the dodging about and uncertainty. It was nearly half past three, and long past lunchtime.

The Rolls swept onto the Hammersmith flyover. It was fairly moving now, with us about a hundred yards behind.

'We ought to phone the office,' I said. The portable radios had only a range of a few miles and the others would probably have returned to the Yard by now.

'Tell them we're heading west.'

'Yeah,' said Nick.

He was slumped in the passenger seat, playing with a cigarette in his little thin-fingered hands. His long bushy hair was sticking out on all sides as usual, like a mane, and what with his slightness, his pale face, his dark glasses, flashy tie and crumpled velvet suit, you might have thought he was connected with drugs, but not on the side of the law. He was twenty-seven. Sometimes he had a moustache or beard to change his appearance, which he often did, as he was employed on a fair amount of undercover work, not only for the Drug Squad. Other departments, like the Flying Squad, might ask him to help them out. At one time he was the only buyer in the Yard – that is, he would visit people dealing in drugs and pretend to have an interest in purchasing some of the stuff – and on account of this thought himself to be quite important. I used to think quite a lot of him myself, until I found out he didn't think much of me. But we got on all right together out on a job.

Nick was married, and lived in West London, not far from Uxbridge. He'd been in the Drug Squad now for a year and a half.

'Hallo,' I said. 'He's pulled into a petrol station. He must be going somewhere.'

'Good thinking,' Nick remarked.

We were both silent as I drove past the station, a BP 24-hour-service one, and saw Palacios get out of the stationary Rolls.

'We'd better call up the Yard,' said Nick. 'Yeah – while he's filling her up. Pull in here.'

I drove into a side-road of shabby Victorian detached houses with small front gardens and Nick jumped out, keyed up to do the dramatic thing of bursting into a private house, waving his warrant card and asking to use the phone. Luckily the house he chose had a telephone and actually belonged to a retired policeman. He was out again in a few minutes. 'Okay,' he said. 'I've told them we're on the A4 heading west. Get going!'

I did so, just as the Rolls glided past the entrance to the side-road. We set off after it in the stream of speeding cars, down to the Hogarth roundabout where, instead of taking one of the westerly exits, Palacios went right around and back the way he had come.

We passed the petrol station again, going the other way.

'Arseholes,' said Nick. 'He must have spotted us.'

I thought so too. Why else after filling up with petrol would he double back towards London? The Mini-Cooper was not all that inconspicuous – it was blue with a white top – and naturally, as the Rolls figured so much in our minds and our forward view, it seemed the Mini must in turn impinge on Palacios's notice.

This idea was strengthened when the Rolls turned off the Great West Road, went under the Hammersmith flyover, crossed the River at Hammersmith Bridge and drove down Castelnau.

'Bloody hell,' I commented. 'He's going to Morland's place.'

But he didn't. He drove straight past it, past the private car park where we had sat in cars most of the previous week observing the comings and goings of Morland and his mates.

'Jesus!' said Nick. 'What's he up to, for Christ's sake?'

There was no answer to that. There was no answer in fact until the following day. But eventually it became clear that Palacios was oblivious of the Mini on his tail and up to something unusual. So it seemed to me. But Nick had reservations about continuing with the job of tailing the Rolls.

While we were arguing, the Mini was held up at the lights on Barnes Common and Palacios pulled away.

'We're going to lose him anyway,' said Nick.

'No, we're not!' I said, and when I could I raced the car across the Common and over a railway bridge, from where we saw the Rolls-Royce slipping over Richmond Road and into Roehampton Lane.

As we approached the crossroads, mostly on the centre white line, with me shouting at other cars: 'Get out of the way!' and 'Piss off, the lot of you!' the lights there changed to red.

'Breathe in!' I said, and with hooter blaring and wheels screeching, gave a few other drivers attacks of angina as the Mini jumped the lights and scooted up the Lane.

'Wow-ee!' I exclaimed. 'How was that? Do I pass the test?'

That bit of excitement cheered both of us up, and after Nick had recovered and lit another cigarette, we discussed the matter more amiably – the discussion being concluded when at the end of the long wide sweep of Roehampton Lane, at a major intersection, the Rolls turned right, in the direction of a signpost saying 'A3 – Guildford – Portsmouth'.

'Portsmouth!' I said. 'Hey! He's going to the coast. Palacios has a boat. Remember? Could be on the south coast.'

'Yeah. Maybe,' said Nick, relaxing as I was, now that we were on the open highway, with the chase at last given some significance.

'All right. Let's follow him. Bugger it.'

2

Our immediate concern as we whizzed along the Kingston bypass was to determine whether or not he would cross the Metropolitan police force boundary into the area covered by the Surrey police. There was not much doubt in our minds that he would. So when we found ourselves driving past Sandown Park racecourse into Esher – a few miles from the police boundary – we were all geared up for some quick action when we got to the police station at the end of the High Street.

We were in and out of it, flashing warrant cards, leaping through the front office into the Communications Room, making a terse phone-call to Nobby in our office, in a couple of minutes. What they thought of our intrusion and appearance – I was pretty casually dressed and long-haired myself – I've no idea. But then we were off again, with Nick driving now. He went like the clappers after the vanished Rolls-Royce, doing up to 100 mph. Fortunately, no Gestapo (traffic-cops) were around to delay our progress.

The Esher halt was delay enough. But it was a chance we had to take. We had to report that we were leaving the Metropolitan area. But there were some anxious moments as we raced along the two-lane road – until the maroon beam-end of the Rolls hove in sight on the other side of Cobham.

We settled down behind it, with two other cars between it and us.

'Christ! Bloody hell!' said Nick.

I asked him what was the matter.

'We're almost out of petrol!'

He swore further and began to complain about my eyesight.

I gave as good as I got, said he'd been slack coming on duty with a half-empty tank, and reminded him that it was his car.

'Keep your eyes peeled for a petrol station!' he said.

'There's one about three miles further on – the other side of Ripley.'

'How do you know?'

'I've been this way before.'

If he had questioned me further, I would have told him that an uncle of mine lived nearby – nothing more, as he might have made a scornful remark if I'd said that this uncle was a Rear Admiral. He was my mother's brother. He lived in West Clandon, a few miles from Ripley, and he died two years later, in 1972. I also had another uncle in the Navy – he was married to my father's sister.

The petrol station was just before a roundabout on the hill-top south of Ripley village.

Nick had the car filled up and collected the Green Shield stamps, while I worked out that over on the right – six miles away as the crow flies – was the village of Chobham where I was born. That was during the War, in 1943. We lived there until I was eleven. It seemed a long time ago.

Minutes later we were belting along the dual carriageway that led to the outskirts of Guildford, where the by-pass took us right about the town through various junctions by any of which the Rolls could have left the A3. Signs to other towns and other main roads abounded, and I felt we had really made a balls-up this time. But we stuck to the signs that pointed the way to Portsmouth, with me peering ahead as Nick negotiated the curves and roundabouts of the carriageway as if it were a race-track.

On the left the modern mass of Guildford Cathedral caught my eye as we entered a huge left bend – at the other end of which was the speeding Rolls.

'Eureka!' I cried. 'Oh! Pardon my French! I have him. Yea. Forsooth.'

From then on it was a very enjoyable ride across the Sussex

Downs. Nick turned on the car radio. Sometimes we sang along with the pop-songs being put out by Terry Wogan.

'Which way are you going, Bill?' we chorused.

'Close to you!' we yelled, making faces at the distant Rolls, wondering whether Palacios was also tuned to Radio One.

I listened to the words of that song and thought of Sam, and became quite sentimental. 'Just like me, they long to be close to you. . . .' Things were going well with us then, despite my job. And whenever I could, I would go and see her. That was almost enough in itself – though not always.

We sped through the English countryside. All the woods were in colours of early autumn, and now and again I forgot I was with Prichard and that we were tailing a suspect to somewhere on the coast.

We reached the coast about three hours after leaving the Cumberland Hotel. With the misty sun now low in the west, the panorama to be had of Portsmouth from Portsdown Hill was quite impressive. But when we got into the city, which is actually on a large flat island and looks as if the Second World War has never ended, I remarked to Nick: 'What a grotty, dingy hole!' He had closed in on the Rolls, keeping only one car between us, and was trying to make sense of the many signs and the wriggling streets.

'Where the hell is he going?' said Nick.

The Rolls ploughed on, ignoring signs pointing to the City Centre, Southsea, the Dockyard, to where the *Victory*, Nelson's flagship, was on show. During the War, my father sometimes passed through Portsmouth. He was a Commander in the Royal Navy, in which he had served all his life, mostly on aircraft-carriers and frigates. He retired when I was eleven. People say I'm like him in appearance.

Suddenly, all that was left was one sign: 'IOW Car Ferry.'

'I say. We're off to the Isle of Wight!' I said in a humorous fashion. 'Oh, jolly good show! Lovely night for a sail – what?'

'The Isle of Wight! Jesus!' muttered Nick. 'We better have something to report at the end of this.'

'We will, we will,' I assured him.

'Have you been *here* before?' he asked.

'No, I haven't.'

'Do you have to book?' he fretted to himself. 'What happens

if we can't get on the ferry? Jesus! What a caper! And then what?'

What happened was that the Rolls-Royce came to a halt in the ferry car park, on the edge of the quay, alongside which was the high white superstructure of the ferry itself, with vehicles already trundling down the slipway, over a lowered ramp, and onto the open car-deck. It was about ten to six.

Palacios got out of the Rolls and trotted over to the ticket office. I left the Mini and followed him, and found myself standing behind him at the counter – pretending to be on another planet, yet straining to hear what he said.

'Return,' he said in his American voice. 'Oh. Yeah . . . A Rolls-Royce . . . No passengers. . . . How much is that?'

He was wearing a fawn polo-necked sweater and brown slacks. Being taller than him by a head I could see that he was going thin on top. He drummed his fingers on the counter. For a crazy moment I wanted to tap him on the shoulder, say: 'Excuse me, sir,' and tell him who I was.

'Thank you,' he said, handing over some pound notes before taking up his ticket. 'Could you tell me what time in the morning the ferry leaves Fishbourne to return to Portsmouth?'

The ticket clerk told him.

'Eight or nine? That's fine. Thank you.'

He brushed past me and went out.

'Return! Fishbourne!' I said, in a hurry. 'A Mini-Cooper S. One passenger. How much?' It came to about £3 10s. 0d.

Nick was impatiently waiting outside in the car. The Rolls had disappeared onto the ferry.

'For Pete's sake! The ferry goes in a couple of minutes!'

It left at six o'clock.

We were in fact the last car on, halting right behind the Rolls, and as we sat there, all keyed-up – bumper to bumper with Palacios – the ramp at the rear of the Mini lifted, arching itself up over us, and the ferry swiftly drew away from the quay and the land and we sailed off into the sunset.

The journey across the Solent to the Isle of Wight took three-quarters of an hour. The sea was calm, and the air was cold, and all the time it got darker.

We remained where we were, smoking cigarettes, unwinding, going over the afternoon's events, which seemed on recollection to become more and more fantastic – though we soon reduced them to basic policeman's prose for our notebooks, which we took the opportunity to bring up to date. This meant consulting the AA Book, as well as each other, so that our facts tallied.

'To be continued,' I said as I signed my name and rank.

Palacios didn't stir from his car. He just sat there, encased in his shining machine and thinking no doubt about *his* day, and the next day. We glanced at him occasionally – almost parentally. Familiarity was breeding a certain scorn.

'He must be as thick as two planks,' said Nick.

I agreed. It was verging on the incredible that after three hours of being followed he still hadn't connected the little Mini parked in the Haymarket, the Mini flitting in and out of his rear mirror, the Mini now stationed behind him, and drawn some unwelcome conclusions.

However, when we disembarked at Fishbourne, driving up a slope flooded with arc-lamps into the unknown island, it very soon seemed as if our suspect had at last become suspicious. For after turning left and taking a road to Ryde, he pulled into an Esso petrol-station.

'He's onto us,' said Nick, drawing in to a dark driveway, where we waited with the lights off. 'He'll carry on and check to see if we're following. You'll see.'

It seemed he was right. The Rolls set off again on the few miles to Ryde, drove into the town, and out again, and then, via a twisting route of badly surfaced secondary roads, made its way to Newport in the centre of the island.

Neither of us knew where we were or where we were going, and we stayed close to its tail-lights, all the while becoming more despondent and certain that Palacios was playing games, though he didn't try to shake us off or speed away.

In Newport he turned into a one-way street, lined on one side by a cinema, the Savoy, which was showing a Beatles double-bill of *Let It Be* and *The Yellow Submarine*. Opposite was a small car park. He pulled into it, and we drove on past, over a cross-roads where the lights were green, and stopped. Looking back, we got that sinking feeling when we saw him reverse out of the car park, come on towards the lights and us, and then turn right, away from us. As he did so, the lights went from amber to red.

That was it. We couldn't follow – the one-way street and the lights prevented that. In any event we were convinced now that he knew he was being tailed. Even so, we drove despairingly through the streets of the town, looking for him – just in case.

It was useless. The Rolls had vanished.

'Fuck it!' said Nick. 'We better report.'

It was nearly quarter to eight. We had been on the job for over seven hours, and were feeling pretty low when we barged into Newport police station, one of those modern, compact, bare and over-lit buildings, and revealed who we were.

But the working atmosphere soon made us more realistic and we realized that as the Rolls must still be on the island, there was a remote chance that one of the island policemen on his rounds might see it. The Chief Inspector was very helpful. He put a message out to the island police force asking them to try to locate the Rolls. While this was being done, Nick telephoned London, where Nobby, who was still on duty, was sympathetic about our efforts and suggested we stayed overnight.

This we had already planned to do, and I found out from the Desk Sergeant where we could get accommodation and have a decent meal. Then it was off to the Wheatsheaf Hotel, a small two-star place in the market square. There we were given a room with twin beds on the ground floor, and having booked in, drove around the corner to Calvert's Hotel, which the Sergeant had recommended for a meal. By now we were more thirsty than hungry, and first had a few drinks in the bar.

I took the opportunity to ring up Sam from a public telephone in the hall, stuffing two of the new five-pence pieces into the shilling slot of the coin-box when the beeps began.

'Hallo?'

There were five other girls in the flat, but I knew her voice.

'Hallo, sexy,' I said.

'Oh. It's you.'

'Who else? I *am* the only man in your life, aren't I?'

'No, you're not. You're one of many. Men are always ringing me up.'

'Brothers, uncles, cousins. . . .'

'Where are you?'

'Can't say. We're onto a big one. Tell you tomorrow though.'

'Why can't you say? It can't be *that* important.'

'Can.'

'Oh, Buzz – as if it mattered. The phone's not tapped.'

'I wouldn't be too sure of that, miss. We've 'ad a few cases recently of pretty young ladies like yourself, miss, bein' rung up by saucy gentlemen who just wants to say they loves 'em.'

She laughed. I could picture her with both hands on the receiver, propped against the wall of the hall. I could just hear the traffic outside the flat, and a radio was on.

'How are you? Taking it easy tonight?'

'Just having a coffee. Trying to do some frantic last minute revision. I don't know a thing.'

'You'll pass.' The next day she had the practical exam of her Finals before qualifying as an SRN (State Registered Nurse).

'Well . . . I hope so.'

'It's time you started working for a living.'

'Working! What do you think I've been doing for the last three years?'

'Waiting for the right man. Here I am.'

'Where?'

'In N—. Crafty! You're trying to take advantage.'

'Me! *I* was the one who was –' The beeps started.

'Love you!' I said. 'Good luck tomorrow.'

'Love you too. Thanks.'

'Night-night. Bye.'

'Bye, love. When will I see you – ?'

The phone clicked, and the dialling tone came on. I gazed bemusedly at the mouth-piece, my mind still full of her.

Samantha Maria Joubert was twenty-one. She was tall and slim, with very thick, lovely, long blonde hair, which she kept very clean and tidy. Her skin was honey-brown, except where her bikini had been, and when she was back in Africa, where her home was, she tanned even darker in the sun, and her hair became golden. Her eyes were hazel. She wore virtually no make-up, which I approved of, and wasn't one to worry about getting her hands dirty or her clothes. This would happen when we visited my elder brother, Bill, on one of the farms which he managed in Berkshire. She liked to be active, as I did, and at harvest-time she helped as much as any man, with tractor-driving, and rabbit-shooting and inoculating cows. London she really detested, and hated living there. This wasn't surprising, since she had been brought up and lived about as far out in the wilds as you can go. This was in Tanzania, where her father had a farm of 1,000 acres near Mount Kilimanjaro. She had come to England to train as a nurse, at the Middlesex Hospital in London.

I had known her now for a year and a half – we met at a party near Lord's Cricket Ground – and I was more consistently fond of her, loved her more, than any other girl. To me she was like a princess – which she was. For although her family, exiled from Poland before the First World War, had altered their name and didn't use titles, they were related to the Polish royal family. She could have called herself a princess if she had wished.

I put the receiver back on its rest and rejoined Nick.

We went into the dining-room, where in high-backed settles we sat facing each other across the table, feeling a lot more cheerful and eager for our long-delayed lunch, dinner and tea. The losing of Palacios didn't seem so bad now, and there was some novelty in being where we were, especially with food at last in sight.

We both had tomato soup, with rolls and butter, then large mixed grills, with a bottle of red wine, followed by apple-pie and cream, and brandies with our coffee. It would all go on our expenses.

Conversation was minimal to start with, until the coffee stage was reached, when we began talking shop as we always did if not being jokey or abusive.

Our subject was the Salahs.

There were five of them – father, mother, son and daughter, and daughter-in-law. The father, Mohammed Salah, came from Pakistan. His wife was English, as was his daughter-in-law. They were an unusual family, and by accident their deeds would eventually have a fatal effect on our lives, and their downfall would eventually bring about ours.

At the time they were not so important to us or so involving as Palacios and Morland. But they had already engaged our professional attentions.

Nobby had mentioned on the phone to Nick that the intercept on the Salahs – at Stoke Poges – would be operational in a fortnight. The intercept, or as Nobby put it, the Tinker-Bell, was a bit previous as we didn't expect the Salahs to do anything interesting until February the following year. But some useful information might be gleaned about their contacts and activities.

In my opinion, the intercept, or phone-tap, was and is an invaluable aid in the detection and prevention of crime. Prevention is as much the policeman's job as conviction after an offence, and in our case prevention was of utmost importance in the cure of drug offences.

In 1966 there were to my mind unrealistic complaints when it leaked out that in one year the Special Branch had intercepts on 12,000 phones. This didn't of course include the phones that were being tapped by the Secret Service, the Foreign Office, the Customs people, and so on. However, no intercept was arranged without very good reason. And each one had to go through a rigid procedure of application. A Detective Inspector applied to his Chief Superintendent, who applied to his Commander, who applied to an Assistant Commissioner, who applied to the Home Office, where the application had to be personally approved by the Home Secretary himself. Many more intercepts were applied for than granted. In London at that time, about seventy phones were tapped every day, out of a population of five or six million – among whom must have been thousands planning criminal actions. The question was: were these persons to be allowed to carry out their nefarious designs and rob, maim, murder, destroy, deprave and corrupt before they could be apprehended? Without such intercepts that were granted, there's no doubt that the rule of Law would have been much less effective.

Indeed, whenever I passed the intercept centre in those days – near Chelsea Barracks – I wished it well, as any policeman would do.

Intercepts were a follow-up. The beginning of an investigation often arose from information received from informants – without whom we would have got very few convictions, most of which were the result of a tip-off of some sort or other.

Informants – we called them snouts – had initially pointed us in the direction of Morland and the Salahs. Their pieces of information were rewarded by favourable statements on their behalf in court, by cash payments (of up to £100), or by some pretended sympathy for the plight of the petty offender.

Most of our informants had been carefully cultivated by our DS, Nobby Pilcher. Nick also had some useful contacts. In our line of business it was just about the only way to get at the distributing organizations. Every month we put away individuals who were in possession of drugs. But we were really after the major suppliers of drugs, the dealers. So we made ourselves agreeable to our informants, bought them drinks, and put it down to expenses. All our meetings with them naturally had to be carried out in a clandestine manner, for our sakes as well as theirs.

It was the arrest of a runner, or peddler of drugs in the streets, that really put us on the trail of the Salahs. This was in July 1970. He turned informant, and when he appeared in court he was fined.

His information was coincidentally and almost immediately confirmed and much expanded by a telex message from the States of Jersey police.

It was received in the Yard at 23.26 hours on Thursday, 23 July, and gave details of the Salahs and their activities. The States of Jersey police must have had a very good snout, or perhaps the Salahs thought they could talk more freely in Jersey. Anyway, the message ended by saying the family were returning to England on 24 July.

We already knew a little about the Salahs. The prosecution at the Salah trial would later make a lot of allegations about them. It was alleged, for instance, that sometime at the beginning of 1970 the Salahs bought a motor caravan called a Highwayman, which was later fitted with a false floor; that in the spring of that year the father, Mohammed Salah, went to Lahore in West Pakistan and bought from a relative 900 lbs of cannabis resin; that the mother, Kathleen, together with her son, John, and daughter, Janet, who were both in their twenties, then left England in the Highwayman and drove through Europe to Pakistan; that Mohammed and John returned to England by air in May, while mother and daughter returned by road; that the cannabis was sold for about £120,000 and that £30,000 was paid into a Jersey bank.

They already had an account in Jersey in which £63,000 had

been deposited in January. Very sensibly they later decided to invest some of their money in two houses, one at Ascot, and the other at Langley near Slough.

It was also said at the trial that John Salah had been convicted for possessing cannabis in 1968.

He was now twenty-six. His wife, Kathy, was twenty-two. His mother, Kathleen, was the boss of the family. She was about fifty, English like Kathy, and Birmingham-born. Mohammed, who was fifty-nine, had come to England before the War, built up a clothing and warehouse business in Birmingham and sold out in 1967 for a large sum. He was now retired. The daughter, Janet, was twenty-four and something of a dusky beauty – quite fanciable in fact.

That was the Salah family; and in the summer of 1970 they were all living in a flat in a large and rambling house called The Meads, in Park Road, Stoke Poges.

The house, like others in the once salubrious area, was going seedily downhill. It was set back from the road, partly screened by a high hedge, a fence, untidy trees and a tangled shrubbery.

On a certain, cool grey summer evening, Nick and I, garbed in tie-and-dye shirts and jeans, drove openly up to the house, parked the car, went to the side door, and rang the bell to the Salahs' flat.

I left it to Nick, who was more experienced at this kind of play-acting, to do the talking.

What follows is word for word what I told the court at the Salah trial, in answer to questions put to me by the prosecution.[1]

Question: On Monday, 27 July 1970, with the last witness, D C Prichard, did you go to The Meads, Park Road, Stoke Poges? – Answer: I did. Yes.

Q: At about what time did you get to the premises? – A: At about 7 p.m.

Q: Did you go to the door? – A: Yes.

Q: After either ringing or knocking, was the door answered by somebody? – A: Yes.

1. Adam was one of the police witnesses for the prosecution at the trial. His evidence was largely based on notes in his police pocketbook, from which he was allowed to read aloud. These notes coincided in nearly every detail with what he wrote in his statement for the purposes of the trial. Much of what he said in court was denied by the Salahs. – G.H.

Q: Who was that? – A: John Salah. . . .

Q: What conversation took place? – A: DC Prichard talked to John Salah and said: 'Can we talk to you?' John said: 'Sure. Come in.'

Q: Did you go in? – A: We did go in. Yes.

Q: Where did you go? – A: We went up some stairs into a living-room.

Q: Who did you see there? – A: There was Mrs Salah, Mr Mohammed Salah, and Kathleen Muriel Salah.

Q: What happened then? – A: DC Prichard said: 'A mutual friend has suggested that I come and talk to you. He says you may be able to help us.' John Salah said: 'Look, man – come straight to the point. Are you after some hash?' DC Prichard said: 'Yeah. But I did not want to say anything in front of everybody.' John Salah said: 'Don't worry. We all know about it. We all work together.' DC Prichard said: 'I have contacts in the States who have put £30,000 at my aisposal. Can we do any business together?' Mohammed Salah said: 'No, we can't. You know it is all spoken for.' DC Prichard said: 'Are you in a position to supply this sort of amount?' Mohammed Salah said: 'Yes. But not at the moment. We must honour obligations.' John Salah said: 'Look – if you are seriously interested, will your people wait?' DC Prichard said: 'Yes. There is no hustle on this. They are prepared to wait for a reasonable time.' John Salah said: 'We intend to return in January, and if you can place a sufficient order we will bring that back on top of what we have already decided upon.' DC Prichard said: 'Okay. Can we talk some sort of price?' Mrs Kathleen Ruth –

Q: That is the mother? – A: Yes.

Q: What did she say? – A: 'No. Don't discuss any price yet. We don't know how much per kilo we will have to pay for it.' DC Prichard said: 'That's fair enough. We will contact you at the end of January.' The mother said: 'No. Leave it until mid-February, because we cannot guarantee what the weather conditions will be like coming back.' DC Prichard said: 'Okay. That's agreed. I will contact you next year.'

Q: Then eventually did you leave the house? – A: Yes.

Q: What sort of time? – A: About 7.30.

We returned to the car and drove away – out into the road and out of sight of the house, when it was toe-down and go, all the way down to the cross-roads and then left. We met up with Nobby and Nigel Lilley, the other DC in our unit, and told them what had happened. Then we went to the nearest public-house for a welcome drink.

From that day on we kept the Salahs under constant observation, aided later by intercepts – waiting to see what and where their next move would be.

In the dining-room of Calvert's Hotel, Nick and I were having a laugh remembering our visit.

'We must send them a card at Christmas,' I said.

'Mr Prichard?' asked the waitress. She looked from me to Nick.

'Yeah?' he said.

'There's a call for you. The telephone in the hall.'

He was back in less than a minute.

'We're off again,' he said and grinned. 'They've found the Rolls. At Cowes.'

3

We reached Cowes about 10.30 p.m., reported to the police station there, and PC Donellan who had found the Rolls took us to where it was, a couple of hundred yards away. It was parked on a quay in Groves and Guttridge boatyard.

If it had been parked in a garage or under cover, the Rolls might never have been found. But there it was, a grand and beautiful sight to us, carelessly abandoned on the quay beside a slope of steps leading down to a pontoon on the water.

The yard was an extensive boatyard right in the middle of Cowes. The area was occupied by several huts, sheds and edifices like hangars, with the paraphernalia of boat-mending and boat-building all around, not to mention stranded motor-cruisers, sailing-boats and yachts upright in giant iron cradles, with their masts towering to the moon. It was a weird scene, though the music and chatter of a party going on in a yacht beside the quay, and the loquacious presence of PC Donellan, who was telling us about his own little boat, made everything more normal.

Once he had shown us where the Rolls was, he strolled off to continue on his beat.

We scouted around, keeping an eye on the car and the boats offshore, while trying to overhear the conversations of the merry-makers in the party and on the quay when they came and went. Of Palacios there was no sign at all.

Having re-established contact with the Rolls-Royce, we could not now let it out of our sight. However, there was no point in both of us keeping an eye on it – we had to get some sleep. So we decided to take the watch in turns. If anything happened while one of us was away, if Palacios returned and drove off again, the other could soon alert the Cowes and Newport police. We didn't think this was likely to occur, on account of the fact that I had heard Palacios ask about the times of the ferry's return to Portsmouth in the morning.

At 11.30 I left Nick hunched in the shadows of a shed, and speeded back to Newport. Fairly whacked I got to bed in the Wheatsheaf Hotel about 12.20.

An alarm clock startled me awake at 2 a.m. I returned thick-headed to Cowes and relieved Nick, who drove off to Newport. I settled down to wait and watch.

The moon was full in the south. Everything was in shades of grey-blue, with the shadows the deepest black. No lights showed. The party on the boat had ended. The only sound was the lapping of the tide as it ebbed.

At 4.45 a.m. I was suddenly aware that a light was shining dimly out on the water, coming from one of the boats moored not far away. Muffled sounds of movement within it could be quite clearly heard.

At 5 a.m. Nick joined me. We crouched at the corner of a repair shed, straining to see in the darkness. The moon had sunk out of sight. We told ourselves not to get too worked-up.

Fifteen minutes later the cabin-door on the boat, a catamaran, was opened and a man emerged. In the light from the cabin we could see a man who had to be Robert Palacios.

He started bringing boxes out of the cabin and putting them in a dinghy. He rowed to the shore and transferred the boxes to the boot of the Rolls. Then he rowed back to the catamaran and vanished into the cabin. There was a pause, and then about 5.55 a.m. he reappeared on deck with some more boxes which he also proceeded to load into the dinghy. Again he rowed to the quay, carried the boxes over the pontoon and up the steps, put them in the boot of the Rolls and returned to the boat. At about 6.40 a.m. he re-emerged from the cabin with more boxes, put them in the dinghy, appeared to secure the cabin-door, and switched off the light. For the third and final time he rowed to the shore. This time only one box was put in the boot, which now seemed to be full, and two boxes were placed on the back seat of the car.

At 7 a.m. Palacios climbed into the Rolls and drove away.

In the dawn light we followed him to Fishbourne, and saw him board the ferry, which left at eight o'clock for Portsmouth.

I don't know how many boxes were loaded in the Rolls – about nine or ten. They were large white cardboard boxes tied up with string, and we were pretty certain what was in them.

As we drove back from Fishbourne into Newport in the early morning sunshine, with Tony Blackburn doing his nut on the car radio and us joining in the choruses of *You can get it if you really want it*, and *Gasoline Alley Bread*, we were very wideawake and looking forward to ringing Nobby in London. It now seemed that nothing could or would go wrong.

'He's on his way!' I heard Nick say on the phone in the police station. 'Yeah. And he's loaded.' Then he gave Nobby all the details.

After that there was nothing to do but hang about until we got word that Palacios and his pals had been arrested. It would take the Rolls about two hours to reach the London area where our people would be waiting to shadow the car, which would hopefully proceed to Morland's address. In the meantime we went out and had a hearty breakfast.

Back in the station, we wandered about from the CID room to the front office and back again. Two of the DCs were discussing *Softly, Softly*, which had been on TV the night before, unaware of the really dramatic events of the night and the approaching denouement in London. We were still keeping the details of the importance of our investigation to ourselves.

It was not until lunchtime that the word came through.

First we heard that Palacios had been apprehended after making a call from a public telephone-booth. He threw the car-keys over a wall in an attempt to disassociate himself from the

Rolls-Royce, but one of our men saw him do this. On investigation the boxes in the boot and on the back seat were found to be full of cannabis. Then we heard that he and the Rolls had been taken to Morland's house, a search of which revealed some more cannabis. During this, two men arrived at the front door and walked into the Drug Squad's arms. The four men, and Morland's wife, were arrested.

Cock-a-hoop, Nick and I went with D C Bailey to the customs office at Cowes, and were taken out with one of their officers in a customs' launch to the blue-hulled catamaran – the *Letitia* of San Francisco. We clambered onto the stern of the boat, and I soon took the padlock off the cabin-door by means of a screwdriver from the launch. We crowded inside.

The interior of the catamaran was rather untidy, with a double bunk not properly made, and books and sailing equipment scattered about – so we didn't have to be too careful. There were bulk-holds on either side of the cabin. In the starboard hold was another bunk and also some shelves, on which were sheets and blankets. Among the sheets I found a block of cannabis, which weighed about a pound. On a shelf in the other bulk-hold a box containing about twenty blocks of cannabis was discovered. We also found the log-book, which gave the details of the *Letitia*'s journey from Morocco.

All this was just what we wanted as evidence, and there was a lot of jubilation on board the catamaran.

Having gone through it with a fine toothcomb, we left the boat about two o'clock, replacing the padlock as best we could, as we didn't want anyone else breaking in.

The air of jollity continued on the trip back to the Custom House and in the Gloster Hotel nearby where we all adjourned for a celebration lunch.

Nick had phoned Nobby, telling him what we'd found, and he had told us to bring everything back with us to London. When we told the customs officers this, they weren't at all pleased, and said everything on the boat, which had now been officially detained by them, was their property. Naturally, they were a bit sensitive about the London Drug Squad finding a boat-load of cannabis on their doorstep, and weren't too keen on losing the little they had got their hands on. The Customs and Excise people, who were long-established in search and detection, didn't care too much in general for our activities, regarding them as amateurish, interfering and fairly useless. So there was something of an argument – and as we were only DCs and couldn't blast their superior officers, we had to phone up London again and say that the customs people were being very stubborn and wouldn't release our evidence. Nobby got on to our Chief Superintendent, Mr Barnett, a very dour Scotsman. He phoned up the customs in London, told them we were going to take what we wanted, come what may, and that they could go and get stuffed. Somehow this worked.

The log-book, the block of cannabis, the box, documents about the boat and bills were handed over – though we had to sign a mass of forms for them – and having put them in our car, we said our farewells to the local law, and the customs, and drove away from Cowes. We called in at Newport police station to say our thank-yous before driving on to Fishbourne, where we got on the five o'clock ferry to Portsmouth feeling like kings.

But the greatest moment – when it really hit me on the way home – was after we had driven at a leisurely pace through Portsmouth up onto the Downs and into the ribbon development south of Horndean. On our left the sinking sun shone red through gathering mist. Inside the car the radio had started blaring out the *Sounds of the 70s*. It was six o'clock.

'Hey! We might have made the news,' I said. 'Switch over.'

'That'll be the day,' said Nick, and did as I suggested.

We listened as the BBC voice read brightly about the price of steel . . . about Government Ministers and Ministries . . . the collapse of a bridge in Melbourne . . . the hijacking of a Russian jet . . . the cancellation of Trudeau's visit to Russia. . . .

'There's nothing,' said Nick.

'*A police drug squad*,' said the radio, '*has seized three hundredweight*' – 'three hundred! Jesus!' said Nick – '*from a red Rolls-Royce*' – 'It was maroon!' – '*in southwest London. A Customs and Excise officer said the haul was worth a king's ransom, in terms of the number of cigarettes*' – 'What had *they* got to do with it?' – '*Scotland Yard officers tailed the car from London to Southampton*' – 'That's not right!' – '*and back again, before they stopped it*' – 'Who did?' – '*At Cowes, in the Isle of Wight, earlier in the day, customs officers and police, engaged on the same cannabis hunt,*' – 'It was later' – '*found between thirty and forty pounds of the drug in a yacht.*' – 'It's here, you bastards! In this car! We've got it! Us!' – '*are said to be helping the police with their inquiries. . . .*'

Nick carried on some more about the mistakes the news item contained and about the customs people getting in on the act and about the size of the consignment, of which we had had no clear idea, and then he shut up.

I was also silent. I had made no objection to his comments as I was not able to speak, having become all emotionally disturbed. I stared out of the window at the setting sun and I'm not ashamed to say that there were tears in my eyes.

What I had accomplished this day would please my parents very much when I told them, when they read of it in the papers. But the newspapers couldn't of course reveal the names of officers in the Drug Squad, not in association with any success.

'It was *us* they were talking about on the news,' said Prichard thoughtfully. 'Me, and you.'

'Yeah. . . .'

'It was on the news,' he repeated.

'Yep. . . .'

'It will be in the papers,' he went on. 'Headlines!'

'Yes,' I said. 'We're going to be famous.'

4

'You're what!' said Robert Palacios. '*You!* You got to be kidding.'

'We're police officers,' repeated Nick, taking off his sunglasses. 'You're coming with us to the charge room to be formally charged.'

'I thought you were going to *join* me in here. You don't look like the fuzz.'

'We're in the Drug Squad,' I added.

'Jesus,' said the American. 'The enemy in our midst.'

He came out of the cell, smoothing his thinning hair.

'Now, look,' he said. 'You look like nice guys. No rough stuff. Honest. I want to look good in court.'

'You will,' I said. 'Your mother won't recognize you.'

'Jeez,' he said. 'Aren't you London policemen wonderful!'

We were silently killing ourselves over the fact that he'd made no sign that he'd seen us before, as we guided him into the charge room of Cannon Row police station, where he had been taken after the arrest.

It was now half-past nine. Morland and the others had already been dealt with, and put away for the night. But Nobby had had to wait for our return with the evidence from the catamaran before Palacios could be charged. Also in the charge room were a uniformed Inspector and a Sergeant – respectively the Duty Officer and the Station Officer.

Nobby had told us that the immaculate Nigel Lilley, who was on a few days' leave and had heard about the arrests on the radio, had telephoned the office, full of envy and some annoyance that we had bust Morland & Co. while he, Nigel, was away. Our Detective Chief Inspector, Vic Kelaher, who had also been much involved with this job, was also away, in Paris, having discussions with the American Bureau of Narcotics.

Everyone in the charge room was laughing as we entered, but quickly assumed a serious aspect for the business in hand. It was almost like a party, with Palacios the lucky winner of the prizes neatly laid out on the desk. These included the box and the block of cannabis, and the log-book. Beside them was a large envelope, containing the arrested man's personal property, such as his watch, comb, cash, and car-keys, which had been taken from him earlier.

The Inspector sat behind the desk with the charge sheet in his hands. It had already been written out by Nobby, while Palacios was having his dabs (fingerprints) taken.

'Stand in front of the desk,' said the Inspector.

'Okay,' said Palacios, and saw the articles we had removed from his boat. He sighed.

Nick and I took up positions in front of him.

'Detective Constable Acworth and myself are police officers,' said Nick. 'Do you recognize us?'

'Recognize you?'

'Have you seen us before?' I asked.

'Well . . . What *is* this? A quiz?'

'Answer the question.'

'Was it at Buckingham Palace?'

'Don't try to be funny, Palacios,' said Nobby.

'We made a search of the catamaran, *Letitia*, moored at Cowes,' said Nick. 'On board we found these articles on the desk. Do you recognize them? Before you answer I must warn you that anything you do say will be taken down in writing and may be given in evidence.'

'Thanks. Yeah . . . It looks like now you've got it all . . . Congratulations.'

The Inspector then read out the precise details, date and place of the charge, also the regulations of the Dangerous Drugs Act, 1965, that had been contravened. He told Palacios that he would appear at Bow Street magistrates court the following morning. He then asked Palacios to check through the lists of personal property and property found elsewhere to see that they were correct, and sign his name where indicated. Nick and the Inspector added their signatures. Then I proudly wrote my name under Nick's in the box of 'Persons Charging'. I was interested to see that Palacios had described his occupation as 'pilot'.

Nobby beamed at me, looking like the man in the moon. He had already said what a grand job we had done. 'God bless you!' he had said. I wanted to tell him that if it hadn't been for my insistence Nick would never have followed the Rolls-Royce out of London and we would never have made our arrests. But I couldn't split on him like that, though it had been provoking when he kept saying 'I' not 'we' and acted as if he had made all the decisions.

'What happened to the *Letitia*?' asked Palacios.

'She's been seized by the customs,' I said.

'Oh, no. Not my boat. I put out a lot of bread on that boat. Ten grand. I really loved her.'

'You'll never see her again,' said Nick. 'They'll take the Rolls as well.'

'What! But I only bought her yesterday!'

'We know that,' I said.

'Jesus-Christ-Almighty! What a lousy deal.'

'Lock him up,' said the Inspector.

'You bring bad news,' muttered Palacios as we led him back to his cell.

'How did you know about the Rolls?' he asked as I opened the cell door. 'I mean – that I bought it yesterday?'

'We were there,' I said.

'You were. . . .' He still didn't understand.

'Go inside,' ordered Nick.

'We followed you from the Cumberland Hotel to the Isle of Wight,' I explained – casually.

'You followed me!' He looked at us both in amazement and sat down on the mattress-covered wooden boards that served as a bed.

We stood in the doorway and between us told him all about our journey.

He had had absolutely no idea that we were on his tail from the moment he left the Cumberland until we lost him in Newport. His expressions of astonishment multiplied as we described every move he had made. He couldn't believe that I had stood behind him in the ticket queue for the ferry, that we had parked behind him on board, that we had watched all his activities on the catamaran that morning. But it was our turn to be surprised when he revealed the motives for some of his movements. He was talking quite freely now.

'The A4,' he said. 'Oh, yeah. I pulled in to that filling-station to check on my direction. Not for some gas. The car was loaded. No – I'd taken the wrong road. So I had to double back to get on the A3.'

'Why did you make for Ryde?' I asked. 'Then Newport. Instead of going straight to Cowes?' I leaned against the wall.

'Did I? Oh, yeah. Well, I was looking for some action. I wasn't going to turn in that early. And I was really enjoying the drive. That Rolls-Royce –! Oh, shucks!'

'You stopped in a car park at Newport.'

'At Newport? Yeah. I went there as there was no scene going in Ryde. Would you believe it –? I thought I would take in a movie. There was a Beatles film showing in Newport. So I pulled into a car park by the cinema. Then I changed my mind.'

'You changed your mind?'

'That's right. I reckoned it was time I got back to my boat. Hadn't seen her for some days. Besides, I had to get my arse out of bed before dawn.'

He grinned at us. I felt sorry for him. He was a fairly affable bloke and had some style. And if he hadn't been so unobservant we wouldn't have had such a success.

'I guess I did a great job for you fellows,' he said. 'You owe me a lot.'

'Fuck you, Jack,' said Nick. 'We owe you nothing! But Morland may feel you owe *him* something. So watch it.'

'I was only doing a job.'

'That's what they all say,' I remarked. 'Blame it on Hitler. Ve vas only obeyink orders.'

'What will I get?' asked Palacios.

'What you deserve,' said Nick. 'And I won't be sorry.'

'Could be ten years,' I said.

'Yeah,' said Nick. 'But, if you cooperate, it might be a fine.'

'If you play your cards right. Ten years more likely.'

'I don't think I'd like that,' said Palacios, looking about the cold cell and at the bucket in the corner.

We were being deliberately nasty. There was a chance that someone like Palacios would become a prosecution witness to avoid a prison sentence.

'Come on. Let's go.' Nick jangled the keys. 'We can't hang about all night chatting to the accused.' He put on his dark glasses.

'See you,' I said to Palacios. 'In court.'

He stood up as we left the cell, trying to be nonchalant. He didn't want to be left alone.

'What time's breakfast?' he asked.

'What breakfast?' I answered. 'You expect to get fed?'

'Bread and water, man,' said Nick, and banged the door shut. He rammed in the bolts and turned the key in the lock.

I rang the doorbell loudly several times.

'Open up!' I called into the letter-box. 'This is a raid!'

Suddenly the door opened. It was Sam, and I flung my arms around her.

'Oh, Buzz –!' She couldn't say any more as my mouth was on hers. She struggled out of my grasp and lurched against the front door and shut it. 'People will see us.'

'I don't mind,' I said. She was wearing her usual off-duty gear, a shirt and jeans. In the bright light of the entrance hall I noticed now the sparkle in her eyes and her shiny forehead.

'You're pissed!' I cried.

'No, I'm not!' she retorted. 'But *you* are.'

'Charming! What a way to greet a national hero.'

'What hero? You're more like a randy gorilla.'

'Bloody charming! I'll show you. But first, you fabulous sexy beast – come here.'

'No,' she said and smiled.

'All right. . . .'

I approached her carefully, prepared for some resistance. But she responded very thoroughly. Her breath was sweet. She had evidently been drinking. A couple of sherries and she was away.

'Oh, Buzz,' she said softly. Then her voice altered. 'You smell a bit strong. Where *have* you been?'

'Haven't washed for two days,' I said.

'You'll have to have a bath,' she said. 'And your clothes – And your hair! It's filthy. Where have you been?'

'To the Yard. Just having a few drinks with Nobby and Nick, celebrating the greatest achievement of the Drug Squad since it was formed. Oh, yes! And all because of little Adam. Read all about it. Read all about it!' I cried, waving a folded *Evening Standard* in front of her nose.

'Come inside,' she said, being efficient. 'I'll make you a coffee, and put the hot water on for a bath. I'll have to boil a kettle for your hair. Come on.'

The flat was on the right of the main entrance hall. Its door was open, and we went inside, across the narrow hall where the telephone was and into the sitting-room. There, three of the girls, all nurses off-duty, were sprawled about in the sort of domestic chaos that only bachelor girls can create. The record-player was spinning out something from *Swan Lake.*

'Evening all,' I said. 'What a bloody sordid scene!'

'Hallo, Adam – Hi – Evening, copper,' they said, continuing with painting their nails, eating cheese and biscuits and sewing a strap on a bra. Sam went into the kitchen.

I remembered that the Finals of their SRN exams had been that day.

'How did it go? Did you pass?'

'It went. It's over. That's the main thing.'

'That's good,' I said, and added, seeing the empty glasses and a bottle: 'Hallo! You've been having a party.'

'Just the six of us,' said Caroline, her hair hidden under a bath-cap. 'Drowning our sorrows.'

'Where did you get the booze? Brandy!'

'It's duty-free,' said Sam, returning from the kitchen. 'And it's empty. Bunny's father brought it back from Germany. He's in the Air Force.'

'Where is she?'

'Gone to bed. So has Jane. It's after eleven, you know – and we're all a little bit tired.'

'How did *you* do, love?' I asked, putting my arm around her.

'I don't know. It wasn't too bad!' She started picking up empty coffee-cups and glasses. 'You can have your coffee after you've had a bath. Hair first.'

'But I haven't told you about the big adventure!'

'You can tell me in the bathroom.'

'You're not going to wash his hair for him again!' Linda's expression was suitably scornful.

'Why not? I like doing it,' Sam replied.

'And I like her doing it,' I said.

Sue and Caroline giggled. 'Whatever takes your fancy,' Caroline said.

'They're only jealous,' said Sam. 'Come on, lover.'

'Right. But here –! Read that!' I slapped the *Evening Standard* down on the table with its back page uppermost. 'That's me!'

'You?' queried Linda.

'What does it say?' asked Sue.

Caroline picked up the paper. ' "£50,000 drugs in ambushed Rolls".'

Sam looked at me inquiringly.

'I'll tell you in the bathroom,' I said, and I did, while she washed my hair – though the story echoed oddly with my head in the sink and was somewhat disjointed, being interrupted by my protests at the extremes of hot and cold water poured over me, by Sue bursting in and asking questions until chased out, and by the warming awareness of Sam's arms touching my bare back. She worked fast, and wasn't rough, and asked a few questions herself.

That bathroom was even more indescribable than the living-room. Umpteen coloured towels obscured the rails, door and chair. Toiletries and cosmetics were piled on shelves. Six tooth-brushes sprouted from mugs below the inadequate mirror that served them all. Stockings, panties, bras and God knows what hung from a system of clothes-lines above the bath. The walls were peeling. The door wouldn't lock. In the mornings that bathroom was hell.

The flat, on the ground floor, was on a corner of Gloucester Place, a very busy road. But its traffic couldn't compare at times with that in the flat. A kitchen and two bedrooms – four girls in one bedroom and two in the other – completed the accommodation. They couldn't afford any better and were each paying £4 18s. od. a week. It made the section house where I lived seem like the Savoy Hotel.

Sam left the bathroom while I had a bath – some liberties she wouldn't take or liked to be taken. She didn't mind too much what the other girls thought. But it was important to her that we respected each other.

After splashing about a bit and trying out a different soap on each limb, I dried myself quickly, combed my hair and emerged from the steam and chaos in a towel. I swaggered into the sitting-room with a hand upraised in greeting.

'Hallo, fans,' I said in an African accent.

'You Tarzan, me Caroline,' said Caroline trying to be flirtatious. 'Come and sit in my tree.'

'Oh, God,' said Linda. 'Another naked body! As if we didn't see enough of them all day.'

'Go and get dressed,' said Sam.

'But my clothes will make me pong again,' I protested.

'Can't have that,' said Linda.

'All right,' said Sam. 'Borrow my dressing-gown. Wear that.'

'Thank you very much,' I said in an Indian accent, and bowed out with several 'Salaams'.

When I returned, clad in Sam's long white towelling dressing-gown, the five of us sat in the glow of the red-hot bars of the electric fire, drinking cups of coffee. With Greig's *Piano Concerto* as background music I told the girls about all the action of the last two days.

Being informal with the girls was a situation I was used to, having visited Sam in similar circumstances in this and other flats shared by nurses during the eighteen months I had known her. In fact, I met her when she moved into a flat also occupied by a nurse I'd been going out with for over two years, Chris.

But this wasn't until Chris had been in America for some months. While she was there, I was somewhat at a loose end, waiting for her to come back. Then two of the other girls at the flat, in Notting Hill Gate, asked me to come to a party. This was really so that I could give all of them a lift there in my car – which I did, and so met the new girl in the flat, Sam. When Chris returned, Sam didn't want to get in the way and stopped seeing me. She also left the flat. But then the affair between Chris and myself folded up, and I made it my business to get back with Sam. However, she didn't really feel sure of me for some time, especially as I still saw Chris now and then, just as a friend, and took her to a dance at Christmas as Sam couldn't come. There was a big row. Then all of a sudden Sam had to have an operation – in the Middlesex Hospital where she was training to be a nurse. She was in bed in a ward there for two weeks. I went to see her every day. This impressed her, I think, and from that time on we saw a lot of each other. She spent her twenty-first with me on Dartmoor, literally on the moors. It was in May. We drove there – it was her idea – and on her actual birthday, after we'd laid out all her presents on a rock on top of a tor, she opened them one by one. I gave her a transistor radio. In the summer of 1970 we went on a proper holiday together for the first time. As she had never been to Scotland, she said she would like to go there. I agreed with this, and so we set off in my car, via the Lake District and the west of Scotland to the north, then down the east coast and back to London – all in a week. Before I went I told my parents, who objected considerably, as it was obvious we wouldn't be sleeping in separate bedrooms. This didn't help relations between Sam and my parents, and because of it, she always felt they slightly disapproved of her. I didn't, of course – on the contrary. I would see her every day if I could, or telephone if I couldn't, and whenever my duties and hers permitted, I would spend my time with her. She was more than a girl-friend. She was, I suppose, outside my family, the best friend I had.

'It's quite a story,' said Caroline.

'Thrilling,' said Sue. 'You must be very pleased.'

'What a clever boy you are!' said Linda. She was always being sarcastic. 'Will they give you a medal?'

Sam said nothing. She was sitting on the floor at my feet, and had said very little throughout my telling of the Rolls-Royce saga.

The other three girls now trekked off to bed, yawning and pleading tiredness and the ghastly prospect of getting up early in the morning. It was almost midnight. They were tactful about leaving us alone, even Linda, and drifted away without any meaningful remarks, just – 'Good night.'

Sam and I sat on in silence, after the piano concerto had come to an end in crashing semi-quavers, listening now to the lessening sounds of traffic outside.

I was a little disappointed that she hadn't been more excited about my success. Perhaps she was worried about her exam results.

'I bet you passed,' I said.

'What? Oh, I wasn't thinking about that,' she answered, and switched off the record-player. 'I was thinking about us.'

'What about us?'

'You like it in the Drug Squad, don't you?'

'Very much. You know that.'

'Yes. And this business with the Rolls-Royce is a feather in your cap.'

'I hope so.'

'Promotion?'

'Could be.'

Two years earlier, shortly after joining the CID, I had sat a written exam for promotion to Detective Sergeant and had got the pass-mark, 60 per cent. The next step would be an appearance before a selection board, for which one could be summoned at any time.

'Oh, darling,' she said leaning her head and an arm on my knee. 'I'm being very selfish. I really am very pleased for you.'

Actually, the problem was that she didn't like me being in the police force. Apart from the fact that it took up so much of my time, and interfered with my spare time, and might be dangerous, she didn't consider it to be a very decent profession, or the people in it to be very decent. I think myself that she was influenced in this by police behaviour in Africa. She was just anti the police. Perhaps it was because she also identified them in this country with London, which she didn't like at all. What was bothering her was that if I did particularly well in the

Drug Squad, there was less likelihood that I would leave. And this, though she never said so, was what she hoped I would do.

She once said, when we were at some police function: 'I could never marry a policeman.' 'But I'm a policeman,' I had said. 'That doesn't matter *now*,' she replied. 'For I don't intend getting married until I'm at least twenty-five. It doesn't too much matter what you are now, love. But anyway, I mightn't marry *you*.' 'You said you would.' 'No, I didn't – I said I might. But I might not. It won't be a policeman though,' she stated, and added: 'You won't still be one when I'm twenty-five. Will you?'

To that there was no answer. I didn't know then. There was a time, several times, when I thought of leaving. But once I'd joined the Drug Squad, I was never happier at my work.

'Sometimes you make me feel so guilty,' she said.

'Guilty?' I stopped stroking her hair.

'It's like . . . Well, you don't notice things so clearly as I.'

'You mean I'm stupid.'

'No. You're not. You're not. More . . . innocent.'

'Innocent! Blimey! I know a thing or two. You wouldn't believe some of the things I've seen and learned about in the last six years.'

'But you haven't *learned* from the experience,' she said, looking up at me.

'Yes, I have. I've learned a lot.'

She looked at me searchingly. I had become a little worried at her remarks, which seemed to suggest I was somehow not up to her standards – which I wasn't of course. My parents, however, considered I had matured a lot in recent months.

I leaned towards her. 'Are you making a complaint, madam?' I said, aware of her body pressed against my thigh.

She shook her golden head. 'No complaints. It's you that should be complaining. . . .'

'Me? Never! What about?'

'Well . . . Sometimes, I'm afraid I take advantage of you.'

I looked at her in amazement. 'You?'

'Yes.'

'*I* don't know – Women!' I said, with a dramatic flourish of my hands, which disarranged the dressing-gown and dislodged it from my legs.

'You're not wearing anything underneath,' she said accusingly.

'Oh, dear!' I said. 'What a disadvantage I'm at!'

She smiled. I bent down and kissed her nose.

'You wouldn't want to take advantage of me now?' I said and grinned. 'Would you?'

Half an hour later we went to bed – tired and happy, as the saying is. We were very quiet and didn't disturb the other three girls in the bedroom. Sam's bed, though only a single in a corner along the wall, was comfortable enough. I lay on the outside, and she lay against my back, with an arm around me.

'Night-night. Sleep well,' we whispered to each other in the dark.

'Congratulations!' she breathed in my ear. 'You really did very well.'

I think she was referring to the Rolls-Royce caper. I smiled to myself.

In the minute before I went to sleep, scenes from the tailing of the Rolls flashed triumphantly through my head. It had been a triumph, no doubt of that. It was also something more. It had been my greatest achievement in the police – even in my life. . . .

PART TWO

There is a kind of character in thy life
That to the observer doth thy history
Fully unfold.

5

Adam Buzzard Acworth is my full name. Sam, and most of my family friends, used to call me Buzz for short. Later, it was sometimes Buzz the Fuzz. I am 6 feet 1½ inches in height, and weigh 12 stone. My hair is brown; my eyes are dark blue; my complexion is fresh.

I was born, the youngest of four children, at Chobham in Surrey on 17 July 1943.

At an early age I was renowned for biting people, especially on their calves when they were least expecting it, like when they were having a meal. Of course there'd be a very large yell, for what to everyone else was no reason at all.

When I was young I used to be fairly round and tubby and have fair, curly hair.

Father: He was a chubby little fellow, unassuming, and affectionate, but also a powerful little chap.

Mother: Very powerful, and very restless.

Father: His nanny used to talk about him having 'ants in his pants'. He would never sit still.

Mother: This was his big problem. He didn't walk into a room. He fell in.

Father: He was a very active spirit. His interests were very much out of doors, to do with anything that moved or had action. He was for instance extraordinarily proficient on his tricycle. It had three wheels, but Adam only needed two. The first time he had a bicycle, I took him out on the lawn and said: 'Let's have a go,' and he got on it, and suddenly I heard him say: 'Dad! Look!' And there was Adam sitting absolutely upright on an entirely stationary cycle. He had, and has, an extraordinarily good sense of balance. He's also less frightened of danger than most people. Or maybe he is frightened, but doesn't show it.

Mother: He made less friends than the other children, probably because he was the fourth, and also because he was shy and unsure of himself. With visitors he was difficult, and self-conscious. He wouldn't hide from them. He'd want to be there, and be noticed, which couldn't be helped as he never sat still. But he used to say nothing. Fortunately, there was always plenty of company around. At one time there were twenty-three of the family in the village of Chobham – fifteen of them were children. If he wanted friends, he didn't need to look for them anywhere outside.

Father: I remember when we used to play croquet on our lawn. When the others weren't looking, this small boy would edge up to his ball, and a little foot would be put on top of the ball and remove it, so that it was in a better position to strike when it came to his turn.

Mother: Sometimes at croquet he would get really angry, and swing his mallet round and round him. The chances were he would then let go. So everybody fled from him as fast as they could. He never bore anyone any grudge however much he was punished – as he was, regularly. He was shut in his room, and spanked, and denied this and that. But nothing really made very much difference.

When my father retired – when I was eleven – we moved to a dairy-farm, with pigs and poultry, at Stanford-in-the-Vale, in Berkshire. I used to have a room in the attic where I played with my electric trains. Up to the age of fifteen if I'd been naughty and my parents got very annoyed, I used to come upstairs and shut myself in for as much as twenty-four hours.

Father: He was got at maybe too much when he was naughty – which he was, quite frequently. But once the row was over, it was forgotten. He never bore any resentment. He was amazing.

My mother used to try to coax me down for lunch or supper. But I refused, and might go without food for hours. I used to read – though I never cared for reading – or play with something, or just lie on my bed, possibly crying and being very selfish.

Being on the farm was very enjoyable as well as instructional, and it meant being out of doors, which I loved. I was frequently present when calves were born, and piglets, and saw them being delivered. This sometimes involved me helping out, by clearing out their mouths and putting them to their mother's teats. Also, I was present at the castration of pigs and bullocks and generally helped the vet by holding the beasts, though he didn't in fact let me do the cutting. Then there were the tractors. I've always enjoyed driving them, and anything to do with them, be it ploughing, harrowing, rolling, harvesting and the like.

After being at a day school, I went to a prep school, Frilsham House, where I didn't do very well. I was caned on two occasions. Once for breaking a light bulb in a pillow-fight in the dormitory. The reason for the other beating I can't remember. But this time it was administered with a miniature cricket bat autographed by the current England Test Team.

Then I went to Gordonstoun and found it very tough.

Father: Academically he didn't get on as well as we had hoped. There was always a struggle. Basically, he had great trouble with reading, and accordingly found it very difficult to learn because he couldn't read.

Mother: We're pretty certain that nowadays he would have been classed as having a certain amount of word blindness – dyslexia. He was tested for this, but they never actually used that word. If he had been at school now, he would have received much more sympathetic treatment and individual help. But in those days they were inclined to think it was laziness, which discouraged him and gave him quite a complex.

Father: In an unconscious way, I think, he knew it wasn't so much laziness – he just couldn't read. And when he wrote, he wrote words the wrong way round. He couldn't understand what was wrong – why people kept on at him. He felt that he was being got at unfairly, and had rages of frustration. But in time he learned to write properly and to read.

I enjoyed sports and I played all that were going. I was best at cricket, being very active in the field, and was renowned for spectacular catches in the deep and near the wicket. The only prize I ever won was for throwing the cricket-ball. I was in the First XI for three years as an all-rounder. In the spring term there was hockey. This I thoroughly enjoyed and made the hockey First XI for two years. In fact at the end of my school career I stayed on an extra term in order to play hockey. As for rugger – normally I was in the Second XV, in the scrum.

My nose has been broken three times. First at my prep school when I was skating on a lake. I fell, and landed on my nose. The next time was at Gordonstoun – when a big boy whom I'd been ribbing during a physics lesson thumped me one. The third time was much later, after a ball near Sevenoaks. About 2 a.m. four of us decided to have a swim in the pool of the local prep school. I dived in at the deep end and found it wasn't as deep as I had thought. My nose got bent on the bottom. Luckily I didn't concuss myself. But when I got out, covered from head to toe in blood, the two girls, who were both nurses, weren't too keen on coming to my rescue. I've had no after-effects at all, except that jokey remarks about my nose are sometimes made. In fact most females seem to think it's fairly distinguished.

With girls, to begin with, I was, however, somewhat backward. At Gordonstoun there was virtually no contact with them, and in the holidays very little, apart from female cousins. Most of my time I spent working on the farm. If I thought about girls at all I thought they were idle, childish and stupid. The only things I learned about them were picked up from other boys' stories. I suppose I could have been regarded as fairly naïve.

Mother: There is a very definite tendency in our families for late maturity, and in Adam's case this obviously applied. But Gordonstoun undoubtedly helped him to develop. He didn't enjoy it to start with. But he never made any fuss about going there, about being shoved in a night train, when he was thirteen, and going away 600 miles. We only visited the school twice in his five and a half years there – for his confirmation and in his last term. There was none of this visiting five times a term that goes on nowadays. He got by, enjoyed the expeditions and games.

The daily routine was getting up at seven o'clock in the morning, going for a run, generally in shorts and gym-shoes, and coming back for a warm shower then a cold shower. Then we dressed, and had a prep period until breakfast-time, which was at half-past eight. Classes started from about nine and went on till 1 p.m. when there was an hour for lunch. After lunch, two afternoons in the week were devoted to sports, and another to activities of various kinds. These were aimed at promoting self-reliance, initiative and leadership. I did life-saving, mainly in the sea. There was also sailing and mountain-climbing. Each term each class went on a three-day climbing expedition to somewhere like the Cairngorms, often in very bad weather, including blizzards. One would get to the top of a mountain and down again without seeing further than ten or fifteen yards. We very seldom, surprisingly, got into any difficulties. This was because the masters were experienced climbers themselves.

The headmaster, Mr Chew, had also been a mountaineer and in his time was a very good athlete and sportsman. Soon after I had passed my driving-test – my father taught me to drive – I was asked by Mr Chew to drive his car, to take him about and also people who visited the school. He asked me because I think he realized that I wasn't going to get particularly many O- or A-levels – if any. My three O-levels I got by the time I was seventeen, and the masters had more or less given up with me. After that, although I sat a number of exams each term the exams were on, I always failed the lot. This didn't worry me, and no one insisted that I should study, so even when I was supposed to be working I would go out shooting with one of the masters or do some driving for the Head.

I got on well with the masters – but perhaps they should have pushed me harder to pass my exams. As it was, in my last two years I managed to get away too easily with doing what I wanted, and not what I should have done. When I left school I hadn't the first clue what I was going to do.

My brother Bill, who's nine years older, was managing two farming estates of about 3,000 acres near Hungerford in Berkshire. I went and helped him for five months. What he was doing I would have liked to have done as well, that is, farming. But my father didn't think it such a good idea, having all one's eggs in one basket, for he and Bill were both farming already. Besides, although I had a look at the Agricultural College at Cirencester I didn't have enough O-levels to get in. Again, the family tradition of going into the Navy couldn't be followed, as I had even less A-level qualifications for that.

Mother: It was my suggestion that he joined the police. He toyed with the idea, then turned it down.

So my parents thought it would be a good idea if I went

abroad for a year to think things over. Father knew of someone in Toc H, and someone who had contacts with VSO (Voluntary Service Overseas). Through them I got a job as a games-master at a school in Pakistan, not far from Hyderabad.

I was nineteen, and had never been abroad before, apart from school and skiing trips. I had never been in a plane. My parents saw me off at London Airport, and I arrived in Karachi early on an August morning. Here I was met by the headmaster, a short, round, bald, moustached ex-colonel, who sweated profusely. He picked up provisions in a truck and we drove off into the desert.

Father: The first job he was given, the first night he got out there, was to keep awake and see which boys were stealing cameras and watches. He also went out and shot mad dogs that had rabies. It was a pretty difficult year.

The school was a boarding-school for the sons of well-off Pakistani businessmen and servicemen, supposedly run on the lines of an English public school, and aimed at getting the boys into the Services. We got one into the RAF while I was there, but he was thrown out after three months. Of the twenty masters, two were English. I stayed with one of them, a Mr Hurley. We were supposedly looked after by a Pakistani boy whose English cooking left something to be desired. Apart from supervising games, like cricket and hockey, sometimes in temperatures over 100, my job meant taking the boys on expeditions. They were never very keen on this, as they saw no purpose in it. They were much more keen on their book-work. After three months I got dysentery, and in four days lost two stone. The school doctor came and looked at me, but that was about all. I never met anyone outside the school, as the place was so isolated. In fact I became very lonely. I made no friends with the Pakistanis – I didn't trust them. You could spend all day trying to get them to tell the truth about what they were doing or what they had done. It was impossible. Occasionally, Mr Hurley and I would escape in his car, an old Peugeot, to Hyderabad for a drink. But as I was earning £7 10s 0d. a month – though admittedly this was pocket money – we didn't have many. Beer was 15s. a bottle. We had a couple and just came back.

But in the spring of 1963, in the vacation, the two of us and another young chap, a police cadet who had joined us, drove up to Lahore, then along through Rawalpindi and Peshawar to the Khyber Pass and the Afghanistan border. Unknowingly, we must have passed lorries laden with cannabis on its way to England.

At the end of the summer term Hurley gave in his notice, and I helped him drive back to England, via Iran, Turkey, Bulgaria, Yugoslavia, Germany and Belgium – along one of the routes drug-smugglers used to get their stuff to England. There were riots in Iran, and floods in Turkey, where Hurley got dysentery, and on the way there we had twenty-one punctures, which I had to repair in the heat of deserts. In the end I could do the repairs, though dripping with sweat, in ten minutes flat. It was quite a journey. At the end of it I had three baths, one after the other, to rub off all the dirt.

I returned in time for a cousin's twenty-first birthday party, which was in the village of Chobham. At this I felt very lost and confused, being with relatives and females once again, who all wanted to hear what I had done.

At home the next day the first question was – What was I going to do?

Mother: When he came back in July, he toyed again with the idea of joining the police. His father encouraged him.

Father: Having been in the Navy, I reckoned that the general set-up in the Forces was the sort of thing for Adam. With his lack of academic qualifications, however, he couldn't get into any of the three Services.

Mother: He could only have got into the ranks.

Father: But he could get into the police. It was very much a man's job. And we felt, I hope not smugly, that the police could do with some public school trained boys like Adam. We took a great deal of advice on this, as none of our relations had ever been in the police force.

Mother: We went to see Colonel Croft, who was head of the Cadets, and we went to see David Holdsworth who was at that time Deputy Chief Constable in Devizes. He advised us that if Adam wanted a career as such, he should enter the Metropolitan police, where he'd gain experience much faster. We talked it over with Adam, and one day he said: 'I think I will have a go.'

Father knew a chap in charge of recruiting and I went to see him in London, at the Recruiting Office in Borough High Street. I was not terribly keen, but I thought – Well, at least I can give it a try and see what happens.

There was an interview, a medical, and some written tests. Soon afterwards I was accepted.

On 20 January 1964, I reported to the police training college at Hendon.

6

'Good-bye,' said Sam, standing at the door of the flat in her dressing-gown. She gave me a kiss. 'See you tonight. Bye.'

I whisked out of the entrance hall, out of the house, into the early morning cold and the growing grinding row of the early morning rush-hour. It was just after eight o'clock. Some of the girls in the flat had got up at 7 a.m. to go on duty, and of course this meant that everyone had to get up, get dressed, and leap in and out of the bathroom and the kitchen, where there was only time and room for a coffee and bread and marmalade. Sam was on night-duty now. She had the day off, but would have to report to the hospital at 8 p.m.

I found my Volkswagen and manœuvred my way across town, through Bloomsbury to the Barbican, on the edge of which was Golden Lane and the section house where I lived.

This one was the ultimate of its sort, being a modern, five-storied building, with plenty of coloured glass about, and you had your own fair-sized carpeted room, with underfloor central heating, wash-basin, writing-desk and chairs, in addition to the usual bed, cupboard and chest of drawers.

A section house is home to bachelor coppers. Actually, it was more like a third-rate hotel – though the accommodation was free. You paid for your meals and contributed 10s. a month towards the cost of papers, magazines and TV hire. But the residents certainly didn't behave as they would at home. The place was known by them as the Sexual House. Not that there was much of that around. For one thing, girls were not allowed to enter coppers' rooms and had to be met in a glass-encased visitors' room by the entrance hall, where only exhibitionists would have had any fun. There was more talk than action about sex, and most of the action consisted of playing card-games, billiards, coming back drunk and puking, putting on records or the radio very loud, shouting and swearing, horseplay, and having rowdy games of football and cricket in the corridors, all as late as four in the morning.

Most of the 125 inmates were PCs straight from training, aged nineteen or twenty. At times they were extremely childish, noisy and thoughtless, acting as if they didn't care for anything or anyone at all, and as *they* were the Law, they weren't too concerned about breaking the regulations of the building. This went as far as thieving, which was made easy by the fact that none of the bedroom doors had locks. Thefts at the Golden Lane section house were fairly regular entries in local police station crime books.

Having parked the car, I dashed inside, ran up the stairs to the first floor and entered my room, 101. There I got rid of my tie-and-dye shirt and jeans, had a proper wash, shaved, and got dressed in a respectable dark suit, white shirt and tie, ready for my appearance at Bow Street magistrates court.

We always had to look like smart and sober citizens in court – it helped our image and pleased the judges. My long hair, down to my shoulders, of course ruined that illusion.

Downstairs, there was just time for a coffee and a slice of toast in the canteen, and a quick look at the newspapers that were laid out there. One or two of the spades behind the self-service counter were as shirty as usual, and as usual among the forty or so fuzz at their feed were one or two young uniformed sods with their personal radios on, making a hell of a noise with police calls and messages yakking away – which are the last things you want to hear when you're not on duty.

I grabbed some newspapers and parked myself in a quiet corner to study them.

I had just found what I was looking for in the *Daily Mail* when a young copper with his radio on came and sat near me.

'Turn that bloody thing off, for Christ's sake!' I said with my mouth full of toast.

He made some kind of protest, and I told him quite forcibly that I wasn't very interested in what was happening on his beat, and if he was, why wasn't he there?

As he was only a PC and couldn't tell what rank I was – though he could see I was older – he soon shut up and switched off his radio.

This increased the good feeling I'd had since returning to the section house that today I was not just a common DC – a feeling much justified by my perusal of the papers, which were saying that the drug haul was worth £200,000.

The *Daily Mail*'s story – 'Red Rolls in big drug raid' – was headed by a photo of the Rolls outside Cannon Row police station. It had several details I didn't know about – that Morland's sculptures were made of glass fibre and that he'd exhibited in West End galleries. It also said that Palacios's boat, the *Letitia*, had formerly been called the *San Giorgio*, and had been owned by an Italian yachtsman, who had recently entered the *Sunday Times* round-the-world race in another boat.

I opened the *Daily Express*. Later in the day I would take cuttings from all the papers about the Rolls-Royce story, after checking with the Warden. They would go into one of the desk drawers in my room, to be added to the only other cuttings I had, which were about an occasion, two years before, when I was shot at by some robbers.

'Hallo! Hallo! What's all this then? Going to cut them out for your scrapbook?'

It was Mike Edmans. He was a DS from the provinces, and one of the few fellows I was friendly with at Golden Lane.

'How's our hero?' he inquired. 'May I sit with you? Or do I have to ask the Commissioner first?'

He plonked his tray on the table and sat down beside me. Mike was a very genial fellow – very tall and dark, and somewhat crazy. He was always on the go and full of laughs.

'Oh,' I said. 'Have I been promoted already?'

'No. But Prichard has.' He hooted and shook with mirth and began to wolf his bacon and eggs.

I told him what I thought about Prichard's contribution to our success, and then answered Mike's questions about some of the details.

He said, through gulpings of tea and munchings of bread and butter, that the story had been on the television news last night and that all the lads had been talking about it. I had myself noticed that a card-playing quartet near us had been eyeing me

– one of them had even nodded. They were playing *Vingt-et-un*, and from the way cups, beer-bottles and ash trays littered their table looked as if they had been playing cards all night.

'Well – chalk that one up for the Drug Squad then,' said Mike. 'Very impressive. You'll now be telling your new boys how to do their job.'

He was referring to the fact that at the beginning of the week the Commissioner, Sir John Waldron, had, according to *The Times*, decided to increase our strength by moving in another Chief Superintendent and have two WDCs (Women Detective Constables) work full-time with the Squad. This was something of a laugh. Morag McGibbon had already been working with us on a full-time basis for some months. Another Chief Super was just a gesture. We did get another DC and a DS later, but what we really needed was another twenty men with the drive and ability of Nobby Pilcher.

I said: 'The only one who really knows the job back to front is Nobby.'

'What about Kelaher?'

'He knows the game,' I agreed. 'But Nobby *is* the Drug Squad. Got to go,' I added, finishing my coffee. 'See you.'

Mike I saw nearly every day at work. He was with Provincial Force inquiries at the Yard, in C9, right opposite our office.

I charged out of the section house, and drove through the height of the rush-hour via the Old Bailey and Ludgate Circus to the Embankment. I was supposed to be at the office at 9 a.m.

What I had said about Nobby being the Drug Squad now struck me as being a very true remark. This was what was so crazy about the organization, that most of the work that got the best results in drugs was done by a Chief Inspector and a Sergeant, helped out by Nick, Nigel and myself – us against all the villains in the London drug scene. At least that was how it seemed to us.

When I joined the squad at the beginning of the year, I was supposed to be working with a Sergeant and another DC. The Sergeant, who had been switched to us from another job, didn't seem to me to have the great dedication required for the drug side of police work. After several months I slowly slid over to Nobby's group, though this was never made official. Apart from these two groups of three, there was a group of four, and three other officers whose special task was to see to Heathrow Airport. Gatwick was outside the Metropolitan area. There were also two first-class sergeant-clerks, who were in charge of all the books and administration, and gash people who were now and then attached to us or borrowed. In overall charge of the office were two DIs (Detective Inspectors) who answered to two DCIs (Detective Chief Inspectors) – one of whom was Kelaher – and then to the Chief Superintendent, who had just been doubled. But as I said the most effective unit was Nobby's, and so I began to work with them.

The others in the office often called us the Whispering Squad, as we would invariably go into a huddle or into a corner to discuss our plans. This didn't please the others too much, as we generally wouldn't let them know what we were up to, and wouldn't answer their queries. I suppose it was partly because we were in competition with them. But mainly it was because they might repeat what they knew of our plans in places and to people they shouldn't. In short we didn't altogether trust them.

The Volkswagen went bombing along Whitehall, past Big Ben, about Parliament Square, past the House of Commons and Westminster Abbey, and then into Victoria Street. The October sunshine gave a lift to the buildings and brightened the day.

Pleased with myself as I was that morning, Mike's reminder of the addition of brass to our numbers was somehow dispiriting. It seemed like a move to pacify the politicians or the Press – who were trumpeting about the menace of drugs to society. We didn't want to be lumbered with the off-loading of senior officers who were waiting to pick up their pensions.

The Yard was fairly full of thick-skinned, thick-headed senior officers in cushy numbers, enjoying their perks after their exhausting, thankless and brutalizing years on the beat as a PC and DC. I couldn't really blame them. Dealing with the dregs of humanity would only improve a saint. Moreover, these tired old sods very probably didn't have the specialized knowledge required or care much for their new appointments. How could they? – when they knew that in a year or so they'd be posted somewhere else, or promoted.

This applied to everyone of course. No one was supposed to

remain in the same place doing the same job for too long. The maxim was – two years and out. This wasn't strictly maintained. Nobby had been for five years with the Drug Squad for instance. But as it took about a year to pick up a new job, no one was fully effective for very long. Naturally all this moving about bred a certain instability, and could lead to apathetic indifference. It really was a very strange system. The idea behind it was to prevent police officers becoming too familiar to and with the locals, and to prevent them becoming corrupt.

Apart from all this, however, my main reason for feeling somewhat cynical was the recollection that in any event drugs weren't all that important in the Yard, for we were dealing with a non-statistical crime.

When a crime was reported to the police it got recorded in a crime book – black ink for alleged offences, and red for arrests. It was also classified. Theft was 'Theft'; rape was 'Rape' and so on. A drug offence however went in as 'Not recorded as a crime'. The reason for this was that no one complained about or made allegations about *drugs*, as only those people mixed up in them or actually taking drugs came into contact with the stuff, and generally they wouldn't inform on each other. Even if one of them, or a member of the public, said that at a certain address there was some pot, this would be regarded as information, not as an alleged offence, and would not go into the crime book. Drug offences were non-statistical, and therefore the powers-that-be weren't all that interested in them, though the Press had made it an issue. If it hadn't been for the Whispering Squad, Customs and Excise would have had it all their own way. But it was we who made the headlines; and, though I say so myself, without us the Drug Squad would only have been a name, not a force to be reckoned with.

New Scotland Yard is housed in two great blocks of glass and concrete at the junction of Broadway with Victoria Street, not far from Westminster Abbey. I drove boldly up to the entrance of the underground car park and waved a round red pass at the man there. He grinned, and I drove on down.

The car park was vast. Not all the vehicles there, however, were actively engaged on police business. Most of those that were belonged to the Flying Squad – or Sweeney Todd as

Nobby called them. Some were available for general use by each office in the Yard. But also there were senior officers' cars, normally chauffeur-driven, and many private cars belonging to civil servants, who outnumbered the CID men.

It was typical that because of this there wasn't enough room for the cars of the officers on duty – which inevitably led to petty infringements. For either you broke the law by leaving your car at a parking-meter, unavoidably getting a parking ticket – which could be squared up if you wrote a report out – or by some fiddle you managed to get hold of an official pass. This is how I had got in. The pass I had used was one we had, unofficially, in the office. Sometimes we had three, and by chopping and changing around we could get up to six cars in the car park – all against the regulations.

I took the lift to C 1 on the second floor of the Victoria Block, a long eight-storied building, divided by corridors running end to end, with offices on either side.

Our office, overlooking Victoria Street, was one of the severely functional sort, with strip lighting that emphasized the stark angles of office equipment and the general untidiness of the desk-tops. Despite the fact that we all worked here, apart from the Chief Inspectors and the Chief Supers, there was far more office furniture than people. There were, for instance, two dozen desks, not to mention all the filing-cabinets and the cupboards that kept the official forms. Nearly all the desks were parked in groups beside the windows. The only cheering item was a drinks cabinet, which we kept replenished with spirits and beer and so on by having a whip-round in the office now and again. Technically we were not allowed to drink on duty at all. But this was overlooked on occasions when there was something to celebrate – as on the previous night. Having a drink during the day was fraught with danger as a Chief Super might come in and inquire what we were doing. However, on Friday evenings, we would quite regularly have a drink together before going home.

It was on such occasions that the plants in the office were watered with beer and gin. These were cannabis plants that had been taken from addresses which had been searched, and after being analysed at the laboratory they would come back to us and we would keep them on the window-ledge until such time that they were needed at court. They were large, not particularly attractive plants, with sprays of saw-toothed leaves. But they were female – you can't make pot from a *male* cannabis plant – and added a touch of colour to the office.

At the end of the room were two glass-partitioned offices, occupied by the two Detective Inspectors – one of whom at the time was DI Bolton. They were seldom there for more than six months and we had really nothing to do with them, though they checked our paperwork before passing it on to a DCI, normally Kelaher. In one of their offices was a safe where valuable property and prisoners' property were kept. In the other office was a display cabinet of items used in the drug scene – all kinds of amphetamine tablets or LSD, cannabis, syringes, cigarette papers, pipes, powders, cocaine, heroin and how to make it. There were also some souvenirs: a hookah used for smoking pot, and a very long, highly decorated pipe which had belonged to a famous pop group.

This was the office in which I had been working for about eight months.

When I barged in that morning, my breezy entrance was somewhat spoiled by a near-collision with the black tea-lady who was dispensing her wares inside the doorway.

The DCs who had assembled around her nodded at me and made the odd comment, which was more than I got from Nobby and Nick, sitting side by side at their desks.

Nobby was on the telephone, and Nick was writing up his police diary.

'Morning!' I said.

Nick grunted. Nobby put a hand over the mouth-piece. 'Get me some coffee,' he said.

The only welcome I got was from Ada and Betty, the two civilian ladies next to us who did some of our typing and so on, and answered general phone-calls.

I offered to buy them their teas, and joined the other DCs who were ribbing the tea-lady.

'What are you selling today, Blondie?' inquired one of them jokingly, poking among the snacks.

'The usual,' she said, offhandedly flushing the cups.

'I could do with a bit of the usual,' said the DC. 'How about you?'

She giggled nervously and said: 'How much you going to pay me?'

The coloured tea-ladies were played up quite considerably at the Yard. Some of them got quite cheeky in return. They all wore blue nylon coats which had on the breast-pocket the initials 'MPCS'. This was always good for a witty interpretation. 'Mustn't Poke Coloureds or Sambos' was one. Or there was 'Make Pilcher Commissioner Soonest'. This was Nigel's contribution. The letters actually stood for 'Metropolitan Police Catering Service'.

Another version, currently popular, was 'Mustn't Pinch the Canteen Spoons' – a reference to a recent memo that had gone the rounds deploring the theft or disappearance of large numbers of metal spoons.

Ada and Betty were duly grateful for my attentions, more so than Nobby, who was still engaged on the phone.

'Quite an adventure you've 'ad,' said Ada, the elder civvy, stirring her tea. 'I nearly fell off the sofa I did when it come on *News at Ten*. I was so excited. "It's us!" I said to Alfred, I did. "It was Nobby and his boys who did that," I said.'

'How did you know it was us?' I asked.

'Well, Nobby was talking about you and Nick going after a Rolls-Royce – that was on Wednesday when he come back from the Cumberland Hotel. And yesterday, I *knew* something was up about that Morland who you've been observing for so long. Nobby was *never* off the phone. Was he, Betty?'

'No,' said Betty. 'It was really quite exciting, just *being* here.'

'Makes it all seem worthwhile,' I remarked.

'Oh, yes,' said Ada. 'I know how hard you work. Such long hours. And you meet such wicked people! Really dreadful – corrupting young persons with dangerous drugs.'

'Disgusting!' commented Betty.

'It's a very good job you're doing,' continued Ada. 'Very beneficial. Don't you think so, Betty?'

'Oh, yes,' said Betty. 'It's quite like social welfare. Do you know what I mean?'

They would have gone on in this way, but I interrupted them, cheerily saying: 'You're not doing such a bad job yourselves. No, indeed.'

Their main job was to collate information and type out the cards for the Index of Drug Offenders, all those in Britain, which was in our office. They didn't do shorthand. If we wanted to dictate a report or statements, we had to send for one of the shorthand typists from the typing pool. A lot of them were coloured and not perhaps as efficient as they might have been – as indeed were a large number of the civilians employed at the Yard – and when they returned with the typescript it often had so many mistakes that the whole thing would have to be retyped. Even then there would still be mistakes on every page. It saved time to bash away at some typewriter with two fingers ourselves, which we generally did, though none of us, and hardly anyone in the police force, was taught to type.

Ada was a bit of an old dear, and when answering outside calls to the Drug Squad would answer questions put to her as best she could.

We couldn't help civilians overhearing some of our conversations, and their presence was another reason for us being known as the Whispering Squad.

It was also a reason for some of the belated and incomplete entries in the duty book, which sat on a small table at the foot of the typists' desks. Each of us was supposed, daily, to write in the time of our arrival in the office and the time of our departure, also our destination when we left. This was so that our superiors knew where we were and roughly what we were doing. It also meant that anyone else in the office could tell at a glance where we were. Districts and courts were described in a simple code, the first letter being that of the police division – DP was, for instance, Paddington; CB was Bow Street Court; CD was West End Central police station; FF was Fulham. But Stoke Poges was Stoke Poges, and actual streets and businesses were spelt out. Necessarily, our entries were somewhat vague and often not filled in until the end of the day, or the day after. When we didn't come into the office we rang up, and someone else, usually one of our unit, wrote in the details for us.

'Who's stolen the duty book?' I inquired, noticing its absence.

'I've got it,' said Nick.

He was using its abbreviated entries, as we all did, as a reference for the expanded and detailed day-by-day entries in his personal police diary.

Our diaries had to be kept up to date as they were checked through every Thursday morning by a Chief Inspector. Not that he actually read through *all* the thirty diaries of the officers in the squad. His main concern was to see they'd been filled in and were in order and to countersign our claims for expenses.

Our pocketbooks or notebooks were hardly ever looked at.

I sat down at my desk opposite Nick and pulled the duty book towards me.

At the top of the right-hand page, in the box beside my name, I wrote – 'Off. eng. 9–10 am to CB Ct. Bk later' – which meant 'Office engaged from 9 to 10 a.m., then to Bow Street Court. Back later.'

I knew that we'd leave the Yard about 10 a.m., in order to get to the court in time for the hearing of the charges against Palacios and the others. We would probably return to the Yard afterwards.

'It doesn't let up for a moment,' said Nobby, replacing the telephone receiver. He swallowed some of his untouched coffee.

'Arrgh!' he said. 'It's horrible. Still, it's warm and wet, as the bishop said to the actress. Are you making more misleading entries, Acworth?' he continued. 'Putting down 9 a.m.? You were never here then, my son. Nice of you to drop in though.'

'Yes, I was!' I said in mock indignation. 'Straight. DC Prichard will vouch for me. Won't you, DC Prichard?'

'What? Yeah. Oh, sure,' said Nick.

'Conspiracy!' said Nobby.

'Oh, Sergeant,' I said. 'How can you doubt the word of a gentleman *and* a policeman?'

'Experience, mate. That's all – which also leads me to believe you've been having it off again. You looked shagged out, you bleeding deb's delight. Who was it this time?'

'Sorry. Can't tell you,' I answered. 'Official secret.'

'Lady Cynthia, was it? Amazing what poor taste these titled titties have,' he remarked to Prichard. 'How does he do it?'

'Maybe with his truncheon,' said Nick.

'Well,' said Nobby thoughtfully. 'He can't have much else to show them.'

I protested a bit, as this quip was rather unjustified.

Nobby was a very likeable and sociable bloke. He was thirty-five, a Londoner, married with two children, and lived in Bexley. In appearance and manner he was an archetypal sergeant. Of average height and weight he was a fast mover, and seldom at a loss. His bright eyes were undershadowed and lined with all the late hours he kept, mostly in the way of work. We relied on him a lot. 'Leave it to your old dad,' he would say – and I felt I could.

He was always taking the michael out of me, in particular my accent, the hunt-ball scene, and the kind of girls I associated with. It wasn't easy to retaliate – him being a sergeant, with no known failings apart from a weakness for fast cars, football, and an occasional flutter on the horses. But I did my best.

I turned the conversation onto yesterday's events.

'We were bloody lucky,' I said.

'Lucky, my arse,' said Nobby. 'Teamwork. Taking chances. Perseverance. That's what did it. And some exceptional thinking from a couple of thick DCs.'

He grinned at me.

'What's it feel like to be famous?' he asked, and before I could answer said: 'I'll tell you.' He whispered: 'It feels like any other fucking day in the fucking office.'

He raised his voice. 'There's work to be done! Not only by yours truly and Shortarse here. Now!' he said and got to his feet. 'What *you* can do is give me a hand with the property lists. And you,' he said to Nick, 'you can get onto the fingerprints office and see if they've got a record of Palacios's dabs – when you've finished your memoirs.'

He peered over Nick's shoulder at the diary.

'It'll never be a best-seller,' he said. 'Not enough sex.'

Nobby picked up the pink copy of Palacios's charge sheet and we went into the DI's office that had the safe. It was a huge, deep affair, with many shelves.

He began to twiddle the knobs and soon gave up, saying: 'You bloody do it. I can never remember the combination.'

While I did as he asked, he got out the red register in which the times of opening and closing the safe, and by whom, had to be entered, and filled it in.

We set about listing in the property book all Palacios's personal property, which was in a large brown envelope, and listing all the cardboard boxes of cannabis and other exhibits, each of which had to go into a polythene bag and be labelled. This took some time.

Much of our office routine, in fact of all police work, was paperwork. The night before, when we returned from Cannon Row, apart from filling in the duty book and bringing our pocketbooks and diaries up to date, we had had to make out a Specrim (Special Crime telex message), which would be sent to the Commissioner, his Assistants and Deputies, and to the Commanders. This Nobby did. Then an entry, taken from our copy of the charge sheet, had to be made in the Arrest Book. Three other forms had to be filled in: Lab Form 1, which had to go to the laboratory with the drugs; a legal aid form, to let the Yard's solicitors know that an arrest had been made and that a prosecution was being prepared; and a detailed form called a Crimsec, which had to be sent to the Home Office. Finally, at some future date a full report, with statements and so on, would have to be made before the trial.

I often felt that it wasn't our job to be clerks. Nor were we trained as such. I also felt that the mass of forms could be simplified. A master charge sheet, for instance, containing all kinds of detailed information, could be made out at a police station, photo-copied – carbon copies being out of date – and sent to all the departments and people concerned, who could then themselves extract such particular information that they required. They had secretaries. We had not. To me it seemed absurd that we should be doing their job for them – especially as the average policeman didn't spell or write too well. And it was downright stupid that an already overworked, understaffed police force should be loaded with clerical matters.

'Thank Christ that's bloody well over!' said Nobby as we slammed shut the door of the safe.

'It's like a bank,' I said. 'With all that stuff in it worth a fortune on the black market. Would it really fetch £200,000?'

'What's the rate now? No. Nearer £150,000. But it's still more than you or I will ever put away. Do you realize it would take me, on my salary, all my life to earn that much? Shocking. Isn't it?'

'Diabolical,' I said. 'It's just as well we're on the level.'

We returned to our desks. With the aid of the occasional receipt and a word with Nick, I began adding up my Isle of Wight expenses before putting them in my diary.

They came under three headings: *Refreshments*, *Travelling*, and *Incidentals*. Under the first, you could claim 7s. 6d. for an extra meal if you worked over nine hours. If you worked more than twelve hours, you could claim for two extra meals and get 10s. 9d. *Travelling* included petrol for the official use of your own car, plus taxis and trains if you used them. *Incidentals* covered the buying of refreshments for informants. Officially that meant people who provided information in an investigation – but it could be and was interpreted as meaning any member of the public with whom you had a natter in a pub.

While I was doing this, Nick was still making faces over the entries in his diary, and Nobby was answering another phone-call. This one was briefer.

'That was our dear old Commander,' said Nobby at its conclusion. 'He says he is very well pleased and wishes you both to know it. A notable achievement, he says. He can't drop in and see us at the moment. But he's going to put on a bottle for an office celebration before lunch – when we're back from Bow Street. You're both invited.'

Nobby grinned expansively.

'Gee, that's wonderful,' commented Nick. 'I dig that man.'

'We must tell Nigel,' I suggested. 'He ought to be in on it.'

'Good idea. Give him a ring. But later on. Pack up what you're doing now. We're off to court.'

Before we left the office, there was yet another call for Nobby, at the end of which he was much quieter and thoughtful, not answering our questions until we were in the lift and on our own going down to the ground floor.

'It's all go,' he said. 'The Salahs are moving from Stoke Poges. It seems they've gone and bought a house at Ascot.'

7

Robert Palacios, Francis Morland, Michael O'Shea and a fourth man duly appeared in the dock at Bow Street magistrates court and were remanded in custody for another week, until Friday the 23rd. Morland's wife was allowed out on bail of £1,500. This process of being remanded while a case against them was fully prepared would continue until 23 November, when all five were sent for trial at the Old Bailey. The men were committed in custody, while Mrs M. was again allowed bail. The charges against them, now specified, were that the four men had conspired together with Patrick Craig Newson and others unknown to import cannabis resin. The Morlands were also charged with possessing cannabis and LSD. Palacios and Morland were further charged with importing and possessing cannabis resin.

In the meantime, during the rest of October and November, the Salahs and their activities began to occupy more and more of our time and thoughts and talk, and we became correspondingly more secretive and sensitive about our plans and all the watching and waiting we had to do. For after our triumph in the Rolls-Royce affair, we were determined to do even better. In this we thought the Salahs might be able to help us.

None of my excitement at being involved in this operation could I reveal to Sam, who only knew that I was frequently working in the evenings, and as a result used to turn up at Gloucester Place knackered, late or not at all. There were rows – especially when I couldn't make some of our dates for parties, evenings out and cinema shows. She wouldn't go out without me, nor did I want her to, and the fact that she was on night duty every three weeks didn't make things easier. But occasionally, at weekends, we got away together – as we did on 18 October, the Sunday after the first appearance of Palacios and his pals at Bow Street.

It was a very beautiful autumn day, bright and warm and sunny. We drove out of London in my Volkswagen to Hertfordshire, to the home of my younger sister Jane and her husband.

They had recently returned to England from Kenya, where he had been a warden on four of the game reserves, one after the other, and now lived in the village of Benington. There was roast beef for lunch; and afterwards Sam, who had been on duty the night before, slept on the lawn on a rug. We went for a walk through the hilly fields, with leaves falling about us and underfoot. On the way back to London the brakes, which had been dodgy on the run out, packed up completely, and we travelled back using the hand-brake only.

On the next day, Monday the 19th, Nick and I were in the thick of it once again, checking out the information that the Salahs had bought a house. It was one of the busiest days we had spent on matters relating to them since that July day which ended with us ringing their doorbell.

In Nick's car, as mine was now out of commission, we drove to Slough, which is west of London and Heathrow Airport and across the Thames from Windsor. Stoke Poges, two miles north of Slough, was in effect one of its suburbs. Flashing our warrant cards, we visited the Town Hall Housing Department, the GPO and local estate agents. Our inquiries soon ascertained that the Salahs were not buying one, but *two* houses – the second at Langley, another village surrounded by suburban development. Contracts had been exchanged. The family were going to split up, and both parts were apparently going to move out of the flat in The Meads, Stoke Poges, and into the two other houses in November.

At first we feared that they might have been tipped off about us, or that Nick and I had somehow overplayed our hand in July, or that for some reason they had become suspicious and were moving to throw us off the scent. Then we swore because the intercept on The Meads – zealously applied for and grudgingly granted – was going to be a wash-out.

But the move, besides being a sensible investment by the Salahs, was as it turned out very much in our favour. For when the intercept on the phone at The Meads began, it proved to be less than satisfactory. The phone was a public one in the hall and was used by all the tenants in the house. For this reason, most of the calls didn't apply, and in any event the Salahs seldom used the phone themselves. When they occupied *two* houses however – both with telephones – it meant not only that they were more active in going out and visiting each other, but also that they rang each other up more often. This gave us more food for observation and investigation. But it also gave us more work.

The intercept on The Meads commenced on 27 October and was withdrawn, after providing nothing relevant to the investigation, on 7 November.

Two days earlier, on Guy Fawkes Day, the Salahs moved out.

The younger couple, John and Kathy Salah, took up residence at 29 Mapledene Road in Langley.

This was a fairly nondescript, pre-war, grey-tiled house in a nondescript road, with a mock-tudor gable, white front door, a garage, and a high hedge around the small and scruffy garden.

From 13 November, all their phone-calls were intercepted – and continued to be so for four months.

The parents, Mohammed and Kathleen Salah, with their daughter Janet, went to live in a very desirable brand-new property at Ascot.

The house, which cost them about £25,000, was on a pleasantly wooded estate, with landscaped gardens and white palings, at the far end of the Ascot Racecourse's straight mile. Beeches, firs and pine-trees lined the approach road; horses grazed in paddocks; rhododendrons grew thick and tall. Most of the other houses were still in the process of being built. The Salahs' home, called Kier Park House, was a solid red-brick establishment in the Georgian style, with a green-tiled roof, a double garage, a portico with sets of twin white pillars at the front, and white-painted windows with shutters on the first floor. At the back there was a small lake.

The phone at Kier Park House was tapped from 4 December until February the following year.

But it was the intercept at Mapledene Road that, six days after its inception, first put a gleam in Nobby's eye and gave purpose to our endeavours.

Mrs Kathleen Salah made a call to her son, John.[1]

1. The extract and the information obtained from this intercept and from all the others that follow are taken from the transcripts in evidence at the Perjury trial and put before the jury. They were not put in evidence at the Salah trial. However, they make the narrative easier to follow if they take their place here rather than later in the book. It should be borne in mind that the transcripts are only allegations made at the Perjury trial of what the police claimed had been recorded by the phone-tap. – G.H.

Mum: Hello, John.

John: All right, Mum?

Mum: Yes. Ni-Ar's [sounds like] had his letter.

John: Yeah.

Mum: He said if you want the pants and vests [emphasized] you must give an order for two and a half months before.

John: Yeah.

Mum: He said it's very bad in Afghanistan now for white people.

John: Yeah.

Mum: Well – I don't want to go, John. I think it would be better if your father went.

John: Yeah.

Mum: He said that there are customers for the pants all the time, and that much of the stuff that is sold is of very inferior quality.

John: Yeah.

Mum: You know – so he said if we want to order these vests, I have to put down 50 per cent first.

John: Yeah. That's all right.

Mum: I've been today about the van. It still hasn't come.

John: It's due though, isn't it?

Mum: It's due – but it hasn't come in. . . .

John: Shouldn't talk on the phone, Mum, really. Right. I'll come round tomorrow afternoon and we'll have a chat about it. . . .

They then had a general conversation about the dog having a rash.

The words in brackets were the telephone-typist's comments. 'Ni-Ars' was in fact Niaz Ali, a relation of Mohammed.

Two hours later Mum was on the phone again.

Mum: John, I've just read this letter again, and what they want is 50 per cent deposit and also the price is up 50 per cent.

John: Oh.

Mum: Where I had the letter from he said that there is other people who grow it specially – you know, the wool.

John: Yeah.

Mum: Like – it's fleecy-lined.

John: So it's gone up.

Mum: They said half as much again.

John: That's no good, Mum.

Mum: Yeah. Your father's a bit upset about it.

John: That's been cooked.

Mum: Looks like it.

John: To put us off.

Mum: No. Not to put us off. To get a cut.

John: A cut for [*sounds like*] *Ni-Ar-Zally* [*phonetic*]. *Or he's wrote to the old man. Or the old man's wrote to him behind our back to tell him to write that letter.*

Mum: No, he hasn't. That's nonsense.

John: Is it?

Mum: Yes.

John: Well, you'd better write back then, and tell them it's got to be at the old price or to forget it.

Mum: Yes . . . We'll sort something out. . . .

John: If it's a little bit more, it doesn't matter.

Mum: It does matter. The price will have to go up anyhow.

John: Yeah.

Mum: That's why it's costing more. Because the price has gone up. They just took us for a ride, you know, with the last lot.

John: Yeah. . . .

A few minutes later John telephoned his mother, and advised her to '*play along with the old man. . . . If Dad goes out there, he'll come to some arrangement with them anyhow.*' To which Mum replied: '*Yeah. I can't afford to cross him.*'

Mohammed very seldom used the telephone. Now that he was retired, he had few interests, and seemed to be the passive partner in the organization of the journey to Pakistan. His wife, Kathleen, was hard as nails. She appeared to be the boss of the family and was more often on the phone than anyone else, apart from John. He seemed to be rather a neurotic person, with a fairly effeminate manner and voice. He had longish hair and a moustache. Kathy, John's wife, a placid, pleasant creature, wasn't involved in any of the business arrangements. Her telephone conversations were generally moans about the weather, the cleaning woman, the price of dresses, the amount of chlorine in the water, the state of John's health and that of their shaggy dog, Khan, the fact that the drains smelled, and other domestic matters. Janet was something of a chatty flirt and seemed to think she was the bees'-knees. Her role was vaguely secretarial. As far as we knew she didn't work for a living. Neither did John, though he described himself as a motor dealer. The only one who had an ordinary job was Kathy. She was a hairdresser. They seemed to quarrel among themselves quite a lot, and appeared to be under some kind of strain.

Throughout November and the next two months we paid frequent visits to Slough and Ascot, mainly in the evenings when the Salahs were at home. We sat for hours in parked cars in the dusk and in the dark, smoking cigarettes, with the radio switched on low. In rain, drizzle, mist and fog we watched and waited for what little activity there was. Most of it outside their houses we provided ourselves, when we took a stroll to ease our cramped limbs, breathe some fresh air and peer at their front doors and lighted windows as we walked slowly past, wondering what they were doing inside. Sometimes they went to the cinema. Mostly they stayed indoors in comfort and warmth, making meals, eating them and watching television. About ten or eleven at night we would retire, cold and yawning, to the nearest pub before phoning the office and booking ourselves off duty.

In our observations on the Salahs, Nobby, Nick, Nigel and I were not always together. Each of us was also employed on other matters during the day. Sometimes we visited Ascot, Slough, and the other locations alone. Sometimes we joined another of the squad already there, or were joined by someone coming out later from the office or from another job. Mostly we worked in pairs. A twelve-hour day was not unusual.

To get about we used, of necessity, a variety of cars. Some we borrowed from the Yard supply of 'nondescript' cars, which were vans of various types. More often we used our own cars turn-about. Nick had his Mini, and Nobby a souped-up Lotus Cortina. By this time I had part-exchanged my Volkswagen for a new one, red in colour. Nigel had learned to drive in July and also had a VW, an orange one called a June Bug, with all the trimmings. Unfortunately he couldn't use it too often as the Salahs had one exactly the same. In fact between them the Salahs had two VWs and a black Mercedes sports, which belonged to Mrs Salah.

As time passed, their whereabouts, activities and movements became as engrossing as a television series.

National and international happenings were only of passing interest – except when they actually affected us, like the council workers' strike, which ended on 5 November, and a series of power cuts and black-outs in mid-December. The state of the weather, MCC cricket scores in Australia and football results were matters for idle discussion during observations. The death of General de Gaulle, pay disputes, sea-tanker collisions, Common Market discussions, Northern Ireland disturbances, the renewed American bombing of Vietnam, the release of the kidnapped James Cross in Canada, earthquakes in Peru and a Soviet spacecraft on Venus – all these were merely noted and soon forgotten.

The major excitements of any day were the events at Ascot and Slough, and the news, via C11 on the fourth floor of the Yard, of any significant phone calls made by the Salahs.

Their first main problem was the acquisition of a suitable vehicle to take them to Pakistan and back. This turned out to be quite a bother.

At the end of November, Mrs Salah telephoned her son.

Mum: I am sorry, John, I cannot understand the questions you have asked me. There is about ten or fifteen diagrams in here, and neither Janet or me understand them to answer the questions you have asked.

John: You can see the line, and it tells you.

Mum: Really, John, I can't.

John: The vans we are interested in are the same cubic capacity inside. Exactly the same. All but an inch, we think. The vans we have seen are the same inside as the transit, like.

Mum: Yeah. We'll wait until tomorrow to see what happens. . . .

John: Okay. We'll get something sorted out, as there's not much time – is there?

Mum: Leave it today, John. It's Sunday. Have a bit of a rest.

John: Okay, Mum. See you tomorrow.

The following morning, John, evidently a late riser and somewhat forgetful, telephoned Kier Park House.

John: Hello, Mum. John here.

Mum: Yeah?

John: Are we going out this morning to have a look?

Mum: Well – we're waiting for you actually.

John: Okay. I'll be over in about half an hour. I'm ready now. I'm just going to have some breakfast. Then I'll be over.

Mum: Make yourself look nice if we're going to London, eh? Put a suit on or something.

John: Oh. I haven't put a suit on.

Mum: You get more attention if you're nicely dressed.

John: Well, you get the attention and don't worry about me. Okay?

Mum: Okay. Ta-ta.

John: Bye.

It was in this mood that they went to London to look at some vans.

The search for a suitable vehicle wasn't easy. Apart from London, it took them to High Wycombe and to Birmingham, where apparently a new transit van had been ordered as far back as September. Three months later it had still failed to materialize – so the order was cancelled.

Janet lent a hand. Calling herself Mrs Mason, she telephoned the Rover Motor Company and asked what size of Landrover would be needed to pull a fourteen-foot trailer carrying two tons of personal effects and four people overland to Australia. She also rang the AA about the technical and legal difficulties of taking a Landrover, four people and a trailer to India. The AA said they would send her a useful leaflet.

Meanwhile, Mrs Salah senior got a letter from Kabul, which had been sent to their old address at Stoke Poges.

She telephoned John and reported that '*if we want those carpets, they will start making it now. But there is nothing about any prices.*' She went on: '*I think he's going to pull a fast one. . . .*'

John reassured her and asked her to come round to Mapledene Road – there was a place fifteen minutes up the road that he wanted her to visit.

This must have been the boatyard and marine chandlers called Crevald's Services Ltd, which was on the south bank of the River Thames near Old Windsor – a row of huts and sheds, with cars and cabin-cruisers parked beside the A308 that connected Staines and Windsor. It was here that they, and we, came to see how the trailer being made to their specifications was progressing.

The next piece of news from abroad was a telegram – from

Niaz Ali. It was addressed to 'Kathleen Masoon, Kier Park House, Ascot', and said: 'Top quality NW wool is available at 83 shillings per pound.'

In the first fortnight of December, while John was worrying about his health, Mrs Salah was making calculations about profit and loss, and the wives were discussing Christmas shopping. On the 14th, a Monday, the news was that the maps had come, that there was no letter from Pakistan, and that a Landrover, which they appeared to have purchased, couldn't be picked up that day as it needed a new oil gauge. On the morning of the 15th, Mrs Salah telephoned John and told him that the Landrover was now ready and that she would collect it at four o'clock that afternoon.

That call was made at 9.22 a.m. Soon afterwards, C11 telephoned down with the information.

My evidence at the Salah trial about what happened next went as follows.[1]

Q: On Tuesday, December 15th, 1970, were you and DC Lilley and other officers at Kings Avenue, Brixton? – A: Yes.

Q: In Kings Avenue, Brixton, are there some premises of Wilson's, motor traders? – A: Yes.

Q: Are those showrooms, or just a plot of land? – A: There are a number of caravans for sale and also some workshops and offices.

Q: As far as the offices are concerned, did you see anyone in the offices? – A: Yes. I saw Mohammed and John Salah and another man whom I did not recognize.

Q: About what time was that? – A: It was about 4 p.m.

Q: Then a little later on, did you see anyone in the garage of that firm as opposed to the offices? – A: I did not see anyone in the garage as such. No.

Q: What did you see? – A: I saw a Landrover there.

Q: What was happening in relation to the Landrover? – A: It was being fitted out with accessories.

Q: Did you see anybody there? – A: Yes. All three persons were in fact looking at the vehicle as well. . . .

Q: Who are the persons to whom you are referring? – A: John,

1. Again, in this and the next extract from the proceedings at the Salah trial, Adam was answering questions put to him by the prosecutor, Mr Corkery. – G.H.

Mohammed, and this third person I do not know. They all left at 4.30 p.m.

Q: When they left, did they go off in a vehicle of some sort? – A: Yes. They went off in a blue Mini, as far as I can remember.

Q: Do you remember who the driver was? – A: The third man, whom I did not recognize.

Mrs Salah didn't in fact turn up that afternoon, and the Landrover wasn't taken away. By the way, the other officer with me and Nigel was Detective Inspector Bolton. He was also with us when, on the morning of the 16th, we once more bombed over to darkest Brixton, where a cold wind kept the streets from looking their dismal best. We hid ourselves behind and among the bulky bodies of motor-caravans that were parked there.

Q: At about nine o'clock in the morning, again with DC Lilley and other officers, did you go back to the same area? – A: I did. Yes.

Q: Did you see the Landrover on that occasion – A: I did. Yes.

Q: Had you, either on that occasion or the earlier occasion, taken the registration number of the Landrover? – A: Yes.

Q: What was it? – A: EMG 456J.

Q: On this following day, what had you seen happen? – A: It was driven to the main offices of Wilson, which is in Acre Lane.

Q: Did you see any other vehicle there? – A: Yes. There was an orange Volkswagen, registration number RPP 24H.

Q: Who was by the Volkswagen when you saw it? – A: Mrs Salah, Janet and John.

Q: Mrs Salah being the mother? – A: Yes. They drove in a Landrover back to Kings Avenue offices and John was driving.

Q: Then what happened? – A: About fifteen minutes later John drove the Landrover himself, and Mrs Salah and Janet followed in the Volkswagen.

That night, Nigel and I hung about Kier Park House for over four hours. There was a bitterly cold wind and it was very dark, for the road was still unlit. It was also fairly dangerous, for among the unfinished houses piles of earth, bulldozers and building materials made the going awkward. We prowled about the lighted windows of the Salahs' pseudo-Georgian residence, stumbling and cursing, and wondering where the hell the Landrover was. It *had* to come to Kier Park House – there wasn't room for it at Mapledene Road. But although we put up with the cold and the tedium until after 11.30 p.m., after Mohammed and Mrs Salah and Janet had gone to bed, no Landrover put in an appearance.

It was not until the next day that we realized the Landrover had only been taken out for a run-around on the Wednesday, before being returned to the garage.

In fact it didn't come to roost outside the house at Ascot until the following Monday, 21 December – by which time I had happened to meet Prince Charles.

My brother Bill's farm-estates near Hungerford produced a good quantity of beef and corn, and dairy products from herds of black and white Friesian cows. One of the owners also reared pheasants – for shooting. They were also of course for eating. But the main idea was to provide a day's sport in the winter months for his guests. It was a well-planned and expensive pursuit. At mating-time, in March and April, the birds were captured in the woods where they roosted and put in pens, one cock with five or six hens. As the eggs were laid – many hundreds in all – they were gathered up every day and put in an incubator in an outhouse. When they hatched, the chicks were eventually transferred to very large open pens in the woods, where they were carefully fed and reared until they flew off on their own. But they didn't fly far and they continued to be regularly fed and protected from foxes throughout the summer. But with the onset of winter they were fair game for any gun.

This is what took me tanking along the A4 on Friday night. On the Saturday there was to be a pheasant-shoot, and the chief guest was Prince Charles.

I wouldn't be doing any shooting myself, although I'd done a fair deal over the years – on my father's farm, at Gordonstoun with the masters, on Bill's estates – with a 4.10 or a 12 bore. I wasn't bad at it. In the police force, using a Webley .38 revolver, I had qualified as a marksman. But on this occasion I was to make myself useful as a picker-up of dead birds, and an unofficial bodyguard to HRH.

The morning was fair and dry when the shooting-party, of eight guns, assembled outside the landowner's mansion at about 9.15. There was altogether quite a crowd, what with the thirty or so beaters, hired for the day at 50 shillings each, and the loaders, one for each gun, who did just that – loading the pair of double-barrelled 12 bore guns that each man used. There were also a few helpers and dog-handlers, not to mention the gun-dogs themselves. Prince Charles's man had four black labradors which were superbly trained and turned out to be much better than me at finding and fetching the kill.

We all moved off, and parked ourselves in the lee of a wood while the beaters went about it and entered it at the other end. They then proceeded to walk towards us through the wood, making a fearful racket, sending the startled pheasants like chattering rockets out of the trees, into the open and towards the line of guns.

Each gun was at a fixed post, about twenty-five yards apart. Each was numbered. The positions on the first drive were drawn for, and on the other drives – there were seven in all – everyone moved up two.

After four drives we all adjourned for lunch in a special long shed by the gamekeeper's cottage, and were served with platefuls of steaming Irish stew and great slices of home-made tart – all washed down with mugs of beer and cider.

Although the Prince was with us, he was not among us, being hedged by his hosts and the higher gentry. All eyes were on him, observing if he was enjoying himself. He was also on our tongues. For the night before an alarm had gone off accidentally in the house of the landowner's father not far from where host and guests were sleeping. The house was empty at the time. No one heard the alarm or went to investigate – except HRH, who padded out into the frosty night, attired in his royal nightclothes, to check that all was well. It was, but the vision of the Prince of Wales in his pyjamas, game to do battle on his own with burglars, provoked much admiration.

It was after the next and fifth drive, as we moved off to another wood, that the Prince, who turned out to be a very good shot, asked me who I was and what I did. I told him. He seemed very interested and asked a lot of questions. We talked together for about twenty minutes while the beaters got in position for the drive. I tried to find out what he thought of Gordonstoun and what he did there, but didn't have much luck.

At the end of the day, about 800 pheasants had been killed.

Prince Charles got over a hundred, and was presented – as was each of the guns – with a brace of pheasants for himself.

As he stood there, at the centre of the shooting-party, who were loudly comparing notes and trophies on the darkening field, it struck me that he would one day be crowned king – Charles III no less.

I smiled, remembering the day I had worn that crown myself.

It had happened eleven months earlier, in January that year, and arose out of the fact that I was a trained police marksman.

I was asked, with two other TDCs, to go to the Tower of London and keep an eye on the Crown Jewels while they were being cleaned. This was done every January, and it took about three weeks. In fact during this period I was posted to the Drug Squad. The three of us TDCs, armed with Webleys with six rounds in them, and under instructions to use them if necessary, sat with the jeweller in the Jewel House, which at the time was being refitted with a more sophisticated security system. We helped him to take the regalia out of the cabinets. We also helped him to clean them. I helped with the diamonds, which had to be taken out of their sets before being treated and cleaned with chemicals, then dried in hot sawdust. The gold and silver were polished.

At some stage it was suggested that I might like to wear St Edward's crown, and be king for a minute – all as a joke. Of course I agreed.

The crown, which was very heavy, was put on my head.

The others said 'Hail!' and 'Long live the king!'

For a moment I felt very royal and strangely important. Then the moment passed and I became aware that I was doing something wrong.

I carefully removed the crown, knowing that it was a sacred object, and that the man who wore it had to be someone made special by the church and state and by his birth.

Prince Charles walked away from the beaters and the other guns with his brace of pheasants, raising his hand, wishing everyone 'Merry Christmas!'

I wondered what he'd have said if I had told him about my crowning. I thought he might perhaps have been amused.

8

'You've no idea,' said Sam. 'It's the most wonderful place to be at Christmas-time.'

She was talking about the hospital, where she would be working throughout the Christmas period into the New Year, having volunteered to do some extra days.

We were in the flat in Gloucester Place on our own, munching our way through the plateful of buttered toast that was our supper. There were apples for dessert, chocolates to follow, and sherry to drink, all of which were presents from her patients. She sat at my feet, in the full glow of the electric fire, this being the only illumination in the room apart from the lights on the little Christmas tree in the window. The girls had spent a lot of time decorating it and the room, which was crammed with colourful streamers, tinsel, seasonal set-pieces, sprays of holly and masses of cards.

It was Christmas Eve.

'Everyone relaxes,' she went on. 'The doctors call you by your christian name, and the patients –! They're so kind, so cheerful, even the really ill ones. You should see their faces – and their eyes. There's so much love around.'

She had been on duty all that day, helping, among her other tasks, to put up the decorations in the wards. They would only be up for two days, coming down on Boxing Day because of the fire risk.

She was now a 'black belt', and Acting Staff Nurse, having passed her SRN Finals with flying colours. The results had been announced at the beginning of the month. Another result of this had been that she had decided to go home to Africa in three weeks' time.

I felt very bad about that when she told me – especially as she had already booked her flight. And it wasn't just for a holiday. She said she might get a job out there.

I couldn't actually believe that she would go away and leave me – I didn't want to – so we didn't discuss it at any length. I thought that she would change her mind, or that I could change it for her by making her realize that I loved her, and needed her, and wanted her to marry me.

In the meantime the issue was avoided. We were both very busy at work and Christmas was approaching. But there were times at the office when I became suddenly depressed, with a very hopeless feeling.

On Christmas Eve we were all harmonious. But I couldn't help asking, when she said: 'There's so much love around' – 'Does that include me?'

'Of course it does,' she answered, and then continued with what she was saying. 'They'll be going around the wards now, some of the nurses, with their capes turned inside out so that the red's on top, and singing carols.'

'Away in a manger,' I sang, more loudly than necessary.

'Oh, stop that!' she said, sharply. 'You'd spoil anything. There are some things, beautiful things, you just don't appreciate!'

I said: 'Sorry,' and was so hurt for an instant by her rebuke that I couldn't speak. What she said wasn't true. I did appreciate beautiful things, like classical music, and her. I was only trying to make her smile. I didn't like it when she was so serious.

'Poor Buzz,' she whispered, kneeling beside me with her arms around me and her face close to mine. 'You always do the wrong thing, don't you? The wrong thing at the wrong time for the wrong reasons. But there's no need to be sorry. It's not *your* fault. Is it?'

'Sorry,' I repeated.

'Ssh . . . no,' she said. 'It's not your fault. It's mine. I'm so horrid sometimes – without meaning to be. I didn't mean to snap at you. . . . But – Oh, there we go again,' she said, retreating to the floor and choosing an apple. 'Talking about *us*. Why don't we talk about something else? Like – what would happen if there was a black Prime Minister in England. Do you want an apple?'

'Waste of time,' I murmured. 'Yes. Thanks.'

'Why? It might happen. It's interesting.'

'No, it's not. It's a load of codswallop. A black Prime Minister! Bloody hell!'

'One day it could be a very important issue.'

'One day. Now, it's not. Now, there's us – and *that's* important. . . . Anyway – what's wrong with talking about us?'

She stopped eating and looked up at me.

'There are many other people in the world, Buzz,' she said. 'They have many, many problems and quite a few lead dreadful lives. We have to remember them. And think about them.'

'All right. But there's nothing we can do about them.'

'If everybody thought that, the world wouldn't be a fit place to live in. People would be dying in the streets. But they aren't. I know they aren't – working in a hospital. People care about people!'

'So do I. About you.'

She looked at me, and her expression softened. But she said nothing.

'You're important to me,' I added.

She looked away. I leaned forward.

'And you're the right person for me. I'm not wrong there.'

I took her face in my hands and kissed her nose.

'It's glowing like a bloody beacon, your nose,' I said and grinned at her.

'It's the sherry,' she murmured. 'Am I really the right person?'

'Yes. Have some more,' I said, and filled up her glass.

'Your nose . . .' she frowned up at me. 'Your nose is like a squashed cucumber.'

'Wow. Thanks. You say the nicest things.'

'Do you know –?' she began, and gazed at the apple in her hand. 'Do you realize that your name is Adam?'

'Holy Moses. Then you must be . . .'

'No. I'm not. I'm Sam.'

'Pleased to meet you. Very.'

'Did I give you that apple?' she asked worriedly.

'Yes.' I finished it off.

'Oh. Then it's too late. We are lost. Paradise lost.'

'It's never too late,' I said and smiled at her.

She smiled back, got to her feet and stood and stretched her arms above her, outlined by the fire-light. Then she did a pirouette and held her hands out towards me.

'Shall we go to bed?' she said offhandedly.

She moved away, swaying from side to side, moving in time to a tune she was humming.

I stood up, somewhat amazed at her forwardness, but eager to comply.

'What's that song called?' she asked, dancing away from me and towards the bedroom.

'What? Oh. Isn't it *Woodstock*?'

'Oh, yes . . .' She smiled at me, and then sang the words: 'We are stardust, we are golden. And we've got to get ourselves back to the Garden. . . .'

'Away in a manger', sang the choir, in beautiful female harmonies, their voices filling the hospital chapel.

We couldn't see them – they were behind us up in the organ gallery. But there was a lot for me to look at, apart from Sam. There were glittering golden mosaics all over the vaulted roof, marbled walls, and masses of holly and ivy below the windows, not to mention what was going on in the candle-lit altar end. The chapel was very high church – there was bell-ringing and incense – and it wasn't very big. But it was packed with nurses, medical students and patients, some of whom had been brought from their wards in wheelchairs and thronged the back of the chapel, looking very decrepit and ill, one or two with drip-bottles hanging above them.

I felt somewhat awkward being there. But Sam was really enjoying herself, and singing loudly.

She was wearing her full blue and white striped nurse's gear, with cape, cap, and black belt.

'I can't go out like *this*,' she had said, referring to her shirt and jeans. 'And I'm not going to get all dressed up.' Though this of course was what she did, taking a lot of time and trouble in the process. Meanwhile, I was yawning my head off. I would myself have preferred to have gone out for a drink, or to a party. We couldn't afford a meal, both being broke after all the buying of gifts and festive spending. But she was feeling sentimental about Christmas and the hospital, which she was leaving in two weeks' time, and she said it would do me good to go to Midnight Mass. When I questioned whether she needed to put on her uniform she said: 'I'm a nurse. We're going to a place of worship in my place of work. And I don't want to be *out* of place.' I couldn't complain. She looked fantastic all kitted out. No wonder all her patients loved her and gave her presents. I wondered if she would like the set of white stone Casa Pupo goblets I had bought her.

'Be near me, Lord Jesus,' she sang. 'I ask thee to stay close by me for ever, and love me, I pray.'

She was holding her hymn-book with her right hand. My book was in my left. Our disengaged hands were touching, with fingers interlaced.

'Bless all the dear children in thy tender care, and fit us for heaven, to live with thee there.'

It was nearly midnight. The priest asked us all to turn about and face the crib which was in one of the alcoves at the rear. Gathered about it under an illuminated star were large plaster-of-paris statues of Mary, Joseph, angels, shepherds, and animals, gazing adoringly at nothing. The crib was empty apart from some straw. I wondered why the plaster infant was missing.

Behind us, the priest said: 'Let us remember that stable in Bethlehem where was born of the blessed Virgin a child who would save mankind – the Son of God, who would live and die and live again and give us life eternal. The moment of his birth approaches.'

This was quite the wrong thing to say in a hospital. One of the medical students near us said quietly: 'Push. . . .'

There were giggles and sounds of stifled mirth all over the chapel, and when the altar-boy tinkled his bell at midnight, there were other whispered comments of a crude nature.

Then a nurse, who wasn't expecting such a vocal reception, emerged from the dressing-gowned patients with a very new-born baby in her arms. With a nervous smile she placed it in the crib. This should have been a magic moment. But the baby belched, or something.

The chapel filled with subdued choking noises and snorts. I whispered to Sam: 'It must have been the sherry.' She was trying not to laugh.

The situation was saved when the choir in their red capes, burst out singing *Gloria in Excelsis Deo* and startled us all.

I enjoyed the rest of the service as much as Sam. Everyone in fact sang very joyfully, and when it was over, the hospital corridors outside the chapel rang with chatter and laughter, which turned into loud exclamations when we got outside.

It had been snowing. It was still snowing, and everything was covered in spotless white.

'That's wonderful!' said Sam. 'A white Christmas! I've never seen one before.'

She stood still, with her face upturned and her arms outstretched trying to catch snowflakes with her lips as well as her hands.

'Come on,' I said. The snow was resting on her uniform and on what showed of her plaited hair. 'Or do you want to be a snow-woman?'

I added: 'That was snow-lady, that was my wife.' But she didn't seem to hear.

The short drive back through the muted traffic to Gloucester Place passed in something near silence. The snow muffled sound and made everything look strange. I happily skidded the car around snowy corners, with my foot on the accelerator, so that the rear-end slid all over the shop.

'Must you?' she said. 'Let's get home safely.'

'I know what I'm doing,' I said.

In the flat there was a sort of party in progress, rather raucous, with the record-player going non-stop and presents of wine and sherry being drained away. However, as the girls who were there were working the next day, it didn't go on too long – they had to get to bed. I had myself to get to Stanford-in-the-Vale, where I was spending Christmas with my family.

I tucked Sam up in her cosy bed, kissing her several times, as I was pretending to be Santa Claus and his reindeer who all wanted to kiss her goodnight. My present I left at the foot of her bed in a pillow case together with a box of crackers and a box of chocolate liqueurs.

'Happy Christmas, love,' she whispered. 'Bless you.'

'Night-night. Sleep well. Love you.'

At 2 a.m. on Christmas Day I left the flat and drove home through the snow.

I didn't return to London until 30 December, after the usual round of visits and parties, which meant meeting all the cousins, aunts and uncles, apart from my brother's and sisters' families and their children. Everyone asked me questions about my job, and I told them what I could.

It was the snowiest Christmas period I ever remembered, and we all had a jolly good time, indoors and out.

One morning, over coffee, my parents got me alone and had a little go at me about my future. My mother wanted to know what the situation was between me and Sam – whether I intended to marry her, and if so, when. She rather suspected that I might pack in my job, push off to Africa, and live in sin with Sam among the blacks – which I assured her would never happen. She said she hoped I wouldn't leave the police force, as I was now doing so well and making a go of it. My father took this further, and suggested that I should re-sit my sergeant's exam, get a higher mark, and then go to the Police College, Bramshill. He said that I had now been with the police for seven years and that it was time I got myself promoted.

I wouldn't have minded that and thought it would happen next year anyway. But I wasn't particularly keen on Bramshill. In my opinion, it wasn't a good thing for a CID officer to be too rapidly promoted and accordingly never really know his job, which he could properly learn only through experience. I wasn't very keen either on going back to school, or on the prospect of becoming a desk man, which most of the inspectors and upwards seemed to be. I wasn't even sure that I wanted to stay in the police force.

This wasn't something I could say to my father or mother as they would have been fearfully disappointed. The previous year, some months before I joined the Drug Squad, I had become so generally fed up with the police that I decided to chuck it all in. I came home on a Friday evening and said: 'I'm handing in my papers on Monday. I can't take it any more.' Father said: 'For God's sake, son, hold on a bit!' So I did. I wasn't being reasonable and was depressed.

Being with the Drug Squad changed all that, and my parents were pleased, commenting on the fact that whenever I went home I was always singing the Squad's praises. But then, when I got really fond of Sam after her illness and she of me, I began to have doubts about continuing with the police. If I'd mentioned this to my parents, they would of course have wanted to know why I felt like that, and any answer would of course have involved Sam, who didn't care for me being a policeman. So I said nothing. But everything rather depended on what she wanted, and this wasn't very clear. What was clear was what she *didn't* want – that is, to settle down, live in England, marry before she was twenty-five and marry a policeman. The trouble was I couldn't offer any alternative. There was nothing else I could do or wished to do against my parents' wishes. But if she had actually asked me to leave the police and live with her in Africa – married or not, I think I would have done so. But she didn't. So I stayed where I was and waited for something to happen, or for her to change her mind. Anyway, there was so much going on, at work and off duty, that it was easy to be optimistic. We were always with people, even when we were together. So any heart-to-hearts, even if we had wanted them, were easily avoided.

On New Year's Eve we went to a party behind the Cumberland Hotel.

'Happy New Year!' we wished each other, as if she wasn't going away, as if we would be together throughout the year.

On New Year's Day – Sam worked in the morning – I picked her up in the afternoon and we drove to Bristol, where there was a dance at the University that night. Christian, Sam's younger brother, and his girl-friend came too. We all drank far too much, stayed the night on someone's floor and felt shattered the next day. It was also very cold.

That was on 2 January, a Saturday. After lunch Sam and I drove back to Hungerford, to see Bill and Sue. We stayed overnight at the farm. Then it was back to foggy London as Sam was working on Sunday afternoon.

She worked every day for the rest of the week – Friday being her last. I saw her whenever I could.

On the Monday, 4 January, my parents asked her to have tea with them in the Guide Club in Belgrave Square. My mother was a Brown Owl for five years. I was a bit apprehensive about the occasion – rightly, as it happened. When I met Sam afterwards she was livid. She had gone along for a sociable chat and had taken a lot of trouble with her appearance and clothes – she had borrowed the best bits and pieces from the other girls in the flat. What she got, she said, was a lengthy interrogation. She said she had been cross-examined about her intentions concerning me.

'They don't want me to lead you astray! Of course I didn't say it was the other way around. I tried to smile, sweetly of course, said "Gosh" and "Gracious" and practically had to apologize for loving you. It was dreadful. I've never known a family as possessive as yours!'

After that she went right off my parents, and the next time she met them she was very cool.

Also during that week – with two of the girls from the flat, Bunny and Sue – we saw a film at the Empire, *Ryan's Daughter*. I liked it, and was quite moved by it. Sam described it as 'sex education at its most picturesque'. After it we went on her suggestion, and the other girls came too, to a Greek restaurant in Charlotte Street for kebabs and bottles of retsina. Bunny got quite tight, and waved at all the cars in Park Lane. For some reason she was staying at home then. I stayed the night with Sam.

Soon afterwards we went out again – after I had bathed and shaved at the flat. She insisted on this as I was looking particularly shaggy and unshaven on account of the special job I was on then – nothing to do with the Salahs. We had a good night-out at Haddies, a discotheque and restaurant in a basement near South Kensington tube. They played all her favourite smoochy records, and though I'm not good at dancing, she enjoyed herself so much and moved so well that I enjoyed myself just watching her and holding her close.

On the way back to Gloucester Place we were racing through Hyde Park, trying to get to the other side before the gates closed at midnight, when the Gestapo stopped us. They said I was speeding. I explained why, and made a joke of it. They thought I was just being smart and became quite nasty. So I showed them my warrant card. They thought I had stolen it, and refused to believe I was a DC until I correctly told them what floor my office was on, the Commissioner's name and the office number of Criminal Intelligence at the Yard, C11.

'They were going to arrest you,' said Sam. 'Oh, gosh. How funny.'

'They would have, if I hadn't been one of them,' I said. 'Being a policeman has its uses.'

That night I stayed with her again.

This was in fact not all that usual – staying the night. But as she was going away, she let me. However, during the weekend it all went wrong.

Friday, 8 January, was her last day at the Middlesex Hospital. It was also very busy. When I got to the flat she was lying on her bed, listening to Bruch's *Violin Concerto*, and feeling very low. Farewell presents from patients and nurses were piled on the dressing-table. I tried to cheer her up, but didn't succeed too well. Fortunately, as we were going to my sister Jane's house in Hertfordshire for the weekend, she had something to occupy her mind. But as this was also an occasion for farewells, it didn't really help. She was fairly subdued. This was despite the weather, which was unusually mild for January – almost like spring – except it wasn't. We went for walks in the fields and lanes, did some jigsaw puzzles that Jane happened to have, and on Saturday evening there was a party with gallons of beer.

The following morning Sam still hadn't made an appearance by the time the others went to church, so I took a breakfast tray up to her bedroom. She didn't get around to eating – the reason being that as we were alone in the house I took advantage of the situation and of her. It was a big mistake. I really blotted my copybook that time. Not that she reacted immediately – after a bit of a struggle she just gave in. But when we got back to London, after driving over to my parents for tea and then on to dinner with Bill and Sue – it was all good-bye – Sam said she had a headache, was tired, and as it was late, would I mind not coming in, not even for coffee? I of course agreed and sympathized and said I would see her tomorrow.

I didn't – not for three days.

I rang her up on the Monday.

'I just want to be on my own for a few days,' she said. 'I've so many things to do.'

'But you're not working,' I said. 'What about the evenings?'

'There are people to see – friends – before I go. Christian for instance.'

'Your brother?'

'He's taking me out to dinner.'

'When?'

'Tuesday.'

'Oh. What about Wednesday?'

'I'm going out.'

'Oh. I could see you at lunchtime. And drive you about if you wanted to do any shopping.'

'Thank you, but I can manage on my own.'

It was no use. She seemed to be right off me, though this was very difficult to bear and even believe after all we had done together and said to each other.

'What's the matter?' I said. 'Is anything wrong?'

'No,' she said. 'I've told you – I just want to be on my own.'

I gazed at the mouth-piece of the receiver, imagining her at the other end.

'Shall I see you on Thursday?' I said. This was the day before she left. She *must* see me then. There was a long pause, which made me very miserable. I had to say something.

'I love you,' I reminded her.

Her voice said: 'Yes. All right. On Thursday.'

Those three days were like three months. But as I was rushing about London like a blue-arsed fly on police work, driving between the office and Windsor, Ascot, Chelsea, Muswell Hill in North London, and places south of the River, I didn't get too worried. In between, I reserved a table for two at a restaurant called Spot 3, where they played classical records as background music. I also bought Sam a going-away present, a ring – not an engagement ring, but a signet ring with S-A-M on it – the initials of her full christian name with mine in the middle. She had always liked my ring with the family crest on it – a rampant griffin.

It was good to see her again when I called at the flat. She asked me in for a coffee. She was wearing a long high-waisted dress, a new one, and her hair hung loose on her shoulders. In honour of the occasion I had also dressed myself up a bit, and was wearing my green suede jacket and a golden tie she had bought me. Until she came along I had never taken much interest in clothes. But she liked me to look reasonably up to date, and used to go shopping with me in King's Road and advise me on what to buy. The funny thing was that she wasn't all that interested in clothes herself. Not that it mattered as she looked fabulous in anything.

'What are you looking at?' she said. We were seated in different chairs on either side of the electric fire.

'You,' I answered and grinned. 'You look terrible.'

'Oh. I thought you had noticed.'

'What?'

'You *haven't* noticed. Look at my eyes.'

'I'm looking.'

'Well?'

'Come closer,' I said, reaching out for her. 'I think –'

'No,' she said and sighed dramatically. 'And it cost a fortune.'

'What did?'

'I've had my eyelashes dyed.'

She had – dark brown. I burst out laughing.

'Whatever for?' I chortled.

'To give me a degree of sophistication when I go home – a touch of the woman of the world. Obviously, I've failed.' She was sending herself up.

'No,' I said. 'It makes your eyes all mysterious – like pools of brown swamp-water.' We laughed together.

'Fool,' she said.

Everything seemed all right. But she hadn't kissed me when I arrived, and there was a distance to her, as if she were already half-way to Africa.

We drove to Spot 3 in Chelsea. It was normally a very good place to take girls, to put them in a romantic receptive mood, with all the Tchaikovsky, Rachmaninov, and so on that tinkled away in the background. But although Sam clearly enjoyed herself and said everything was super, she wasn't somehow being loving, just very affectionate and kind, as if we were very good friends and not much more.

There were occasions when I said to myself that I would never understand women. I tried. I worked away at it. But sometimes, as on this occasion, the fact came home to me – that women were basically another species.

Sam was chatting away enthusiastically about Africa, and about what we would do when I went there. This had been discussed before, at New Year, and was now a definite plan which was very welcome to me. The idea was that once the Salah business gave me a moment – when they set off overland for Lahore – I would then fly out to Nairobi for a holiday at Sam's home, probably for a month. I had been to Africa before, to Kenya, two years before, when I stayed with my sister Jane and her husband who was at that time warden on a game reserve of one and a half million acres. That was really something I would have liked to be.

Sam said I should investigate the possibility while I was with her.

'It would be wonderful,' she said, leaning forward, 'if you could get a job out there. You'd love it. All that space and freedom. Everything *here* is so small and confined – it really is – with people travelling like clockwork toys between home and work and work and home, with little excursions to see other people now and then. And it's all so superficial, conventional. All the wrong things matter, like what you wear and what you say, and how you say it. You've no idea. Well, I suppose you have. But in Africa everyone is so much more genuinely friendly. It's a happy country. The Africans are a very happy people, always laughing. And people are more interested. And interesting! You can meet and talk to such different kinds of people, from ambassadors to hitch-hikers. And if you're a girl you can talk to a man without him wanting to get you into bed.'

'Cor!' I said. 'What's wrong with the chaps out there then? Letting the side down rather – what?'

'There's nothing wrong with them,' she said. 'It's just that they have respect.'

'Respect? Oh. Sorry about last Sunday,' I said.

'Don't be sorry,' she answered. 'I've no regrets.'

She smiled.

As I've said – women are sometimes difficult to understand.

At the end of the meal, over coffee and liqueurs, I produced the ring from my pocket. It was in a small box.

'What is it?' she said, somewhat anxiously.

'Have a look,' I said.

She opened the box very cautiously and inspected the contents.

'It's a signet ring!' she cried. 'Oh, how lovely! With – what's written on it?'

I explained about the initials. 'Put it on,' I said.

'No – you do it.'

Unfortunately, it didn't fit any of her fingers.

'It's too big,' she said. 'And I can't wear it on my thumb.'

'I'll have it altered.'

'No, no. I'll do that.'

We argued a bit about that, until she got her way. She put the ring back in its box.

'Thank you, Buzz. Thank you very much. . . . You're always giving me things,' she said with a small frown.

'I *like* giving you things.'

She looked at me, very seriously.

'You're such a lovely man,' she said. 'A nice, kind, lovely man.'

'I agree,' I said. 'I love you too.'

By the time we got back to the flat, we had both had quite a lot to drink.

It was a cloudy night and cold, but in the sitting-room, with the fire on, it was warm and snug. Alone, as the other girls had all gone to bed, we lay on the sofa with our arms around each other, not saying anything for a while, not doing anything either.

I was feeling fairly miserable. Some slow symphonic theme was trundling round my head. There was no doubt that tomorrow she would go. In the car I had jokingly said that unless she agreed that we went off then and there and found a vicar to make an honest woman of her, I would drive the car off Tower Bridge into the Thames. She said she wasn't too keen on that, and anyway, what was the point? – we would see each other again. In the meantime out in Africa I suspected she would be seeing a lot of other blokes. Some fellow would come along with more brains, money and position, and sweep her off her feet. In England there had been only me – and she had been only mine. I'd made sure of that. But more than anything I was going to miss her – seeing her, hearing her, touching her, just having her around.

She was very warm against me. I could feel her breath on my neck. Everything about her was reassuring and loved.

'We've had some good times, haven't we?' she said.

I thought about them – all the good times we'd had – and that everything was coming to an end. I couldn't help the tears coming to my eyes, and running down my cheeks, though I managed not to make any sound.

'I shall miss you,' she said. 'And your family. . . . It's been a long time. I mean, we've known each other a long time. . . . And you were the first who – the first boy I –'

She noticed I wasn't breathing properly, and looked up at me.

'Oh, Buzz . . . Buzz. . . . Please don't cry.'

'I can't help it,' I said with difficulty. 'I'm going to – lose you. . . .'

'No, darling. No. Oh, love, love. Please don't. Please don't!'

In a few moments she was in tears as well, and making undying and incoherent protestations of love and devotion – as I was to her. I said she didn't have to go – I didn't want her to go. She said it wasn't for ever. I said I was afraid it might be and that I didn't know when she was coming back.

'Oh, what are we going to do?' she sobbed.

Eventually, we realized there was nothing we could do, and a cloud of misery settled over me, added to by my shame at having been so foolish as to cry. I didn't stay much longer. I embraced her very passionately once and left the flat.

I was back at 7 a.m. the following morning to take her and her luggage to Victoria Station, where she would get a train for Gatwick Airport and there a flight to Nairobi.

It was still dark night, and raining. One of the other girls came with us. I could hardly speak.

At the station I put her luggage on the pavement, gave her a kiss and got back in the car. I didn't even say good-bye.

I somehow drove to the Yard, hardly seeing, breathing deeply and feeling half dead.

Without quite knowing what I was doing I walked about New Scotland Yard, saying things, writing up my diary, signing forms.

At the end of the day I drove in my red Volkswagen to Muswell Hill, with £25,000 in a brief-case, and a revolver in a shoulder-holster under my jacket, and Nobby by my side.

9

Early in the New Year – I think it was on Monday, 4 January, the day that Sam had tea with my parents in the Guide Club – I was asked by the Flying Squad to do a job for them. They wanted someone to pose as a buyer, and as Nick was engaged on another inquiry, nothing to do with the Salahs, they sent for the first time for me.

I was very chuffed about this as it was to be a solo effort and meant I was getting to be recognized as a useful bloke to have around. Working with the Flying Squad was also a step in the right direction. It didn't mean that I discontinued my Drug Squad activities, nor was I officially seconded to them. I was just borrowed.

They wanted me to assist in the busting up of a set-up that, as they believed, manufactured drugs at one of the universities. It wasn't that unusual for them to deal with matters relating to the drug scene. They dealt with all kinds of organized crime, usually of the big-time sort, and had all kinds of informants. Not all informants in our line came to us. It depended on personal contacts and recommendations. In this case the informant had gone to the Flying Squad. Everyone in the Yard, and in the police generally, was very protective, even jealous, about informants, who were cherished and treated with more consideration than some policemen's wives.

The first thing I did was to meet the FS informant, who was also going to be my contact man.

The meeting took place in a nondescript van where, in the dark interior, lightened by slits near the roof through which one could observe unseen, we were introduced to each other as Buzz and Bernard, which wasn't his real name.

He was about my size, a very long-haired, lanky fellow and pretty scruffy. Beside him, I looked almost trendy, though I was dressed quite casually, in dark-brown cords, tie, and a leather jacket.

The van was parked in one of the back streets of Muswell Hill, a suburb in North London. I had been driven there by two Flying Squad men, one of whom had then collected Bernard.

The two of us, having discussed who I was supposed to be – ex-public school, wealthy, well-travelled, jobless, and after some easy money – left the van and walked past the shops of Muswell Hill Broadway, which is on the ridge of a hill near Alexandra Palace and has very fine views of London, over Hornsey and Islington to the East End, where I was a PC.

We were to have lunch with a guy who, I was informed, could bring us in contact with a drug-maker.

He had been told by our Bernard, acting on Flying Squad

instructions, that I was loaded and was willing to pay £25,000 for 200,000 capsules of LSD. This was a fairly low bid. I was offering to buy each capsule for 2s. 6d. On the black market at that time one capsule was worth at least £1. Two hundred thousand would therefore fetch as many pounds. Theoretically if I sold what I had to pushers at 10 shillings a capsule, I might have made a profit of over £75,000.

The rendezvous was in a small restaurant. Near the door was a bar, where Bernard introduced me to the contact, Martyn Wetherup. He was a television camera-man, aged twenty-eight. He seemed friendly enough and was well-dressed in the moddish way, and was also wearing a leather jacket.

He bought us drinks. We sat down at one of the shiny-topped tables and ordered a meal. Outside, I knew that the nondescript van with the two FS men inside it was parked in sight of the restaurant. I had seen it arrive as we went inside.

So I settled back to enjoy the meal, if not the company, feeling that I held all the cards.

The other two clearly weren't as relaxed as I was. Bernard was in fact rather jumpy, and kept playing with the cutlery. I was able to joke about this and play him up, saying to Wetherup that Bernard was always on the look-out for fuzz and had a guilty conscience.

Wetherup asked me some questions about myself, but as I was the one with the loot, I had a right to be cagey. I told him however that I'd been in Africa and also mentioned the fact that I'd been in Pakistan and had driven back to this country overland. 'A hell of a journey, man,' I said. 'But worth it.' I also sketched out a plan I had for buying a yacht, and bringing a cargo of cannabis from Morocco to the Isle of Wight. 'Those customs haven't a clue, man,' I said.

He had no reason to be suspicious – despite my somewhat stagey manner. These people often caricatured themselves, especially in their language, with which I was fairly well acquainted, having learned it mostly from Nick – words like *acid* for LSD, *bread* for money, *caps* for capsules, *gear* and *stuff* for drugs. During most of the meal, however, we discussed football and the disaster at Glasgow Rangers' football ground the previous Saturday in which sixty-six people had been killed when crush barriers gave way as spectators left Ibrox Park.

Bernard remained silent, until we somehow got onto Vietnam and the war there, which he denounced rather bitterly, despite the fact that some 60,000 American troops were being withdrawn according to Wetherup. 'But the bombing goes on,' said Bernard. 'Jesus. It's vile. Really vile.' Political conversations were not much to my liking, so I said: 'Where's the stuff then?' which shut them up.

I asked, as instructed, for 200,000 capsules of LSD and indicated that I could pay £25,000.

Wetherup blinked a bit, but said nothing one way or the other.

We arranged to meet again. I said I would give him a ring and fix a date. I couldn't give him my telephone number, I said, as I didn't have one. He accepted this, and gave me his home number. Apparently he lived not far away. He paid for the meal and the three of us went outside.

'*Ciaio*,' I said, with a cheery wave and a grin as Wetherup left us.

Bernard and I walked off to a nearby pub, where I was collected by the FS men, who were eager for a drink, food and information in that order. Bernard went off on his own.

I had a few other meetings with Wetherup over the next ten days. They were necessary as he wouldn't, very wisely, talk over the phone – not that he had much to report when I saw him, which was mostly at my insistence and mostly for coffee. I tried to chivvy him along, saying I needed the stuff *now*, and talked about making other deals in the future. I said I knew someone who had a light aircraft and regularly popped over to the Continent – a useful way, I suggested, of avoiding customs and getting the stuff secretly into the country. A small plane, I said, could land nearly anywhere. The 'someone' was in fact one of Sam's cousins who had a private aircraft.

Shortly before my last night out with Sam, I drove to Muswell Hill accompanied by DS Nobby Pilcher, who was posing as my 'minder' but was really guarding the brief-case full of bank-notes on the back seat. He was armed with a .38 Webley revolver and so was I. We went in my Volkswagen, which was shadowed through the streets by a nondescript van loaded with FS men, more anxious about the money than about our personal safety. The cash had been very meticulously counted out, handed over and signed for. Half of it was real money, mostly in ten pound notes and twenties. Half of it was bent.

Nobby and I joked together about giving the nondescript van the slip and catching the next plane to the Bahamas. We had the feeling we were both in the wrong business.

I parked not far from Wetherup's flat, got out and strolled along Muswell Hill Broadway, casually peering at the lighted shop-windows. Nobby remained in the car. The FS men in their civvies kept an eye on both of us.

Arriving at my destination, I rang the front doorbell, and was let in. The flat was fairly large. But I didn't stay there long enough to examine it.

'The bread's below,' I said.

Wetherup came outside with me to the car. I explained who Nobby was, or rather wasn't, on the way, and for good measure I addressed him somewhat rudely when we got there. Nobby looked suitably surly and said nothing.

Wetherup got into the back and I into the front beside my minder. He opened the brief-case, and the three of us gazed with wonder on all that lovely money. For a moment I think we forgot our roles. When we spoke our voices were hushed.

'Christ,' said Wetherup.

'Amen,' I said. 'Isn't that something?'

After a brief discussion he left us.

On Friday, 15 January, on the afternoon of the day on which Sam left me, I drove in the rain and gloom to Muswell Hill more miserable than I had been for years. Nobby was beside me again, and again we were both armed. On the back seat was the brief-case containing £25,000.

It was like a dream. It would have seemed strange at the best of times, like a scene from a film. But a part of me was still with Sam, and with her as she flew homewards in her father's monoplane from Nairobi over the hot dry bushlands of Tanzania to the cooler slopes of Kilimanjaro.

I parked the car and walked swiftly along the Broadway in the rain. I entered the building where Wetherup lived, and rang his doorbell. He let me in. He took me to a room at the back. On the way there I observed that in the sitting-room were four people. I saw a quantity of LSD, some of it in capsules, some of it loose in powder form in plastic bags – as the police found it later. Wetherup switched on the single ceiling light. What he said made me angry. For a moment I really hated him and the people who traded in drugs. The revolver under my left arm-pit pressed against me, reminding me I was licensed to kill. I swore very loudly. I complained that he was inadequate and inefficient. He apologized and left the flat with me, to check that I had the money. This time he didn't get in the car. Nobby opened the brief-case for his inspection, and then he left us.

I slumped into the driver's seat, trembling, and drove the car, as planned, to where the nondescript van was parked. We sat there, waiting, for an hour.

What happened in the interim was this. Two FS men had entered the building after Wetherup and I had gone out. Everyone then left in the flat was arrested.

An hour later, as arranged and in order not to lose my cover, I returned to the flat and rang the doorbell.

An FS man opened the door, and grinned. I asked him if Mr Wetherup was in and was told that he wasn't, and that his friends were no longer there.

'Is everything all right?' I inquired.

'Couldn't be better,' said the FS man. 'Thank you for calling, mate. But we've nothing to sell today.'

That night after the money had been returned to the Yard, where it was checked and counted before I was issued with a receipt, I drank the night away, in celebration of a successful job and in sorrow at the loss of Sam.

I heard later that a woman and three men appeared at Highgate magistrates court charged with possessing dangerous drugs. The four, three of whom were students, appeared at Middlesex Sessions on 19 April. I wasn't a witness at the trial – the identity of Buzz the Buyer had to be safeguarded. The prosecutor said that when police raided the flat they interrupted the making-up of drug capsules and found LSD worth £50,000 in bulk or about £150,000 if sold in small quantities. He also said the LSD was stronger than any previously examined at the Metropolitan police laboratory. Apparently it had been manufactured by one of the accused, a student called

Eric Adler, at his university. He pleaded guilty to the unauthorized possession of 4,284 tablets containing LSD and 433·8 grams of the same at the flat. The two other students, and another man, pleaded not guilty. The latter also denied possessing 1·53 grams of cannabis and 1·3 grams of cannabis resin. He made a statement, saying he was only the middle man.

On 23 April, Adler was sentenced to eighteen months' imprisonment. The two other students were acquitted. The fourth man was fined £100 after admitting possessing a small quantity of cannabis. The judge having decided as a matter of law it would not be safe to convict, had previously directed the jury to return a verdict of not guilty in the case of the charge against the fourth man of possessing LSD.

So that was that.

Before all this, back in January, the only cloud was Sam's departure. I got over that, for I knew I'd be seeing her again. Besides, I had a lot of other things on my mind to do with my job – mostly to do with the Salahs, whose preparations for their trip to Pakistan were now reaching a climax.[1]

Mum: I've just had a letter – from faraway places.
John: Yes.
Mum: Everything will be ready at the end of February. All right?
John: Yes. [sounds half asleep] . . . Can you bring £7 over, Mum?
Mum: No. Your father's got to go to the airport – Niaz Ali's leaving for England on the 10th. He's got to go and book his ticket.
John: Okay.

Their conversation was on the morning of 1 January. John wasn't too well. Apparently he was suffering from a chemical deficiency of the brain which was causing some nervous disorders. That's how the intercept summed up one of the many chats about his health. Kathy wasn't well either. She had flu. And she wasn't at Heathrow Airport with the rest of the family on 3 January to wave good-bye to Mohammed, who, according to the intercept, was flying off to Pakistan. However, he didn't get off the ground – the flight was delayed because of fog.

Mohammed and his wife, and Nigel and I, returned to the

1. Again, the extracts that follow are taken from the intercept transcripts given in evidence at the Perjury trial. – G.H.

Airport on the 4th. The same thing happened again. At the Perjury trial a woman who worked for PIA witnessed to the fact that M. Salah, on 5 January, swopped a BOAC ticket for a Pakistan International Airlines flight to Karachi. The flight was delayed by fog for some hours, but eventually left Heathrow Airport that afternoon.

The day before, a Monday, John rang up his sister Janet in the evening for a chat about the trailer under construction at Crevald's boatyard.

John: I've just spoken to the builders, and he said the interior depth will be just over three feet. It won't be enough, Janet.

Janet: It won't be enough.

John: We will have to make it bigger. It's eleven feet long and five feet wide. I said I'll be in in the morning. . . .

Janet: Well, if we make it higher and put a mirror in, it will look as though we are using it for our clothing and camping equipment. . . .

John: I'll pop round and we can finalize it for tomorrow morning.

Janet: Yes. Okay then.

John: And can you come with me? – only I'm taking the Landrover with me. About nine.

Janet: I don't know.

John: Well, look – you must soon make your mind up because he only has ten or twelve days to do it.

Janet: Well, I've got to see about the flight. Well, look – we'll scrap the boat idea, and have it done nice inside.

John: Yes. Okay – I know what we want. . . .

The boat idea seemed to have been to take an actual boat on the trailer to Pakistan and back – in fact not such a bright idea, even somewhat crackpot. Perhaps they had considered using it to row from France to England on the way back, thus outwitting us all.

The next morning, 5 January, Kathy rang the boatyard to tell them John wouldn't be able to collect the trailer until about 11.30 a.m. It wasn't in fact collected until the following week.

In the meantime, on the 7th, Nobby Pilcher found the Highwayman van, which the Salahs at their trial were alleged by the prosecution to have used on their previous venture to Pakistan and back in the spring of 1970. As a result of inquiries Nobby went with WDC Morag McGibbon to Chadwell Heath on the eastern edge of London, where he examined the van, PBH 24H and found that it was fitted with a false floor. The vehicle was later photographed.

It was just another possible piece of evidence to add to the mass we were accumulating almost daily.

On Tuesday, 12 January, John telephoned his mother in the afternoon about his health. He said he was going deaf and thought this was probably caused by the tablets he was taking. He also told her that the trailer would be ready on Thursday the 14th.

On the 13th, at about 8.30 p.m., Mrs Salah telephoned back.

Mum: Hallo, John. I've got the flu now.

John: Have you?

Mum: I just want to ask you a very simple question.

John: What?

Mum: You know if you've got four library books and you put them on top of each other and you measure them – but on the other hand, if you put two one side and two on top of one another you're not taking up so much space, are you?

John: You are – because it doesn't matter. Because they are still equal amounts.

Mum: But I've just measured them, and they are ten inches high. And if you take the other two the other way – you see what I mean – you cut it down to five inches high.

John: You haven't – because you're still taking up the same area width-wise. So therefore it doesn't make any difference. You can't put a pint of milk into a half-pint jug.

Mum: No. But you can stack a thing away, so that –

John: Yeah. I know what you mean. And that's the way I'm doing it, Mum. . . .

The phone was then handed over to Janet for another nutty conversation, between her and John, about measurements and materials and about what time and in what vehicle they should go to the boatyard on the following morning. How they ever got as far as Pakistan was sometimes a wonder to us. A decision was eventually made.

John: You come over about nine.

Janet: Okay, then.

John: Look – I can't order any wood until I've got it and can measure up myself, you see.

Janet: All right then. I thought you knew how you were going to put chests on the floor.

John: Yeah.

Janet: Well, I had a better idea of putting them up the side.

John: What?

Janet: Chests – cupboards.

John: Well, we'll work it all out, Janet. It should take about a week to build it all in. Come over about nine then.

Janet: Okay. See you in the morning.

John: And I'll change the colour. I'll paint it dark blue.

Janet: Oh, not blue. It will clash with the vehicle.

John: Or green.

Janet: Dark green.

John: All right then.

Janet handed the telephone back to her mother, who said to John that she was worried about him looking so pale.

John: Look, Mum. My nerves are a bit on edge – because I've got a lot on my mind, you know. Just come over at nine o'clock. All right?

Mum: Will you go to bed then now?

John: Yes. All right, Mum. See you tomorrow.

We didn't, however, as she never put in an appearance at the boatyard that morning. It was really extraordinary how nothing ever seemed to turn out as they'd planned. I gave the following account of what happened next at the Salah trial.[1]

Q: Have you a note for an incident on January 14th? – A: Yes.

Q: A Thursday? – A: Yes.

Q: On that day, with DS Pilcher and other officers, were you once again keeping observation in the vicinity of Crevald's boatyard? – A: Yes.

Q: Did you see the Landrover again? – A: Yes.

Q: At what time did you see it? – A: About 9.45 a.m.

Q: Who did you see in it? – A: John and Janet.

1. The next two passages in italics are taken from Mr Corkery's examination of, in the first instance Adam, and in the second, Nobby Pilcher. Kelaher's evidence largely corroborated Pilcher's as to what took place in the morning. – G.H.

Q: Where did they go? – A: They entered the offices of the boatyard and stayed there until about 11.10 a.m.

Q: Then did you see a trailer? – A: Yes.

Q: Did you take a photograph of that trailer at that time? – A: Yes.

Actually I took several photographs before John and Janet went off in the Landrover towing the trailer behind them. The photos were taken from inside a nondescript van with my own camera, a Zenith; I was using a small tele-photo lens. But as I was shooting through wire-meshed glass and as it was a foggy morning, the photos weren't all that good.

That weekend I went home, exhausted, and slept most of the time.

But the indefatigable Nobby never let up. Most of *his* Sunday was spent at Ascot, with DCI Kelaher. This is how he described his day to the court at the Salah trial.

Q: Coming to January 17th, the Sunday, with DCI Kelaher did you go to Kier Park, Ascot? – A: Yes.

Q: The time? – A: About 10.20 a.m.

Q: Did you see the trailer again? – A: Yes, sir – in front of the garage, just outside the house.

Q: Did you keep observation generally on the premises until about noon? – A: Yes, sir.

Q: Did you see anything happening in relation to the trailer during that time? – A: During that time I saw John, Kathleen Ruth – the mother – and they were working on the trailer with Janet.

Q: John, Janet and Kathleen? – A: Yes.

Q: What were they doing as far as you could see? – A: They appeared to be altering the inside of the trailer.

Q: What articles or tools were they using? – A: I saw John with an electric drill and I saw pieces of wood being handled.

Q: And later on did you see the Landrover? – A: Yes, sir.

Q: What time was that? – A: That was about 9.30 p.m. the same evening.

Q: What did you see happen then? – A: That was being driven by John. It left the house at Kier Park. . . . The trailer remained behind.

I was back at work again on Monday, 18 January.

It was all go, as apart from the watch on the Salahs, there were three or four other jobs to be taken care of every day – other inquiries and investigations, not to mention office work, which prevented us from leaving London. But at some time or other we all – Nobby, Nick, Nigel and myself, and occasionally Morag and Kelaher – trotted down to Ascot and Slough to see how the Salahs were getting along.

Generally speaking, John Salah kept the Landrover at the house in Mapledene Road, and the trailer was parked on the open space in front of his parents' home.

I later told the court myself at the Salah trial that on Wednesday, 20 January, I saw John, Janet and Mrs Salah senior working on the trailer and that on the following day John and Janet started painting it the agreed shade of green. I also told the court that on the Friday morning I was at Ascot with Kelaher, where we stayed until about 3.30 p.m., watching John fiddle about the trailer.

The main action of that day involved Nobby, Nick, Nigel and Morag, who arrested a woman for possessing cannabis in SW4 – nothing special, just the kind of thing that happened all the time.

Two days later, on Sunday, 24 January, Nobby and Nigel were at Heathrow Airport, when Janet Salah took an afternoon flight to Jersey in the Channel Islands. This was where the Salahs had a bank account. Probably she went over to draw out some money to pay for the coming trip – the start of which we expected any day now.

Mohammed was still in Pakistan, making business deals no doubt in connection with carpets, coats and vests. Preparations in England for the journey seemed to have been completed. Activity at Ascot and Slough was at a minimum. Even the intercepts had little to report.

Then, on the night of Thursday, 28 January, John's wife, Kathy, telephoned her mother in Birmingham.

She complained about her health. Her mother reassured her, saying she would be coming to stay the following Monday. She asked when John was going. Kathy said Sunday evening. But she wasn't sure what time. He's going to be away about a month, she said. He's driving out and flying back.

That conversation was on the 28th.

A week before, in Lahore, Mohammed had allegedly written

in a panic to John. It was an air-mail letter and the stamp was franked on the 22nd.[1]

Dear John, I am sorry to say I am not wrote to your letter soon when I reached in Pakistan. John I have been to Pershore 9th January and came back 10th January night about 8.30 p.m. 13th January I was taken ill. I had very bad flu & temperature. Since 13th Jan. I never get of the bed and I don't know what is going on. So Doctor came to see me he spend about 1 hour to examine me. So I start treatment. Take me seven to eight days to get better. So I feel real weak. Please tell Jan & your mother DO NOT *start 31 Jan. & 1 February. I have cancelled everything. We will start fresh again.* DON'T *start till you hear from me. I find out everything. Why should we pay NR (New Rupees) 9½ thousand Deposit to get the goods. They want to put there profit fist away and to start make goods. So I said* NO. *Don't worry I will get my own terms on time. When the time is come. It will come soon. I am not coming back till I find proper place and right price. Wish you understand my point. Don't worry. Thing will turn better. I feel the* KHAN *is very big dog now. Please let know has he growing . . . Anyhow remember me to Khan and Kathy. How is Kathy. Is she still under Doctor. And look after your health. Give my love to Kathy & to you & Jan & your mother. Love from Dad.*

The letter could never have reached Mapledene Road in time to have any effect – unfortunately for the Salahs, and for us. For on 20 January, the day before Mohammed put pen to paper, post office workers in England went on strike. Official mail deliveries stopped, and weren't resumed until 8 March, when the strike ended.

Blissfully unaware of Mohammed's alarms and cancellations, the Salahs in Slough and Ascot continued with their final preparations for the journey to Pakistan.

On Sunday, 31 January, Kathy rang her mother again, at lunchtime. John, she said, had left about half an hour ago.

Nobby and I were on duty. It turned out to be a thirteen-hour day. In my diary afterwards I noted that at 2 p.m. I went to Slough and Ascot and engaged in observation on the Salahs. Then I drove with Nobby to Dover and was 'engaged on observation re suspect vehicle' until 6 p.m., when we had a meal. We were further engaged re suspects between 6.30 and 8.30, when we had another snack and a drink. This break lasted a bit longer – until 9.15 p.m. The observation then continued

1. What was alleged to be the original letter was read out in court at the Salah trial by Mr Corkery in the following italicized words. – G.H.

until 1 a.m., when we took time off for a coffee before returning to London.

This was somewhat amplified by the statement I made later and by what I said in court at the Salah trial.

Q: On January 31st, 1971, a Sunday, together with DS Pilcher, did you go to the car ferry terminal at Dover harbour? – A: I did.

Q: Was this a question of following a vehicle all the way to Dover, or did you in fact start observation at Dover? – A: I started observation at Dover.

Q: In the car ferry terminal there at about 10.30 p.m. in the evening, did you see the Landrover? – A: I did.

Q: The same Landrover which you have described already? – A: Yes.

Q: In what part of the terminal was it? – A: It was in the outward-bound car park.

Q: Was the trailer attached? – A: Yes, it was.

Q: Who was near the Landrover and trailer? – A: There was John, Janet and Kathleen, the mother.

Q: Did you see the Landrover and trailer boarding the ferry? – A: Yes. I did.

Q: Did the ferry leave Dover? – A: It did. Yes . . . at about 12.30 a.m. on February 1st.

Q: So it is in the early hours of February 1st the ferry left. At any stage during your observation had the Landrover been taken off the ferry before the ferry left? – A: No.

Q: Was the ferry bound for Ostende? – A: Yes.

We stood on the quayside waving good-bye. The night was cold and clear. The sea wasn't rough. They would have a good crossing.

'Send us a postcard!' called Nobby.

'Be good!' I shouted. 'Don't do anything I wouldn't do!'

'Come back safely!' bellowed Nobby. '*Auf wiedersehen!*'

'*Au revoir!*'

'*Arrivederci!*'

'*Ciaio!* Bye! See you!'

Nobby pushed his hands deeper in his corduroy jacket pockets.

'See you come back all in one piece,' he said. 'We'll be waiting.'

We watched the ferry's lights diminish in the night. It was

difficult to realize that very nearly a year's constant work had come to a temporary stop. We couldn't follow them any further.

'When will they be back?' I said.

'Middle of March – about then,' Nobby answered. 'You should know. How long does the journey from Pakistan take?'

'Two weeks? Depends on the weather, punctures, riots, floods, earthquakes – and the driver,' I said with a grin.

'Two weeks there, and two weeks back – with a week in between to load up and to rest. And all we can do now is bloody well wait.'

He turned his back on the sea and began to walk towards the car park. 'Come on,' he said. 'Let's get back to the Yard.'

On the road going back to London, we heard on the car radio that Apollo 14 had been launched, forty minutes late, and was on its way to the moon.

We talked about it a bit. Everything was up in the air, so to speak – the Salahs, the astronauts, and us.

'Imagine,' Nobby said. 'Them up there. In nine days' time they'll have returned. They'll have been to the moon, and back. It's amazing, isn't it?'

'Fantastical,' I said, peering through the windscreen at the sky. 'It's *all* amazing.'

We eventually signed off duty at 3 a.m.

Two days later, I signed off work for a month.

On Friday, 5 February, at about the same time as Apollo 14's lunar module landed on the moon, my plane touched down at Nairobi. And the fifth man on the moon stepped onto the moon's surface as I walked on the slopes of Kilimanjaro with Sam.

PART THREE

We must not make a scarecrow of the law,
Setting it up to fear the birds of prey,
And let it keep one shape, till custom make it
Their perch and not their terror.

10

The Apollo 14 astronauts returned safely to Earth and splash-down in the Pacific on 9 February.

John Salah and his father Mohammed returned safely to England on 26 February, leaving Mrs Salah and Janet to drive the Landrover and its load across Europe.

In the meantime I was down on the farm in Africa, where it was summer. But at 6,000 feet or so it wasn't too hot. Kilimanjaro, at over 19,000 feet, is the highest mountain in Africa, and its broad top is always mantled with snow. It covers an area the size of London and loomed in the background of our brief safaris into the bush to look at and live among the animals. We camped out on two occasions and no one carried any guns. Lions made themselves heard nearby at night, but only a leopard took a stroll through our camp. On another occasion we drove the four hundred miles to the coast, to Mombasa and Malindi, and did some deep-sea fishing from a catamaran. Sam caught a sail-fish and was very pleased with herself.

It was a magnificent holiday, and I had a very good time. Very bronzed and fit I returned to England myself on 3 March after a tearful farewell with Sam at Nairobi Airport, and on the freezing morning of the 4th, a Thursday, I signed on duty again.

It was as if I had never been away – apart from the confusing fact for me that in my absence English currency had been decimalized. Shillings, florins, half-crowns, and sixpences were going or had gone, and in their place were the new pence, which now included three cheap-looking bronze coins worth supposedly a half-penny, a penny, and two pence. They took a lot of getting used to. So did the frosty weather. In fact, that night there were flurries of snow.

But the office chat was quite unchanged. Excited, but whispered, conversations were going on between Nobby, Nick and Nigel in which I was immediately involved. For the night before, John Salah had received a long-distance call from Turkey.

According to the intercept it had been an excruciatingly bad line.

The call was from Janet. She said she was bogged down in very heavy snow, fifty miles from Bulgaria, at a small place called Babaeski. The nearest big town was Edirne. Janet said she didn't know when she'd be home and complained about the difficult driving conditions. John wasn't very sympathetic. She said she would ring again.

We crowded together in front of a map that had been stuck on the office wall showing the possible overland route from England to Pakistan, and back. There was much speculation about Janet's and Mrs Salah's progress. Edirne was on Turkey's border with Bulgaria and Greece. They had already crossed the Hellespont and passed through Istanbul. Asia Minor and the Middle East were behind them. Basically, only the English Channel separated them from us. We reckoned that, given the delay of a week, they should be back in London about 15 March.

There had only been two other significant telephone calls while I was away – both at Mapledene Road. The intercept on Kier Park House had been terminated the day after Mrs Salah and Janet left the house.

On 26 February, John rang Kathy to tell her he had just landed and would come straight over to Slough bringing his father with him. He had a lot to tell her, he said. Everything had gone okay – but it was like a James Bond film.

On the 28th, a Sunday, the intercept revealed something of what he meant when, in the evening, he telephoned a certain doctor.[1]

1. This extract from the intercept transcripts, like the previous ones and like those that follow in this chapter, is taken from evidence given in court at the Perjury trial.

Doctor: Hallo. How did you get on?

John: Terrible.

Doctor: Did you get there all right?

John: Yes. But the Landrover is busted up. We picked the worst time of the year.

Doctor: What? – the Landrover isn't fit to come back?

John: It's been through quite a bit. I was in the middle of nowhere, trying to flag down three flaming Arabs as I went off the road. Nobody would stop. My feet and hands started to freeze, it was so cold. And all the gas froze up inside the Landrover. About five minutes later, six Landrovers came round the bend – all full of American students. They had all the winching equipment, and they got me out in ten minutes. Otherwise we would have frozen to death.

Doctor: How long did it take you to get there?

John: Two weeks. . . . They wouldn't let us in. . . . Then there was some trouble at the borders. Apart from that . . . two chaps have been killed. . . .

Doctor: What? Out there?

John: Yes.

Doctor: Oh, crumbs.

John: I'll have to explain when I see you.

Then followed a general conversation about John's ailments, which included stomach trouble and the fact that he had strained his back passage. John seemed to be after some buckshee medical advice. But the doctor was still curious about the trip.

Doctor: When did they leave?

John: Monday.

Doctor: You stayed on for a few days, did you?

John: Yes – but we have had a lot of trouble, a lot of trouble.

Doctor: How is the car now?

John: It's going all right. It's been off the road a few times. We've had a lot of trouble among ourselves. I'm worried to death, as two people were killed with the consignment. I'll have to explain to you when I see you.

Doctor: But the consignment you've got.

John: Only half of what we want because a lorry was hi-jacked and they were shot dead.

Doctor: Is it enough to make it worthwhile? That's the thing.

John: Just about, I think. But you know, it's a lot of trouble.

Doctor: So you didn't need the trailer really.

John: No. As it turned out, we didn't. I'll tell you when I see you. I don't want to talk on the phone, you know. . . .

Doctor: Well, if you hear anything, let me know.

John: I don't think I will. I tried to send a telex to my wife and did everything possible to get a message in, but it's just hopeless. I paid somebody £5 to send a telex, and they said that she would get it. Of course I arrived yesterday and she hadn't heard anything. She has been worried to death.

Doctor: So really they left on Monday – which means if they are going along well, they should be approaching Turkey by now.

John: Yes. But Janet said to me if the conditions are that bad, she's going to stop and wait until it gets better. It's so dangerous out there. . . . She's only a girl you know. The driving – I've never seen nothing like it in my life. Anyhow, I'll tell you all about it on Friday.

We never found out exactly what the doctor's involvement was. We would have investigated further, but the occasion never arose. At the time we were of course full of imaginings. But there were other more important matters in hand.

I could well imagine the difficulties Janet and her mother were having, although my journey along their route had been in summertime, not in early spring. However, they were over the worst of it. The snow that had bogged them down as they entered Europe was an unlucky break, though it was to be expected at that time of year. I vaguely remembered Edirne as a check-point, shabby and sparse, where everything and everyone went at half-speed.

We still had to keep a daily eye on John and his father. There was no telling when or how they might get a message, revise their plans and perhaps even do a bunk. I went down to Slough and Ascot in all weathers to observe, usually with Nigel, in case something happened.

It did, on Tuesday, 9 March, when a telephone operator rang Mapledene Road at 11.20 a.m. with a telegram for Mason, a Salah pseudonym. Kathy took the call.

The message was from Svilengrad in Bulgaria and read: DELAYED BULGARIA UNTIL END OF MONTH – MUM.

Within minutes John telephoned his father at Kier Park House, Mohammed wondered what was wrong. John didn't know. '*It's going to be too late*,' he said. '*You think it comes too late, eh?*' said Mohammed, and went on: '*What can we do now?*'

They really had no alternative – they couldn't do anything. Neither could we. We also wondered what had happened, and what had gone wrong. How serious was it? What was the explanation?

We looked up Svilengrad on the map and found that it was a small town a few miles from Edirne, on the Bulgarian side of the border with Turkey. We had some anxious discussions on the 9th and 10th. So did Mohammed and John. For nine days, from the 11th to the 19th inclusive, they telephoned each other with the question: '*Is there any news?*' The answer was always: '*No news yet*.' Once John said: '*I think that there is something terribly wrong*.' He and Kathy were planning to go on holiday in April. Kathy, we heard, was newly pregnant.

There were a few ribald remarks about that – about which of us was the father. It was decided that in any event we would all go to the christening and be fairy godfathers, as almost inevitably one or more of us had been on duty, observing 29 Mapledene Road, when the seed had been sown. Otherwise, there wasn't much to smile about.

At 1.45 p.m. on Friday, 19 March, a man called Sid rang John, who described some of his adventures abroad and told Sid he was very worried because he'd had no word. '*I'm going out of my mind with worry*,' said John. '*I'm just sweating it out*.' He said that other complications had arisen which they (Janet and Mrs S.) didn't know about. But it was important that they knew. He couldn't tell Sid – it was very involved. Sid said he didn't want to know. John told him to phone again in a week. Neither knew then that only six hours later John would be returning Sid's call with some fatal news.

Kathy returned from work at the hairdresser's shop about 5.30 p.m. John was watching the television news. She asked him how he was. She didn't need to ask if there had been any news – his attitude told her there'd be none. She went into the kitchen to prepare a meal for them both before he went out to see the doctor.

The news ended. The telephone rang.

Man: Is that John Mason?

John: Speaking.

Man: You don't know me – but I've just hitch-hiked through Bulgaria, and I've got a message from your mother.

John: Yes?

Man: She has been detained in Bulgaria by the authorities.

John: Yes.

Man: Janet is in jail.

John: In jail!

Man: Yes. Apparently there was some dispute with an American about the trailer, I believe, and the police got to know. Anyway, I think your mother tried to bribe them, and they confiscated the car and the trailer. Your mother is under arrest, but she's in a hotel. Janet is in prison, and they're trying to make her confess. Do you understand?

John: Yes. Yes. Oh, dear. Do you know where they are?

Man: No. I'm afraid I've forgotten the name of the town. But it's on the border somewhere.

John: All right. Thank you.

Man: That's all I can tell you. Apparently your mother can't write, or anything like that.

John: Okay. Thank you. . . .

It was disaster – for them, and for us.

News of this conversation reached Nobby, Nick and myself as we sat about the office, relaxing with a Friday evening drink or two after having spent the afternoon making an arrest and filling in the usual forms. Nigel was out at Slough.

The three of us stared at each other in utter dismay as Nobby put the phone down. Our previous mood of banter and jokes was ended. We slumped or sprawled at our desks in the shade of the spiky cannabis plants in the window and began debating what to do. One thing was certain – what we had imagined might have been as much as a ton of cannabis, the biggest consignment ever to reach England, would never be seized by us. And the ghastly irony of it was that our plans had been foiled by other policemen.

We said some fairly nasty things about the Bulgarian fuzz. We swore at Mrs Salah and Janet for getting into an argument and wrecking the whole show. We deduced that they must have been picked up before the 9th, the day Mrs Salah sent or was allowed to send the telegram.

Why Janet was in prison, and her mother only detained in a hotel, was somewhat baffling. We wondered whether the police out there might be giving Mrs S. the chance to try to obtain her daughter's release. The longer Janet was in jail the more Mrs S. would very likely do to gain her daughter's freedom. We thought about the messenger, the hitch-hiker. How had she persuaded him to trek across Europe to deliver a message that was to be the ruin of us all?

In the neon glare of the office we prowled about, all attentive when the gist of every phone-call John Salah made that night filtered down to us from C11.

John must have driven over to Kier Park House to deliver the bad news personally – there was no telephone call to Mohammed from Mapledene Road. He must also have tried to get in touch with Sid from there.

But John was in his own house when Sid telephoned just before eight o'clock.

Sid: Did you want to speak to me?

John: Yes. They've been done.

Sid: For certain?

John: Yes. For certain. A hitch-hiker told me. In Bulgaria. Apparently they've got Janet in jail. I'll have to go out there, Sid. Care to come? I could use some help now.

Sid: When are you thinking of going?

John: Monday. I think I'll go by car. It'll take about three days.

Sid: I'll come down tomorrow afternoon, John.

John: I'd be very grateful. I don't even know the town. It's really very serious.

Sid: Okay. I'll come tomorrow about one. . . .

Soon after this Mohammed phoned John to ask about his plans for going to Bulgaria on Monday. John wasn't very coherent, and must have gone to bed and taken some pills, for between 8.30 and 10.30 Kathy three times rang a number in Chiswick – she was trying to get hold of the hitch-hiker. She also made a fruitless call to Worcester.

It wasn't until about 11.20 p.m. that the hitch-hiker telephoned John, who by now was in a terrible state.

He wanted to know the name of the town where his mother had been arrested. The other man said he would try to find out. Then John had to hear the tale of his mother's and sister's arrest all over again – which he did, and went to pieces, swearing they were innocent, and that it was a frame-up. He couldn't have slept much that night. In the meantime we had decided what we must do.

In the morning, the Bulgarian police were contacted. Information was exchanged. We had now no alternative but to come out into the open. Search warrants were taken out, and preparations for an arrest were made.

Late on the sunny morning of Saturday, 20 March, an hour as it happened after the hitch-hiker made his last call to John with the information that the town, he thought, was Svilengrad and that there was only one hotel there, we set off in our cars from New Scotland Yard for Slough and Ascot – not to observe this time but to apprehend.

Nigel and I drove to Kier Park House, but nobody was at home. We hung about a bit outside, then proceeded to Slough, with Windsor Castle in view much of the way.

Meanwhile, Nobby, Nick and Morag had gone to the house in Mapledene Road. It was nine months after Nick and I visited The Meads, Stoke Poges. Now Nick found himself for the second time face to face with John Salah. The shock of meeting must have been the same on both sides.[1]

Q: Did you keep observation on March 20th, 1971, a Saturday, this time at the address: 29 Mapledene Road, Slough? – A: I did.

Q: Did you go there at 12 noon? A: I did.

Q: With whom? – A: With Sergeant Pilcher and Woman Detective Constable McGibbon.

Q: Who answered the door? – A: The door was answered by John Salah.

Q: Dealing with this matter, did you make notes at the time or soon after? – A: We made our notes – The proceedings we are coming to are divided into separate parts and at the conclusion of each part we made our notes.

Q: It is right to say that basically there was an interview with John

1. What follows is Nick Prichard's account of what happened next – as given in answer to questions by the chief prosecutor, Mr Corkery, at the Salah trial. Much of his evidence was later contested by the defence. – G.H.

Salah, and then an interview with Mohammed, and then an interview with Kathleen, the wife of John? – A: Yes.

Q: Separate matters dealt with, you say, by notes separately? – A: Yes. . . .

Q: Taking the first matter, was the door, as you told us, answered by John Salah? – A: Yes.

Q: And Detective Sergeant Pilcher took up the conversation? – A: He did.

Q: What did Sergeant Pilcher say? – A: Sergeant Pilcher told John Salah who we were and that we had a warrant to search the premises for drugs.

Q: Did you enter the premises? A: We did.

Q: Did you see in the front room Mohammed Salah? A: I did.

Q: Was he told the reason for your visit by Detective Sergeant Pilcher? – A: He was.

Q: While John and Mohammed were together, did Sergeant Pilcher take up the story? – A: He did.

Q: What did he say? – A: Sergeant Pilcher said: 'We are making inquiries into the arrest of other members of your family in Bulgaria who have been found in possession of a large quantity of cannabis.' Sergeant Pilcher cautioned them, and John Salah said: 'Yes. We have had a phone-call to say they had a hundred kilos. They are innocent. It is a frame-up.' Sergeant Pilcher said: 'We have been keeping observation on you all for some months and we have seen you purchase a Landrover and a trailer.' John said: 'No, not me.' Mohammed Salah made no reply. Sergeant Pilcher said: 'You were seen making alterations to the trailer at Kier Park.' John said: 'No. You did not see me.'

Q: Were the premises then searched? A: They were.

Nick went on to tell the court in some detail that in a drawer Nobby found a number of cards which had figures and sketches on the reverse side of them – they were basically hairdressing cards with the name 'Kathy' on the other side. When Nick was handed the originals (Exhibit 1) he agreed that one of the cards referred to '12 across, 11 down, blocks of 3' and had the measurement '4¾' and then '1¼ depth', also '72 × 14'. He agreed that another card was headed '14 blocks down, 12 blocks across, 3,000 pounds', and had various calculations. On two other cards he agreed that there were drawings which were clearly drawings of a trailer, and that yet another card had on it '3 pieces 2 in wide 3 in depth 5 ft length', and the words 'wine', 'beer', and 'crisps'.

Nick said that Nobby also found in the drawer a visa (Exhibit 2) issued by the Royal Afghan Embassy in London bearing a photograph of John Salah with a moustache.

Q (referring to the visa): The purpose of the journey is set out a little further down as that of pleasure? – A: Yes.

Q: The border of entry – in other words, going from Iran into Afghanistan. Means of transport – Landrover? – A: Yes.

Q: Approximate date of arrival – February? – A: Yes.

Q: Duration – one month? – A: Yes.

Q: And if a previous visit made to Afghanistan give date. And the date given is May 1970? – A: Yes.

Nobby, it was said in court, found three more cards (Exhibit 3) on a sideboard. Nick agreed that on one of them was written in red ink 'passport', 'money', 'car' – also '5 days', 'first town from border', '20 miles west', 'detained', '100 killows' (kilos), and some names and telephone numbers. It was also said that on another of the cards was written: 'Sdilengrad Bulgar delayed until end of month'.

Then John Salah was searched, said Nick, and in his coat pocket were found a letter (Exhibit 5), a list of telephone numbers (Exhibit 6), and three notes (Exhibit 7). The letter was addressed to 'Mr J. Mason' and the sender's name was 'M. Salah' whose address was given as being in Lahore, W. Pakistan.

After Mr Corkery had read out this letter to the court and the contents of the notes had been explained, Nick's examination continued.

Q: After that, did you in company with Sergeant Pilcher see John Salah in the kitchen? – A: We did.

Q: Did a conversation then take place? – A: It did.

Q: Was Mohammed in another room at this stage? – A: He was in the lounge.

Q: First of all, what did Sergeant Pilcher say? – A: Sergeant Pilcher said: 'I have already told you that we have been keeping observation on you and your family for some time and we know that you put a false floor in the trailer you bought in order to ship a large quantity of cannabis from Pakistan.' Sergeant Pilcher cautioned him, and he said: 'No, not us. It is all a frame-up.' I said: 'What do these figures and notes refer to?' I then showed him the notes, Exhibit 1. . . . He said: 'That's for some building work I was having done.' Sergeant Pilcher cautioned him. I said: 'Do you remember when I came to see you on July 27th last year, you told me that all the cannabis that you had had then was accounted for and that you intended to make another trip in January this year. If you remember, you and your mother said that I would be able to purchase as much of it as I wanted when you got it back. What do you want to say about that?' John Salah said: 'I thought I recognized you. I deny that that conversation took place, and my family will back me up.'

Nick said that John Salah was then shown a list of telephone numbers and that Nobby pointed out a reference to 'Niaz' and a number in Lahore and stated that this was the number of Niaz Ali who was supplying drugs to him. John denied this and said that Niaz Ali was a judge. Nobby, said Nick, then showed John Salah the airletter, Exhibit 5.

Prichard: Sergeant Pilcher said: 'Your father travelled to Pakistan in order to purchase the drugs. What does this letter refer to when it mentions goods?' John said: 'You will have to ask my father.' Sergeant Pilcher said: 'You travelled to Pakistan earlier this year and flew back with your father. How did you get out there?' He said: 'I flew out.' Sergeant Pilcher said: 'On February 1st I saw you, Janet, and your mother leave Dover with the Landrover and trailer.' He said: 'Yes, all right, that's right.' Sergeant Pilcher said: 'From inquiries we have made it is obvious that you and other members of your family bought the Landrover and trailer, rebuilt the trailer with a false floor, travelled to Lahore in order to bring back to this country a large amount of cannabis. Whilst travelling back through Bulgaria, Janet and your mother have been arrested in possession of about 900 kilos of cannabis.' Sergeant Pilcher reminded John of the caution, and he said: 'No. We are innocent. They were framed.' I said: 'Our information is that you travelled to Pakistan early last year and brought back 1,000 weights in the false floor of your van.'

Q: What is 1,000 weights? – A: 'Weights' is an expression used by people involved in drugs to describe a block. Normally a pound weight is described as a 'weight' and not a pound. It would mean 1,000 lb in weight.

Q: And the answer? – A: He said: 'No, not us.' Then Sergeant Pilcher showed John, first of all, photographs of the van PBH 24H and said: 'We have traced this van which you purchased new last year, put a false floor into and used to bring drugs back into the country.' John said: 'No. We did not put that floor in.' Sergeant Pilcher said: 'My information is that you kept the drugs in a garage which you and your mother rented.' He said: 'No. We have never rented a garage.'

Q: Did Sergeant Pilcher then point out to him the note, Exhibit 4, which is addressed to Kathy, which amongst other things, in the second sentence, asks her to pay the rates for the garage? – A: He did. Sergeant Pilcher said: 'What about this?' John said: 'I know nothing about it.' Sergeant Pilcher then said: 'As a result of the inquiries we have made, you are being arrested for conspiring with the other members of your family to contravene the provisions of the Dangerous Drugs Act, in other words, to bring into this country the drugs which have been found in the possession of your mother and sister.'

Q: Was he cautioned? – A: He was. And he replied: 'You can't touch us here. We have not got anything.'

Q: Then after that did you go and see Mohammed Salah with Detective Sergeant Pilcher? – A: I did. . . . John was taken back into the lounge and Sergeant Pilcher and I went back and made the notes, in the kitchen . . . Mohammed was still in the lounge. Then Mohammed was brought to the kitchen and we interviewed him in the same circumstances as John.

Q: What did Detective Sergeant Pilcher say to Mohammed? – A: He said: 'We have been keeping observation on you and your family for some time now and you travelled to Lahore recently. What was the reason for your visit?' Mohammed said: 'We went there to get some coats.' Sergeant Pilcher said: 'My information is that you went out there to purchase a large amount of cannabis.' Sergeant Pilcher then cautioned Mohammed, and he said: 'No. I went to buy coats.' Sergeant Pilcher said: 'We have found this letter in the possession of John. Was it written by you?' He was then shown the letter from Pakistan.

Q: Did Mohammed read the letter, Exhibit 5? – A: He looked at it. I do not think he read all of it. I cannot remember.

Q: At all events, he was shown it, and he was asked if he wrote it. What did he say? – A: He said: 'Yes.' Sergeant Pilcher then said: 'You received a telegram last December from Niaz Ali which quoted a price of 83 shillings per lb. What did that refer to?' Mohammed made no reply.

The telegram was produced in court. It was addressed to 'Kathleen Masoon' at Ascot, referred to 'Top quality NW wool' and was signed 'Niazali'. Nick continued with his evidence.

Prichard: Sergeant Pilcher then said: 'My information is that you purchased about 900 kilos of cannabis in Pakistan. If that is correct, that would work out to about £9,000 and you refer to nine and a half thousand in this letter.'

Q: A kilo is how many pounds? – A: A kilo is just over two pounds – 2·204. . . .

Q: Did Sergeant Pilcher caution him again? – A: He did. . . Mohammed replied: 'I am sorry. My wife make the arrangements with Niaz Ali and I went there to pay for the goods. I don't understand how you know what happened.' Sergeant Pilcher said: 'You are now telling us that you did go to Pakistan to buy the drugs?' He cautioned him, and he said: 'Yes. You know what has happened, but it was all I do with this.'

Q: Would you say that sentence again? – A: He said: 'Yes. You know what has happened, but it was all I do with this.' Sergeant Pilcher said: 'Last year you and your family went to Pakistan in a van, and you returned with another load of cannabis in a false floor.' Mohammed said: 'Yes, but that was arranged by them.' Sergeant Pilcher said: 'You have a large amount of cash in a bank in Jersey. It amounts to £82,000. Can you account for that?' Mohammed said: 'Yes. That came from my business which I sold.' Sergeant Pilcher said: 'You are now living in the house at Kier Park. How was that paid for?' Mohammed said: 'My wife paid for that from her money.' Sergeant Pilcher said: 'How much did you sell your business for?' Mohammed said: 'I think it was about £45,000.' Sergeant Pilcher said: 'How can you account for the other money in Jersey?'

Q: That being the difference between £45,000 and £82,000? – A: Yes.

Q: Which is just under £40,000? – A: Yes. He said: 'I can't remember now, but I can account for it all.' Sergeant Pilcher said: 'Is Niaz Ali related to you?' He said: 'Yes, he is. He is the man who sell all this stuff.' Sergeant Pilcher said: 'As a result of the inquiries we have made, you are being arrested for conspiring to contravene the Dangerous Drugs Act, that is, to bring into this country the cannabis which has been found in the possession of your wife and Janet in Bulgaria.' He cau-

tioned him, and he said: 'Yes, but are they all right? Will they come home?'

Q: Then did you make notes as to that conversation? – A: Yes. . . .
Q: Did you later on see Kathleen? – A: We did.
Q: That is, Mrs Salah junior? – A: Yes.
Q: Was she in the house at the time? – A: No.

Nigel and I arrived at Mapledene Road a little before one.

It felt rather strange walking boldly into the house and into the living-room without any attempt at concealment and then confronting John Salah. He was sitting down, and looked somewhat worried. Morag was with him. The Salahs' shaggy dog, Khan, bounded about when we entered the room and was something of a bother. We discovered that Mohammed was being interviewed in the kitchen. We had a chat with Nick at the kitchen door, and as the house still hadn't been properly searched – Morag had had to keep any eye on John and Mohammed – Nigel and I did so while we waited for Mohammed's interview to end.

Before long Nobby emerged from the kitchen, had a chat with us and told us to take Mohammed back to Kier Park House and give it a going over. In the meantime, Nick and Morag would fetch Kathy from the hairdresser's where she worked.

It was about 1.15 p.m. when Nigel and I left Mapledene Road with Mohammed. With Nigel driving – it was his Volkswagen – and with Mohammed on his own in the back, we set out on the return journey to Ascot in thoughtful silence.[1]

Q: During the journey was any comment made by the police or by Mohammed? – A: Yes. Mohammed said: 'Today is the day of judgement for us all. I am glad it is all over.' I said to Mohammed: 'Did the other officer tell you that you did not have to say anything unless you wished to?' Mohammed replied: 'Yes, but it does not matter now. I am an old man of nearly sixty, and they cannot do much to me now.'

He had been gazing out of the car window, seemingly oblivious of the castle and town of Windsor. He was silent as we

1. The account, in italics, of what happened next and what was said is taken from Adam's evidence at the Salah trial. Again, much of it was later disputed by the defence. – G.H.

drove across Windsor Great Park, where the trees were still leafless and the grass dun-coloured and coarse.

Q: Later on in the car did he make some other comment? – A: Yes. He said: 'This is bad for us. Everything has gone wrong. Do you know about my wife and daughter in Bulgaria?' I said: 'Yes. We do.' Mohammed said: 'What will happen to them?' I said: 'I don't know. I wish we could say, but nobody can tell you the answer to that.' Mohammed said: 'If I thought anything would happen to them I would drive the thing over myself, you know. But I am too old for that. John should have driven – but the women said they must drive.'

We arrived at Kier Park House about half-past one. Nigel parked his June Bug on the very place that John used to park his Volkswagen and the Landrover. We waited as Mohammed groped in a pocket for the front-door key with his head bowed. In his sloppy jacket and baggy trousers he didn't look as if he owned the place. I wondered if he was aware, as we were, that he probably wouldn't enter the house again for some time.

Inside, a nasty little dog, a poodle, came yapping towards us. Mohammed hushed it, and stood still as we looked about, opening doors and peering into rooms. The whole place was very well turned out, with expensive fittings and furnishings which we later discovered had come from Harrods. In the hall there was a telephone.

Q: Did DC Lilley make some comment to Mohammed? – A: Yes. DC Lilley said to him: 'This is a large house and it will take some time to search it all. I want you to stay with us as we search the house, starting at the top.' Mohammed replied: 'Yes, but there is nothing for you upstairs.'

The three of us went up the thickly carpeted stairs. The dog came too. Nigel asked Mohammed which was his bedroom. He showed us and sat on the double bed fondling the dog as we made a quick search of all the drawers and fitted cupboards and obvious hiding-places in the room. It was rather unlikely that they would have taken any special precautions. But we made a thorough search none the less, without messing things up too much.

Nigel found a black brief-case, unlocked.

Q: Did Mohammed acknowledge that it was his? – A: Yes. He said: 'That's mine.'

There was a large pile of correspondence, bank books and personal documents inside it. We emptied it out onto the bed, and sifted through the contents. Mohammed helped us by identifying some letters to a bank in Jersey.

Q: When those letters were found, did Mohammed make any comment about them? – A: Yes. He said: 'I have told the other Sergeant about that.'

Q: Then did DC Lilley pick out the bank book, Exhibit 10? Did Mohammed make any comment in respect of that book? – A: Yes. He said: 'That is my personal money in Pakistan.'

Nigel pointed to the name inside it – Mr Rahmatulla.

Q: What did Mohammed say about that? – A: He said: 'That's the name I use there. I have that account because when you buy hashish it is best to pay from an account out there. It is cheaper. It is business.'

Q: Then did Mohammed pick up a passport? – A: Yes.

Q: Did he go through the pages and make any comment? – A: Yes. He said: 'That's when I went to Pakistan last. This' – he was then pointing to page 11 – 'is where I landed at Karachi, and there are others. Look – this one in Pakistan . . . And these would be going and coming from Pakistan.'

We put everything back in the brief-case and continued with our search of the other rooms. There were four bedrooms. Apparently Mrs Salah had a room of her own. I didn't care to spend too much time going through her and Janet's belongings.

Mohammed led the way when we went downstairs. He was becoming somewhat impatient by now, and went ahead of us into the living-room.

From the top drawer of a sideboard he produced six packets of colour photographs and a pencil drawing of a motor-vehicle.

Q: Were you also given by Mr Mohammed Salah from the sideboard two keys on a ring with their tag marked Landrover? – A: Yes. He said: 'This is the only thing you want. There are many photos of this,' pointing to the sketch, 'from when we drove it back with the stuff hidden in the bottom last year. See how John had the bottom made. Lots of space . . . We never had any trouble, not like this time.' He then said:

'These are the keys to the Landrover. I hope the women will be all right. I must have some coffee. Do you want any?'

'Okay,' I said, and went with him into the kitchen, which I searched as he got out cups and coffee and put on a kettle. Nigel joined us. We said very little to him, and generally only spoke to him when he asked us questions. I imagine he found our diligence and silence somewhat disconcerting. We supped our coffee as we went along.

Eventually we completed our search of the ground-floor rooms. Then we went outside to check over the garage. Inside it was the black Mercedes sports car, which Mrs Salah normally drove. Mohammed had used the white Volkswagen to travel to Slough that morning. In the glove compartment of the Mercedes we found a starting-pistol in a holster.

We returned to the house, and collected what we had found. I told Mohammed that we had finished and that he would now be taken to Cannon Row police station.

Q: What comment did he make then? – A: He said: There is nothing more to find. I have told you everything. It is all over now. I am too old for all this. . . .'

He wanted to know if he needed to take anything with him, like his razor, toothbrush and pyjamas. I told him it wasn't necessary.

Before we left he remembered to put some dog-food into a bowl in the kitchen.

In the hall he paused, looking about. At the front door he paused again.

'Will you look after my dog for me?' he asked.

I assured him we would.

The door shut behind him, and Nigel held out his hand for the front-door key.

11

That afternoon John's wife, Kathy, was also arrested and taken to Cannon Row police station. She denied any involvement in the trip to Pakistan. She said that what her husband did was his own affair, that work done on the trailer had nothing to do with her, and that although she knew what was going on she wasn't involved.

All this was very much in agreement with our own findings, and in view of this and of her condition, she was released on bail. But John and Mohammed were refused bail and put in Brixton Prison.

This was done on Monday, 22 March, on the very morning that the trial of Palacios and his pals began at the Old Bailey. Meanwhile the intercept on Mapledene Road continued to report on all the phone calls that Kathy made and received.

On that Monday, after one o'clock, she rang Directory Inquiries for the telephone number of Brixton Prison. She dialled the prison and asked when the visiting hours were. She was told: 10 a.m. to 11.30 a.m. and 1 p.m. to 3.30 p.m. except Saturday.

At five o'clock on the same day Mrs Salah telephoned from Sofia in Bulgaria. Her news was that she had been released that day and that Janet would be freed on Friday. Everything was all right, she said, unaware of what had happened in England. Kathy told her.

Mrs S. apparently didn't or couldn't take it in. She rang again later on that night, and Kathy had to go over the whole story of the arrests. She also warned her mother-in-law about returning to England. Mrs Salah asked Kathy if it would be safe for her to go to Jersey, and added that there was nothing to worry about as it was all a load of rubbish.

Very early the following morning, Kathy's mother, who was keeping her company now, telephoned Slough police about Mohammed's car. The neighbours had been complaining. She wanted the police to come along and move it into the drive.

The Drug Squad, she said, had the car-keys. They said they would see what they could do.

Soon after six o'clock that evening a man, presumably Sid, telephoned the house.

Man: It's me. Don't say my name. Okay – I came round on Sunday. What happened?

Kathy: Well, John and I was taken away. There is a lot of trouble. I'll ring you at your Mum's in a couple of days.

Man: You know your phone is tapped.

Kathy: Yes. Well, I know now. . . .

Half an hour later Mrs Salah was on the line. But not for long. Kathy told her to ring a call-box on the corner.

'*Is my husband all right?*' asked Mrs S. Kathy said she had seen him and John that morning and continued: '*There are certain things I must tell you. I'll go now. Okay?*' '*Tell me now,*' insisted Mrs S. '*I can't. Don't be silly,*' said Kathy.

On Thursday, 25 March, a woman rang about a boat that had been advertised for sale. She would call round that night. If she did it was probably before Mrs Salah rang from Sofia once again.

Mrs S.: I've been in touch with the British Embassy here, but there's very little I can do. . . .

Kathy: How is Janet?

Mrs S.: I haven't seen her.

Kathy: I see.

Mrs S.: But things are moving. Something might happen next week.

Kathy: I see.

Mrs S.: Don't worry, Kathy – because I'll come back and sort this lot out . . . There's going to be a lot of trouble when I get back.

Kathy: Yes. All right.

Mrs S.: All my love – give my love to my husband and my son.

Kathy: I'll write to your mother.

Mrs S.: All right. Just tell her I'm on holiday, and we have had a bit of an accident with the car and we are stuck.

Kathy: Don't worry. I'll write to her and explain to her.

Mrs S.: I'll ring next Tuesday.

Kathy: We are going to court on Tuesday. . . .

On Tuesday, 30 March, Mrs Salah telephoned after half-past

six wanting to know how Mohammed and John had got on. Kathy told her they had been remanded until 20 April. She added that she would rather talk to Mrs S. from a friend's house, and gave her the number.

On April Fools' Day, 1971, the intercept on 29 Mapledene Road was discontinued. In all it had reported on nearly 500 calls.

It was really odd how the appearances of the Salahs at the magistrates courts coincided with both the Palacios and Muswell Hill trials. Adler and his mates appeared at Middlesex Sessions on Monday, 19 April, and on 20 April, John and Mohammed and Kathy were committed for trial at the Old Bailey later that year.

A month before this, on 22 March, the Salahs had appeared for the first time in the magistrates court on the very day that the Rolls-Royce trial began at the Old Bailey.

On that day I took all the relevant exhibits from the Drug Squad safes to the Old Bailey and hung about outside the court, West Court 4, until I was called to give evidence.

The prosecution had a very good tale to tell. The chief prosecutor, Mr Mathew, who happened to be a friend of my father's, said that the Morlands' home in Barnes had been the clearing station for huge quantities of drugs, probably being shipped to the United States. In August of 1970, said Mr Mathew, Palacios was in Morocco with his £6,000 catamaran, *Letitia*, which had originally been built for the 1968 transatlantic yacht race. He was introduced to Francis Morland, who was alleged to have been involved in highly professional and organized smuggling. Mr Mathew said that the Third Secretary at the Liberian Embassy in Rome and other diplomats were part of an international drug smuggling ring which had 'stacks and stacks of hash', as he put it, hidden in the Moroccan mountains. Morland, said Mr Mathew, asked Palacios if he would be interested in smuggling drugs to England in his catamaran. Palacios agreed. He was then taken to a house in the Moroccan mountains and 200 kilos of drugs were loaded onto the catamaran. In London, at the Cumberland Hotel, Morland handed Palacios £2,000. But, said Mr Mathew, the whole operation was being watched by the police. He said that at

Morland's home Palacios was asked to ship a ton of cannabis to the Bahamas in the catamaran, to some man who owned an island there. Palacios refused to do this and demanded that the cannabis in his boat should be removed. It was arranged, said Mr Mathew, that Palacios, who was to pick up a £1,700 1958 Rolls-Royce for his father, should drive it down to Cowes, load it with the cannabis, and take it to Morland's home. He was arrested in London, and the police found in the car cartons containing a vast amount of cannabis.

It all sounded like the synopsis for a film. But from my point of view the ending wasn't all that satisfactory, and just about as disappointing for me as the result of the Muswell Hill trial.

To begin with, Morland, who for some reason had been allowed out on bail after numerous applications, had done a bunk. He had fled the country, and wasn't in court to answer the charges against him.

The following week his mother and the family doctor who had stood bail for him were each ordered by the judge to forfeit £4,000 within a month, or go to prison for nine months in default. Mr Sherrard QC, for the defence, said Morland had originally been remanded in custody, but was later granted bail in his own recognizance of £1,000 and with two sureties, each of £5,000, put up by his mother and the doctor. The QC said Morland was a man of the highest character, and that both Mrs M. and the doctor were as much taken by surprise as anyone else by Morland's absence.

His recognizance of £1,000 was also forfeited, or 'estreated', as they put it – a very fair price in my opinion, for his freedom. His wife, who had admitted the unlawful possession of herbal cannabis and cannabis resin, was fined £500, with six months to pay.

Robert Palacios, our quiet American, was dealt with just as quickly. For the last five months he had been remanded in prison – as much for his own protection as a penalty for breaking the law. Threatening letters had been sent to him. But in the interim he had very sensibly decided that English prison life wasn't for him. He turned Queen's evidence and became a witness for the prosecution.

It was nice to see him again, though he looked somewhat pale. He had done us proud.

When he stood in the dock to answer the charge of conspiring to smuggle cannabis resin into the country, and was asked how he pleaded, he said: 'Guilty.'

He was fined £4,000 and given twelve months to pay. The fine was later paid by his father, a San Francisco magnate, who had flown to England to save his son and take him home. Actually if they had just left the country and not paid the fine within the year, very probably nothing would have been done. Mr Palacios did the proper thing. However, he couldn't rush off with his son back to the States straight away. Palacios junior still had to give evidence as a prosecution witness. To make sure he did so, all in one piece, Nick and I were detailed to look after him for a couple of days.

After he was sentenced and freed, we both accompanied him to a hotel in Queen's Gate where it had been arranged that he should stay until his evidence had been given.

At this secret address, which was known only to the police and Palacios senior, we spent the afternoon, lounging about each other's bedrooms – Nick and I had a double room – and chatting about Bob's flying and sailing days. In the evening we were joined by Bob's dad, and the four of us went out for a meal.

By common consent, though I think it was our idea, we dined at the Cumberland Hotel. It seemed a fitting and suitably ironic place to end the Rolls-Royce affair – that is, where it began. Mr Palacios turned out to be an affable little man, very wealthy, and wonderfully well-disposed towards us. Besides thinking the Drug Squad had done a fair bit of sleuthing, he was generally full of praises for our methods of work and our attitude towards arrested persons. It was quite an evening.

When eventually he left us at Queen's Gate to go to his own hotel, he shook hands with Nick and me and thanked us for looking after his son. He actually wanted to give us a present of some sort.

'How about a Rolls?' I joked.

Feeling very brotherly we accompanied Bob to his bedroom and made sure he was safely locked inside. Then after warning the night porter to wake us if any stranger called and asked for Bob, we flopped onto our mattresses and had some kip ourselves.

The next day we three had breakfast together, and having gathered up Bob's few bits and pieces we transported him to the Old Bailey. There we stayed with him until he was called to be a prosecution witness, when we all shook hands and said good-bye.

'If you're ever in San Francisco, look me up,' said Robert Palacios, and turned and waved before he entered the court-room.

I never saw him again.

It was a week after this that John and Mohammed were remanded for the second time, on 30 March.

Two days later, the intercept on Mapledene Road was discontinued.

On the following day, Friday, 2 April, Nobby saw Janet Salah in Sofia Central Prison.

He had gone to Bulgaria with DI Bolton. They travelled by plane from Heathrow Airport. The purpose of their visit was to verify that the stuff was in the trailer and that Janet had been arrested in possession of it. The Landrover was in her name. Bolton, who had hardly ever involved himself in our activities, went with Nobby as someone of a higher rank than a DS was needed to deal with the Bulgarian police. The two of them did so with help from the British Embassy in Sofia, in the form of a Mr Lacey.

Janet had now been in prison for a month. Nobby and Bolton saw her briefly. Without her make-up she didn't look so good, and wasn't her usual self at all. She was sullen, and didn't have much to say.

Earlier, they had been able to examine the Landrover and the trailer, both of which were locked up in the prison yard. Photographs were taken of both vehicles. It must have given Nobby a bad feeling, seeing the vehicles in such circumstances. The last time had been at Dover.

The trailer still contained a large quantity of cannabis resin, in packets or blocks of three. Nobby testified to this at the Salah trial. He also said at the trial that he reckoned there were in all 616 packets in the trailer, that he took possession of one of the packets which contained three smaller blocks, that he labelled it, gave it to the Bulgarians, and that the Embassy arranged for it to be sent to England.

It was later established at the Salah trial that the packet

didn't reach the Foreign Office until the beginning of May, that Nobby himself collected it from the FO on the 5th, and that on the 10th it was sent to the forensic laboratory.

On the morning of 3 April, he and Bolton met Mrs Salah in the British Embassy. She made and signed a statement, which was however never used in court.

Nobby and Bolton then returned to England.

Janet was tried and sentenced to eighteen months' hard labour. She appealed, and was given two and a half years' hard labour when the appeal failed. The prosecution at the Salah trial claimed that soon after this Mrs Salah went to Ireland and had about £90,000 transferred from the Salah account in Jersey to a Dublin bank. She then returned to Bulgaria.

Later, Janet was pardoned and released.

In the meantime, Nobby, Nigel, Nick and myself, along with Morag and Kelaher, had started preparing and formalizing the evidence against the three Salahs we had arrested. Our statements were typed out and signed on 14 and 15 April.

On 20 April, Mohammed and John and Kathy were sent for trial at the Old Bailey.

By this time I had rather lost interest in them, for Sam had stopped answering my letters.

12

Towards the end of April I couldn't take Sam's silence any more. I telephoned her one weekend evening from my parents' home, putting a call through Dar-es-Salaam to her father's farm. In the long pause before she answered, while I wondered if she would, I thought about Kilimanjaro and the African night. The Jouberts seemed to be having a dinner party – there was a background noise of merry voices and cutlery in action. By the time Sam came to the phone, I was feeling very dejected.

She spoke slowly and in a non-committal way, as if she could be overheard. She said it was lovely to hear from me and what did I want? Was something wrong? No, I said, and asked how she was and what she was doing. It wasn't until we'd exchanged some polite social chit-chat that I asked her if she had got my letters. Of course she had, she said. You haven't written for a month, I said. Oh, haven't I? she replied and said she hadn't noticed it was that long – she must have forgotten. She had meant to write, she said, and she would. I asked her if she was returning to England in the summer. She was, it appeared, in June – but briefly. She wasn't sure. She asked me how I was.

'Be good,' she said. 'Night-night.'

I heard the line go dead at her end as I slowly replaced the receiver. The room I was in, the study, seemed foreign to me, and I stared at a large framed photo of myself on the desk, showing me as a PC with a silly grin on my face, and felt very unhappy.

When she wrote to me it was to say that she felt differently about me. She also said that when she came to England she would be visiting several friends and relatives and mightn't be able to see me all that often – if at all. She would if she could, but three weeks wasn't long.

Afterwards I learned she had spent most of the three weeks with her new boy-friend, a wealthy young Englishman, whom she'd met in Tanzania. Together they went to the Shetlands, where he had a cottage. I saw her twice – once at dinner, when she visited an aunt of hers who happened to live near Chobham. I just asked myself along. The other time was at the flat of friends of hers in London, where she spent most of the time on the phone to this other man. By now I had got over being hurt and was fairly livid. But I couldn't show it, or tried not to, as she would never have forgiven me or seen me again.

When Sam returned to Africa, we were still friends as far as she was concerned and that was all.

She sent me birthday cards and Christmas cards, and was usually quite good at replying when I wrote – which wasn't often. I heard more about her from mutual friends. But their news wasn't good. After the Shetlands boy-friend she had another, a rich young farmer, and this one was much more serious. In fact they nearly became engaged.

I didn't see her again for over a year.

June was a bad month. Sam left England on the 30th, and on the 11th Nobby left the Drug Squad. So did Nick. Their departure probably wasn't unconnected with something that happened that same week, which was going to work against us from now on.

Two days earlier, at Middlesex Area Sessions, Kelaher was named by the prosecution as the senior Yard detective seen by customs men talking to a suspected drug smuggler, Basil Sands. This was at the trial of Sands and four others, who had all been charged with conspiracy to get possession of 24 lbs of cannabis. They pleaded not guilty. One of the four was a girl, Sands's girl-friend. The others were a West Indian, a Burmese, and a Persian. Kelaher was brought into the trial as a witness for the defence.

The arrests and the trial arose out of an investigation by the customs people back in March.

They were following up the discovery of cannabis hidden between the slats of two packing cases which had arrived at Heathrow Airport from Damascus. These had been addressed to a 'Mr Royde Thompson', and a man using this name telephoned Heathrow and asked for the cases to be delivered to a hotel in Earls Court. This was done by a customs officer posing as a BEA worker. Other customs men were watching and noticed Kelaher in conversation with Sands in Earls Court tube station. They later arrested Sands and his girl-friend and also picked up Kelaher. Although they knew who he was they took him to a police station, where he was detained and questioned before being allowed to go.

This was on 5 March – the very day that Mrs Salah and Janet were detained in Bulgaria.

On the 16th, Kelaher was transferred from the Drug Squad to another squad in C1. At the time he was up for promotion to Chief Superintendent, and the move didn't do him any good. More than that, it was a serious blow to all our efforts, and meant that Kelaher wasn't with us at the time of the Salah arrests. Nobby had to take most of that responsibility on himself. It also meant that Kelaher was made to seem suspect in some way, though he wasn't suspended or anything like that. I thought it was a rotten way to treat a man who had done so much to combat drug trafficking, who in two years had helped to prevent drugs worth £21 million reaching the market. It was the Law's loss and the drug offenders' gain.

We couldn't help feeling bitter towards the customs people.

They had never taken too kindly to our good results and successes. Nor had they particularly welcomed what must have seemed to them Kelaher's advanced ideas on international co-operation in fighting the drug traffic and the adoption of some of the modern American methods. Now he was out of it, out of the way, and practically accused of being involved in drug smuggling himself. For at the trial of Sands and the other four civilians in June, a senior customs officer said he had recommended that his superiors should consider the possibilities of prosecuting Kelaher.

When Kelaher gave evidence, he told the court he was investigating the arrival of a consignment of cannabis at Heathrow which was to be conveyed later by means of small hotels to the people who were going to collect it. His information, he said, had come from Basil Sands, who had been his informant for some time. Kelaher said he went to the hotel concerned, whose proprietor he knew, and where two parcels believed to contain cannabis had arrived. He inspected the invoice, telephoned Sands, and arranged to meet him in Earls Court Underground station. Shortly afterwards a taxi arrived and the driver took the parcels away for delivery at another hotel.

It was then that Sands, his girl-friend who was with him, and also in effect Kelaher, were arrested by the customs men.

The idea, said Kelaher, had been that Sands, who was keeping an eye on the drugs, would tell him when they got into the hands of two Lebanese drug smugglers whom he, Kelaher, had been trying to catch. Sands, he said, was acting with his approval in dealing with these people.

This was typical of Kelaher, who wasn't too concerned about making the easy arrests of runners and pushers and the grabbing of small amounts of pot. He was after the big dealers and the big consignments.

He was then questioned by Mr Lloyd-Eley QC, who was defending Siamuk Ardalan, a young Persian, one of the accused.

Lloyd-Eley asked Kelaher about a gold watch worth £285 which he had helped the wife of a man in prison to buy. Kelaher had in fact helped to convict the man. The wife had chosen one of six watches which Kelaher, knowing a dealer in Hatton Garden, had brought along for her inspection – she was working in clubs and wanted jewellery. This had been in 1967.

On 15 December 1970, four months before the Sands arrest, customs men and policemen had visited the woman's flat – she was now divorced – and found Kelaher there, also another man. The place was searched, and among the furs and jewellery found was the gold watch, which Lloyd-Eley claimed the divorcee had said had been *given* to her by Kelaher – which he refuted.

Lloyd-Eley later on suggested to Kelaher that he had refused to make a statement to a customs officer not because he was concerned about the safety of his informant but because he wanted a guarantee that he wouldn't be charged. Kelaher of course denied this.

He also categorically denied Lloyd-Eley's allegation that the reason why he had given the evidence which he had on certain matters was because he 'was in league with Sands in connection with the delivery of the cannabis and the transaction which was to follow'.

As usual it amazed me what defamatory allegations could be freely made in court about a person's intentions or character. Policemen were of course especially vulnerable to this kind of attack – as I would soon enough discover for myself.

Another view of what had gone on was given by another defendant, Alfred Nicholson, a West Indian, aged forty. He was an exporter. He said in evidence that Sands had told him he was acting as an informant to a police officer named Victor, 'Chief of the Drug Squad'. Victor was Kelaher's first name. Nicholson said he refused to become an informant himself, and became very angry later when he heard from Sands that drugs addressed to a 'Mr Thompson' were being sent to his address. 'Vic' apparently recommended that the drugs be sent to the hotel in Earls Court. Nicholson later alleged that when he was in Brixton Prison, he was told by a customs officer that the officer would recommend that he, Nicholson, should get bail, if he made a statement. The customs man had added: 'Even Sands is not important. I want Kelaher.'

Nicholson's counsel, Mr Myerson QC, said his client was an honest man who had become the victim of circumstances.

'Like most of us,' said Mr Myerson, 'he has become a spectator of a bitter fight over the honesty and integrity of a senior police officer.'

Ardalan, the Persian, whose QC, Mr Lloyd-Eley, had alleged that Kelaher was in league with Sands, told the court that he had come to Britain from Sweden some nine months earlier, hadn't been able to get a job, but had got money by gambling. He was introduced by Sands to Kelaher who said he wanted Ardalan to play the part of a contact man. This meeting took place at the Hilton Hotel and other police officers – Nobby and Nigel in fact – were present. Ardalan said okay, and was sent for on two occasions, on one of which he was late. On the other the potential buyer didn't arrive. He said he wasn't paid anything, but had agreed to help because Sands had allowed him to have a room at his flat without any charge. Sands, who was forty-one, and his girl-friend, who was twenty-five, lived in a flat at Draycott Place in Chelsea.

When Sands went into the box he denied that Kelaher was to get money after a consignment of cannabis had been sold and said that Kelaher had been perfectly straight with him. Sands's girl-friend said she had gathered from him that he had been caught in the cross-fire of a gun-battle between police and customs.

Of Kelaher, she said: 'He told me he had explained over and over again to the customs. They just wanted a case, and it did not matter whether it was a good case or a bad case.'

It was bad for Kelaher. Nothing was proved against him. Nothing was said against him by four of the accused – which they might very well have done. The supposition that a Drug Squad chief with all his expert knowledge should act so foolishly over such a small amount of stuff and so imperil his career was never questioned. It was only established that he had been associating with an informant and some non-Europeans. But the prosecution and the defence combined to make some very damaging remarks in their closing speeches.

Mr Marriage, prosecuting for the Board of Customs and Excise, more or less told the jury not to believe Kelaher's evidence.

'Do not in any circumstances,' he said, 'use his evidence against any of these defendants.'

At no stage, said Mr Marriage, had the prosecution sought to rely on Kelaher's two statements, and in fact hadn't questioned him.

He went on: 'The more those of us who were concerned in this matter thought about the matter and those statements, the less we came to the conclusion that Mr Kelaher could be believed.'

Mr Lloyd-Eley QC, defending Ardalan, actually said that Kelaher was corruptly involved with Sands in a conspiracy.

'I could not and cannot tell exactly what their purpose was,' said Lloyd-Eley. 'I can only tell you that it was concerned with their obtaining possession of what they thought were 10 kilos of cannabis for their own purposes. The obvious inference is that it was to be sold and the proceeds shared in some way between them.'

These remarks, which we read in newspaper reports of the trial, made it seem as if Kelaher himself was in the dock. He couldn't however answer back, and had to suffer these allegations in silence. I thought it was damnable.

It was left to Sands's counsel, Mr Williams QC, to restore some balance. He spoke of a bitter conflict between the police and the customs.

He said: 'It is no use Mr Lloyd-Eley or the prosecution in their conduct of the case saying – "Look at the customs officers. Are they the sort of people who would carry this vendetta to the point of crucifying Mr Kelaher?" – because the fact is that they have done it.'

Mr Williams went on to say that the prosecution had begun by saying that they did not accuse Kelaher of being corrupt, but they had fed the defendants who were hostile to Sands with all the dirt they could find. Whatever the truth, he said, it was a terrifying picture.

Judge Trapnell, the chairman, in his summing-up said that a forthright attack had been made on Kelaher's character and good name. It was right, he said, that he should remind the jury that Kelaher had been attacked without anyone representing him.

He told the jury: 'Whatever your belief about him – and some hard things were said about him – these customs officers never cautioned him, and they would have done if they had reasonable grounds to suspect him of committing an offence. . . . If he is to be judged, let him be judged properly by another tribunal on some other occasion.'

Little did I know then that another occasion for another tribunal would be found – through Nobby, Nigel, Nick and myself before the end of the year.

The trial of Basil Sands and the other four ended on Tuesday, 20 July. It was one of the longest drug trials in legal history, the hearing having lasted thirty days. It cost over £50,000. Sands was sentenced to seven years in jail. Ardalan and Babet, the Burmese, each received a three-year sentence. The girl-friend and Nicholson each got twelve months. All five lodged appeals.

Judge Trapnell, in sentencing the five, said: 'I think it must be made clear . . . that in cases where people smuggle or endeavour to smuggle drugs into the country, whether as couriers or whether they be the front-line reception people, it is essential that there are sentences which are to a degree punitive in order to make clear the view that is taken of this kind of offence.'

He also said that he hoped the disagreements said to have arisen between the Drug Squad and the customs people would be ironed out by amicable discussion.

Meetings to this end were arranged. But the threat to such harmony, and to drug traffickers at large, had been removed, and the Drug Squad ceased to be as effective as it had been under Kelaher. Without his expert knowledge and experience and his contacts and those of Nobby and Nick, who were both transferred in the first week of the Sands trial, Nigel and I could do very little. The squad as a whole, which had never received that much support or actual practical help in its endeavours, was firmly put in its place, as a sort of Cinderella of the Yard. We were out of favour, under a cloud. No one wanted to know us.

On the day after the Judge's sentences on Sands and the others, an inquiry was set up by the Commissioner, Sir John Waldron, into the allegations made at the trial. The investigation was to be headed by the Assistant Chief Constable of Lancashire, Mr Prescott. The Home Secretary, Mr Maudling, approved the move, and was reported to be much concerned at the grave allegations made against a Yard officer in a highly responsible position.

I think we had been fighting a losing battle all the time. Apart from drug offences being a non-statistical crime and therefore not rated very high in official reports, we were spoiling a lot of permissive people's fun. We had prevented millions of pounds worth of cannabis reaching the market, and by May of 1971, cannabis was in very short supply and very expensive – up to £15 an ounce. The customs people of course said this was all the result of their own successes and intense activity. We, that is Nobby, Nick, Nigel and I, had also arrested about twenty persons a month, and several of them were fairly well connected. Drug offenders at that time were mainly of the student intellectual sort from middle- and upper-class backgrounds. If we had gone around like average working-class policemen, picking up the working-class who'd committed offences, we'd have been doing all right by our bosses. But we didn't. In chasing after drug offenders we entered some rather smooth establishments, and found ourselves apprehending some rather well-to-do people and sons and daughters of the same. Some had friends in very high places.

We certainly tried hard. We spent in fact hours on the job. Apart from the Rolls-Royce affair, my own effort at Muswell Hill, and the Salahs, there had been many other arrests and successes of a minor nature.

The year before, on my birthday, I was on continuous duty for forty-eight hours, at the end of which three men about to set up a laboratory for the making of mescalin were arrested and all their equipment seized. Then there was a raid on a flat in West Kensington, when we picked up two men and 60 to 70 lbs of cannabis in polythene bags, worth about £32,000. Another time we raided a house in South London, where we found 60,000 amphetamine tablets, called 'blues'. One of the four characters we arrested there was nicknamed the Poison Dwarf. Two were just off to the Isle of Wight Pop Festival where they'd have done a roaring trade. In fact we'd volunteered to visit the Festival ourselves and sniff out what was being pushed about. But the local coppers, the Hampshire Constabulary, weren't keen on us showing them what to do.

We even had a go at clearing up the heroin trade in Gerrard Street in Soho. A junkie would call at the back door of a Chinese restaurant, hand over some money and go elsewhere and wait. We never knew when or where or how the heroin would be passed to him. It would happen in a flash. We could always pick up the junkie with the goods on him, but it was impossible to find out the source. A thorough search of suspected premises was way beyond our resources, and even if it had been laid on, we still wouldn't have found out who was behind it all. Heroin doesn't take up much space, and any restaurant proprietor would have denied any knowledge of it. The operation was abandoned.

The last time Nobby, Nick, Nigel and myself went out on a job together was on Friday, 11 June.

Nick was having a farewell party in the office to celebrate his promotion to Detective Sergeant. He had been transferred to Q Division and would start work there on the following Monday. We were all fairly cheerful, especially myself, as my own chances of promotion would naturally increase with Nick's departure, as well as my status in the squad. The naming of Kelaher in the Basil Sands trial earlier that week hadn't taken on too much significance. Nor did it seem much more than the usual bloodymindedness and a bureaucratic balls-up when Nobby turned up at the party with a long face and Police Orders in his hand to say that he'd been posted, at only three days' notice. He was to report for duty at Clapham on Monday morning.

Nick, Nigel and I gathered around him. It was bad news, and we were all somewhat confused.

Nobby was fuming. He relieved his feelings by swearing loudly. It really was the limit. All his years of careful work within the Squad were cancelled in a moment, without warning – and without him and also Nick, Nigel and I would be at a disadvantage.

The others in the Drug Squad who were at the party heard the news of his posting with something like glee. They knew they'd now have less competition. First Kelaher had gone. Now it was Nobby and Nick on the same day. Our celebration was well on its way to becoming a funeral party when a phone call brought us back to life again.

The call was for Nobby – from one of his informants.

We remained near him, supping our whisky doubles and gins, resolving we weren't going to tear our guts out for anyone again. The others in the room were busy shouting their mouths off, not caring what we were up to any more.

Nobby raised his voice – he was being short with his caller.

'No! Sod you,' he said. 'Swan off!'

'Must be the Commissioner,' said Nigel.

We three laughed. Nobby scowled up at us, and then as if someone had flipped a switch his expression changed.

'Bugger it,' he said and pounded the desk. 'Let's go out in a blaze of glory! What do you say?'

I looked at him expectantly, ready as we all were to fall in with his suggestions.

Nigel said: 'What's up, Nob?'

But Nobby was now checking details with the informant. He slammed the receiver down, and sprang to his feet, showing his teeth in a great grin.

'We'll show them!' he said. 'We can pull it off. Any time we want. Can't we? Fuck them. Right! Let's go!'

We downed our drinks and followed him and slid out of the office without another word.

It was early evening and sunset was still three hours away. In two cars, Nobby's and Nick's, we zoomed off to Holland Park, where we hoped to intercept a pusher with the stuff on him.

I was with Nick. He parked his car at the Addison Gardens end of Elsham Road, a street of shabby houses, fronted with small yards or gardens and backing onto railway lines. Nobby and Nigel drove further down the road and also parked. Before long, we observed a black man and a white man go into a house about midway between the parked cars. The stuff was being collected.

Nick and I got out of the car and hovered by it until the black and white suspects reappeared. Whitey now carried a hold-all.

The two of them came towards us, and we approached them as Nobby and Nigel came up behind them.

Suddenly Whitey rumbled who we were, lost his bottle (nerve), and flung himself sideways into the front yard of No. 51 or 52. He hurled the holdall away and himself down some steps into a basement. The door wasn't locked and he careered on into the house. Nick was close behind him and disappeared after him into the basement.

I remained outside in case Whitey came out through the front door. Sounds of pounding feet and banging doors within the building could be heard. I was poised near the front door steps with one eye on the basement. There was a commotion in a ground-floor room on my right – a woman squawked. A window shot up, and Whitey, moving like greased lightning, was out on the window ledge before I knew where I was. I got to him as he jumped diagonally over the basement area and into the next garden and managed somehow to grab his hair as he fell back. He didn't fall in fact, but I did. He broke loose. I overbalanced, crashed into the basement headfirst, and knocked myself out.

As I found out later, Whitey, who had already slowed up Nick with a right-hander inside the house and alarmed the residents by barging into their front room while they were watching TV before exiting by the window, charged into the next-door house, followed in a moment by Nick, and got out the other side by smashing through a window. He then ran through the back garden, climbed over a wall, and dropped down onto the railway tracks. Nobby and Nigel, who had managed to lose the black man, now joined Nick. But by this time Whitey had disappeared.

Being only temporarily stunned, I soon joined them on the nearby railway bridge, where Nobby was jumping up and down, trying to see over the parapet, shouting: 'Where is he? Where is he?'

We pulled ourselves together, with anything but sympathy coming my way, and while Nobby put out a call to the local police saying where our suspects might be, Nigel pacified the startled residents, telling them how to apply for compensation and no doubt dramatizing the dangers of our job.

Equipped with the holdall, containing cannabis as we thought, we then marched to a house nearby, where we knew Whitey had been shacked up.

We knocked and rang and ordered whoever was within to open up. A girl upstairs told us somewhat rudely to go elsewhere. Nobby kicked in the door – at least, that was the intention. He miskicked, and put his foot through the glass panel. But we got inside.

There was what looked like cannabis in one of the rooms and we arrested the rude girl, carting her off to the nearest police station.

In the meantime, some local coppers had picked up Whitey

in a housing estate across the railway tracks. A sharp-eyed kid had spotted him and given him away.

The cannabis was later found to be duff, a substitute – though this didn't stop charges being made out against Whitey for the possession and pushing of what he also thought and said was cannabis. He turned out to have escaped from Maidstone Prison, where he'd been doing time for robbery.

This little escapade wasn't our finest hour – but we got our man. More than that, we finished as a team on a note of success.

When we returned to the Yard, some hours later, the others had gone. They didn't know of our achievement, but it didn't matter. We toasted each other amid the debris of Nick's promotion party.

'To us!' we said. 'And bugger the others!'

The occasion might have become somewhat sentimental, even sad. But Nobby reminded us that although we'd been split up, several of our cases were still to come before the courts and we'd have to follow them through by preparing reports, making and taking statements, and giving evidence in the witness box. It was all something to look forward to. We'd still be meeting, socially and in court.

Before long we were reminiscing about the good times we'd had and all the laughs, and recalling our triumphs. We raised our glasses to those we remembered and drank to some of the arrests we had made.

'Whittome and Cox!' said Nigel.

'Morland and Palacios!' said Nick.

'Palacios and Morland!' I replied.

'Perman!' 'Long!' 'Harris!' 'Sworder!' 'Clark!' 'Robinson!' 'Roy!' 'Scott!'

'The Salahs!' said Nobby. 'God bless them!'

'The Salahs!' we chorused and drank to their downfall.

13

'I swear by Almighty God that the evidence which I shall give shall be the truth, the whole truth, and nothing but the truth.'

'What is your name?'

I answered: 'Adam Acworth, attached to the Drug Squad, New Scotland Yard.'

It was after twelve noon on Friday, 10 September 1971. I was in the witness box at the Old Bailey.

The Judge, Mr Gillis QC, was on my right. The jury were opposite me. More or less to the left of me, in the dock, sitting in a row, were the Salahs, John, Mohammed and Kathy, who by now was very pregnant. They were attended by two warders. Their QCs and solicitors' representatives were in the well of the court between the Salahs and myself – as was the prosecution, whose leader, Mr Corkery, having established who I was, paused and arranged his papers.

He had just finished re-examining Nick Prichard, who had been in the witness-box the whole of the previous day and most of that morning. It was now my turn as a witness for the prosecution to give my evidence against the Salahs, who'd each pleaded not guilty on Tuesday, 7 September, to three charges of conspiracy to import, possess and supply cannabis and cannabis resin.

'We are now in 1971,' said Mr Corkery. 'Can you help us as to your general hair style in July 1970 – namely, the date, July 27th, when you went to The Meads with the last witness?'

'It was fairly long,' I said. 'But not quite as long as it is at the moment.'

In fact, as it hadn't been cut for a year and a half it was now hanging down my back. I had washed and brushed it carefully for my court appearance and clipped my sideboards. My suit was a dark-grey pin-stripe and I wore my Gordonstoun tie.

Mr Corkery continued: 'On Monday, July 27th, 1970, with the last witness, Detective Constable Prichard, did you go to The Meads, Park Road, Stoke Poges?'

'I did. Yes.'

'Did you make a note as to the happenings at those premises?'
'Not personally. No.'
'What happened?'
'Detective Constable Prichard made notes and I countersigned them.'
'Before you countersigned the notes, did you satisfy yourself that his notes were accurate?'
'Yes.'
So, for me, it began.

On the previous day, Nick had told Mr Corkery about what happened at The Meads on the evening of the day when he and I went there. His account was based on the notes he had made in his notebook and of course on his statement, which was virtually the same as mine.

He then described, from the same source, how he and Nobby had seen Mrs S. and Janet arrive at 29 Mapledene Road in a black Mercedes at about 3.10 p.m. on 13 January.

He stated that he and I had been at Kier Park, Ascot, on 18 January at about 9.45 a.m., when John Salah arrived in the Landrover. Photographs of the cars and the Salahs were looked at. Then Nick told about the arrests on 20 March of John, Mohammed and Kathy – this being based on his and Nobby's statements, which again were identical.

Exhibits were now produced. Exhibit 1 was the batch of hairdressing cards with Kathy's name on them. On the reverse side were figures, drawings and writing. Exhibit 35 was a block of cannabis that Nobby had taken from the Landrover at Sofia Prison.

Mr Corkery sought to relate the measurements on the cards to the block of cannabis, to the floor of the Highwayman van, and to a trailer.

Next John Salah's visa for Afghanistan was entered as evidence. It showed a visit to Afghanistan when the approximate date of arrival was February 1971, and referred to a previous visit in May 1970. Three more cards, Exhibit 3, were then dealt with. On them were various words, together with two names and two telephone numbers – one name was that of the hitchhiker. The other was of a town in Bulgaria.

Nick confirmed that John Salah had been searched by Nobby

and that on him were found an airmail letter, a list of telephone numbers, and three notes, one being an instruction to a bank in Jersey, signed by Janet and Mrs S., that in the event of their death, all moneys in their account in Jersey would go to John. Another note, signed by Janet, gave John the authority to sell at his own discretion the two houses at Kier Park and Mapledene Road.

After the search, as Nick revealed in detail, John was further questioned by Nobby. Then it was Mohammed's turn. Both were questioned in the kitchen. Later Kathy was also questioned.

Mr Corkery, his examination of Nick now over, sat down.

So far so good. But then it was the defence's turn. John Salah's QC, Mr Hudson, was the first of the three defending QCs to cross-examine.

Referring to Nick's evidence about our visit to The Meads on Monday, 27 July, Mr Hudson said: 'So that you have no possible illusions about my questions, I am suggesting you have completely made it up and what you say is absolutely untrue. Do you follow?'

'I understand,' said Nick. 'These notes are true.'

Mr Hudson continued: 'I want you to understand I am suggesting they are lies – or you have told lies in the witness box. Do you follow?'

We were, of course, expecting this. It was a common tactic employed by the defence – to impeach the veracity of prosecution witnesses. Policemen were always fair game in this respect. And not only would your truthfulness be questioned by the defence. They could, and if allowed would, make implications that you were lying and even a bad lot yourself, and generally speaking they would do what was permissible to confuse the prosecution witness and sometimes even the issue. It was all done in the course of justice. But it seemed to me to be very unfair. The average witness, especially the average policeman, couldn't think as clearly and quickly as a QC, and sometimes couldn't help becoming mixed up and creating the wrong impression. Accordingly, the trial ceased to be about a defendant's guilt or innocence. The issue at stake was the QCs' expertise – whether the prosecution or the defence were more convincing and could score the most points. It was almost a tennis match between them, with the Judge as umpire and audience. The witnesses and the defendants were only rackets and balls.

Mr Hudson implied it was absurd to think that two hippie types (Nick and me) could turn up at someone's house, unintroduced, unnamed, and be let in and start talking about business deals involving £30,000.

He suggested that Nick's evidence about what happened and what was said in The Meads on 27 July was 'absolute nonsense'.

He said: 'You made this conversation up, because you did not get any information at all. Did you?'

'Yes,' said Nick.

'I am going to suggest to you what really happened,' said Mr Hudson. 'I suggest that when the door was opened, one of you said to Mr John Salah: "May we see Mr Salah?" And the reply that you got from John Salah was: "Which Mr Salah do you want to see?" And you replied: "The elder one." That is what happened, was it not?'

'No.'

'John Salah then told you that his father was out but was expected back shortly and asked you to call back. Is that true?'

'No.'

'One of you then pressed him to say that you could wait for him, and you were then let into the house?'

'No.'

'You were almost immediately asked: "What do you want?" And you, not Acworth, said that you wanted to buy some charge. Do you know what that word "charge" means?'

'Yes,' said Nick. 'It's an old-fashioned expression.'

'It means "hash"?'

'It means "cannabis".'

The Judge interposed. 'Did you say that?' he inquired.

'No,' said Nick.

Mr Hudson continued: 'John Salah then said to you: "What do you mean by that?" And you replied: "You know, man – hash"?'

'No.'

'And whilst these preliminary inquiries were taking place, the mother and father, that is to say, the defendant Mohammed and his wife, returned to the house, and the son, that is, John, immediately said to his father: "Do you know who these men are?" And the father said: "No, I do not".'

'No.'

'And then when you went upstairs you then said you had a friend who was prepared to put up $40,000 US for hash and that "if we were in a position to get it we could all do business"?'

'No.'

'I suggest the mother started shouting at Sergeant Acworth, telling you both to get out of the house, and that if you did not get out immediately she would call the police?'

'No.'

'And I suggest then that when you got that reaction . . . you realized that you had in fact come across a difficult position?'

'No.'

'And I suggest you then said you had made a terrible mistake. And then more or less – I would not say they chased you out of the flat – they abused you as you quickly beat a hasty retreat?'

'No.'

Mr Hudson then went on to suggest at some length that Nick's version of what happened at the *arrest* of John Salah and afterwards wasn't true and that John had been threatened and badly treated.

Hudson's error of getting my rank wrong and calling me Sergeant was the sort of slip-up that barristers make quite often. Names, ranks, titles, dates and times would sometimes be incorrectly given in the hot pursuit of a line of argument.

Next on the attack was Mr Lloyd-Eley QC, who had defended Siamuk Ardalan in the Basil Sands trial and made several serious implications about Kelaher's involvement.

This time he was defending Mohammed Salah.

Mr Lloyd-Eley was much more flash than the portly Hudson. He was a distinguished-looking, grey-haired, bespectacled man, and when his cross-examination continued the following morning he quite unknowingly took the first steps that two years later would result in the utter reversal of our roles that day.

He was trying to establish whether there was any other written evidence or report that would substantiate Nick's statement and the notebook from which the statement had been made.

However, it was the Judge who actually asked the vital question.

'Do you keep any record of your activities other than any entry which you may make in a notebook?'

'I keep an official diary. Yes . . .' said Nick.

'Have you your official diary for July 1970?' asked Lloyd-Eley, and some minutes later made a fateful request.

'I would invite the prosecution to make available to this witness that particular document, so that in due course I can have sight of it.'

This was granted.

He went on to question how and when what Nick had written in his notebook came to be made and why neither Nick nor I had an official pocketbook on us.

In fact, pocketbooks were very seldom carried. And as they were hardly ever checked over by senior officers, they weren't always up to date and weren't always written up at the scene or at the time of a particular observation or arrest. They should have been.

Lloyd-Eley chewed over the fact that Nick's statement and mine said we left The Meads at about 7.50 p.m. – while his note said 7.30 p.m.

He wanted to know how both *statements* contained the same error. Nick couldn't tell him. He also implied we were breaking the law by inviting the Salahs to commit an offence by indicating we would pay for drugs. He re-stated Hudson's contention that John was on his own when we arrived and that we were thrown out. He further claimed that Mohammed would never have said the things recorded in our statements as his English wasn't good, and that when he was arrested he wouldn't entirely understand what Nobby was asking him and wouldn't be able to express himself well in reply.

Nick's response was to say that although Mohammed's speech wasn't perfect, he understood and spoke English perfectly well.

Lloyd-Eley concluded his cross-examination with a detailed refutal of nearly everything that Nobby and Nick had written in their statements about Mohammed's answers to their questions.

The third defending barrister was Mr Ronald Shulman, a suave, thin fellow, aged thirty-six. He would be named the following year as the third alleged plotter in the 'shilling will' trial. The other plotters were found guilty of conspiring to forge the will, which was contested by Penny Brahms. Shulman fled the country, and in August 1973, his legal peers found him guilty in his absence of conduct unbecoming a barrister and expelled him from his Inn.

He was appearing for Kathy.

He had referred to her as 'the lady defendant' three times when the Judge interrupted.

Judge Gillis said: 'I have never heard of a female defendant referred to, in the years I have been at the Bar and Bench, in the terms that you are employing. The correct way to refer to a defendant is either by name or, if you wish, to refer to a *female* defendant. You do not refer to lady defendants or to men defendants. You have been long enough at the Bar to know how to refer to defendants.'

Mr Shulman apologized. From then on Kathy became 'the third defendant'.

She was clearly not as seriously implicated as the other Salahs. Nevertheless Mr Shulman did his best to discredit and cast doubt on the evidence of the witnesses for the prosecution – us. The circumstances of her being collected from the hairdresser's and later questioned at Mapledene Road were queried. Again, it was suggested, as with John and Mohammed, that Nick wasn't present while Nobby put his questions.

'Finally,' said Mr Shulman, 'before you left Mapledene Road, did you hear John Salah say to Detective Sergeant Pilcher: "Why are you dragging my wife into this?" '

Nick said: 'No. I didn't hear it.'

'I suggest that was in your presence. Did you hear that?'

'No.'

'Did you not reply to that: "It is up to you, John. You have just got to cooperate and she can stay at home"?'

'No.'

'There was no question of using the third defendant in order to get cooperation from her husband?'

'That is immoral and wrong,' said Nick.

Shulman then returned to the matter of who was where and

when in the house. His suggestion was that Kathy had been 'interviewed' as they called it, by Nobby and Morag, and that Nick wasn't in the kitchen at the time. He also suggested that Kathy hadn't been cautioned, wasn't told she was being arrested and said practically nothing of what she was stated to have said. He ended by suggesting, with reference to the interview, that Nick hadn't heard one word of it.

He said: 'You copied it from another police officer's notebook?'

'That is untrue,' said Nick.

When Nick was re-examined by Mr Corkery, he had a chance to try to clear up some matters the defence had muddied.

He said: 'It is quite common, from my experience, for either the buyers or the sellers to remain completely anonymous. . . . The other side wouldn't want to know anything about the people who were buying. All they are interested in is the cash. . . . Nobody really wants to know too much about the other people, in case arrests are made . . . even the business men, when dealing in drugs, will still have the same attitude of business – they wouldn't pursue the matter as they would normally if they were doing legitimate business.'

Obviously, he agreed, he couldn't say where he could be found, or give an address – it might have been dangerous for his wife. Also, when working undercover he couldn't carry anything on him that would associate him with the police and couldn't steer conversations so that they kept precisely to the rules.

Nick said: 'I have gone in with the knowledge that drugs are available and have been put out or advertised on the market. . . . With that knowledge I go in and I attempt to find out where the drugs are being kept in order that the police can get hold of them. . . . Should I even attempt to control the conversation, then the whole point of me going in would be lost, because it would be found out that I was not who I said I was.'

All this was really pretty obvious. Nick went on to say that Mohammed's English was good, though not perfect, that his wife was English, as were his children, that he had lived here for twenty-five years or so, and that he never indicated he was having difficulty in understanding what people were saying to him.

Lastly, Nick described how notes were made after the suspects had been questioned.

'Sergeant Pilcher and I stayed in the kitchen where there was a dining-table. We sat down at the table, and then started writing and saying to each other something like: "The first thing I said was this." Then we would both write it down. "And his reply was this." "Yes, I agree." And that would be recorded, and so on, until the end of the interview.'

'Between you, you discussed what was said?' asked Mr Corkery, adding later: 'At the end of it all you would expect that the notes would obviously be the same?'

Nick agreed. He said: 'The notes would be accurate because obviously one person by himself cannot remember verbatim everything that was said. But by both officers going through their notes one gets a very accurate recollection of what has taken place. . . .'

It was not far off the lunch break when Nick withdrew. Then it was my turn.

I told the court what happened at The Meads on 27 July 1970, also what happened at Brixton on 15 and 16 December, at Crevald's boatyard on 5 January 1971 and on 14 January, at Kier Park on 18 January and on 20, 21 and 22 January, at Mapledene Road on the evening of the 22nd, at Dover on 31 January, and at Slough and Ascot on 20 March. All this was generally just a repeat of what I had put down in my statement.

Then Mr Corkery went through the exhibits that Nigel and I had found in Kier Park House on 20 March – the letters, bank-book, passport, photos, sketches.

All that took up the afternoon, and my examination had to be continued on the following Monday, when the entries in the passports of the three defendants were gone through in detail. I was more able to assist in this than the others as my own passport had some similar stamps from the time I drove home from Pakistan through Europe.

The easy task over, I now faced cross-examination by the three defending QCs.

Mr Hudson, after suggesting that I gave 'an utterly false

account' of my visit to The Meads with Nick, became somewhat derisive about the details.

He remarked: 'You arrived and left without giving one single tiny, weeny clue as to where on earth you had come from.'

'From a mutual friend,' I said.

'That is not a clue, is it?' returned Mr Hudson. 'According to your colleague you were never even asked who the mutual friend was.'

'No,' I said.

'Is that right?'

'Yes.'

'And you had never had any dealings with the Salahs before?'

'No.'

'You were a total stranger to them?'

'Yes.'

'And you openly discussed the purchase of thousands of pounds worth of cannabis with them without disclosing anything about it?'

'Yes.'

'In the gear of a hippie?'

'Yes.'

There was no point trying to explain. As we had learned at training-school, the safest way to answer questions in court was to say 'Yes', 'No', and 'I don't know'.

Mr Hudson made further derogatory remarks about the conversation at The Meads as reported in my statement, and implied that we were encouraging the Salahs to commit an offence.

He suggested that when we got a hostile reception we 'fled like frightened rabbits'.

He went on to claim that on 21 January I never saw John Salah painting the trailer.

'It was a cold day,' said Mr Hudson. 'Not the sort of day you want to put paint on at half past four at night and leave it in the open air.'

His final allegation was that a diagram of a vehicle that Nigel and I found at Kier Park House had been tampered with.

He said: 'I suggest that there was no diagram of any false bottom there when you found that document. . . .'

The Judge said: 'You are suggesting that the part in ink was not on the diagram when the officer discovered it?'

'Yes, my Lord,' said Mr Hudson.

He sat down a few minutes later.

Having got through the first cross-examination all right, I felt more confident, and was able to return Mr Lloyd-Eley's opening remark with a strong denial.

He said: 'The first matter that I want to put to you is that a large amount of the evidence which you have given affecting him [Mohammed Salah] is untrue . . .'

His follow-up however quite winded me.

He said: 'When you were at the premises at Kier Park House on March 20th in the company of Mohammed Salah, but in the absence of Detective Constable Lilley, at that time you asked Mr Mohammed Salah for £5,000?'

I was astounded. 'No, sir!'

Lloyd-Eley then suggested that in making this demand I had used such words as 'if you do not want big trouble, you co-operate with us and give us five'.

I couldn't believe my ears. It didn't sound like me at all. It was in fact so far-fetched I almost smiled.

'That is not true, sir,' I said indignantly.

Lloyd-Eley continued with his 'truthful account' of what took place on 20 March. He dealt with the car journey from Mapledene Road to Ascot. Nigel and I were in the front. Mohammed was in the back.

Lloyd-Eley said: 'On the journey did you say to him: "Did you know me?" . . . And did he say: "No"? . . . Did *you* then say: "I am the man who came to The Meads with my friend" . . . "and your wife threw us out"? . . . Mr Salah said: "Yes, I remember." . . . Did Detective Constable Lilley say: "I was sitting outside in my MG sports car"?'

I didn't only deny that question. I answered it, and was pleased to do so.

'I do not think he is likely to have said that, sir, because he has not got one.'

Nigel never had an MG, only an orange Volkswagen which was delivered to him on 1 August 1970. In fact he didn't learn to drive until that July and he actually got his driving licence on the day of our visit to The Meads. It was his car that he, Mohammed and I were in on the afternoon of 20 March.

Considering the Salahs had *two* Volkswagens and a Mercedes sports, Mr Lloyd-Eley's next suggestion was a bit unlikely.

He said: 'Did you say in the course of that journey when the discussion was about the car: "We are not like you people. We can only afford small cars on our wages"?'

'No, sir,' I said wearily.

There was much more to come. Lloyd-Eley implied we had searched Mohammed in the kitchen and later prevented him from fetching his reading-glasses when we were looking through the contents of his brief-case in the bedroom.

Then he repeated the suggestion that I, alone in the living-room with Mohammed, made a demand for £5,000.

He said: 'When you made that demand –'

'I did not make that demand!'

'I must put it to you that Mr Mohammed Salah said: "What do you mean – five?" . . . And at that stage did you catch hold of him by the shirt front and tie and say: "I will choke you – you know what five is"?'

It was incredible. 'No, sir!'

A few minutes later he was suggesting that Nigel went into the kitchen and came out with two kitchen knives, put Mohammed into a state of fear and that I said: 'We want to cut your throat.'

'No, sir,' I said for the hundredth time.

Later on, Lloyd-Eley alleged that when we took Mohammed to Cannon Row police station I said: 'When we get to Cannon Row, we will put you in a cell, and you will hear Big Ben strike for the rest of your life.'

'No, sir,' I said . . . 'I have never said any words resembling that, sir.'

Then followed a long interrogation about how and when and where pocketbooks were written up, a repeat of the allegation that Nick's note made on 27 July was concocted, and a new allegation that we had conspired to fabricate written evidence.

Lloyd-Eley next went over some of the exhibits found in Kier Park House and finally suggested that on 15 December 1970, Nigel and I were observing the wrong premises in Brixton.

It was with some relief, but as much amazement at what QCs could suggest in court about one's actions and motives, that I stood down when the trial was adjourned for lunch.

After the lunch break, Mr Shulman had just one question – whether I had addressed any remark at any time to the third defendant.

The answer was 'No.'

Then it was Nobby who, after answering Mr Corkery's questions, had to be Aunt Sally for the defence.

He stood up to Mr Hudson very well, and firmly denied the latest allegations, which included threats, attempted bribery and blackmail. It was suggested that Nobby said to John: 'Tell us what we want to know, else we will nick your wife', and that when John asked to phone his solicitor he was told by Nobby: 'Sit down. Do as you're told.' All these things were of course denied.

Earlier, there had been quite a to-do between the Judge and Mr Hudson, who had been questioning Nobby about the block of cannabis he had removed from the trailer in the prison yard at Sofia. Mr Hudson became quite heated as he wasn't getting anywhere with his witness.

He said, somewhat forcefully: 'You cannot say – can you? that this piece of cannabis here is the piece of cannabis that you selected? Can you? You cannot – can you?'

Mr Corkery, the prosecuting counsel, stood up. 'Let him answer,' he said.

'Please, Mr Corkery,' retorted Hudson.

Nobby explained. 'I did not mark the cannabis itself.'

Mr Hudson hammered on. 'I can follow your reasoning if you had stuck the label onto the cellophane and that cellophane label was still on when it was opened by the laboratory assistant in London. Do you follow?'

'Yes,' said Nobby.

'But there is nothing there. In fact, the label is in an entirely different place to where you put it.'

'Yes, it is.'

'And you did not stick it either.'

Judge Gillis said: 'What is your question? And please formulate it if you want an answer.'

'I am asking a question,' said Hudson.

'There are a number of questions in the paragraph which you were just concluding,' said the Judge.

'I hoped I was trying to assist the witness.'

'I cannot talk at the same time as anybody else, Mr Hudson, and when I speak others must remain silent. Will you put the series of questions which you wish to put and pause to allow the witness to answer?'

'They were not a series of questions.'

'They were. There is no need for argument. You will be given every opportunity of putting each question you wish. . . .'

'I have been asking my questions in such a way that the witness can be perfectly clear as to what is being asked.'

'But it can still remain one question,' said the Judge. 'May I say when I address Counsel I require them to remain silent. I cannot speak at the same time as others and we cannot hear one another. . . .'

'May I speak now? I have only asked one question and I am going to ask it again since I have been rebuked.'

'You have not been rebuked,' said the Judge. 'I am surprised it is necessary for me to intervene more than once. I am making this position quite clear. This is the way the trial will proceed – introduce whichever questions you wish and give the witness an opportunity to reply.'

And that was that.

Mr Lloyd-Eley now had a go.

It was during his cross-examination of Nobby that some of our diaries which had been asked for arrived in the court – mine for July 1970 was missing. It had been lost.

The available diaries, Nick's and Nobby's, were handed over to Lloyd-Eley, and the Judge said he could peruse them and if need be question witnesses further about them.

This questioning was done half-way through the afternoon, after Mr Shulman, defending Kathy, had ended *his* cross-examination.

Lloyd-Eley rose to his feet and requested permission to cross-examine about the diaries. His manner, always assured, was now doubly so.

Nobby was handed his diary for the period 8 May 1969–29 July 1970.

He was asked to read out the entry for 27 July.

It said that between 1 p.m. and 4 p.m. he had been at Slough and Park Road, Stoke Poges, that he had returned to Scotland Yard and remained there till 5.30 p.m. when he went to Kensington. Then he had a meal, until 6.30 p.m. when he went to Earls Court Road. He was thereabouts until 9 p.m. Then he went on to Brompton Road, where he was until 11 p.m. at which time he signed off duty.

Nick and I were watching proceedings from seats at the back of the court. We cast puzzled glances at each other. Why did the entry make no mention of Nobby being at Stoke Poges in the evening?

Lloyd-Eley leaned forward and smoothly inquired whether Nobby still said he was at Stoke Poges about 7 p.m. and saw us there.

Nobby said he was and he did.

'Is it not right,' insisted Lloyd-Eley, 'the narrative in the diary clearly puts you in the area of the Earls Court Road from about 6.30 until 9 p.m.?'

'During this time, on this day, I was at Slough,' said Nobby firmly, though his mind must have been in a whirl. 'My only reply is that *this* is a mistake I have made when making up this diary.'

A few minutes later he was saying that he never returned to London on the 27th and that he stayed at Stoke Poges throughout the day. Every entry *after* the entry about going to Stoke Poges at 1 p.m. was therefore wrong. Nobby said so.

At this point Nick and I were asked to leave the court.

Neither of us could understand why Nobby's diary had no note about him being at Stoke Poges when we were there. We were also worried as the omission might cast doubt on our evidence about visiting the Salahs. It was an unexpected and potentially disastrous error.

So it later proved to be. But not in the way we imagined.

The rest of that afternoon was taken up by Mr Corkery's re-examination of Nobby – mostly about the cannabis exhibit acquired in Sofia. Then Nick was recalled and further cross-examined by Lloyd-Eley.

He asked Nick to look at his diary entry for 27 July.

It said in brief that he was at Slough or Stoke Poges between 12.45 p.m. and 4 p.m. and between 6 p.m. and 9.20 p.m. This fitted our account of the visit to The Meads. His diary also said that his observation at Stoke Poges ended at 8.30 p.m. when he went to the Cherry-Picker pub nearby and purchased a meal for himself and refreshments for an informant. He was there until twenty past nine.

Before 6 p.m. on that day the diary showed Nick had been at London Airport on an inquiry. The questions asked about this helped to ease the tension and brought the afternoon session to a strangely merry close.

'You were dressed as a hippie with a tie-and-dye shirt?' asked Mr Lloyd-Eley.

'Yes,' said Nick. 'London Airport is crowded with such people.'

'Then you meet your informant dressed as a hippie?'

'Indeed, sir, when I meet my informants they do not want to be recognized with a police officer.'

'Of course,' said Lloyd-Eley. 'A person who wears an ordinary suit such as you are wearing now would not be identified as a police officer?'

'In certain circumstances,' said Nick, 'a criminal can pick a police officer out very easily.'

Lloyd-Eley quipped: 'It used to be by the size of his boots.'

Judge Gillis added: 'That was when they were wearing uniform.'

Everyone laughed and fell about, and the court was adjourned until the following morning.

In the interval the mystery surrounding Nobby's apparently misleading entry in his diary was solved.

It wasn't misleading. He hadn't made a mistake. The error lay elsewhere.

14

On Wednesday morning Nick Prichard returned to the witness box. He was asked to confirm Mr Corkery's reading of Nobby's diary entries for Monday, 27 July, and Tuesday, 28 July 1970.

The entry for the 27th said that Nobby was in the Earls Court Road area between 6.30 p.m. and 9 p.m. The entry for the 28th said that he was at Slough and Stoke Poges between 6.30 p.m. and 12 midnight.

Nick then read the equivalent entries in his own diary. On the 27th he was at Stoke Poges between 6 p.m. and 10.20 p.m. On the 28th he was at Stoke Poges between 6 p.m. and 12 midnight.

Mr Corkery paused before addressing himself to the witness, who was even paler than usual.

'You were in court and you heard other evidence, and you have now seen your own official diary for the two days, the 27th and 28th?'

'Yes, sir.'

'As it affects your diary, have you any comment to make?'

'Yes, sir.' Nick breathed in and steadied himself. 'From looking at my diary for Tuesday, July 28th, I now believe that the day that I entered the premises at The Meads was the 28th, and *not* the 27th. I can only apologize to the court, my Lord. My notes which were made when I came out of the house I dated the 27th. What would appear to have happened was that when the defendants were arrested and statements were made, the only reference regarding that day's observation was the note that I had made in that unofficial book, and the date was taken by all officers as the 27th. . . .'

He continued: 'There is nothing in the original notebook which would indicate a mistake. The note commences at "7 p.m., 27.7.70". I have noticed in my *diary*, from looking at it this morning, that . . . I had originally put Tuesday, July *27th*, 1970, which I changed to read 28th.'

Judge Gillis peered at Nick through his glasses: 'Do you say the "7" has been altered, officer?'

Nick turned to him. 'From my writing I would say that I have written the 27th and changed it. I realized my mistake and changed it to the 28th.'

'Because of the Tuesday?' asked the Judge.

'Because it was Tuesday the 28th, and not Tuesday the 27th, sir.'

Mr Corkery had a few more questions.

'In the official diary,' he said to Nick, 'you put the day of the week – Sunday, Monday, Tuesday, Wednesday, and so on?'

'Yes.'

'In the notebook, how did you start off?'

'The note starts "7 p.m.". Then "27.7.70". There is no day.'

'Nothing to indicate the day?'

'No.'

Poor blighter, I thought. What a bloody fool he must feel.

I didn't feel too happy either. For I had also been with Nick when he made his notes. I had read them through and countersigned them, and I never noticed that the date he put was wrong.

My heart sank when Mr Hudson got to his feet. We were in for it now. The defence being given an inch would take a mile – given one stupid error they'd imply a hundred others.

'I do not know where to begin,' said Hudson. He frowned at Nick. 'You realize what you have said this morning, don't you?'

'I do,' answered Nick.

'You realize, as an experienced officer, the absolutely crucial importance of that conversation in July 1970?'

'I do.'

'And you realize that right up to about ten minutes ago everybody has been spending hours and hours and hours in checking this particular conversation?'

'That is correct.'

'You are now saying to this jury that it never took place on Monday the 27th, but took place on Tuesday the 28th?'

'I am.'

John Salah was half smiling. Mohammed was head-up and attentive. Kathy's eyes were wide.

Oh, my God, I thought, they're going to get away with it after all.

Mr Hudson, with a genuine bone to worry, was in his element. He now suggested that Nick had admitted his error in an attempt to cover-up Nobby's confusion over his diary entries the day before. He suggested that Nick and I had gone to The Meads on *Monday*, the 27th. What was true was alleged to be false, and vice-versa.

It became very complicated, but Nick kept his head. Before long Hudson was pretending to be confused and asking Nick to repeat his explanations. Then he switched his attack and suggested that Nobby had given false evidence which was inconsistent with his diary.

'No,' said Nick. 'He has made a true entry, and has given truthful evidence to the best of his ability. The mistake has been wholly on my part, in that the date is wrong. . . . I put down the 27th when it was the 28th.'

That was well said, I thought admiringly. Perhaps we'll pull through.

When Mr Lloyd-Eley cross-examined again he went over what Nick had said to him towards the end of the afternoon session the day before.

Nick said that when he was recalled he was aware of a probable error, but wasn't conversant with the full details. Later he said that he was certain, though not positive, that the 27th was *not* the day he had entered The Meads. He said that after the court had risen he spoke briefly with Nobby and me and checked over Nobby's and Nigel's diaries, and communicated the full details of his error about 4.45 p.m.

Lloyd-Eley suggested that Nobby and Nick got together yesterday to decide which of them should accept responsibility for the error.

'The truth of the matter,' said Lloyd-Eley, 'is that you are not telling the truth about it and that you were giving evidence in order to endeavour to explain away the impossibility, according to Sergeant Pilcher's diary, of his being present at the time when the meeting at The Meads took place?'

'No, sir.'

Then followed a long and involved discussion about when and how the diary entries for the 27th and 28th were written, including the expenses for those days.

My Lloyd-Eley concluded: 'If, as you have already said, you could not make up your entry for July 27th at the end of the evening, but would have to do it the following morning, July 28th, then you would have made out the details which we see on the right-hand side of the page, showing again the date of July 27th in your own writing, before you went out on July 28th?'

'Yes.'

By this time they had well and truly lost me. I was glad it wasn't me in the witness-box.

Shulman, who stood up next, went off on another tack, about who had actually arrested Kathy and where her arrest was recorded.

It wasn't mentioned in Nick's diary. Nor was Mohammed's. John's arrest was.

Mr Corkery, who then re-examined, summed up this problem in a sentence, putting it to Nick that he was 'the arresting officer in respect of *one* accused, namely John?'

'Yes,' said Nick.

Mr Corkery then produced a piece of paper which Nick had written on while he was outside the court *before* he was recalled. The note had been given to Mr Corkery.

It said:

Sir, I think I have the answer to the discrepancy. As far as I can see, all officers – Pilcher, Prichard and Lilley, show at Stoke Poges on 28.8.70. My notes show 27.7.70. This is possibly an error on my part. The date should have shown 28.7.70. The fact that all statements show the 27th is because my note had to be relied on for the time –

At that point Nick had been recalled to the court.

'What you are saying in the note,' said Mr Corkery, 'is that it may well be that you had made a mistake as to the date, which was, as it were, magnified by the other officers taking the date from you?'

'Yes.'

'Have you in any way tried deliberately to mislead the court and the jury about the dates of that interview?'

'No, sir. I have not,' said Nick.

The Judge tidied things up. He required confirmation from the defence that when Nick was first cross-examined there was no suggestion of any kind that the date of Monday the 27th was the wrong date, and that there was no suggestion that the 'interview' at The Meads did not take place.

The defence agreed no suggestions of this sort had been made.

Nick left the witness-box. The court was adjourned for lunch, and everything, as far as we were concerned, was back on an even keel.

'Well now,' said Lloyd-Eley. He was half-way through his cross-examination of Nigel, who having entered the witness-box the afternoon before, and having been examined by Mr Corkery, was now on Thursday morning being cross-examined. As usual Nigel looked like and spoke like a successful city executive.

I wasn't myself in court that day, but heard what happened afterwards.

'Well now. In addition to the notebook, as you have already told us, you kept an official diary.'

'Yes,' said Nigel.

'Is the diary a document which you keep for the purpose of record and with accuracy?'

'No, it is not.'

'You do not keep it accurately?'

'No, I do not.'

'Why is that?'

'Because sometimes I am vague by necessity. Sometimes I show things in there which I might not have done. It depends on the inquiry I am engaged on. It depends on the amount of security that might be necessary surrounding the particular inquiry. . . .'

In view of what was to follow this was a superb answer. Nigel might have been reading Lloyd-Eley's mind.

The QC continued: 'Your diary is only available within your station to your superior officer and colleagues. That is right, is it not?'

'Yes.'

'And, indeed, it is laid down in police instructions that it must be kept accurately, is it not?'

'Yes, it is.'

'It is countersigned by other officers at the end of each week – your superior officers?'

'It is indeed.'

'With a view to ensuring it is accurate. That is right, is it not?'

'Perhaps – yes.'

'Did you obtain any dispensation *not* to set out accurately in your diary matters concerned with your investigation?'

'Yes, I did.'

'From whom?'

'From my Detective Sergeant – Pilcher.'

'Were the instructions in writing?'

'No.'

In a few minutes Mr Lloyd-Eley, perhaps disconcerted by Nigel's forthright replies, came straight to the point.

'I suggest that you have put forward that explanation because you know if one goes to your diary one finds entries which are wholly inconsistent with the evidence you have given about observations. That is right?'

Nigel didn't answer.

Lloyd-Eley re-phrased the question and Nigel said: 'I haven't seen this diary for many months. I couldn't tell you.'

Mr Lloyd-Eley began producing examples of inconsistent entries.

He said that Nigel had said in evidence that he and Nobby on Sunday, 24 January, saw Janet go through the departure gate at London Airport to board a flight for Jersey at 3.30 p.m.

The diary showed he had had a day off.

'I was due on weekly leave on that date,' said Nigel, 'as I was on most other Sundays. But I worked it, as I did on most other Sundays.'

Lloyd-Eley went further back, to 15 December, when Nigel said that at about 4 p.m. he was at Brixton in the garage yard and that at about 4.30 p.m. he saw members of the Salah family leave.

The diary showed that between 4 and 4.30 p.m. he was having refreshments.

Nigel said: 'They do allow us a little time to eat.'

Lloyd-Eley then turned to what Nigel's *notebook* had to say. It referred to 'Salah the elder and two others'. His *statement* about this observation, made on 15 April, specifically referred to Mohammed and John.

Nigel said he should have put Mohammed and John in his note, but didn't. He had made a mistake.

The next date examined was 16 December. The *diary* said that Nigel had been at Brixton between 9 a.m. and 12.30 p.m. His *notebook* said he saw Mohammed, John and Janet standing beside an orange Volkswagen. His *statement* said that Mrs Salah, John and Janet were standing beside the orange Volkswagen.

Nigel agreed that he had no recollection of seeing Mrs Salah standing by the orange Volkswagen. He said he had made another mistake.

Lloyd-Eley moved on to 5 January, when Nigel had said he saw Mohammed board a Pakair flight to Bombay which took off at 12.45 p.m. His diary showed he went to Heathrow Airport at 10 a.m. and returned to the Yard at 1 p.m. Lloyd-Eley asked how Nigel was able to ascertain the flight left at 12.45 p.m. when he must have left the Airport between 12.15 and 12.30.

Nigel said the diary entry must be incorrect.

In fact, said Lloyd-Eley, the Pakair flight, PIA 702, never went to *Bombay* – Pakair didn't fly planes to Bombay, because that was in India. Moreover, it didn't leave at 12.45 p.m. Lloyd-Eley said that Mohammed left on PIA 702 at 2.15 p.m., and flew to Karachi.

'I have a note,' said Nigel, 'that I was informed, as everybody else in the terminal was informed, over the loudspeaker, that PIA 702 to Bombay left at 12.45.'

Mr Lloyd-Eley referred to another date, 19 January, on which day Nigel had said he was outside 29 Mapledene Road at 9.20 a.m. and saw Mrs Salah arrive in the Mercedes.

The diary showed Nigel to be on duty at 7 a.m., when he went with some customs officials to Surbiton, where between 10.30 a.m. and 11 a.m. he had a meal.

Nigel agreed he was at Surbiton post office at 7 a.m., where he met the customs officials. They were going to intercept a parcel. He said they all went to an address in Tolworth Rise, and that he wasn't there very long. He said he left and went to Mapledene Road, getting there about nine o'clock.

'Why not enter it in the diary?' asked Lloyd-Eley.

'I do not know,' said Nigel.

He was asked if there was any claim shown for mileage between Tolworth Rise and Slough, or from Slough back to the Yard. There wasn't. The diary showed details of a journey to VS Section, then Surbiton, twenty-six miles – there and back.

'Mr Lilley,' said Mr Lloyd-Eley, 'are you saying that it was just an error on your part that you did not record the journey on to Slough and the observation there?'

'Yes.'

'Was this intentional or a mistake?'

'I don't know. It was either intentional or a mistake. It was one of the two.'

'Can you not assist us as to which of the two it would be?'

'No, I can't,' said Nigel.

It's just as well I wasn't actually there to see and hear Nigel being too clever by half. I would have bitten my fingers to the bone or made an exhibition of myself by shouting: 'Stop acting like a bloody fool!'

All of a sudden he did, and at the same time seemed to lose some of his usual fluency and sureness.

Mr Lloyd-Eley inquired: 'Well, how would it come about that it was *intentional*, on that particular occasion?'

'Well,' said Nigel. 'Well, because of the security of this particular inquiry which we had decided, and Sergeant Pilcher had said to me on certain occasions it is up to me – we will not always show when we go out to the Salahs. We spent a great deal of time – a great deal of interest was shown in them. Other inquiries of a similar nature, because of indiscretions, had been stopped. People had got to know we were interested in them. We did not want this to happen on this occasion. We ensured that there was no indiscretion. . . .'

He then agreed he had gone to London Airport at 5.30 p.m. that same day and had shown an observation on the Salahs and had named them.

Lloyd-Eley asked why Nigel had concealed the morning entry, by saying he was at Surbiton, but not the evening one. Nigel replied that he didn't know what state of mind he was in when he wrote the diary and that it was some time ago.

Lloyd-Eley followed up other dates. He established that whereas Nigel's diary for 20 January showed he was at the Yard between 10 a.m. and 10.30 a.m., he had said in evidence that he, and I, were at Ascot at 10.40 a.m. The diary for 21 January showed he had gone to N22 at 4.30 p.m. In evidence he had said he was at Ascot at 4.30 p.m.

The cross-examination returned to 24 January when the diary showed a day off.

Nigel had said in his statement and in answer to Mr Corkery's questions that he had been at London Airport.

He now explained that he had worked on most of his days off in his ten years as a policeman, and that he had spent most weekends in or around Ascot, Slough and London Airport, watching what the Salahs did. He had made no entries in pocketbooks or diaries about these occasions as they were of no value to the court, only to himself.

It was not until Lloyd-Eley came to 26 February, when Nigel had said that he and Nobby had seen John and Mohammed arrive at London Airport at about 8.30 p.m. – the diary showed he was in a pub at Westminster about that time – that Kelaher, who initialled the diary entries and expenses, was finally mentioned and said by Nigel to have approved of all this.

'Would he have approved of your putting in these false entries?' asked Lloyd-Eley.

'Yes,' said Nigel. 'That is what I understood from Sergeant Pilcher.'

'What you are saying is that all the entries that one finds to be inconsistent with the notes in your official notebook are false entries in the diary. . . . Made quite deliberately? . . . And backed up by claims for expenses which are wholly fictitious as far as those precise details are concerned?'

'Yes,' said Nigel to all these questions.

'And you say that both Sergeant Pilcher and Detective Inspector Kelaher *knew* of this practice and approved of it?'

'Yes, I do.'

There it was – and there it rested for the time being.

Mr Lloyd-Eley moved on to question Nigel in detail about the day of the Salah arrests. Then Shulman asked him questions relating to Kathy.

Mr Hudson, speaking out of turn, got further explanations from Nigel about the false entries – namely, that Nobby had given the instruction, some time before November 1970, that there had been a security leak which prompted the giving of the instruction, that it was up to us to say not too much about what we were doing, and that Kelaher, Nigel presumed, knew what was going on.

By now Nigel was enjoying himself. Some of his answers had successfully irritated the defence and made his audience smile – they were later rebuked for this by the Judge.

The high spot came when Nigel, referring to 'long-haired, moustachioed, hippie-types' of policemen who carried no identifying material on them, said of himself: 'I have always been a fairly short-haired, ordinarily dressed individual.' To which Hudson responded: 'Short-haired and smartly dressed individual, it would appear.'

Nigel must have liked that.

He stepped down at lunchtime. After lunch it was the turn of our leader, Detective Chief Inspector Victor Kelaher.

15

Kelaher's father had been a policeman, a Detective Sergeant, who died when Vic was three years old. He was brought up in a Metropolitan Police Orphanage and in his teens he went to work as a clerk in Scotland Yard. After doing his National Service in the RAF he then became a policeman himself. He was now forty-one, married with three children, all girls.

In the panelled courtroom he stood in the witness-box looking as relaxed as usual. He wore his dark blue suit and a thin blue tie. His face was tightly composed, slightly flushed, and his eyes gave nothing away. His voice was light, with a trace of an accent, but firm. I can't remember any mannerisms, just that he rolled his eyes a bit and tilted his head back a little when considering a reply. When he smiled, which wasn't often, he looked friendly and kind.

Not so friendly were some of the faces turned his way in court – at least, not obviously so. Among them were two or three senior policemen, the team of Lancashire officers set up to investigate the allegations made against Kelaher at the Basil Sands trial. Not that they were hostile, just impersonal and cold. They were very attentive, as was everyone else, wanting to hear what Kelaher would say.

Mr Corkery briefly took him through the three observations on the Salahs in which he had been involved, on 17, 18 and 22 January – which were also described in his statement. He had of course made others, but he hadn't thought them relevant to this particular case.

This was established by Mr Lloyd-Eley.

Kelaher explained further: 'I put in my pocketbook matters which I consider should be given in evidence. It does not necessarily mean I make a note of all my observations.'

Then he was asked about diaries, where they were kept and what they contained. He said he merely signed the diaries of his subordinates, after they'd been checked by a DI, and he would only look at the contents if he wanted to query something.

Naturally he wouldn't have had the time to go through the thirty or so diaries brought to him for signing once a week.

'Mr Kelaher,' said Lloyd-Eley. 'Did you ever allow any of the officers who were serving under you in the Drug Squad to make wholly false entries in their official diaries?'

Kelaher paused before replying. 'You may well be getting at instructions which I gave earlier on in the course of this inquiry, when I conferred with Sergeant Pilcher and I told him that for security purposes it would be as well if the officers did not show the places where they were keeping observation.'

'Can you tell us when that would be approximately?'

'Very early on. It was in 1970, early on after we started the investigation.'

Lloyd-Eley pursued the matter, concluding: 'You gave them instructions enabling them to set out wholly fictitious entries saying that they had had wholly fictitious expenses?'

'For security reasons, yes – that they should not say the particular area they were doing the observation.'

'And did you also give them authority to claim for moneys apparently spent on these fictitious journeys?'

'They would claim the money they had incurred on refreshments or expenses, whatever it might be.'

Lloyd-Eley raised his voice: 'I suggest you would not have given those instructions had you been acting honestly?'

'Are you suggesting I was acting dishonestly?'

'Yes.'

'Then you are wrong.'

He said that with great emphasis. It had been Mr Lloyd-Eley who had made most of the serious allegations against Kelaher at the Basil Sands trial.

The QC now turned smoothly to another matter.

He said: 'When we go to the diary of DC Acworth, as he then was, one finds in the diary substantial agreement with the observation which he has given evidence about?'

'Maybe. Yes.'

'And disclosure of the precise place of observation and the people on whom observation was being kept?'

'Maybe. I haven't seen the diary.'

'As far as DC Lilley is concerned, one also finds in his diary on a number of occasions *explicit* statements as to where he is keeping observations and the people on whom he is keeping observation?'

'Well, this may be so.'

'What would be the purpose of his making this disclosure in his diary, and yet giving completely *fictitious* details on *other* occasions on which he said he was keeping observations?'

Kelaher briefly glanced at the ceiling. 'It probably depended on what period of time they referred to, because, as I stated earlier on, it was *earlier* in the investigation I gave the instructions. But later on, in fact, I had reason to believe that there were no foundations in my suspicions.'

He added that he had formed this view by 26 February. When asked if he thought it necessary for superior officers to know what a subordinate was doing, he said that *he* was the superior and *he* knew what they were doing.

'I would be at home,' he said. 'And I would get a certain phone-call, as a result of which I would contact him. That would be on the day in question.'

Kelaher was now referring to the intercepts, which he or Nobby saw twice daily. If they couldn't, and if some conversation seemed important, the details were telephoned to their homes. But he couldn't mention this in court for security reasons – and offered to put it in writing for the Judge. This was declined.

'Are you saying,' inquired Lloyd-Eley, 'that these were occasions when you directed someone to work, and show himself on weekly leave? Were there other occasions that you phoned up the officer and directed him to make a fictitious report?'

Kelaher said: 'I wouldn't say to him: "Make a fictitious entry in your diary." If I rang him up I would tell him to go from his address and keep a certain observation, whatever time of day or night it might be, whether it was his day off or not.'

All that was common knowledge to us, but I suppose the jury, and indeed the QCs, were interested in our methods of work, which were characterized by long and irregular hours.

My Lloyd-Eley next reverted to the question of security leaks.

'Tell me,' he said, 'a little more about the security matter which led you to give these instructions? Are you saying that it was – as we have already heard – suspected that a police officer was the possible leak?'

'Not necessarily,' said Kelaher. 'I was concerned only in possible indiscretions in conversation, etc.'

'How could the entries in the diary affect that?'

'These are left lying around, and anyone can pick them up – civilians or police officers.'

Then followed several questions about the running and manning of the Drug Squad office, and about expenses.

Finally, Mr Lloyd-Eley reiterated that it wasn't necessary for accurate entries to appear in the diaries of Nobby, Nick, Nigel and me, because Kelaher knew exactly what we were doing.

To this he agreed, saying: 'They were working under me.'

'And they would have been acting on your instructions in everything they did?'

'Yes,' said Kelaher.

Mr Hudson's cross-examination was brief and confined to an inconclusive questioning about 22 January.

Mr Shulman pursued the matter of when and where Kathy was questioned, detained and charged, and who collected her from the hairdresser's.

He established something I'd forgotten about – that Kelaher actually went on leave on the day the three Salahs were arrested, 20 March, and that when he returned, on the 31st, he had left the Drug Squad – having actually been transferred on the 16th.

There was a curious postscript to Kelaher's appearance in the witness-box that day. After the jury and the witness had retired from the court a short discussion took place. Then they were allowed to return.

Lloyd-Eley rose again to his feet to cross-examine further.

This time his questions related to 5 March – the day on which Kelaher and Basil Sands had been detained by customs officials at Earls Court. On the very same day Kelaher and Nigel Lilley had together observed John Salah visit a doctor.

Kelaher was asked to read from his *notebook* entry.

'Friday, March 5th,' he said. 'With DC Lilley to observation, eight o'clock. John Salah in Volkswagen (orange).'

The *diary* entry said: 'At 7.30 to CO, and with DC Lilley to West End re observation.' Then it said that Kelaher entered a public house and purchased refreshments for himself and an informant. The next entry said: 'To Earls Court area' – though no time was given. He finished duty at 1 a.m., the lateness having been caused by him being interrogated by the customs people.

Lloyd-Eley suggested that Kelaher had made up the Salah observation to explain his departure from the Earls Court hotel at 7.30.

'And I suggest to you that the account which is set out in your notebook, and in the diary, is to your knowledge contrary to the observation of customs officers at the hotel?'

Kelaher responded: 'That is completely untrue – as I gave evidence before you at the Middlesex Sessions and told you so.'

'I think that is as far as I can take that matter, my Lord.' said Mr Lloyd-Eley,

Kelaher left the witness-box.

That is also about as far as the whole matter of false entries went, although details varied with individuals.

Morag McGibbon, our WDC, was next in the box and gave evidence in her soft but precise Scottish voice about two observations concerning the Salahs, on 5 and 14 January 1971. She had made no notes about the arrests on 20 March, and though Mr Shulman asked her endless questions about Kathy's movements on that date, Morag really didn't have much else to add to what the court already knew.

Her evidence continued until late on Friday morning, when I was recalled.

Mr Lloyd-Eley wanted to take me through the observations I had described in my statement and given in evidence and compare them with the diary entries for the days in question – as he had done with Nigel.

The observations and my evidence tallied on 15 and 16 December 1970, when I was at Wilson's garage in Brixton. On 5 January 1971, they didn't.

I had said in court that at about 9.40 a.m. I was at Crevald's boatyard when I saw John Salah and Janet arrive, and that about 10.40 a.m. I saw Mrs Salah arrive.

My diary entry said I was on duty at the Yard at 9 a.m. and engaged in the office until 10.15, when I went to Paddington.

I said this was a false entry, made for security reasons, at Nobby's direction, though also at my discretion.

Lloyd-Eley wondered why I hadn't claimed any expenses for driving there. I said I didn't claim for driving.

I wasn't going to help him by saying I wasn't authorized to use my car. He could find that out for himself.

His next bit of wonderment concerned the fact that on the previous day, the 4th, my diary entry named the Salah family as being the object of an observation at London Airport between 6 p.m. and 10.30 p.m. This was the day before Mohammed flew to Pakistan.

Lloyd-Eley said: 'Why should you have put that entry in, if you were seeking to conceal by fictitious entries the following day you were keeping observation on them?'

'I do not know,' I said, and indeed I didn't. The entry was nine months old, and I didn't remember much about the why and wherefore of that entry or any others. Flipping through the diary brought back certain memories, and made me curious to read on for myself – though of course I couldn't as I had to answer questions.

What really worried me wasn't so much the absence of Salah observations in the diary but the almost daily inaccuracy of the entries, especially about times. The absent Salah observations had a fairly simple explanation – which I had just given. The other inaccuracies might, I imagined, lead to tricky situations which my memory couldn't explain, and there was the whole inexact business of booking and phoning on duty and off duty, and of course one didn't put *everything* down, like going out for a haircut, or to the post office, or shopping, or quick drinks with friends and visits to see them. The diary was just a general guide to our whereabouts and wasn't always true.

Some errors in it arose inevitably out of the existence of a detective's duty allowance, whose maintenance actually required us to make false entries about overtime. It was quite unofficial, and unofficially quite accepted. Senior officers knew of it, but if questioned about it would very likely deny the existence of such a practice – as they denied the existence of much else that shouldn't have been done but was.

As members of the CID we didn't get paid individually for the overtime we did. But each week the amount of hours every

DC, DS, etc., had worked overtime was added up and made into a grand total which was then divided by the number of CID officers in the force and paid out to each of us as a monthly detective's duty allowance. It was felt that this was the most democratic way of dealing with the matter, as some officers didn't have the same opportunities as those who were on special jobs or inquiries to earn any overtime. It was also supposed to prevent individual officers from faking claims for large amounts of overtime pay. In practice it meant we were required to make up fictitious entries about overtime in our diaries, so that the overall average and the duty allowance would remain about the same.

For example, if an officer just signed off duty at six or seven every day of the week, a DI would be sure to remark on this and suggest he was slacking. So, for the good of all, officers would sometimes extend daytime observations into the evening and phone off duty at 11 p.m. or midnight.

It was easy to put vague notes in the *duty book* about '7 p.m. to Chelsea section. Back later', which an officer could expand in his *diary* into 'At CO till 7 p.m., then to Chelsea and Kensington re suspect addresses. Engaged till 8.30 when purchased refreshment for informant and meal until 9.15 p.m. Then further engaged on observation till 11 p.m. and off duty.' In fact the officer might very well be somewhere other than Chelsea or Kensington – for instance at a cinema or in a restaurant, from where he could telephone the Yard at some point and ask the reserve officer to show him off duty in the duty book at 11 p.m. Often the entries about overtime were real. Sometimes, however, they were not. The whole system of making diary and duty-book entries was open to error, and a defending QC, chancing on any discrepancy, could make things awkward. It was this that made me more nervous than the missing entries about the Salahs.

If Lloyd-Eley had got hold of our duty books he would of course have found that they tallied with the diaries, and that the absent Salah entries were duplicated in the duty books. The defence would then have had two guns to fire at us. But the duty books were never produced in court – not on that occasion.

All this was somewhere in my head while Lloyd-Eley cross-examined me.

He was now busy pointing out that I had identified the Salahs by name many times – which I had already admitted. I mentioned them on 4, 7, 12 and 14 January, and didn't on the 5th. On the 18th I mentioned them in the evening observation but not in the morning one.

'Why?' said Mr Lloyd-Eley.

'I do not know,' I said. 'I cannot say what I thought then – I obviously did not think there was any harm in putting it in.'

He moved on to 20 and 21 January.

I had said in evidence that Nigel and I were at Kier Park on both days at 10.40 a.m. and 4.30 p.m. respectively. The diary said that on the 20th I was at Notting Hill and Chelsea between 10.30 a.m. and 1 p.m., and that on the 21st I was in the office until 4.30 p.m. when I went to N22 – as Nigel had also said. On neither day had I mentioned any observation about the Salahs.

I did on the next day, the 22nd, and later, on the 27th, and of course on the 31st when they left Dover.

Lloyd-Eley put it to me that apart from these specific instances, there were a number of other references to the Salahs in my diary, from October 1970 to March 1971.

'That is correct,' I answered.

'Again,' said Lloyd-Eley, 'I ask you what could be the point in making wholly fictitious entries in the diary when you were making a whole series of references to the family?'

'Exactly as I have said about four times already.'

'Is the truth of the matter, officer, that the evidence you have given about observations is untrue?'

'No, sir.'

'Just as the evidence which you gave about July 27th and the going into premises at The Meads was untrue?'

'No, sir.'

'And the evidence which you have given about March 20th, 1971, and what took place on that occasion is untrue?'

'No, sir.'

The cross-examination ended with another suggestion that I had demanded £5,000 from Mohammed, which I again denied, and some questions about a diary entry on 20 March that said: 'Kier Park House. Meal 1.15 to 1.45. Further engaged until 4.30.'

'Tell me,' said Lloyd-Eley. 'Whilst you were at Kier Park House, did you take half an hour for refreshments?'

'No, I did not.'

'Does the diary show that you took half an hour for refreshments?'

'Yes, it does.'

'Well, is that a false entry?'

'Yes, it is.'

'Why make a false entry about that?'

'I do not know.'

'Officer, surely you know why you make false entries?'

'I have told you why I made false entries.'

'Why did you make *this* false entry?'

'As far as I can remember, I might have had a cup of tea, and that would have been a meal, would it not?'

To my surprise Mr Lloyd-Eley sat down. The questioning was over. I was allowed to withdraw.

Not much more emerged from the further cross-examination of Nobby Pilcher except that he had made false entries on 13 January (as had Nick) and 19 January (as had Nigel) and that on two occasions when he'd given evidence about being at London Airport with Nigel, on 24 January and 26 February, his diary showed him to have been off duty.

Nick was then recalled. He was questioned about the false entry relating to 13 January, involving the same observation as Nobby's, and about one on the 18th, involving an observation at Kier Park with me.

The question of not claiming mileage expenses for these observations was raised again.

Nick answered: 'If I had claimed for all the mileage I did on this inquiry, the bill would have been phenomenal.'

This took us to the end of the Friday session.

The trial resumed on the following Monday, and then on Tuesday, 21 September, Kelaher and I were recalled.

Kelaher was asked by Mr Corkery about the renewing and storing of diaries and said that no record was kept of either in the Divisional Office where new ones were issued and where old and used ones were supposed to be kept for two years.

My diary up to 15 October 1970 – which included the visit to The Meads on 28 July 1970 – was missing. Mr Lloyd-Eley thought this somewhat suspicious, and I was recalled so that he could make the allegation that my diary had been deliberately suppressed. This he did. I denied it.

Mr Corkery put the matter in perspective by pointing out that only one date in the diary, 28 July, was relevant to this particular case, and that my existing diary, which *had* been produced, had many more relevant dates – 15 and 16 December, 5, 14, 18, 20, 21, 22, 31 January, and 20 March.

Judge Gillis turned to me and said: 'Officer, have you any recollection when you last saw the diary which preceded the one that you had in October?'

'I would think on that last date, sir,' I said, meaning 15 October. 'I can't think of it since then.'

He continued: 'Can you remember whether you obtained the one you now hold or someone did it for you?'

'I would think I would have gone to the store and got a new one, sir.'

'What about the completed one?'

'Quite what happened to that I can't remember, sir.'

'Yes,' said the Judge. 'Very well.'

And it was. With that our evidence at the Salah trial was concluded.

There were several other witnesses for the prosecution, including the Salahs' housekeeper at Kier Park House, a man from Crevald's boatyard, and a man from Wilson's garage.

I didn't hang around to hear them. I walked out of the court that Tuesday and bought an airline ticket to Ibiza. Nigel and his wife were already there on holiday. He had telegrammed me, saying the hotel had a vacant room and he'd reserved it for me. 'Join us,' he said.

On Friday I did, leaving the Salahs to what seemed to be a fairly certain fate – and leaving the team of policemen investigating Kelaher with now more than *his* fate in their hands.

Before I left I heard that their investigation had broadened. The allegations made by the defence that the whole business of false entries was a lie had raised further questions about Kelaher's conduct. Lloyd-Eley's damaging allegations were to be examined for any truth in them – with the result that Nobby,

Nigel, Nick, myself and Morag were also now being doubted, and our evidence was being viewed with some suspicion.

It wasn't very nice. For if the investigators could prove any misconduct by Kelaher before or during the Salah trial we would also be called to account. If they somehow reached a conclusion that Kelaher had lied, that conclusion would embrace us, with very serious results.

'United we stand,' as Nobby once remarked. 'Divided we fall.'

PART FOUR

Alack, when once our grace we have forgot,
Nothing goes right; we would, and we would not.

16

There wasn't much sunshine during my fortnight in Ibiza. The weather was generally bad, with gales and rain and flooding in some places – Benidorm for one. We spent most of the time in a hired car driving around the island, which didn't take very long. The rest of the time we ate and drank and wondered what was happening in England.

We returned on Sunday, 10 October.

The next morning I drove from the section house to the Yard as usual to find that I was no longer with the Drug Squad.

I'd been transferred to Illegal Immigrants and Passports, to an office further down the corridor towards the Interpol room. The transfer had already been effective for a week. The order must have been made out and sent to me soon after I flew out to Ibiza. It was like Nobby's transfer all over again, made without warning while I wasn't looking and at very short notice. Now the Whispering Squad were finally uprooted, with me, the last to join Nobby's team, being the last to leave the Drug Squad.

I wasn't sorry about the move. At least I wasn't leaving the Yard. But I wasn't too happy about the new posting, as it involved mostly paperwork and not much activity in the way of detection, observation or arrests.

This I found out soon enough. But the first morning of my return was taken up with handing over various papers and responsibilities to someone else in the Drug Squad after I had breezed along to my new office and got myself introduced. Nine other policemen worked there, and once I had been told roughly what they did and had sized the place up I knew I wasn't going to like it all that much.

With the excuse that I still had a ton of outstanding cases and documents to dispose of back in the Drug Squad office, I nipped out of the building and sped off to the Old Bailey, where I'd been told Judge Gillis was doing his summing-up.

I got there just before the court adjourned at one o'clock for lunch, and when this happened chatted with various people and caught up with the progress of the trial.

Then I went out and had a haircut.

Sitting in the barber's chair watching my Drug Squad image in the mirror being cut away seemed a very significant thing. It was also rather necessary, as the Passports Sergeant had suggested that he didn't want any big girls in hairnets working in his office. In the barber's mirror I watched the transformation curiously. After over a year with hippie-length hair I'd forgotten what I looked like underneath – thin-faced, and rather like a convict.

I suddenly knew what Samson had felt like, apart from chilly around the ears and neck. I felt less confident, more exposed, as if I'd regressed a couple of years.

Back in the Old Bailey, where everyone was reassembling after lunch, my shorn appearance aroused so much surprise and so many jokey remarks about me having become a prison-guard, or getting myself convicted in the lunchbreak, or selling my hair to pay for a pint, and so on, that I cheered up very quickly and decided that it wasn't so bad being back in grey old England.

But the trial itself no longer had the same fascination. I no longer felt so involved. As I sat in court that afternoon I thought more about my future and the new move than about the Judge's summing-up. What happened to the Salahs was no longer of such interest as before, and wouldn't be, unless the unexpected occurred and they all got off.

Much more interesting was an item in the *Evening Standard* which I bought when I left the court at 4 p.m. and read over a cup of coffee in a café opposite the Central Criminal Court.

It said that Francis Morland, a sculptor, had been arrested in New York. The fact that he had skipped bail and had failed to appear at the Old Bailey in March on drug smuggling charges was mentioned. Scotland Yard, the paper said, confirmed the news of his arrest but didn't know where he was detained or on what charges.

This was very cheering news. I couldn't help grinning as I studied the item and recalled the Rolls-Royce affair. I wondered what Robert Palacios would think of this turn of events. The wheel had come full circle once again, just before the Salahs' day of judgement.

There was more news about Morland in the *Evening Standard* sixteen days later. The item said that Morland

> and five other men pleaded guilty in a Federal Court in New York to being members of an international drug-smuggling operation. They were remanded for sentencing. It was alleged that the 46 foot ketch, *Beaver*, owned by Morland, was used to bring in 1,500 lbs of hashish, worth about £830,000, from Casablanca to New York. The six men were arrested after the two-masted boat was boarded by customs agents on 30 July at the Hudson River basin . . . The other accused were all Americans.

Afterwards I learned that our office at Scotland Yard had been able to provide the American police with some useful information about Morland.

It wasn't until the New Year that he was sentenced. He was fined about £6,000 and sent to prison for eight years. On his release he would be extradited and brought back to England to face charges here. He was now thirty-seven. If he got done again, he could be inside until he was fifty.

Was it worth it? I wondered. Why should a man who had so much going for him chance it all and throw it away? He can't have thought about it very much. He can't have thought he was doing any wrong or any harm. And he must have thought he would get away with doing what he did.

I felt sorry for him – that a man of his background, education and opportunities should have gone so far astray.

I even felt sorry for the Salahs. After all, I had known them now for over a year. The crime they were charged with wasn't that demonstrably awful – they were basically charged with trying to better themselves and make some money by taking some frightful risks. And again, they hadn't done anyone any harm. All in all they didn't seem like criminals any more.

The jury were out all day on Wednesday, 13 October.

When they returned that night at about 7.45 p.m., Nobby, Nick, Nigel and myself were all in court.

It was always a sobering moment when the jury gave their verdicts. A fatal, final decision was made after months and years of investigation, after hours, weeks and months of prosecution and defence. In a few words, twelve people, chosen at random and sitting in judgement on persons much like themselves, made a mighty choice that would alter the defendants' lives – be they guilty or not guilty.

The foreman of the jury stood and was asked the usual questions – whether they had reached a verdict, if it was unanimous, and finally what it was.

Mohammed Salah and John Salah were found guilty of conspiring to import, possess and supply cannabis.

Mohammed was jailed for five years. John for three.

Kathy was found guilty of conspiring to import cannabis, but not guilty of possessing or supplying cannabis. She was sentenced to nine months' imprisonment – suspended for three years.

Both men also had to pay costs – Mohammed £2,000, John £1,200.

Kathy and John were in tears after the sentence. They clung together, moaning. Mohammed blindly followed the prison guard out of the dock. He and John were taken to Wormwood Scrubs that night.

The four of us who had brought about their downfall went out and had a drink.

It was more an occasion for reminiscing than for celebration. We stood in the panelled bar of the Magpie and Stump, the local boozer opposite the Old Bailey, and recalled the high spots of the Salah investigation. There was definitely a feeling of satisfaction – that justice had been done and seen to be done – but also a little unease. For the senior officers looking into Kelaher's conduct had also been in court to hear the sentence.

Nobby was certain that no inquiry would pin anything on our boss, Vic Kelaher.

'Besides,' he added, 'they've got nothing to go on. No facts. No proof. Nothing but fucking slanders. It's an outrage.'

'Why are they gunning for him then?' I asked.

'I can't imagine,' said Nobby. 'Look at his record.'

'He's too much of an individualist,' said Nick. 'A lone wolf.'

'No,' said Nigel. 'It's his autocratic manner – he behaves as if everyone else was a step behind, as if he were something special.'

'He's not the only one, is he?' said Nobby. 'But you're wrong about Vic. Compared with the others, he's just too bloody good.'

They were confident nothing would come of the inquiry, and very soon I was of their opinion. We drank to a job well done and to the quick apprehension of Mrs Salah and Janet. Then Nobby told some jokes, beginning in his usual fashion with: 'Have you heard this one?'

We heard about Janet and Mrs S. sooner than we expected. In fact we heard *from* them.

Two days after the trial ended, on the Friday, the Interpol office at the Yard put in motion the machinery for their arrest wherever they were outside Britain. Warrants already existed. Now pictures, information and documents were sent out to other Interpol offices in Europe. The hunt was up.

That weekend the *Sunday Mirror* carried a dramatic story about 'the world's two most wanted women', and displayed photos of them. The photos were from holiday snaps of the Salahs which Nigel and I had picked up at Kier Park House, and showed both Janet and Mrs S. smiling sweetly at the camera. Mrs S. had a scarf arrangement around her head and the sun in her eyes.

Towards the end of the following week Nobby got a phone-call from the Salahs' solicitors. Mrs Salah and her daughter were in London, at the solicitor's offices in Wimpole Street. Would he like to see them?

He got on the phone to Nigel and me. We met at the Yard, picked up the warrants and shot off to the solicitor's as soon as we could.

In an upstairs office, in the presence of a solicitor, Mrs Salah and Janet were formally cautioned and arrested and asked to come with us to Cannon Row police station.

They were very composed about it all and not too bitter about Mohammed and John being in prison. Janet was more forthcoming than her mother, and loosened up enough to say that she'd had a dreadful few months in the Bulgarian jail where, she said, she'd been fed on soup and bread and been ill-used.

It was odd seeing them again. The last time I had seen them was nine months before, on 31 January, at Dover. A lot had happened in between, both to them and to us. It was in fact the first time I'd spoken to Janet – and I'd only encountered Mrs Salah once before, on that confusing evening in July the previous year, when Nick and I visited The Meads. I wondered why they had given themselves up, and was forced to credit them with more sense and family loyalty than I'd imagined they possessed. Mrs Salah had of course told Nobby and Bolton in Sofia that she was prepared to return to England. She'd been very worried about John's health and concerned about Mohammed. Perhaps she thought after the miracle of Janet's release from jail that more might follow in this country. Perhaps she had looked in a crystal ball and seen no danger – to them.

The day after the arrests she and Janet both appeared at Bow Street magistrates court and were remanded on bail. Later on they were committed for trial at the Old Bailey. The trial never took place.

In the meantime, on 3 November, three weeks after judge and jury made their pronouncements on the Salahs, father and son, another announcement was made that would have an effect on many peoples' lives. Mr Robert Mark, aged fifty-four, was appointed to succeed Sir John Waldron as Commissioner of the Metropolitan Police.

At the time it didn't mean much to me – especially as he wouldn't in fact become Commissioner until 1 April next year, when Sir John Waldron retired. For in November I'd made the big decision to move out of the section house at Golden Lane. I was going to get a flat of my own.

I'd been living in section houses for very nearly eight years now – not so much out of choice, but because police regulations said you couldn't go and live on your own until you were aged thirty. However, this rule had recently been altered. Now you could leave off living in section houses after four years' service. It wasn't of course as easy as that. You could go off and live on your own, or with another copper, or with any female you liked, but you could not in any circumstances live with a male civilian, even though he had been well and truly checked out and vetted. This was for security reasons.

Father: One's mind boggles at the intellectual ineptitude of this. I'd have thought that of all the things which would tend to make a copper understand what goes on in the minds of the general public, would be precisely this – to live with some responsible male member of the public and mix with his friends, and so on. A chartered accountant is a very responsible person. So is a solicitor – or any young chap taking up a profession. The daily natter, the exchange of ideas and views, could be nothing but useful and good. To think otherwise is to treat grown men like children – as they do – to isolate these young policemen and make them out to be different from the rest of us, which isn't right.

I didn't want to live on my own, and I didn't want to live with a bird – not unless we were married. Besides, my parents wouldn't have liked that. I wanted to live with a male friend or two who had nothing to do with the police. But this wasn't allowed. It had to be another policeman. This was really the last thing I wanted, as being with policemen twenty-four hours a day wasn't the greatest thrill. That was why I spent as little time as possible in the section houses, and got out and away to my parents' and sisters' and brother's and cousins' places as often as I could, and went out in my free evenings to shows and restaurants and saw a lot of any girl I was going strong with. The company in the section house was just that – company – and somewhat limited at the best.

This didn't apply in a few cases, and in particular with regard to Mike Edmans.

He'd been living in Golden Lane off and on for over two years. He wasn't always there, as for weeks on end he'd be away in the provinces on some inquiry or other. On his return he usually had some scathing things to say about the inmates of Golden Lane, calling them 'automatons' and deriding their idle, cushy existence. He encouraged me to find a flat. So when I did, it seemed natural that he should be the policeman who shared it with me.

My father thought it would be more sensible to buy a flat than to rent it, and so I did – in Battersea, south of the River. Its price was £8,200. Father helped me with the down payment and the rest I got on a mortgage. I then had to borrow £800 from my bank, as the flat was very much in need of conversion.

It was on the fourth and top floor of a Victorian mansion-block of flats called Albert Palace Mansions, Lurline Gardens. The flat faced south across London to the Crystal Palace TV transmitter on the skyline. At the rear were other mansion flats whose fronts faced north and Battersea Park. The mansions were respectable enough, but the neighbourhood was fairly rough. I was lucky to get the flat, as prices were beginning to rocket, and most usefully it was only ten minutes away by car from Victoria Street and New Scotland Yard.

After Christmas spent at my brother Bill's, I moved into my new home at the start of January 1972.

My parents, who had decided to sell the family home in Stanford-in-the-Vale and were going to move to Frilford Heath in Berkshire in March, provided me with quantities of cast-off furniture and household utensils. Mike and I drove down to Stanford in a van he had borrowed and picked up all the stuff in two trips in one day.

Back in Battersea it took ages to unload – mainly because everything had to be carried up four flights of stairs.

For about a month I lived in squalor in the flat, stripping off miles of ancient wallpaper, making good the holes and cracks in walls and ceilings and floors. After a week Mike moved in and we both took a fortnight off work to get the basics done. My agreement with him was that in return for helping me do up the flat he could live in it rent-free.

Dust and dirt and rubble and rubbish was everywhere. Apart from being repapered, the flat hadn't been touched for seventy years. There were gas-jets on the walls and grates in every room. The plumbing was positively Victorian.

I did most of the demolition. Mike filled in the fire-places, used a blow-lamp on the woodwork, mended the sash-cords, and did the more specialist jobs. Then everything had to be papered and painted.

Sometimes we worked very late at night, kept going by cans of beer or mugs of coffee. Sometimes we made so much noise the neighbours complained. One threatened to call the police.

By March, the hard graft was over. The sitting-room was

completed first, then the hall, then the two bedrooms. The bathroom and kitchen were last. I made a mistake with the fitted carpets, putting them down before the central heating arrived, and I repainted the sitting-room when Mike's girl-friend complained about the colour. But when I fixed up my stereo record-player, purchased some reproduction antiques via Mike, and rented a black and white TV set, I felt more like a householder – though some things, like the kitchen wallpaper, didn't get done for a year.

Mike was a very good worker, though after the first month he tended to let me get on with it.

Living with him wasn't too bad, although he was sometimes very exuberant and outspoken. I didn't like it when he made remarks about Nobby, or Nigel, whom I saw quite often – we played squash together. He also made remarks about me, saying that I was 'programmed to impress a female', and 'always waiting for the phone to ring'. He called me Buzzybaby. He was somewhat annoyed when I once took his girl-friend to a party – at her invitation, as he was on duty. I didn't tell him afterwards, not sure he'd be pleased, and he wasn't. When a bird who rather fancied me, a real chaser, had to be given the brush-off, Mike made a song and dance about answering her phone calls and saying I wasn't in. The trouble was that though this girl was a good-looker, and a good cook, she became too possessive – she was always wanting something, attention mostly.

I had of course taken out several girls since Sam's departure – mainly friends of cousins and so on, and purely for social reasons. I had a car. I always paid. I'd be very attentive all evening, smiling at them, asking a lot of questions, ribbing them a bit. They liked that. They liked me. And I liked pleasing them. But when they stopped being friendly and funny and started getting serious, I didn't want to know. I didn't want questions, only a *status quo*.

Sam never asked questions, not directly, not personal ones, yet somehow she understood me. She never made demands, though I always asked her what she wanted. She never tried to own me, though of course she did. There was never anyone who could take her place.

Round about March I heard that someone out in Africa had

asked her to marry him. For really no reason at all I didn't believe she would.

By this time I was generally in a more optimistic mood.

There had been a setback in December when I went before the Selection Board for promotion to Detective Sergeant and failed the oral examination. They said it was because I was the youngest in the group. But out of the nineteen candidates from C1, I was the only public-school boy – and of course under some kind of suspicion as being one of Kelaher's men.

He was still being investigated – and so were the former Whispering Squad. For the inquiry had broadened into a general survey of the methods and activities of the Drug Squad under Kelaher. The investigating team of Lancashire police officers had now been at it since July. Apart from matters arising from the Sands and the Salah trials, they had also taken time off to investigate the Flying Squad.

By the spring these little upsets and worries had faded away – as had the generally dismal national happenings of the winter, with its shortages, miners' strikes, power cuts, and over a million unemployed. A state of emergency had been declared in February, and the troubles in Northern Ireland had been at their worst, with Bloody Sunday in Londonderry, a car-bomb explosion in Aldershot, and several major bomb-blasts in Belfast, one of which injured fifty-one people.

But on Budget Day, 21 March, there was a piece of news that helped to raise my spirits.

After eight months the investigation into Kelaher and the Drug Squad was concluded. A report was sent to the DPP saying that there was no evidence to support the allegations made against him at the Basil Sands trial. He was cleared. And so, as we thought, were the rest of us who had given evidence at the Salah trial.

I learned that Kelaher was now on the staff of the Metropolitan Police Management Services, where his expert knowledge must have been largely wasted, and that he himself was heading an inquiry into the forgery of travellers' cheques. He was still up for promotion to Detective Chief Superintendent.

Coincidentally, a few days later Siamuk Ardalan escaped from Norwich Prison. He was the Persian sentenced at the Sands trial to three years in jail. From his hiding-place he telephoned the newspapers and said he was willing to make a statement that would clear Kelaher in return for his freedom. It wasn't necessary – though an official statement about no action being taken against Kelaher wasn't issued by the DPP until May. Ardalan was never caught.

Everything was now more or less back to normal. The inquiry had ended; the flat was in order; and I had left Illegal Immigrants and Passports.

At the beginning of 1972 I was transferred, on Commander Virgo's orders, to the Obscene Publications Squad. We called it the Dirty Squad.

17

The Dirty Squad was another section of C1 at the Yard, and to begin with in my nine months with them I worked like a black.

Much of our labours turned out to be a waste of time in the changing moral climate. But we did everything we were required to do with a will and lightened the sordid aspect of our task with all manner of japes and jollification.

The Dirty Squad were a great bunch of fellows to work with – as most of the Drug Squad had been – and I had more laughs with them than at any other time. It was probably the right attitude. If we'd taken a serious interest in everything we saw, we'd have ended up like the dirty old men whose fun we were out to spoil.

Basically, we were the DPP's runners, as far as obscene publications were concerned. Complaints about them from the public would be received by him and his department and we would be asked to investigate. Over would come a letter laying out the details of who, what, and where; and in whatever strength was necessary we would steam over to the premises concerned, see what was in store, and whether it might be described as obscene.

It wasn't just shops we visited. Armed with search warrants we called at all kinds of places, warehouses, photographer's studios, printers' firms and private homes, and took away any material that might be used in evidence – mainly magazines and books, but also photographs, slides and films.

If information came to us directly – for instance that a particular bookshop had acquired a load of dirty books – we would raid the place and forward the evidence to the DPP for his consideration. It was up to *us* initially to decide what could be classed as obscene, and then it was up to the DPP to agree or disagree and say if there was a case for prosecution.

Not everything we seized had to be sent to the DPP, only selected examples. But we were inclined to be generous. Crates and boxes of books and magazines would be carted over to the DPP's offices across the way from Buckingham Palace, especially after a warehouse raid, when we would send over half a dozen copies of every issue of large circulation magazines for the DPP's staff to study.

Some of the stuff was kept in a locked section of our office in the Yard. Most of it – in fact tons of it – was housed in wire-meshed vaults under Holborn police station.

Prosecutions didn't necessarily follow the searches and seizings. The DPP might decide to let the purveyor or printer get off with a caution. In which case the person concerned would sign a disclaimer saying that he relinquished all ownership of the books or items – whereupon the DPP had them destroyed. If it was decided to prosecute, the offensive material had to be kept until the trial was over, many months later.

After a successful prosecution all the evidence had again to be destroyed and literally made into pulp. This involved filling up vans or lorries with officially obscene publications and taking them off to the pulping places, of which there were several around London and in Kent. We didn't just leave them there either. The pulping of every piece of porn had to be supervised by the Dirty Squad as well.

Of course in the increasingly permissive atmosphere of the time, it sometimes happened that what we and the DPP considered to be a matter for prosecution was no longer regarded as such by the time it got to court.

In the first five months of 1972, 138 cases for prosecution were submitted to the DPP for his consideration. Action, however, was taken in only nineteen cases, and seventy-five summonses were served against twenty-seven persons or companies. In the same period, a total of 287,243 obscene articles were seized, including 1,407 films. And sixty-four people were cautioned. For a small squad, about twenty men, that all involved a great deal of hard grind.

We spent hours heaving and humping piles of dirty books and mags out of shops and stores and into vans and trucks. We spent hours shifting them out of the vehicles into the Holborn vaults or up to our office. We then spent as much time taking them out of vault and office and piling them into vehicles to be destroyed or returned. On top of all this we spent absolutely ages labelling, listing and itemizing every single article we seized.

The most laborious job in this respect and a real waste of our time was the mail-order business. When we got to hear that such a business was in operation and that unsuspecting citizens were receiving catalogues of objectionable material in their morning post, we informed the GPO, who put a stop on all letters-in-reply going to the mail-order address.

This was usually too late to prevent the letters and postal orders of the speedier and more eager buyers from getting through. So despite our interference the operation was generally worth the sender's while. If outraged citizens had only phoned the Dirty Squad the moment they found something smutty in their letter-box, this particular kind of mail-order business would have had to start doing the football pools instead.

The slower clients' letters which were stopped by the GPO had to be collected by us and itemized, potential buyer by buyer. These people then received in return a letter from the police. It was a warning, saying that it was an offence to send or receive obscene material through the post. They then got off with a caution. Their money was returned to them by hand, by their local policeman no less.

I met some weird and wonderful civvies in my time with the Porn Squad – not all of them dirty and not all of them old – and I saw some very odd sights.

I wasn't shocked, and soon stopped being amazed. After all there's a physical limit to what can be done in the sex act, and basically, when you've seen one dirty book you've seen them all. Even the action with animals – pigs, donkeys, horses and dogs – was so remote from the real thing as to be idiotic. If that was what some people liked, that was their problem. '*Chacun à son* blue', as one wit remarked.

It wasn't for me. And it didn't bother me so long as they didn't do it in the road. What I didn't like were the scenes showing beatings, cuttings and burnings, really vicious stuff that made me feel quite ill. Most of the time the material we saw was just a source of rude comments, comparisons, and cues for jokes. This particularly applied to the films.

In order to find out whether or not they could be termed obscene we had to have a look at them in the office. We had a film projector and a small screen, and at one end of the room with the window-curtains drawn there would be very nearly daily showings of the blue movies we had seized.

Few were longer than fifteen minutes and none would be watched right through. A DS would get one of the clerical civilians in the office to lace a film up and run it, and when the action had warmed up a bit he would wander over and size up the performance. Usually a ten-second glance was enough to give the film a rating.

Occasionally, on a Friday evening, we might have a special showing for selected friends and acquaintances in C1 – a sort of stag party.

During the week we sometimes had a bit of fun with the tea-ladies, accidentally exposing them to something spicey and giving them the giggles.

Whichever way you looked at the Dirty Squad – dull it wasn't. And for a few months I was happy to be useful, active, and working with some very good blokes.

When the news filtered down in March that Kelaher would be cleared of the allegations against him, I began to look forward to a better result at the next Selection Board for Sergeant sometime in June. But, unknown to me, even in March my luck had begun to change, and on 17 April 1972, the ball began to roll steadily downhill.

On that date Mr Robert Mark took up his appointment as Commissioner of the Metropolitan Police.

He had been at the Yard for five years – since February 1967, when he was summoned from Leicester to be an Assistant Commissioner. In May 1968 he moved up to Deputy Commissioner and so became, as it were, heir apparent to Sir John Waldron – the other possible contender for the top man's shoes being an Assistant Commissioner, Mr Peter Brodie. He was head of the CID, a tough Scot and a hard-liner. But Mark had been pushed forward in his career by two Labour Home Secretaries, Mr Roy Jenkins, who'd brought him from Leicester where he was Chief Constable, and Mr Callaghan, who'd made him Deputy Commissioner.

During my own two years at the Yard I'd sometimes come across him in the foyer or in a lift when he was on his way up to the Commissioner's penthouse office in the tower block. He was a shortish, sharp-featured man and wore glasses. Invariably he'd be wearing his executive coat and hat. To me he looked more like a mathematics master than the top cop in charge of 20,000 men.

The Home Office pundits must have thought of him as being more intellectual and more 'with-it' than the average senior policeman. He expressed himself well in public, though he didn't like argument. He was also a good self-publicist in his role as lawman, though not much was known about him personally, except that he came from Manchester, had played lacrosse, read a lot of books, and did *The Times* crossword. His background wasn't exceptional. He'd devised a meterless traffic-warden scheme for Leicester, had been on the Mountbatten prison inquiry, and was one of the advisors to the Hunt Commission on Northern Ireland. It was probably to his advantage that after leaving grammar school he had started as a PC on the beat in Manchester before the War. He was in fact the first Commissioner who had come up from the ranks. Sir John, his predecessor, had been at Charterhouse and Cambridge. It was to his disadvantage in the Yard that he wasn't a Londoner or a Southerner or a crime-buster of repute. He had also been a uniformed policeman throughout his career.

He was appointed, I imagine, because he was an ideas man, and a reformer.

At the time of his appointment, in November the previous year, the *Guardian* described Mr Mark as

> a new type of policeman . . . a dedicated, unaffected professional who wants to find new ways of doing his job effectively. . . . In a

sense he will do to Scotland Yard what Mr Wilson and Mr Heath have already done for Downing Street: ushered in an era of meritocracy. . . . It will be interesting to see what changes his regime will encompass, and particularly whether his own keen intelligence will attract to crime-fighting the sort of man who is just as much at home on a chess-board as in a punch-up.

The Times quoted a quote of his: 'All your doings are publicly known and must therefore be beyond complaint or criticism.' The paper said, bearing this in mind, it was inevitable that some sections of the Metropolitan force would feel a firm hand, both in the exertion of tighter control and more accountability.

The paper praised his thoughtful assessment of fundamentals and priorities as regards the law, and concluded that to his force, he would be a firm man, capable of rooting out wrong relentlessly, where necessary, but eager to encourage the best qualities of the force.

The *Sunday Times*, on 6 November, described Mr Mark's thinking as 'revolutionary', and said that if his views were translated into action

it may mean that within a few years the police function may be split between two distinct bodies. A uniformed body of police would be responsible for public order and keeping peace. But crime investigation would be entirely in the hands of a plainclothes CID, which would seek recruits with higher education. The pursuit of the professional criminal would become a career for technocrats. Neither would have responsibility for traffic control – this would go into the hands of an enlarged and enhanced wardens' service.

The paper also said:

Mr Mark's appointment . . . was undoubtedly made to forestall a Parliamentary demand for a public enquiry into the affairs of the Metropolitan Police. Rightly or wrongly, allegations of corruption – even of participation in crime – prosecutions, loss of prestige, and accusations by outside bodies and other police forces have mounted in recent months. In the coming weeks this tendency may grow. . . .

That's what the papers said. What some policemen at the Yard had to say isn't printable. It was not a popular choice.

In January, Mr Brodie resigned – two and a half years before his retiring age, thus forfeiting about £400 a year of the pension he could have expected had he served his full term. It was said he disagreed with Mr Mark's policies, which were supposedly 'soft-line', and with his reorganization plans.

This didn't really mean much to me at the time, though rumours of dissatisfaction and disaffection reached the lowly levels of the Yard where I worked. They were given a basis when at the end of April, seven days after taking up his appointment, Mr Mark made the first moves in restructuring the force.

They amounted to two basic changes: a partial takeover of the CID by uniformed policemen, and an extension of the practice of moving everyone on every two years. The first change was the equivalent of making membership of the officers' mess and the sergeants' mess interchangeable. It wasn't at all welcome. The second change was even more unsettling – especially to long-service policemen. No worker in any job would care to be moved from one factory, shop, or office every two or three years throughout his working-life. The ideas behind this and the uniformed takeover were that barriers within the force would be removed, a unity of purpose would be achieved, a cross-fertilization of talent would result, officers' experience would be widened, everyone would keep fresh and lively. The results were that morale suffered and men began to leave the force in greater numbers than ever before.

Not all resigned. Some were dismissed as a result of widespread purges now being initiated and carried out.

For Mark, the zealous reformer, another of whose aims was to root out police corruption, had also set up a new department, A 10, to investigate complaints against the police.

It was headed by a Commander and staffed by uniformed and CID officers, who were in no doubt as to the strictness of their unenviable duties. Any attempt at whitewashing was out, as Mark made clear when on 1 May he gave a ten-minute pep-talk to about fifty CID officers at the Yard.

They were members of the Police Federation, the union, as it were, of all ranks below Superintendent. The new Commissioner was reported to have told his audience that the good work of the CID was being offset by wrongdoers, and that he was dissatisfied with the way senior officers were investigating complaints. He said that nobody or nothing would stop him from putting his house in order. The end of his speech was met by a sour silence.

'We were treated like bloody schoolboys,' said an officer afterwards. 'There was no reason to applaud.'

Kelaher had even fewer reasons. The previous month – and several weeks *before* he was officially cleared by the DPP of the allegations at the Sands trial – another inquiry had been set in motion. It was actually the third to investigate his conduct.

During the thirty-day Sands trial, Commander James Crane had had a watching brief. Mr Crane, then head of the Fraud Squad (later he headed the Poulson inquiry), handed over to Mr Prescott and the Lancashire team after the trial.

Now Kelaher was to be investigated again, on the orders of Mr Mark. But he wasn't alone now. The new inquiry would investigate the allegations made at the Salah trial against the main police prosecution witnesses – namely Kelaher, Nobby, Nigel, Nick, Morag and me.

The process began in March. It was slow, and for us, a painful affair.

I don't know when exactly it began, or how and to whom the orders were given. I imagine that Mr Mark read a copy of the Lancashire team's report before it was sent to the DPP. Its conclusion was, apparently, that no criminal action need be taken. However, an internal inquiry was launched straight away to investigate what grounds there were for bringing disciplinary charges – if not criminal ones.

The task was assigned in the first place to a uniformed man, Chief Inspector Ernest Faulkner, a shortish, youngish, slight, quick-moving man with a corporal's hair-cut, who was then at Harlesden police station. He went to work with a will.

On 17 March, one of his uniformed Inspectors, Albert Smith, visited Scotland Yard and took possession of the diaries, commencing in mid-1970, of Prichard, Lilley, Acworth and Pilcher. Back at Harlesden police station, he put them in a sealed envelope and locked them in a metal cupboard in Faulkner's office.

On 22 and 24 March he picked up one of Lilley's pocketbooks, two of Pilcher's, and one of Prichard's, which had been delivered, as instructed, to Willesden police station. He put them all in the aforesaid metal cupboard.

Faulkner then acquired a full-time assistant, Detective Sergeant John Sullivan, another slim and shortish, dark-haired man, with a long, pale face, an okay accent, and again a well-trimmed head.

On 12 April, at Harlesden, Inspector Smith removed the pocketbooks and diaries from Faulkner's cupboard and handed them to DS Sullivan, who also received, from Faulkner himself, Kelaher's diary.

The following week, two days after Mark became Commissioner, Faulkner and Sullivan visited me at Scotland Yard.

Faulkner said: 'Can I have the pocketbook containing the notes of evidence you gave at the trial of the Salahs?'

I said: 'Yes, sir,' and left the office to fetch it.

A few minutes later I returned and handed it over.

On the same day Sullivan collected eleven duty books from the general office, all relating to the Salah investigation.

About this time Faulkner must have established to his satisfaction that evidence given at the Salah trial about two observations – on 13 January (involving Nobby and Nick) and 19 Janauary (involving Nobby and Nigel) – was false. This meant that any resulting charges would not be disciplinary, they would be criminal. Perjury was the crime – lying on oath in court.

The investigation broadened. Detective Chief Superintendent Gordon Mees took over. He was an older, more solid and grey-haired man, though again not tall. He had a brown, potato face, and a mild West Country voice. His helper was Detective Chief Inspector Peter Gittus, tall and handsome, with a pleasant expression and manner.

On 2 May, Sullivan took possession of two statements to withdraw bail made by Wendy Clark and Teresa Gould who had both met Nick at 2 p.m. on 13 January at the Yard.

On 11 May, he and Faulkner saw WDC Morag McGibbon – who was still with the Drug Squad.

Faulkner said: 'I am concerned in the investigation being carried out by DCS Mees concerning allegations made at the trial of the Salah family. Can I have your diary and pocketbook dealing with that case?'

She replied: 'Yes, certainly,' and handed them both over.

Also on that day Sullivan collected seventeen unused pocketbooks from the Stolen Car Squad, and he and Faulkner visited the other Yard offices in Tintagel House, where Kelaher gave them his pocketbook.

In the second half of May, Sullivan went around picking up various other pocketbooks, requisition books and an issue book. He also took Morag's pocketbook and her diary along to the police laboratory, to a Mr Fryd. On the 31st he visited the Regent Street offices of Pakistan International Airlines and collected a passenger manifest and a delay report from a Miss Page who worked there.

In June, Sullivan's travels continued.

With a police photographer, Albert Maughan, he visited Kier Park House, Crevald's boatyard, 29 Mapledene Road, and The Meads, Stoke Poges. At each location several photos were taken.

DCI Peter Gittus then lent a hand. He went to the Old Bailey where he saw the Paper Keeper and had photostats made of the original Section 1 statements of Kelaher, Nobby, Nigel, Nick, Morag and me in the case of the Salahs. These he gave to DS Sullivan on 6 June.

On the 13th, Sullivan took possession of the C1 garage books and collected Morag's pocketbook from the police laboratory. On the 14th he went to the Vauxhall garage and was given two daily books showing the movements of nondescript vehicles. He also returned to the police laboratory with a further pile of duty books and diaries for Mr Fryd's inspection.

So it continued for another month, with Sullivan to-ing and fro-ing, adding more documents to his list of exhibits, including transcripts of shorthand notes made during the trial of *Regina* v. *Salah*, and having some of his acquisitions examined in the police laboratory by Mr Fryd.

Why it took so long, I've no idea. All the relevant documents could have been picked up, even by one man, in a fortnight at the most. But it was four months before they felt a case against us could be proved in court.

In the meantime, knowing very little but only too aware of every rumour, we waited. There was not much else we could do, except get in touch with our solicitors – which we did.

My father's solicitor got in touch with the London firm of Kingsley, Napley and Co., whose offices were in Star Yard near Chancery Lane. David Napley's assistant, Christopher Murray, telephoned me on 15 June, and I met them for the first time on 22 June. Nigel was with me, as he had independently and earlier asked Napley to act for him. There wasn't really much to discuss – it was an introductory meeting more than anything else. The gist of it was that we had to wait and see, while doing and saying nothing that might complicate the situation.

About this time Nobby sent in his resignation, giving the required month's notice. He had had enough. After working with the Flying Squad and the Drug Squad for years, Clapham police station must have seemed very small beer. I think he also wanted to force the inquiry to show their hand.

Three weeks later they did – just before his resignation became effective.

On Tuesday, 11 July, Morag and Nigel were instructed to report to Mr Mees at Paddington Green police station – she in the morning, he in the afternoon.

A prepared set of questions was read out to each of them by Mr Mees in the presence of DCI Gittus, CI Faulkner and DS Sullivan. 107 questions were put to Morag; 165 to Nigel. Neither made any attempt to answer.

The next morning a similar questionnaire was put to Nick – 98 questions. He answered none of them. In the afternoon Nobby was asked a list of 157 questions by Mr Mees. He answered a few.

On the 14th, Kelaher was questioned in the morning. He had taken upon himself, as our boss in the Drug Squad, the responsibility of being the only one of us at the interviews to answer in full. This he did, dealing in his usual decisive manner with the 137 questions that were put to thim.

Kelaher's solicitor, who was with him, asked for a copy of the intercept, and was told by Mees that such a document would be secret, and he doubted if he would be allowed to have it. Kelaher said that the suggestions made throughout the trial were that certain observations were never kept and that 'the intercept would clearly show the need for the observations'. Had he not arranged for them to be covered, he said, he would have been failing in his duty.

His interview started at 10.35 a.m. and finished at 1.40 p.m.

Then it was my turn. Half an hour after Kelaher's exit I entered the room where Mees, Gittus, Faulkner and Sullivan were assembled. I had a solicitor with me – as Nigel, Nobby and Kelaher had also had.

I had been advised by my solicitors that in view of the probable large number of documents that might be put to me in the course of the interview, and in view of the danger that any answer I might give at that initial stage without careful thought and consideration might be erroneous and later used against me, I should refrain from answering any of Mees's questions, as indeed was my right.

I sat in a chair in front of a table on the other side of which was Mr Mees. He took up the sheaf of papers which was my questionnaire and read the opening question. It was in the form of a statement, which he was making now for the sixth and final time.

'I am Detective Chief Superintendent Mees,' he said. 'And I am making inquiries in connection with evidence given in the case of John Salah and others with which you were concerned. As a result of those inquiries, it appears that perjury may have been committed and there was a conspiracy between you and other officers to pervert the course of justice. I now propose to put to you a series of questions relating to that matter. But before I do so, I am going to caution you that you are not obliged to say anything unless you wish to do so, but that anything you say may be put into writing and given in evidence.'

He looked at me – his face was blank. So was mine. I said nothing. Peter Gittus, who was there to record my answers, drew a line against Question 1.

Mr Mees's mouth twitched at the corners. He read out Question 2.

'Are those some of the duty books used by the Drug Squad during the period of the Salah inquiry?'

I looked at the books on the table and recognized the worn and well-used covers and bindings. I said nothing.

Peter Gittus wrote down: 'No reply.'

'Is this your official diary covering part of the period of the observation in the Salah case?'

Mees held it out.

I looked at it – my diary, the pathetic evidence of my months with the Drug Squad, and now a silent witness for the prosecution. I was as silent.

Gittus again wrote out: 'No reply.'

Mees asked me Question 4.

I sat there – they all sat there – for over an hour and a half.

Mees plodded through every question, and paused every time for a reply. I said not a word, or managed to murmur as a change: 'No reply.' In all Gittus wrote that down 154 times.

It was a fairly depressing scene. I hated being there, being interrogated, being faced with heaps of documents I hadn't seen for months, being unable to answer in case I said anything that could be open to misconception. I wanted to protest in some way, to deny what was false and untrue. But I couldn't. I just sat opposite Mees, looking at the table, picking my nails, feeling as if I were six years old again.

Once I glanced at Faulkner and Sullivan. They looked at me with what seemed to be accusation, as if I had let the side down, and with bored contempt. I looked away.

The questions wore on. The time passed. Perhaps even the others wished they were somewhere else.

At last Mees's voice firmed up. He was reading the last few questions.

'I suggest to you that on March 20th, 1971, there was insufficient evidence to prosecute the Salah family for conspiring to import dangerous drugs, and you then agreed with the other officers to fabricate a number of observations in order to support a prosecution of the Salah family.'

He looked at me. I looked at him. Gittus wrote down: 'No reply.'

Mees sighed, and tightened his lips.

In a business-like way he read: 'I now have to tell you that the facts of this case will be reported to the Director of Public Prosecutions, for his information and directions.'

He put his hands on top of the sheaves of unanswered questions on the table. It was over.

'All right. You can go,' he said.

Friday, 14 July, was just about the most desperate day in my life. A criminal case had been made out against me, as a policeman and a person. I stood accused. I might stand trial, in the dock where I'd helped to put many other accused. I couldn't tell my parents. There was no one I could tell. A generally confused feeling of bitterness, shame, frustration, fear and helplessness buzzed in my head.

That night I saw Angela – a girl I'd thought of marrying – and we had a fearful row. In two days' time we were going to fly on a holiday to Crete. I didn't want to go. In two weeks' time Sam was returning to England. I had never been in such a dreadful mess. And on Monday it was my birthday. I would be twenty-nine, and the way things were, the biggest general failure in the world.

18

Angela was badly treated by me – there's no doubt about it. The whole affair was as it turned out a mistake from start to finish. But I was in a very uncertain situation that spring, with in the background ugly rumours about the inquiry flying around, and I needed a permanent someone, a girl to see every day, with whom I could have a good time and forget my troubles. Sam had been out of love with me now for over a year.

On 22 April, the Saturday after Mr Mark took up his new appointment, while the Apollo 16 astronauts explored the mountains of the moon, I had gone to have lunch with a girl cousin of mine and her flatmates, who all lived in one of the other mansion-blocks in Lurline Gardens. That's where I met Angela. The lunch went on a long time – there was a lot of wine – and by the end of it I thought Angela was the prettiest, most desirable bird I'd seen in a month of Sundays. In short, I flipped.

She was small and fair, with big blue eyes, and was very vivacious. She was also very bright, and worked as a personal secretary in the Stock Exchange. At first she wasn't too interested in me. But I gave her a lot of attention, and having monopolized her at the lunch party, I took her out to Spot 3 on the Wednesday and monopolized her all the following weekend. On the Sunday afternoon I took her to see my parents in Frilford Heath where they'd now been living since March, and that night we went to a concert in the Royal Albert Hall.

Perhaps she was swept off her feet. Anyway, from then on, I

rang her up every day, arranged to meet her for lunch whenever I could, and telephoned her whenever I got off duty. She complained a little about all this attention, especially when she was ironing or washing her hair or had another date. But she usually responded to my suggestions and was, I believe, quite pleased to do so.

Before long, what started as a bit of an adventure began to get serious on both sides. I hadn't had any special girl since Sam's departure and Angela was feeling abandoned also, having been recently let down by a bloke she'd been going out with. We needed each other.

In general we got on rather well. There were some small sources of friction, apart from the fact that basically she was just too clever for me. Being an honest person she said what she thought and was sometimes openly critical. She thought for instance that I wasn't very good at catching a waiter's eye and didn't know much about wines, which I didn't. She didn't think I communicated very well. She thought my parents were rather old-fashioned. She couldn't get over the fact that my father sometimes called me 'boy'. 'How peculiar,' she said.

What bothered me about *her* was the fact that she sometimes took pills – tranquillisers, like vallium. I never did so myself, not even aspirins for headaches, believing that it wasn't natural. These pills seemed to make her subject to swift changes of mood, and I sometimes just didn't know where I was. But her liveliness, her sparkle, was one of her attractions.

May was the best month for us. We were good for each other then. And it was springtime.

One Sunday, after we'd had lunch with my sister Sue and her husband at their home in Hertfordshire, we came back to my flat in Battersea, and Angela, after a few drinks, went all quiet. Then she burst into tears. I comforted her, and in between sobs she said I was very lucky, having such a super family.

'I've such a *small* family,' she wept. There was only her mother, who lived in Norfolk, and an older married sister.

Naturally, I was somewhat moved by this, and said she could share my family if she liked. Perhaps, I said, we should get married.

For some reason she didn't accept the idea, but it made her

feel better. She stood on a chair so that our noses were level and flung her arms around me and said I was what every girl should have in her Christmas stocking. Angela was a very volatile person.

That was in May, when we also made happy plans to go on a holiday together to Crete.

In June I got a letter from Sam saying she'd heard I was in some kind of trouble at the Yard and wasn't to worry. And she said she was coming back to England in July.

It was a warm and friendly letter. She said she was going to train as a midwife in Cambridge for six months. Clearly the story that she was going to get married was so much bull. I had always been optimistic about seeing her again and that she would come back to me. Now it was almost a fact. All my old feelings and thoughts about her revived.

It seemed a betrayal of her to be anything more than friendly with other girls. So for a fortnight I stayed away from Angela and didn't telephone her or anything. It was cowardly, but I didn't want to hurt her. Besides, I was very afraid she might suddenly say she'd marry me after all.

Thinking that I could make the break official and turn it to my advantage, I then did a stupid thing. I telephoned Sam in Africa and asked her exactly when she was coming back as I had arranged to take my annual leave from 16 July and thought of going to Crete. Would she like to come? She said she didn't know how she was travelling back, let alone when. She'd thought of driving to Khartoum, and then getting a lift to Cairo. However, she wasn't starting work in Cambridge till 1 August – there was no hurry. She said I should go off and have my holiday and she'd see me later.

I didn't know what to do. At last I rang up Angela and told her the trip was cancelled. She suggested we meet to talk it over.

When we did so, at my flat, she was surprisingly cool. She said it didn't really matter about the holiday as she was now crazy about some fellow in her office and couldn't in all fairness go abroad with me. I didn't know then that in fact this wasn't true – there wasn't another fellow. She also said that anyway she couldn't afford the holiday, and wouldn't be able to go unless I paid. This reluctance of hers, and the competition, naturally made me more keen. But it left me right up the proverbial creek in a canoe without a paddle. I'd gone and booked a trip to Crete for two on a charter flight and had managed to get a fortnight off work. I was very doubtful about Sam being able to come with me, and now Angela suddenly wasn't all that keen on going either. I thought I would end up flying to Crete by myself.

Then I took out another girl I'd known off and on for some months.

I took her out a few times instead of Angela and foolishly began to think *she* might be the one for me, and the answer to all my problems. I mentioned the subject of holidays, but she'd just had one, and as she was a friend of a female cousin of mine it wasn't really on. None of our parents would have approved.

It all seems rather pathetic now – all this thrashing about and clutching at straws. But the inquiry was reaching its climax. We knew now we were going to be questioned, and had a grim idea of what would result.

In the evenings, off duty, I became indecisive. Angela meant complications. The other girl didn't really mean anything much. With neither could I be at ease now. So I stayed at home, where the presence of Mike, a successful copper, made me feel abashed, and watched TV.

It was Wimbledon fortnight. The men's singles final was eventually won by the American, Stan Smith. He beat Nastase. Billie-Jean King won the women's singles for the fifth time. I watched the dull bonk-bonk of the matches in general gloom. On the only day I went to Wimbledon, it rained.

All this time I was waiting for some reply from Sam about when she was leaving. There was just a chance, I thought, a very faint hope, that she might still be able to come with me to Crete, or that she could fly there from Cairo.

Then the week of the questionnaires began.

I saw both Angela and the other girl the Sunday before the questions were asked.

On Monday I telephoned Africa. Sam had left for Khartoum a week ago, her father said, and wouldn't be in England before the 25th. There was no chance of her flying to Crete. I felt she had let me down.

The rest of the week I was right off girls in general. The evenings I spent with Nobby or Nigel hearing how things were going, or went out with Mike or had drinks with the Dirty Squad blokes. Nobby was now thinking of emigrating to Australia when he left the police.

Angela rang the flat several times and Mike was duly evasive. Eventually she rang me at work, on the morning of Friday the 14th.

That afternoon I was questioned 154 times by Mr Mees. In the evening Angela came to my flat and questioned me in turn.

She wanted to know about my intentions. She said what she thought of my conduct. I defended myself. We had a loud and bitter argument about who was being unfair. At the end of it she calmed down and still appeared to be willing and wanting to go to Crete. And she said she would pay for herself. I couldn't understand her. Perhaps she really loved me. But as I felt I needed a holiday more than anything now – as I didn't want to be alone and had asked her to come with me in the first place – it seemed I must see it through. 'Are we going?' she asked. 'Yes,' I said. 'All right. I'll pick you up on Sunday.'

She must have thought I wouldn't. She rang on Saturday and on Sunday morning. She was trying to be bright and cheerful. But by now the nightmarish inquisition in Paddington Green police station was knocking holes in my head. I felt very low, all the more so because Sam hadn't bothered to write or send me a birthday card. Obviously she wasn't as keen on seeing me as I was on seeing her.

On Saturday, I went to a garden party at my former junior school in Chobham. The two headmistresses who'd been there for yonks were leaving, and hundreds of adult ex-pupils were in attendance. I remembered how happy I had been in those childish days.

On Sunday the 16th, in the evening, I picked up Angela from her flat in Brompton Square. She was excited about going away. I didn't care. She prattled away and I answered when required and carried her luggage. We drove to the airport, and as I drove very fast she quietened down.

Once on the plane, which took off just before midnight, she warmed up again and became quite loving. At midnight she wished me 'Happy Birthday' and tried to kiss me. But I couldn't respond, and sat beside her feeling terrible, hating myself for being so unmannerly and so miserable and being what I was. We were silent the rest of the flight.

We arrived very early in the morning – it was still dark.

After a long, uncomfortable drive in a coach to the north coast, we reached Aghaios Nikolaos and the villa, which we shared with three other couples and where we had taken a bed-sitting room for two weeks. Being both very tired, we went to sleep in a double bed that was in the room, but I didn't touch her.

In the afternoon we lay on the beach in the sun.

In the evening Angela, who was becoming quite tense, had a go at being friendly. She put her arms around me. I told her then it was all a mistake – we should never have come – I didn't love her – I didn't want to sleep with her, or even when we got back to England ever see her again.

She sat on a chair and cried. I went out. That night I told her to sleep in a small, single bed that was also in the room. She did, and her crying kept me awake.

I must have been in a very bad way to have acted as I did. It was cruel and unnatural – and really not like me at all. But the questionnaire and everything else had had a far worse effect on me than I'd thought.

For the whole two weeks of our holiday we were like strangers. The three other couples, all married, with whom we shared the kitchen and bathroom, must have wondered what was wrong. I spoke only when necessary, thereby embarrassing them and so adding their embarrassment and Angela's misery to mine.

I don't know why she didn't go home. If she had, then so might I. But I'd paid for my holiday – as she had for hers – and her pride probably made her stick it out. She was a gutsy little lady. She tried to make a go of it none the less, getting me to go on trips, dragging me off to look at Knossos and other ruins, while I only wanted to lie on the beach, and forget the mess I was in.

On Sunday, 30 July, we returned to England. I took Angela back to her flat at her insistence and carried her cases upstairs for her and we said good-bye. When I got to my flat I found among the letters a birthday card from Sam. She'd posted it from Khartoum.

On Monday I returned to work. But although I had recovered some of my self-possession, I was not the same person any more. My enthusiasm in general was less. There seemed no point in slaving away with the Dirty Squad, so I didn't. I let things slide. Whatever happened about the inquiry I knew my police career was finished. I would have got out then if it had been possible, but they wouldn't now have accepted my resignation.

The only thing I had to look forward to was seeing Sam again.

She had written to me soon after her arrival in England on 27 July – nothing special, just about her journey through Africa, across the Sudan, to Cairo. She hoped I'd had a nice holiday, and said she was starting work on Tuesday.

I telephoned her at the maternity hospital on that day, and although she was fairly non-committal she agreed to have dinner with me in Cambridge on Thursday.

'Can't it wait?' she asked. 'You don't have to come all the way up here.'

'I'm not doing anything else,' I said. 'Are you?'

'No,' she answered, rather doubtfully.

'Well, how about it? I'd like to hear about your trip.'

'Is that all?'

'No. I want to know why nobody's married you yet.'

'There've been offers.'

'I know.'

'I see,' she said. 'Someone's been talking.'

'They never stop – the papers have been full of your affairs.'

'Oh, have they? And how about yours? I'm not sure I want to see you again after all I've heard.'

'I deny everything,' I said. 'It's all lies. Not guilty.'

'Well, I'm not so sure. Why are you so eager to see me?'

'I can't imagine. Must be out of my mind. But we're still friends, aren't we?'

'Just good friends.'

'All right then. I'll pick you up at half past seven.'

Suddenly I had the feeling it was going to be all right in every way.

On Thursday I signed off duty as soon as I could and sped across the River back to Battersea and the flat, where I bathed and changed into my smartest gear, clothes that Sam had helped me buy many months before.

The drive to Cambridge was fast and glorious, with the sun setting slowly on my left. But neither the golden countryside nor the gleaming colleges of the city were a patch on Sam when I saw her. She looked absolutely stunning, with her long blonde hair bleached white by the African sun and her skin like *café au lait*. In her pleated blouse and a long floral skirt she looked more lovely than ever.

'Hallo,' she said.

'Hallo,' I said, and it seemed as if she had never been away.

It was an extraordinary evening in that it was quite ordinary and rather self-consciously sociable on both sides.

We had a meal in a Berni Inn – steaks and apple pie and ice-cream. Many months later she told me she hadn't expected to have any feelings for me any more, that she'd even planned to introduce me to another girl who was short of a boy-friend. It came as a shock to her to realize that she was responding to me in the same old way. She resisted this and so was fairly formal. So was I, though I couldn't altogether hide my pleasure. But I wasn't demonstrative, not wanting to put her off or expose what I really felt.

We exchanged polite information about our recent travels.

She told me about her adventurous trip across Africa, about the farm in Tanzania and something of what she'd been doing – she'd been a dental nurse in Nairobi. I told her about the Dirty Squad and about the fact that both I and my parents had moved house. I told her a little about Crete, where I'd gone with another girl. No one she knew, I said, and indicated the other girl wasn't anyone special.

I said nothing about the inquiry. It no longer seemed important.

At one point she said curiously: 'Is something the matter?'

'Hmm? What makes you ask?'

'You're different somehow,' she said with a frown.

'I've lost some weight,' I said, flexing my arms. 'And I've had a haircut since you saw me last.' I was also fairly sunburnt.

'No, it's not that – though the hair *is* an improvement. You're . . . more serious,' she said.

I smiled. 'Me? Don't you believe it. I'm just a hundred years older.'

That night, after taking her back to the nurses' home where she was living, I said goodnight and didn't kiss her and drove straight back to London.

The following weekend she came to London herself and stayed in my flat, which she hadn't of course seen before and said she liked. Everything then that needed to be said was said by both of us, though I told her none of the details about the questionnaire, just about the inquiry, and she didn't insist on knowing any more.

From then on and throughout the summer everything between Sam and me was better than ever before, and I was able to face what was coming with a better heart.

Disaster struck in November, when I came back to England after a short holiday with Sam – my last for a long time. She had had an unexpected tax rebate of £30 or so and decided to blow it on a weekend in Majorca.

'Are you coming with me?' she asked, and of course I said I would, as she wasn't going without me.

We left on the evening of Thursday, 2 November, and after a blissfully lazy time in Palma, where it was actually sunny, we flew back to a cold and windy London on Monday night, arriving back at my flat about midnight.

Mike Edmans was no longer lodging with me. His career as a policeman had prospered as mine had declined. He'd been promoted to Detective Inspector and transferred to a county police station way out west. Sam's young brother, Christian, who was training to be a hotel manager, had moved into the back bedroom. He'd been in the flat since September, and he it was who left a message for me propped up on the telephone in the hall.

It said that Nigel had telephoned. Would I ring him as soon as I got back, however late it was?

What a lovely welcome home, I thought, with a very nasty feeling growing inside me.

Sam came out of the bedroom and said: 'What's the matter, love?'

'Nothing – yet,' I answered and anxiously dialled Nigel's number as she went into the kitchen to make some coffee.

I woke him up. He had been in bed.

'Yes. It doesn't look good,' he said. 'They've been looking for us all day. I've been away as well, you see, and I suppose they thought we'd fled the country. Our worst fears are to be realized, I think. They want to see us.'

'What for?'

'What for? To prefer charges of course.'

'Oh. It's going to happen then.'

'They've taken long enough,' said Nigel. 'The inquiry began in April. But don't get nervous. There's nothing they can prove. Just button up and get onto Napley. I thought you'd like to know.'

'Thanks. How will they –?'

'Don't know. We'll know tomorrow.'

'Tomorrow?'

'Today . . . It's Tuesday.'

In the morning of Tuesday, 7 November, I drove to Scotland Yard, feeling very tense and peculiar, with a sharp awareness of everything as if it were my first day at work. It had rained in the night, and the two great glass blocks of the Yard looked monumental against a cloudy sky.

Sam had telephoned Cambridge, telling them that she was sick and wouldn't be returning to work that day. She stayed in the flat, waiting for my news. She didn't have long to wait.

As soon as I walked into the Dirty Squad office I was taken aside by one of the sergeants and told to go and see Commander Huntley at 10 a.m. He was now boss of C1, having taken over from Virgo on his retirement.

Outside Huntley's office I came across Morag. She looked very pale and could hardly speak. There were tears in her eyes.

'Oh, Adam,' she said. 'We've got to go to Paddington and take our diaries with us.'

'What?'

'Yes. I can't believe it's happening. I must go. I'll see you later.'

She fled down the corridor, holding a hankie to her eyes.

Her distress upset me and made me unafraid of Huntley, who was on his feet when I entered his office. He retreated behind his desk, and I slouched in front of it with my arms folded.

'You wanted to see me, sir,' I said.

He told me that I was to report to Paddington Green police station at 5 p.m., and that he wanted me back in his office at 4.15, when I was to bring my current diary with me.

I asked him what it was all about. He said he didn't know, and that if he did know he would tell me.

You know all right, I said to myself – you're just not telling.

My work for the Dirty Squad suffered that day. In fact it was practically non-existent. I had long conversations on the phone with Sam, who said she would wait on at the flat until I had more news, and with my solicitors. I talked to Christopher Murray, David Napley's assistant. My lunch break was an extended one, and seemed to flow out of and into extended tea breaks. Everyone in the office knew something was up, and showed their concern.

At 4.15 I presented myself, equipped with my diary, at Huntley's office. Morag was also there. Huntley checked that we had our diaries and warrant cards, and said we would be taken to Paddington in his car. It was in fact his official car and was chauffeur-driven. At the time I didn't appreciate the gesture and thought it seemed more a mockery of our position.

At Paddington Green police station, where we joined up with Nigel, we had to wait in the neon-lit reception room for a few minutes until summoned by DS Sullivan.

I looked around anxiously for Chris Murray. He hadn't arrived yet.

Then I was called. It was 4.40 p.m.

'I can't go!' I protested. 'My solicitor isn't here.'

I was taken up to the second floor. In the room in which the questionnaire had been put to me were Mees and Gittus, attended by Faulkner and Sullivan. DCS Mees had some papers in his hand.

'You know who I am,' he said. 'May I have your current diary, please?'

I gave it to him and said in a rush: 'Before we go any further I would like my solicitor to be present.'

He looked at me, looked at Gittus, and said: 'Very well.'

I was asked to wait in an adjoining room, which I did on my own, biting my nails, for three-quarters of an hour.

I was not to know that when Chris Murray arrived, at 5 p.m., he was told he had come to the wrong place and was directed to Harrow Road police station. He went there by taxi and was redirected back to Paddington Green.

In the meantime Morag and Nigel were brought before Mr Mees. Morag was handed two summonses, Nigel three.

I heard later that Mees, Gittus and Commander Clarkson of the Inspectorate had visited Kelaher at his home in Ickenham earlier that afternoon. He'd been handed one summons alleging conspiracy. Half an hour later the three arrived at Nick's front door and delivered three summonses to him.

A warrant for the arrest of Nobby Pilcher had been taken out but couldn't be used as he and his family were on a liner, the *Eastern Queen*, four days away from Fremantle in Western Australia. He had left England the previous month intending to emigrate to Australia and settle down there. When the liner docked on 11 November he was arrested.

Apart from everything involving the summonses, I was weighed down with the knowledge that Mohammed and John Salah had now been released from prison.

It had happened several weeks before. In an unprecedented move the DPP, Sir Norman Skelhorn QC, had advised the Salahs' solicitors to lodge an appeal, which they were told wouldn't be opposed. This they did, and the Salahs were freed on bail after serving less than a year of their sentences.

It looked as if we might be taking their places in prison.

I was in a dreadful gloom by the time Chris Murray arrived, just before 5.30 p.m. I was at once called out to appear before Mees and the others again.

This time there was no avoiding the inevitable.

Mees intoned: 'I have here four summonses to serve on you, one alleging conspiracy to pervert the course of justice, and three alleging perjury at the trial of John Salah and others.'

Four summonses! I thought, as he handed them over to me. Oh, God – they were really out to get me.

Mees continued: 'Do you wish to say anything? You are not obliged to say anything unless you wish to do so. But whatever you say will be taken down in writing and may be given in evidence.'

He and Gittus looked at me, Gittus with his pen poised.

I said nothing – just stood there staring at a wall, until Chris Murray touched my arm, and took the summonses from me.

We left the room, and I was directed into another office, where Commander Clarkson was waiting. He asked me for my warrant card. I was told I was forthwith suspended from all police duties.

Chris and I then went downstairs and joined Nigel. He was taking the whole thing very easily, almost light-heartedly, and was looking forward to 22 January when all the summonses were returnable at the Guildhall Justice Room. In the meantime everything was *sub judice*. We had a few words, and then I went out into the early night, where Commander Huntley's chauffeur-driven car, with Morag already in it, was waiting to take us both back to the Yard.

'Have a nice honeymoon,' called out Nigel, and waved as Morag and I were driven away.

Back in the now brilliantly lit buildings of the Yard, we returned to Commander Huntley's office for an official confirmation of our suspension. He said he was sorry. Then Morag and I separated. We returned to our own offices – which were now no longer ours.

Everyone in the Dirty Squad was very sympathetic. It was well after 6.15, but several people had stayed behind to hear how I got on – to have a word and shake my hand. The DIs and the DCIs were there, even the Chief Superintendent, who after I'd been given a large whisky allowed me to make my telephone calls in the privacy of his office.

The first thing I did was to phone Sam. My hands were trembling, my voice was shaking. I felt very lonely all of a sudden.

'Hallo?' she said. 'Buzz – is that you, love?'

'We've been done,' I managed to say.

'Yes?'

'For – perjury. And conspiracy.'

'What's perjury? Is it bad?'

'Terrible. Lying – telling lies – in court. And I've been – suspended.'

'Yes? Go on.'

'I can't be – a policeman – any more. I'm suspended from duty.'

'Come home,' she said. 'Come home and tell me about it. Oh, love, I *am* sorry.'

'Yes, I will.'

'As soon as you can. Don't worry, darling. You know I'll stand by you. And we all know you're innocent, love.'

'I'll see you,' I choked.

'Love you,' she whispered.

I put the receiver back on its rest, paused, swallowed several times, paused again, took a deep breath, and dialled my parents' home.

My mother answered.

Mother: We were getting ready to go out to dinner when the telephone rang. My husband was upstairs. Adam said he'd been sent for and suspended from duty.

At first I didn't take it in. I said: 'What do you mean, son?' He explained about the summonses, and at the end of it he said: 'I'm so sorry, Mum.' We hadn't expected anything like this would happen. The questionnaire had been a long time ago. The inquiry was over. We thought that the whole thing was finished and forgotten – which is why it came as such a bombshell, out of the blue. I said: 'Hang on, son. I'll get Dad.'

Soon afterwards we went out to the dinner party, which we struggled through in a daze.

I remember that day, November 7th. Like Calais, it's written across our hearts.

When I returned to the main office I had two or three stiff whiskies with the people who were still there. I began to react in a different way, now that my parents knew of the accusations. I began to feel resentful and aggressive. No one seemed to mind when I swore and damned the policemen who had made out a case against me of perjury and conspiracy – and not just against me, against *us*. I said it was bloody, diabolical, a liberty and outrageous, and a lot more.

By the time I got back to Battersea, rather late, I was really fuming, and launched into tirades against the people who were treating me like a criminal. I defended myself vigorously against their imagined and real accusations. Sam was very patient. She had had a drink waiting for me when I arrived – gin and tonic and ice. I said I wasn't drinking gin, not on top of the whisky. But I did, not wishing to offend her. She had also cooked a special fish supper with tomatoes and mushrooms. But I couldn't eat it. She sat and listened while I raved about ingratitude and witch-hunts, and how it was all highly undeserved and unjust.

Then she had to go, to get the last train to Cambridge about 11 p.m. I drove her to Liverpool Street Station and kissed her very passionately good-bye. I thanked her for loving me and for being so good.

When I got back to the empty flat, I felt abysmally sorry for myself and very tired. My head hurt. I couldn't stop shuddering as if I had a fever. I staggered into my bedroom and fell full-length on the bed, still fully dressed. With my fists and my teeth clenched I pounded the pillow and sobbed. Then I curled up tight under the counterpane, with my head under the pillow, and cried and cried until I fell asleep.

In the morning I went back to the Yard and cleared my desk, sorting out papers, handing them over, explaining to someone else what ought to be done with all the things I'd left unfinished. I said good-bye to the blokes who were there. Then I walked downstairs and out of the building and drove away from London. I was going home, to my mother and father.

I didn't know what to tell them. Perhaps they would understand. I'd done my best to please them. I'd had a go. I'd stuck it out. Now I was nothing, not wanted as a policeman.

It was hard to accept that the last eight years of my life had been written off – like me.

PART FIVE

Put not yourself into amazement how these things should be: all difficulties are but easy when they are known.

19

After I joined the police, in January 1964, I was a PC for nearly three years. In December 1966, I became a TDC.

Those three years are not a time I remember all that well, for although everything was new, nothing in particular happened to me and not much that was pleasantly notable. Being a uniformed policeman was like, I suppose, doing National Service – though without the benefit of travel and mixing with different people.

The police training-school at Hendon, where I was for thirteen weeks, was run on very regimental lines. We had to be absolutely spotless throughout the day. Boots, of which we had two pairs, had to be spit and polished, uniforms had to be properly pressed, shirts had to be ironed and the collars starched – all of which you had to do before you went to bed. Reveille was at 7.30 a.m., and we had to parade on the square every morning before breakfast, when we were inspected and given various marks for appearance, smartness, alertness, cleanliness and so on. All the tutors – sergeants and inspectors – kept an eye on us the whole time we were there. Most of the time was spent in classes, learning law, much of which was not all that easy to understand. Basically we just learned various formulas for filling in forms, making arrests, statements, and dealing with criminals and lawyers. There was also the Police Code to learn, and courses in traffic and riot control and first-aid. But we were never taught such basic and very necessary skills as typing and driving. Nor were we taught to write and speak better English.

Most of the twenty or so recruits who joined at the same time as me had not had much of an education. In fact my three O-levels made me seem pretty smart, and together with my posh accent were the object of much mickey-taking. There weren't any other public-school boys in the squad, most of whom had been apprentices in the electrical, plumbing and mechanical fields.

At the end of the thirteen weeks, in April, there was a passing-out parade and we filed past the Commandant of the school. We then all bundled into a couple of police vehicles and were taken to our respective Divisional stations, where the Chief Superintendent welcomed us and gave us a short lecture. After that we went to our police stations.

Mine was at Commercial Street in the East End of London.

Here we were given a number – in my case G465. I already had a warrant number, 153366, which was given to me when I signed on. It would never be issued to anyone else and was mine while I remained in the force. We were then supplied with all our various books, including pocketbooks, accident report books, warrant cards, and various other documents.

Having been shown around the station, I then went out on the beat with a so-called experienced officer who had been in the police force for two years or more. He showed me the ropes for a few days and then I was on my own.

At the time my basic pay as a PC left me with about £13 a week in my pocket. There were extras. For working on a rest day you got some overtime. There was also a London allowance – about £4 a month – and a boot and shoe allowance, which was about a couple of quid.

Although you were provided with four uniforms, consisting of jacket and trousers – two in dark blue serge, one in a light-weight material and another for ceremonial occasions, not to mention two helmets, three blue shirts and two black ties, you weren't provided with vests, pants, socks or boots. These you had to buy. You were also given a very heavy greatcoat, a macintosh as well as a cape, and of course a truncheon and a whistle.

Thus equipped and garbed as a London bobby, I plodded around the seamier East End streets feeling as if I'd gone back a hundred years.

The people in that area, between Whitechapel and Bethnal

Green, were like people I'd never seen before. They swore all day and every day, and generally one had to swear back at them before they would understand what you were talking about. They had to be pushed around, and didn't appear to mind, as it all seemed to have gone on for a very long time.

We generally walked around in twos, even during the day, as you quite often came across people fighting or drunks that were being a menace. I very quickly realized that the way the other policemen dealt with these people was the only way to make sure that you were boss rather than them. You had to be fairly rough at times in order to put them in their place. Otherwise they would have tried to take advantage. Some of the other officers used to use their truncheons more than was necessary. But this was really a last resort, and occurred because you couldn't speak to the locals properly or reasonably. I was never violent with them myself, and in fact never used my truncheon once while I was a PC. What I used to do was to put obstreperous civilians in a hammerlock, forcing their arms behind their backs and pulling them up onto their toes.

Nor was I ever actually attacked, though some people naturally resisted being arrested. Sometimes they thought we were being a bit rough and would object most strongly. But they would probably be drunk and needing something to shout about. As with most East-Enders, unless they had a punch-up at a party or in a pub, they didn't go home happy.

My fellow officers at Commercial Street soon accepted me as one of them, though there was the usual mickey-taking to start with. I tried to fit in and adapt myself, and started speaking as they did. Part of the trick was using their slang, like *The Old Bill* for the police; *guv* for a senior officer; *wallie* for a uniformed officer; *W-Plonk* for a WPC (Woman Police Officer); *moody* for false information; *tom* for a prostitute; and *cross-hand-boogie merchant* for someone accused of gross indecency with another male.

I learned their language fairly quickly and so well that my parents were sometimes amazed at some of the things I came out with. Even today, people tell me I have a slight accent – a cross between Gorblimey and Gordonstoun.

Generally everyone at the station, though somewhat uncouth, was very matey, and from the beginning I was very struck by their loyalty to each other. If at any time a message came over the radio that some policeman was in trouble, everyone would drop whatever they were doing, bale out, and get to the scene as fast as possible, regardless of the danger to themselves. On these occasions everyone really pulled together. But in general at Commercial Street things were rather lax.

There were three shifts, from 6 a.m. to 2 p.m.; from 2 p.m. to 10; and from 10 p.m. to 6 a.m.

On top of this there were other daytime duties, such as traffic control and accident prevention.

Before each shift we stood in line in the parade room, which was in the basement, and a Sergeant would read out from a board which beat we were to patrol. Then an Inspector would arrive and tell us who or what in particular to watch out for and if there was anything special to be done. We had three-quarters of an hour in the middle of a shift for a meal, and although it was unofficial we used to come back to the station *before* the meal for a cup of tea and likewise *after* the meal.

Most of the time supposedly spent out on the beat was in fact spent in the station. If for instance we went out on the early turn, from 6 a.m. until 2 p.m., we would walk around our beat for about half an hour, making sure that everything was in order, trying doors and so on, and then return to the station for about an hour, where we would play cards before going out again for another brief tour until it was time for a meal. The same thing would happen on the second shift. You wouldn't be out for very long before you came back, had another cup of tea and played cards.

As this was the usual practice and openly accepted, hardly anyone bothered of course to be any different. If you were, you soon found yourself without any friends.

The station canteen was open twenty-four hours a day, and a lot of time was spent there, eating, playing cards, and sleeping – which you could do with your head on the table without causing any comment.

On night duty, the best way of passing the time, also to your own advantage, was to go out and arrest someone – anyone. By doing so you could earn some easy extra money. All you had to do was wait until the pubs closed, and arrest some obstreperous or intoxicated civilian. You brought the arrested person back to the station to be charged – which might take some time – and you would then stay there until after you had had a meal, for about three hours. Later on, you would go out again for a short period, return for a long tea break, and then nip out before you finally went off duty to check that everything was in order on your beat. In the morning, you would have to go to court to give evidence about your arrest. This didn't in fact take very long – about half an hour – but it meant that as you were working nights you were given four hours' overtime, which was increased to five and a quarter hours if you didn't take that time off that week.

I don't think Commercial Street in those days was all that unusual. In the police station as in the section house the rules were bent or just ignored – though not of course by everyone and not all the time. However, few officers appeared to think of this as at all irregular, or wrong – as I did. It was a way of life – it was the way things were – and young policemen soon learned from what their seniors did or didn't do how to conduct themselves in a similar fashion.

There were also various perks to be had: free drinks, free meals in various pubs and restaurants; trade prices or half prices on goods and merchandise; handouts or bribes from clubs, betting-shops, and organizations that specialized in stolen goods.

My vocabulary was further increased to take in such words as a *stitch-up*, which meant a case made out against an innocent person; *copping* – taking backhanders or bribes; and *verballing* – attributing verbal statements to an accused person after he'd been cautioned.

At the time, being only a PC and fairly naïve, I was not altogether aware of all the implications of what was going on. I just couldn't believe most of it. But I didn't like what I knew about and found it worrying and distasteful. If I made any comment to that effect, they only laughed. The extent of such 'corruption' if you like, became more clear when I went to the Yard.

In December 1966, I was made a TDC.

This followed an interview before a Board of three senior officers. A few days later I was told by my station superintendent that I had passed. Official notification then appeared in police orders. I was transferred to Leman Street police station, some four hundred yards down the road.

Getting out of uniform was a great feeling. It was in effect a promotion, and as a DC, I would now get anything up to £15 a month extra, this being my detective duty allowance.

The shifts were somewhat different – either from 9 a.m. to 5 p.m. or from 9 a.m. to 10 p.m.

We always worked in twos now, with a regular partner, keeping an eye on suspected persons and the objectives of thieving attentions, such as cars, houses and banks. About every six months there'd be a night duty, when two TDCs, with a DC and a DS, would patrol an area covering seven stations in a car.

This was more interesting and involving than uniformed work – apart from being more active, mobile and more responsible – and things seemed to be looking up when, in February 1967, about a month after I went into the CID, I sat and passed the written sergeant's exam.

I didn't do any work for it until a fortnight before the exam, when I went to my doctor, a police surgeon, and said that I had examinationitis. For this he gave me two weeks' sick-leave, and a certificate to the effect that I had flu. For eight or ten hours a day I studied solidly in the section house with another chap who was also taking the exam. We sat it on a Saturday afternoon in a big hall in Euston, alongside a very large number of PCs, TDCs, and DCs. The first half of the exam required sensible answers to practical problems about police work. The second half required a knowledge of law for which I had had to study from two big books that had to be known from back to front. I got the pass mark, which was 60 per cent.

For just about the whole of 1967 I worked from Leman Street and lived in the Limehouse section house, which was next door to Limehouse police station.

At the end of the year, when Leman Street was pulled down and re-modernized, we all went to Commercial Street, and the officers there were transferred to Bethnal Green.

I was only there about a fortnight when I was moved to Bow Road, where I stayed for the whole of 1968.

It was while I was at Bow Road, sometime in the summer, that I was shot at in a TV-type chase.

A DS, myself and a driver in plain clothes were cruising about the East End in a Q car, in this case a green Vauxhall Cresta, when we spotted a bunch of eight or nine villainous-looking persons walking along a pavement.

We passed them and drove around the block just to see what they were up to. By this time they had disappeared, though we thought we saw two of them go into a block of flats.

We hung about, and very soon two of the villains reappeared on the other side of a demolition site beside us. They were carrying three bags, which appeared to be fairly heavy. We decided to go and question them and once more drove about the block and into a one-way system. As we turned into the road where the bag-carrying heavies had been, a transit van pulled away from the pavement in front of us. The back doors and the side doors were open and a number of persons were being hauled in. We thought this was a bit strange, so we radioed for assistance and set off after them. Unfortunately they must have seen us use the radio, for no sooner had we come up behind them when the rear door opened, a man pointed a pistol at us, and fired. Naturally we dropped back a bit, and the man fired another two shots as the van drove off at high speed.

We gave chase, zooming after them up and around the side streets, until the van slammed to a halt across a road with cars parked on both sides. The gang peeled out from the back and sides, keeping their faces down, wielding an arsenal of weapons. I saw pistols, rifles, shot-guns, and a brand-new felling axe that gleamed in the sun.

They all ran off away from us on the other side of the van, which was blocking the road, and we leapt out of the Q car and went pounding after them. They had a fifty-yard start, and we rather hoped it might be increased and that they wouldn't shoot. Fortunately they didn't, and before we got to them, they had piled into two cars, both Fords, parked on either side of the road and careered off down the street.

We raced back to the Q car to continue the chase, and in order to get around the van, drove up onto the pavement. An old woman who'd been watching all this, was in our way, absolutely rigid. We flashed our lights, sounded the horn and the bells, and still she didn't move. We missed her by inches.

The pavement was luckily a wide one. But on account of the parked cars, we couldn't get off it. A small boy saw us coming and ran along the pavement in front of us, vainly trying to run faster than the car. As we reached him he turned aside into the road.

We roared off the end of the pavement at last – but by this time the villains' cars had vanished.

They were never found. But in their van were found some holdalls and various garments, like caps, overalls, coats and stocking-masks. Clearly they had been about to rob a post office and sorting house which was very near where the van had first been parked. If we hadn't come on the scene a robbery might have taken place and someone might have been killed.

Excitements like this were, however, few and far between. CID work was not quite as *lively* as I expected, partly because any initiative or display of individual zeal was regarded as a dangerous eccentricity by your seniors, who thought you were getting a bit above yourself and making a nuisance. It was enough to do what you had to do.

'Get on with it,' was the attitude. And as no one set any shining examples, as no one inspired or led, no one followed and no one tried too hard.

I interested myself in other activities, like playing cricket, hockey and rugger. I took up squash. I went on a four-day course and became an authorized police shot – a marksman licensed to kill. The daily office routine offered little fulfilment – there was little detection, and masses of documentation.

The only person who kept me going in this period was Alistair Roach, an ex-public school boy with a similar outlook. We had worked together, and lived in the same section houses and I introduced him to an ex-girlfriend of mine, a nurse at the London Hospital, who eventually became his wife. I was his best man, and godfather to his son. After he became a DC he went to the Yard. I followed him six months later. He and Mike Edmans, who was in C9, were two of the few people in the police force whom I admired.

Early in 1969 I became a full DC. I went before a Selection Board at the Yard, where I was interviewed for ten minutes by two high-ranking CID officers and one high-ranking uniformed man. They asked me what I did in the way of sport, what hobbies I had, and interests, what recent experiences in police work I'd had, and how many people I'd arrested.

As a DC I went to Poplar, still in the East End, and three months later the station was closed – one reason being that it was so slack.

Then I went to Limehouse, where I didn't get on too well with the other CID officers and tended to keep to myself. I was there for just three months, and they weren't the best three months I had.

By this time I had been in the police for nearly six years.

I sometimes wondered what I was doing, where I was heading, and whether I should just get out. It frequently seemed a waste of time. For looking at the senior CID men around me, I knew I didn't want to be like them – and couldn't be. My father tried to chivvy me into going to the Police College, Bramshill. But I wasn't keen on this. I just wasn't keen on being a policeman any more – on adopting a life of double standards, on turning a blind eye on the abuses and misuse of power by some policemen. For probably more regulations were broken daily by guardians of the law than by most of those being guarded. I couldn't take this, but couldn't do anything about it. The only way out was to pretend I wasn't aware of what was going on or didn't care. In the end this got me down.

I came home one weekend and said I was handing in my papers on Monday. Father said: 'For God's sake, son – hold on!'

Father: I suppose we probably talked that weekend for twelve hours on the subject. He was plainly very fed up with the goings-on as it were in the post-captain strata of the police, where a lot of very odd things were going on which couldn't directly be called bribery, but clearly were.

Mother: He said that if he carried on in the police he didn't know how he was going to play things, as he was not prepared to go along with their way of doing things. He was very much in the minority, he said, and if he stuck it out, he wasn't going to get anywhere. This was his problem.

Father: We asked him all sorts of questions, and at the end of the weekend my wife and I had a long chat about it, and I said: 'Look, I'm sure Adam is correct, and I'm absolutely certain something should be done.' I accordingly sat down and wrote to a very high-ranking officer whom I knew and asked if I could see him – which I did a few days later. I said: 'Look, what I have to say I believe to be true, otherwise I wouldn't be saying it. For professional reasons you may object strongly to what I say, and if you do, please stop me.' He said: 'All right. Fire ahead.' So I told him what Adam had said, and after about three minutes I said: 'Do you want me to stop?' He said: 'Far from wanting you to stop, I want you to go on. What really shakes me is that although I realize all this, and the senior boys in the force also realize this, we didn't realize that even constables were aware of it.' It was then that he said that steps were being taken to deal with the corruption. . . .

We had a long discussion, during which he made what was to me a very interesting observation. He said: 'When I started off as a youngster, I had great sympathy with the Police Federation view that everyone who reached the top should have started from the bottom. But as the years have gone by, I have become more and more certain, and I now am convinced, that an officer corps is an absolutely vital necessity, and that until we get one, we shall never get any improvement in our standards.'

I was very glad to have my own opinion so strongly confirmed, and by a very senior and experienced policeman.

My father felt that what was wrong with the police was due to the fact that they had no officer corps. It was a view with which I also agreed.

I remember an April morning in 1972 when the memorial service in St Martin-in-the-Fields at Trafalgar Square was held for my uncle, Rear Admiral Sir Anthony Buzzard, who had died in March. A very large number of naval officers attended the service, and when we came out my father said to me: 'It's a pity some of these chaps here couldn't go into Scotland Yard and get things sorted out.'

I replied that it was because they were what they were that the Yard would never have them.

Father: It seems to me, and I may be wrong, that if any service is to be efficient, including a semi-military service like the police, it must be run by people who are leaders, in the proper sense of the word. At the moment the Metropolitan police force, besides being bogged down with bureaucracy and very Victorian attitudes, is like a regiment being run by RSMs. Admirable people up to a point. But beyond that you must have certain disciplines. You must have certain qualities of character that are above the norm, and senior officers you can respect. You must have leaders. In the Navy, there were, I suppose, half a per cent of officers from the lower deck and they were very fine officers. But it was only half a per cent, and I don't think this was accidental.

I know this sounds like sheer snobbery. It isn't snobbery at all. It's the way things are. But the chances are that any discussion on this enormously important subject will be stymied from the start, because people say: 'Oh, well! You've got money. You pronounce your aitches. You've been privileged and protected. You've had all the advantages.' All those sort of things. Someone is bound to bring in the old-boy network and say that that's exactly what is wrong with England today.

A discussion on this subject has to be carried out by very tolerant people. But it has got to be carried out. Otherwise the police will flounder on, compromising all along the way, accepting all the inadequacies and imperfections in the system, avoiding any stand on moral issues, and sinking into the kind of ghastly mess that has made the American people think of their policemen as pigs. That could, I do believe, happen here – unless something is done.

What is required is a very big re-think, almost a total reorganization. The Police Federation, by their very nature, would probably be the last persons to accept this – especially along the lines that I've been suggesting. Therefore any changes must come from the government, and in this case they'd have to have public opinion behind them. But first of all somebody's got to have the courage to raise the issue in the face of all the vilification that's bound to follow and see it through. Then, I think, the government would act.

Something along the lines of the Trenchard scheme could be proposed. It was well designed, but at the end of the War it was out-voted by the Police Federation. The Labour government wouldn't have it either – because it smacked of class distinction, I suppose. But there's no doubt in my mind that a chap who's had a solid education, whose family has never been destitute, whose background has been comfortable and secure, who has been taught to take a strong line on moral issues, on what is right and good and proper – such a person would be more likely to set an example and less likely to be corrupted. An RSM or NCO has no such safety net. His career is his only security. When the crunch comes he has to think of his family, about sending his nippers to school, about earning a living to pay off his HP and his mortgage, and clothe and feed himself and his dependents. And what about his chances of promotion and a pension? If he makes a stand, if he resigns, he's out. Finished. An officer's whole way of life is not so much in peril as an RSM's.

There's one more point. In the Navy, as in the other services, you are never open to 1 per cent of the bribery that you are in the police. But being in the police you are more open to bribery and therefore corruption than any other similar organization. For that reason alone, I would have thought the need for leadership is greater in the police force than in any corporate body of disciplined people in the world.

As regards me, my father felt that I might contribute something to the police. For all these reasons he urged me to hold on.

Soon afterwards I was posted to the Drug Squad.

Father: This was none of our doing. About two years before he actually joined the Squad we were out at a cocktail party with some friends of ours at Stanford, and while this friend was talking to Adam about police work, and I was standing by him, he suddenly said that the people he thought were the biggest sweeps in the world were the drug pushers, and that he had applied to go into the Drug Squad because he would be happy chasing these wretched people. We were delighted. It was the first time I can remember him taking a very strong line. When he eventually got into the Squad he started growing up pretty smartly. He ceased to be a boy. It became very noticeable that he had much more definite views and could explain himself much better.

Mother: He was doing something important, which also made him important. People wanted to know what he was doing, and he was able to talk about something they knew nothing about.

Father: Every time he came home he said it was absolutely marvellous working with a compact team of first-class people, who were really achieving results.

Mother: Without any question, the time he was in the Drug Squad was the time he was most happy.

20

We made headlines on the morning of Wednesday, 8 November 1972 – *Former Drug Squad men accused.*

The newspapers said that summonses alleging conspiracy to pervert the course of justice had been served on five former members of the Drug Squad, including Detective Chief Inspector Victor Richard Kelaher.

The next day some of the papers had another story about Vic. They revealed that he had been awarded the police long service and good conduct medal for 22 years' service which had been completed on 31 October this year.

On the same day the *Daily Telegraph* had a story about Nobby.

> **Yard Talks on Warrant for Ex-CID Man.** Representatives of Scotland Yard's legal department and the Director of Public Prosecutions office met yesterday to discuss possible further moves following the issue of a warrant for the arrest of a former Drug Squad detective sergeant . . .
>
> I understand [wrote the Crime Correspondent] that the warrant could not be used outside Britain and the discussions concerned whether extradition on the two charges was possible and whether further action should be taken to bring him back.

On Friday, 10 November, Mrs Salah and Janet appeared in court at the Old Bailey, charged with conspiring to import cannabis.

Mr Corkery, for the prosecution, told the court: 'The conclusion has been reached that the only right and proper course would be for the Crown to offer no evidence against the two defendants.'

They were formally found not guilty and freed. Costs were awarded to them out of public funds.

Outside the court Mrs Salah hugged her daughter and told reporters: 'This is a tremendous relief.'

The following day, in Western Australia, Nobby Pilcher was arrested on board the liner *Eastern Queen* when she docked at Fremantle. He was taken off the ship and lodged in a local jail over the weekend. His wife and two children were found lodgings elsewhere in the city by the local police. On the Monday Nobby was released on bail of £1,400, while on the same day in England extradition proceedings were started against him.

He had handed in his resignation from the police in June, and left the force in July – soon after the questionnaire and the forwarding of the case against us to the DPP. There was never any secret about his plans to emigrate. Why five months had to elapse between the questionnaire and the summonses, I've no idea. Nobby was allowed to sell up, pack up and sail with his family to Australia – only to be arrested the moment he arrived.

On Tuesday, 16 November, the newspapers were writing about us again. The *Daily Mail* concentrated on Morag.

Whip-round for Morag of the Yard. Scotland Yard detectives have started a collection to hire a top barrister for Detective Constable Morag McGibbon, who is accused of conspiracy to pervert the course of justice.

Miss McGibbon, 28, is believed to be the first Yard woman detective to face criminal charges. She and three other detectives have been summoned to appear at the Guildhall on January 22nd in connection with allegations made during an Old Bailey drugs trial.

Miss McGibbon and one of the other accused officers, Detective Sergeant Prichard, who were suspended from duty last week, were yesterday commended by the Commissioner of Police.

The commendation, published in Scotland Yard orders, is for 'initiative and ability'.

About £500 was raised for Morag, who was one of the most popular persons at the Yard. She worked for all kinds of people, and was always being asked to do this or type that, and go here and there – which she did cheerfully and willingly, although half what she did was beyond the requirements of her particular job with the Drug Squad.

I myself was given about £300. Several collections were made, and the money came to me in various ways at various times. It was all done very quietly. There was a collection on the floor where I worked. Other departments made their own. Even the investigation squad, A10, gave me some money. My own squad, the Dirty Squad, were extremely generous, and one day when I came in to sort something out, one of the chaps in the office just gave me a bundle of notes and said: 'Here – this'll keep you in booze and birds for a while.'

Everyone at the Yard, especially in the Drug Squad and the Dirty Squad, felt a lot of sympathy for us. They realized that the charges against us were based on the sort of things that happened every day. They felt, I think, that it was all unnecessary and that we had been summonsed for no reason at all. Besides this, everyone rallied around as they always did when another policeman or his family were in trouble. It was a really splendid demonstration of solidarity and concern, and made me sorry to be no longer a part of such a company.

On the other hand, I was glad now that at last I knew where I was. For the first time in a year I knew the state of the poll, and where I stood, and having got over my initial unhappiness I was able to face the prospect of appearing in court with some equanimity.

On 16 November – while collections were being made for me and Morag, who had also been commended that day, along with Nick, for initiative and ability – three Appeal Court judges finally reversed the convictions of the Salahs.

Their decision was reached after counsel for the Crown said he had been instructed by the DPP not to oppose the appeals.

Mr Hudson QC, appearing for the Salahs, said the basis of the present appeals was that the jury's verdict was unsafe and unsatisfactory. No criticism, he said, could be made of the conduct of the trial.

Lord Justice Edmund Davies said the 'suspicion' that evidence given against the Salahs at their trial might be unreliable was enough to have their convictions quashed – and they were.

Mohammed, John and Kathy were all cleared and the jail sentences imposed at the Old Bailey on 13 October the previous year were set aside.

I wondered how the Salah family celebrated that night, and whether they drank to our downfall as we had drunk to theirs.

A year would go by before judgement in turn was passed on the six of us.

In the meantime I more or less moved out of London and out of my flat.

Having been suspended on basic pay with no allowances, I was strictly speaking not supposed to do any work. Most of the time I helped my brother Bill on the estates he managed, giving him a hand wherever it was required, mostly with the machines. I also did some building – digging trenches, laying foundations, putting up walls. This didn't get going until the New Year.

Before that I didn't stop going round friends and relations, who were all very good to me and my parents. They had about fifty letters from people and hundreds of telephone calls, all of which were a great help to them.

Sam was working in Cambridge throughout most of the festive season, but she had Christmas Day dinner with me and my parents and I continued to see her every week. She thought I ought to do a course or learn a trade while I had the opportunity. But I couldn't commit myself to anything fully or consider my future until everything was sorted out one way or the other. She left Cambridge in February and moved to Winchester where she was a midwife for three months, helping to bring babies into the world every week. In May she continued as a midwife at Havant until September. She had thought of returning to Africa, but decided to stay by me.

In the New Year's honours Mr Mark was given a knighthood.

Official figures revealed that in the previous year more policemen left than joined the Met – the overall loss exceeding recruitment by 172. Eighty of these had been involved in disciplinary charges and allowed to retire – nearly double the figure for 1971. Eleven others had been convicted during 1972, as against eight in 1971, when five were also imprisoned. In 1972 the figure was nine. Twenty-seven officers, seventeen of them CID men, were awaiting trial.

On 22 January 1973, Kelaher, Nigel, Nick, Morag and I appeared at a special sitting of magistrates at the Guildhall Justice Room. The hearing, which lasted about ten minutes, was adjourned until 12 March.

Nobby was still in Australia. He was now in prison in Fremantle, having been put there when an extradition order was granted. David Napley, who was now acting as *his* solicitor as well as mine and Nigel's, had asked when the extradition application was made that Nobby should be allowed to return voluntarily, rather than as a fugitive offender. This wasn't allowed. Nobby was jailed and Mrs Pilcher, thinking she'd be more useful here, returned with her children to England.

They came back a fortnight before Nobby himself was brought back under arrest. Faulkner, who was now a Superintendent, together with DS Sullivan, flew out to Australia at the end of January.

On the 31st at 2.45 p.m., in Fremantle police station, Faulkner said to Nobby: 'I have a warrant for your arrest.' He read the warrant, and next produced the extradition order. Nobby was asked if he wished to read the documents but declined to do so. He was told he would be arrested and taken back to England to be charged with the offences. He was cautioned, and replied: 'I am not guilty of these charges. I want you to know I'm not saying anything about that or anything else between here and there.'

The three of them flew back to England that night.

On the morning of 1 February they were met at Heathrow Airport by Napley's assistant, the young Chris Murray, and all four proceeded to Snow Hill police station, near the Old Bailey, where Nobby was charged with four offences – one of conspiracy and three of perjury. He was cautioned, but made no reply. That afternoon he appeared at the Guildhall magistrates court and was remanded on bail of £3,000.

On the morning of Monday, 12 March, the six of us appeared together in the Guildhall court for the first and only time.

The previous week, in a gesture of defiance, two seats of justice and government, the Old Bailey itself and Whitehall, had been badly damaged by car-bomb explosions. A third target had been New Scotland Yard. But the car-bomb outside it was discovered just in time and defused. The terrorist attacks had been the work of younger members of the Provisional IRA. Ironically, their targets, the impersonal seats of power, were the targets and the sources of our own real and imagined discontent. But in the Guildhall court all was calm and ordered.

In a small square room in a new grey building we sat on thin metal chairs in two rows, facing the three magistrates raised before us. We were probably the neatest and best-dressed people there. The room was clinical, bright and cool, and equipped with synthetic furnishings. To left and right were our several lawyers and the prosecuting policemen, headed by Mr Mees. At our rear were friends, pressmen and visitors – none in great numbers. Immediately behind us was a walled-off well, with steps going narrowly down to the cells below. My mother and father were present, as was Sam. So were two blokes who'd been done by us on drug charges and had now been released.

One came over to me, although it wasn't me who'd arrested him, and whispered: 'You bent bastards. I hope you get what you deserve.'

The twelve charges were read out against us. The first, of conspiracy to pervert the course of justice, involved all six of us. The others were separate charges of perjury. The matter of bail was discussed. Mr Mees didn't object. We were each allowed out on bail on our own recognizance of £1,000, which didn't of course have to be paid – although we had to fill in forms agreeing to forfeit the said amount if we didn't turn up at our trial. Nobby also had two sureties, friends of his, who each guaranteed to pay £1,000 cash if he disappeared. Then Mees re-entered the witness-box to ask that our passports be handed in. Our counsel objected, saying that we weren't likely to scarper, having stuck around for so long, and besides we might indeed need them to go abroad – for a holiday.

My father was very scathing about this afterwards.

'What an absolute farce!' he said. 'How wet can you get when a chap gets up and says: "Look, we want your passports, but, all right, if you want to go abroad, we'll give them back."'

In the end we were allowed to keep them.

Next, we were told to stand. The chief magistrate announced his decision. We were all committed for trial at the Central Criminal Court, the Old Bailey, at a date to be decided later.

I shivered and felt very strange. A decision had been made. A great iron gate had closed behind us and another been opened. What had seemed unbelievable was now irrevocably true. The next trial we attended would be ours.

Uncertainly we all left the court. It was not yet noon.

My father was talking earnestly to lawyers. My mother was looking worried. She was wearing a blue woollen suit and a cashmere jumper. Like my father, her hair was white.

Sam said to me: 'I thought you looked very good,' and smiled and touched my hand.

Over the following months hours of discussions took place between me and my solicitors, and I was questioned about every detail concerning the case. The sessions with Chris Murray sometimes lasted for as much as six hours. Later, the barristers took over – in particular the QC who was going to defend me, Mr George Shindler. He was a small dark Jewish gentleman with a smooth brown face and penetrating eyes. Sometimes in our discussions he would assume the role of the prosecutor and thump his desk and shout at me.

All the time papers and documents were being prepared and copies were made of everything. Laboriously, and painfully for me, the case for the defence was put together.

The case *against* us was contained in general terms in the Information that Mr Mees had laid for the extradition of Nobby from Australia.

It read, in part, as follows:

The evidence against the Salah family consisted to a large extent of evidence of their alleged conversations with police officers, and of observations of their movements sworn to by police officers. It transpired in the course of the trial that there were very many discrepancies between the officers' notebooks and evidence on one hand and their diaries on the other hand. Following the conclusion of the trial an extensive investigation has been undertaken which has revealed that much of the evidence given by the police of observations kept by them was false. Charges 2 to 12 are selected from amongst a larger number of cases where it can be shown that lies were told. . . .

In addition to those specific offences of perjury in relation to observations, there is a wealth of evidence indicating that there was an agreement amongst all 6 officers to deceive the court about their diary entries. Miss McGibbon appears to have fabricated a notebook for use at the trial, and Victor Kelaher tried to assist his officers when they were caught lying by claiming that he had given instructions to them to falsify their diary entries. . . .

When interviewed by me, Kelaher constantly made reference to a telephone intercept which was kept on John Salah's calls, saying that it would greatly assist his defence. I have been informed by counsel that a perusal of the tape record leaves no doubt that the Salahs were guilty of the offences with which they were charged. But the allegation by the prosecution is not that the defendants did not carry out the movements that the officers described, but rather that in many instances the officers did not and could not have seen those movements, and probably reconstructed them as a result of their knowledge of the telephone conversations of the defendants.

On 17 July 1973, I was thirty.

On Monday, 17 September 1973, I woke very early and lay

in bed looking at nothing. I took a long time washing, shaving and getting dressed. I didn't feel like eating and only had a coffee.

It was two years since the Salah trial and nearly a year since the summonses.

At half past nine I left the flat and walked downstairs and went out into the morning.

The day was unremarkable, but for one thing – I was going to present myself at the Central Criminal Court for the first day of my trial – *Regina* v. *Kelaher and Others*.

PART SIX

Man, proud man,
Dressed in a little brief authority,
Most ignorant of what he's most assured,
Plays such fantastic tricks before high heaven
As make the angels weep.

21

'Not guilty. Not guilty. Not guilty. Not guilty,' I said aloud as I drove to the Old Bailey.

They were the only words I would say in court when I replied to the four charges against me. If everything went as well as it should, and if I didn't appear as a witness for the defence, they would be the only words I would utter in the trial.

The weather was cool and grey that morning. I parked the car in a nearby underground car park and walked, somewhat self-consciously, towards the Central Criminal Court. It was like going to hospital for an operation. I was and had to be optimistic, but anything could happen. In the meantime I wouldn't be able to live my life and would be the object of legal scalpels and clinical skills.

The Central Criminal Court, which takes its name the 'Old Bailey' from the street of that name in which it stands, was looking very large, gaunt and ill-used, with all its windows which had been blown out in the car-bomb explosion in March still masked with polythene sheeting and wooden frames. Such had been the damage then that six months later repairs were still being made. On the dome of the building, the gilded figure of blind Justice holding her scales stood firm, shining out above the scene against the sunless sky.

Above the building's main entrance, which was temporarily out of use, was a bold inscription I'd never noticed before. It said: 'Defend the Children of the Poor and Punish the Wrongdoer'.

Looking like a city gent all soberly suited, I ambled down the street, which was dotted with 'No Parking' cones, to the new court building by the old one. The new one had just been completed, but its façade was still a mass of scaffolding, boarding and polythene-filled windows. Its only entrance was a revolving door which never stopped going round and round, as through it passed, both in and out, all the persons involved in trials taking place in the eighteen courts that day.

Across the road were four other courts in another building and it was there, in West Court 4, that the Rolls-Royce trial had been held. The Salah trial took place in several courts – it not being always the case that a trial sticks to the one court. That of the Salahs was all over the shop.

Our trial was to begin in Court 1 at half past ten. But it didn't in fact get under way until half past twelve.

This was because another trial, involving a little man accused of something else, had prolonged itself until Monday, and sentence had still to be given. It wasn't, as some technical difficulty had arisen, and the case was adjourned.

Up to that point we six defendants had been sitting in the court in front of the rows of jurors-in-waiting from whom our twelve would be chosen. We now joined our various lawyers and QCs and there was quite a lot of milling about, during which more potential jurors arrived. We then heard that the opening of the trial had been delayed while the names on the list of jurors given to the defence were checked against the records held in the CRO (Criminal Record Office). While this was being done there was time for a coffee. So we all trekked upstairs.

My father came with us. He had decided, as much from professional as from personal interest, to attend the proceedings, and had travelled to London that morning by train from Bayford in Hertfordshire where he was staying temporarily with my sister Sue and her husband.

It was not until after twelve noon that we were called back to the court and into the dock, where we regrouped ourselves in the order in which we were to be tried and sat in a line at the front of the dock on some very hard wooden chairs. In close attendance were a male and female prison officer, who weren't particularly chuffed with their job of guarding six police officers.

The dock in Court 1 was high and panelled all about. One small door led out of it into the well of the court. The other exit was a narrow stair to the cells. In front of the dock was a long table at which our solicitors and the police sat. Farther to the right our QCs and barristers were assembling at tables laden with mounds of documents and papers. Below the Judge's dais were the Clerk of the Court and the shorthand writer, in a line with the witness-box. Raised up behind them were five large chairs, all of green leather like the other court seats, except for those in the dock. Above the central chair was the sword of justice, in a red scabbard, and the royal coat of arms. On our left was the jury-box. Below it were seats for the Press. On our right, under the public gallery, were seats for minor legal beavers and family friends.

Above us all was a wide oval of opaque glass that let in the light, which was added to by the concealed lighting that sprang from the half-panelled walls.

This was Court 1 at the Old Bailey, the scene of some of the most famous trials in legal history. It was somewhat daunting, and at that moment very crowded.

At half past twelve an usher shouted: 'Silence, and be upstanding!'

Everyone stood as the Judge stalked out of a side door in his red robe and short wig. He placed a pair of white gloves and a black cap on his desk, and bowed three times to the court, and his legal subordinates all bowed in return.

He then sat down and scowled at us through thin-framed glasses.

The Judge was the Right Honourable Mr Justice Melford Stevenson, a man with a gravel voice and abrupt manner, with a reputation for sternness and decision, for taking a line and keeping to it. He was seventy-one. He had passed sentence at the Cambridge trial of students accused of rioting in a hotel; at the first trial of the Kray twins; at the first trial of George Ince, accused and later acquitted of the Barn restaurant murder; and at the first Angry Brigade trial, at which Prescott was convicted, and Purdie freed. Purdie's counsel had been my QC, Mr Shindler.

The Judge sat down. Everyone followed suit, except for the six of us, our guards, and the Clerk of the Court, who began to read out the charges.

'The first count is against Adam Buzzard Acworth alone. You are charged that on the 10th day of September 1971, at the Central Criminal Court, being a witness at the trial of John Salah and others, you knowingly falsely swore that at about 9.40 a.m. on the 5th day of January 1971, you saw the said John Salah and Janet Salah at Crevald's boatyard, Straight Road, Windsor.'

'How do you plead?'

My voice came out all hesitant and quiet: 'Not guilty.' I adjusted my Gordonstoun tie.

The Clerk read straight on.

There were twelve counts in all. The second was against Morag and alleged she wasn't at Crevald's boatyard at about 9.40 a.m. on 5 January as she'd said. The third and fourth, against Nick and Nobby, alleged that neither was at Mapledene Road at about 3.10 p.m. on 13 January and didn't see Mrs S. and Janet arrive there. The fifth charge, against Nick, alleged that he wasn't at Kier Park with me at about 9.45 a.m. on 18 January.

My name appeared again in the sixth count.

'You knowingly falsely swore that you went with DC Prichard to Kier Park, Ascot, at about 9.45 a.m. on January 18th, 1971, and saw the said John Salah go into Kier Park House.'

'Not guilty,' I said.

I was named again in the ninth count, in which I was accused of falsely saying at the Salah trial that I was keeping observation 'at about 4.55 p.m. on January 22nd, 1971, at Kier Park, Ascot, and saw the said John Salah leave in a Landrover'.

'How do you plead?'

'Not guilty!'

I spoke more firmly now. The Clerk shuffled his papers and ploughed on as if he were reading a weather report.

Nobby was named in the seventh count and Nigel in the eighth – It was alleged they weren't at Mapledene Road on 19 January at about 9.20 a.m. The tenth count and eleventh count were also against Nobby and Nigel, alleging they weren't at Heathrow Airport on 26 February and didn't see John Salah and Mohammed pass through the arrival gate at Number 3 Terminal at 8.30 p.m.

There were three charges of perjury against me. There were three against Nobby, two against Nigel, two against Nick and one against Morag. Kelaher was involved, as we all were, in the twelfth and final count – conspiracy.

'You are all charged that on divers days between the 27th of July, 1970, and the 18th of November, 1972, within the jurisdiction of the Central Criminal Court, you conspired together to pervert the course of justice by falsifying and fabricating official records and documents, and by putting forward at the trial of John Salah and others a false explanation of inconsistencies and contradictions between the evidence of some of you and your records in your official diaries, namely that false entries had been made in the said diaries for security reasons on the instructions of Victor Richard Kelaher and Norman Clemence Pilcher.'

'How do you all plead?'

We responded: 'Not guilty.'

That was it. The charges had all been put and denied. The months, the years of doubt and rumour would now be resolved. The trial was under way.

I glanced at my father, sitting at one side of the court. He was looking at the Judge.

The Clerk read out the names of twelve jurors, who one by one were called on to take their seats in the jury-box.

'Answer your names!' snapped an usher at those who didn't, as they got to their feet from the mass of civilians behind us.

When the twelve were seated in the box, mostly looking as if they wished they weren't there, the Judge leaned forward and asked the prosecution how long they thought the trial would last. The chief prosecutor, Mr Brian Leary, replied that it might go on for six or seven weeks. The Judge said he hoped it wouldn't, and then addressed the jury, telling them that if anyone wished to establish exceptional hardship and excuse himself from serving, he should do so now. None of them did.

We were told to stand and the process of swearing in the jury began.

An usher exhorted the juryman nearest the Judge to take the

New Testament in his right hand and read the card, which said: 'I swear by Almighty God that I will faithfully try the several issues joined between our Sovereign Lady the Queen and the prisoners at the bar and give true verdicts according to the evidence.'

What followed was something of a farce, with an interval for lunch at one o'clock.

Our solicitors and QCs had thought it advisable to screen the proposed jurors and the Yard were telephoned with a list of the jurors' names and asked that these be checked. The Yard eventually came back with the information that a check of the names of the fifty or so jurors in the court revealed that 80 per cent were named in records at the Yard.

There was insufficient time to check whether in fact the 80 per cent were actually the same persons as the proposed jurors. Only the names were the same. None the less we were staggered. We could well have found ourselves facing a jury composed entirely of people not all that sympathetic to the police.

Normally jurors aren't checked out in this way. Normally it would even help defendants to have fellow-sufferers in the jury. But in our case it could have been rather unfortunate. Even so, such a high percentage of co-opted jurors, some perhaps with previous convictions, was somewhat shocking. One man we were told had no less than eleven.

So it was that our several QCs, with the list of the 80 per cent in their hands, started challenging the inclusion of any of them in our jury. At the same time, if any of us didn't like the look of a prospective juror, for whatever reason, we each could raise an objection and nod at our counsel to challenge on our behalf. On top of this, five of the jurors wished to excuse themselves from serving. One said he had a heart condition; another had booked a holiday in two weeks' time; the others didn't want to jeopardize their jobs.

Grudgingly the Judge gave his permission.

The coming and going of jurors took about an hour. Some didn't even get as far as the jury-box before they were challenged. A perfectly innocent Pakistani and a young man with long fair hair inevitably got the nod from more than one of us.

Besides these types, we didn't care to have included in the jury persons who seemed to have difficulty reading the oath –

many documents would after all need to be comprehended – and people who were under the age of thirty. We wanted our jury to be made up of intelligent, prosperous, middle-class, middle-aged people who, we thought, would give us the fairest hearing.

Each of us could object to seven jurors. So in all we could have had forty-two discarded. In the end, apart from the five who excused themselves, the number we challenged and refused to accept was thirty-three.

The jury who were finally sworn in consisted of eleven men and one woman and seemed a pleasant crowd.

The twelve charges against us were read out once again for their benefit and they were handed what was referred to by the prosecution as 'the thin bundle' of documents – copies in photostat and typescripts of extracts from our diaries, duty books, and the transcripts of the Salah trial – everything that the prosecution thought was relevant to their case.

Having done this, Mr Leary began his opening speech for the prosecution by identifying each of us in the order in which we sat and by saying who our counsel were. Mine of course were Mr Shindler QC and Mr Anns. Chris Murray was also there, acting as a go-between for Nigel, Nobby and myself and our separate QCs.

We sat facing the Judge in the order in which we would be sentenced if found guilty. Reading from our right – his left – it was Prichard, Pilcher, Lilley, Acworth, McGibbon and Kelaher.

Mr Leary began speaking at 2.45 p.m.

He had a pained and somewhat aristocratic manner, and spoke with slow precision, as if he were a lecturer addressing an immigrant class. Even when he uttered such strong phrases as 'false entries', 'damning evidence', 'grave charges', and 'tissue of lies', he did so without much emphasis or feeling. His plan seemed to be to let the documents before the jury do the convicting for him. For this reason he was very particular about getting them to look at and compare entries while he interpreted what was written in a way that was not at all favourable to us.

He embarked on this course after telling the jury that C Branch at the Yard was divided into thirteen departments, and that C1, which was one of them, was headed in 1970 by Commander Virgo. Leary detailed when each of us joined the Drug Squad and went on to give a general description of the Salah investigation.

'It was rightly said,' he enounced, 'that this family was involved in drug-smuggling activities.'

He mentioned that we had 'access to a telephone intercept'. But it was left to my counsel, Mr Shindler, to explain to the jury the next day that this was a phone-tapping device.

Mr Leary said: 'The Drug Squad were expecting to arrest the whole family red-handed in the possession of the drugs when they landed in this country. But the plan was frustrated when the mother and daughter were held in Bulgaria. It left the Drug Squad somewhat short of evidence about the involvement of the whole of the Salah family, so they committed perjury. . . . The Crown's case is that a good deal of the evidence they gave at the Salah trial is false. Some of the movements described at the trial may well have taken place. But there is the clearest possible evidence that some of the officers could not possibly have carried out the observations which they swore they had done.'

The defence counsel at the Salah trial, he said, got hold of our desk diaries, and he alleged that we, being faced with them, said we had made false entries in order to guard against a security leak.

'The entries in the diaries were true,' said Mr Leary, raising his voice a little. 'The evidence was false.' And he commented on 'the lamentable fact that police officers attempted to mislead the jury'.

What's new? I thought. No police diary or duty book was ever wholly true. No statement made by a policeman was ever wholly true either. They couldn't be. And if these were quoted in court, of course they'd mislead the jury – inevitably, inadvertently, not intentionally at all.

Again I thought what damage our trial would do to the image of the police force. It didn't expose corruption. Basically it revealed the weaknesses in the system. By the time it ended, none of the QCs present would ever trust a policeman's evidence again – indeed if they ever had.

Mr Leary consulted his notes and continued with his

address. I wondered if he was aware he was prosecuting not just us, but the way every policeman worked.

The first eleven counts against us, he said, were selected instances where the Crown claimed there was adequate proof of perjury. The final charge he said, could best be described as a cover-up operation, led by Mr Kelaher. With his connivance, said Mr Leary, we had concocted a cock-and-bull story to cover up the perjury.

He then used Nobby's diary as an illustration of how a diary was written and what it contained, and went on to explain some of the abbreviations we used.

I could see the jury were fascinated by these revelations of police routine. Their glasses and their gazes were fixed on the photostats and typescripts. They hardly looked at Leary.

The six of us in the dock blinked a bit when at one point he said that duty books were true and accurate. We knew this to be a rather inaccurate generalization.

He then chose to use an entry of mine as an example, comparing it with my diary and with what I had said at the Salah trial. By now he was now getting down to the specific charges against us. Count 1 was against me.

In my evidence at the Salah trial I had said that on 5 January 1971, at about 9.40 a.m., I had been keeping observation outside Crevald's boatyard and saw John Salah and Janet arrive in a Landrover. I had said that I had seen them enter the office and leave at about 10.30 a.m., and that about ten minutes later I had seen Mrs Salah arrive in a white Volkswagen and leave soon afterwards.

Mr Leary said I had never seen any of this.

He asked the jury to look at the extract from my diary that covered that day.

He read it out: 'On duty at CO at 9 a.m. Engaged in office until 10.15 a.m. Then to CD and DP Sections re inquiries until 12 a.m. Return to CO. . . .'

He paused to see if they were attending and then continued.

'Look, if you would for a moment, at the expenses he incurred on that day listed on the other side of the page. Two extra meals. . . . There is no mention of any expenses incurred on a journey to Windsor and back – no mention of mileage and no claim for petrol. Now if you will be so good as to turn to the duty book for that date you will see, on the top right-hand side, what he has written. Can you decipher his writing, and the abbreviations? Let me help you. It reads, in full: "Office engaged 9 a.m. to 10.15 a.m.; to CD" – that is, West End Central police station – "and DP" – which is Paddington – "sections. Back later. Here, 12 a.m. . . ." Members of the jury, there is no doubt that the first line of the manuscript is in his own handwriting and that it must have been written when he was there, at the Commissioner's Office, or New Scotland Yard. The entry in the duty book says he was at the Yard between 9 a.m. and 10.15 a.m. He therefore couldn't possibly have been keeping observation at the boatyard at 9.40 when he claimed to have seen John Salah and Janet arrive there. It was a lie. He never did go to Windsor.'

I couldn't believe my luck. I had listened somewhat anxiously, but nothing could be proved one way or the other. Shindler would shoot the prosecution down in flames. There was no witness to say I wasn't at Windsor. The only so-called evidence was the easily squashable supposition that I had written up the duty book at the times mentioned – which hardly anyone ever did – and that because I hadn't claimed expenses for petrol, therefore I hadn't gone anywhere. Shindler would prove in a flash that I'd made no claim for petrol because I wasn't authorized to do so. I simply wasn't authorized to use my car and could hardly therefore claim expenses for it.

Mr Leary in the meantime had embarked on a similarly detailed explanation of the next four counts.

Taken at face value they didn't sound too good. It seemed indeed that Nobby, Nick and Nigel had never been where they had said they were on three occasions. Mr Leary said witnesses would swear to their presence elsewhere. He also said Nobby had made alterations in his diary and even put in some new pages.

By the time the court adjourned, at four o'clock, I was getting worried again. If the prosecution could really prove their allegations and convince the jury of Nobby's, Nick's and Nigel's guilt, then they might also find me guilty. We were all in it together. David Napley, my solicitor, had warned me of this. 'A case could be made out against some of you,' he had said. 'If two or three of you appear guilty to the jury, they might also add you to the list as being guilty in their minds by association.'

All my old uncertainties returned. I didn't think the first count against me could be proved. But there were two others, not to mention the conspiracy charge that included us all. I had the uneasy feeling it had all been fixed beforehand, and that somehow, by someone somewhere, our fates were part of larger issues and had already been determined.

It didn't help when the petty business of our passports was raised by the prosecuting policemen. This time our counsel madeno objection. As a condition of bail we had to surrender our passports the following day. Apart from this, bail was as before.

The Judge informed everyone that we would assemble tomorrow in Court 8 at half-past ten. Court 8 was more suitable for our purposes, he said, and added with awful joviality that it was air-conditioned.

Resuming his grimmer expression, he rose to his feet.

'Be upstanding!' ordered the snappy usher, wrapping his gown in front of him and saying in double-quick time: 'All persons who have anything further to do before my Lords, the Queen's justices, at the Central Criminal Court, may depart hence and give their attendance again tomorrow at 10.30 o'clock in the forenoon. God save the Queen!'

The jury regarded us stonily, as our guards directed us down the stairs in the dock to the cells below.

22

Friday. . . . I had a sleep this afternoon and have just been out for an enormous dinner as it was/is our last night in Paris. . . . I'm not feeling very literary, my love, tonight. Do so hope all is going well and that Monday won't be too frightening – I shall be thinking of you so hard then, darling, and hoping all my prayers will help you. . . . Must stop, love – Keep Kool – and don't worry – all will be well in the end. Loads of love. Sam.

Her letter reached me on Tuesday morning. I imagined her writing it as she sprawled on her bed in the hotel room, with her hair falling onto her hand. She would have been quite tiddly and tired, and thinking of me amidst all the comfort of her bedroom, and wishing I was there. So did I.

There were other letters, from relatives and friends, wishing me well. But they didn't mean quite so much. Her letter cheered me up a lot. Her father had come to Europe for a holiday and asked Sam to join him for part of it. I didn't mind her going. I encouraged it. For I didn't want her to come to court and hear what was said against me. I'd rather she stayed away until it was all over.

She and her father would now be on their way to the Vosges, near the Maginot Line and the German border, where they would stay for a week. They would then go to Amsterdam before returning to London on 3 October.

I put her letter in my jacket pocket when I left the flat.

The Old Bailey wasn't looking any more friendly when I got there about ten o'clock for the start of day 2 of the trial.

This time we went up to the first floor of the new building and into Court 8. We entered the dock and passed through it and out of it by way of a green door into a short corridor, where there were some stairs and a lift down to the cells. We waited there until it was 10.30 a.m. and time for our re-appearance.

'Prichard and others!' called an usher and one after the other we re-entered Court 8.

It was like a large room furnished for a trial. The walls were half-panelled with pale oak. The other half was white, as was the ceiling. All the fixtures were likewise of pale oak, and the fitted carpet and all the pseudo-leather chairs were dark green. These last were a good deal more comfortable than those in Court 1. The dock itself was more spacious and enabled us to tilt our chairs back against the panelled wall when nothing much seemed to be going on.

We were on the same level as and right opposite the Judge, who was backed by a large and theatrical royal coat of arms. On the floor of the court between him and us were three rows of long tables, at which sat the six defence QCs (each with a junior barrister in attendance) and the three prosecution barristers – all with their backs and wigs to us. The chief prosecutor, Mr Leary, was on the far right of the front row, nearest the witness-box. His profile became quite familiar as he stood by his portable reading-desk, solicitously addressing the jury. Not far from him was a young female barrister, a pretty blonde, who was on a watching brief for the Salahs. My senior counsel,

Mr Shindler QC, had *two* junior barristers to assist him – Mr Bryan Anns, and Mr Christopher Chope. The latter mostly took notes. The three of them were diagonally opposite Mr Leary – that is, in the back row, below us on our left. Along the left-hand wall were two boxed-in tiers for the Press, of whom there were seldom more than three present. Next to them were the jury. On our right, below the public gallery, was a row of chairs against the wall, supposedly for family friends. We were each theoretically allowed two friends or relatives in court. But usually half of the chairs were occupied by interested and high-up policemen, including Commander Clarkson and Peter Gittus. My father was always there. Sometimes he was joined by one of Morag's many friends. There were no wives present. Nobby, Nick, Nigel and Kelaher had discouraged theirs from attending, as I had Sam.

On every available table-top were bundles and mounds of documents and papers, and the indirect lighting that suffused the room meant that everyone and everything was coldly lit and cast no shadows.

It couldn't have been more different from the old Court 1, and wasn't in the least alarming. It was cool – 'antiseptic' as Nigel said – and to begin with seemed a pleasant place to be in. But at the end of nearly every afternoon I had a headache.

The second day of the trial was a big headache in more ways than one. Mr Leary soon got onto Count 6, the second charge against me, relating to 18 January 1971.

First he read an extract of my answers to Mr Corkery from a transcript of the Salah trial. Then he addressed himself to the jury. He hardly ever looked at me, though he sometimes wafted a hand in my direction.

'Acworth says,' complained Mr Leary, 'that he went with Prichard to Kier Park House at about 9.45 a.m. If you will assist me by looking at the extract from his diary, you will see it says: "On duty at CO at 9 a.m., engaged in office until 11.30 a.m." Members of the jury, I put it to you that *that* is a true entry. No one has monkeyed around with it. If it *is* true, he couldn't possibly have been with Prichard at Ascot. The early part of that morning was spent at New Scotland Yard. . . . He was never at Ascot. He was purporting to corroborate the evidence of Prichard. . . . And there is the clearest possible evidence that he was not at Ascot if one looks at the *duty book*.'

Again Mr Leary quoted from it: ' "9 a.m. Office engaged 11.30." '

But this again was no proof of my guilt. My defence was that this was a misleading entry and that I *was*, as I had said in court, at Ascot.

I had to smile when Mr Leary said in injured tones: 'Acworth doesn't claim any travelling expenses for the journey down there.' He was up the spout on that one.

When he came to Count 9, relating to my disputed presence at Ascot at 4.55 p.m. on 22 January, he followed the same line of attack, again reading an extract of what I'd said at the Salah trial, then turning to my diary.

'It's Exhibit 50,' he told the jury. 'If you will turn to page 103 of the *thin* bundle of documents, you will see a copy of the relevant section in his own handwriting. And there, on page 104, is the same thing, typed out, and much more easy for you to read. "4 p.m. return to CO, then to Vauxhall re returning nondescript van until 4.30 p.m. to –" And what appears next is "Slough".'

He said that what had originally been written was 'BD', and that I had actually gone at 4.30 p.m. to BD (Chelsea) section.

He said: 'The Crown suggests that *this* was originally there, and that someone has overwritten "Slough" in order to give verisimilitude to his evidence. Acworth certainly wasn't at Slough at 4.55 p.m. He couldn't have been there. He was in Chelsea.'

What he didn't comment on – which I expected – was that 'Slough' was, unusually for me, written in capital letters and occurred nowhere else like that.

Mr Leary directed the jury to look at the duty book once again. He read the typed-out copy.

' "Here" – that is, at Scotland Yard – "at 4 p.m. To Vauxhall and BD sections. Back later. Rang 7 p.m. and off." That is a true report on Acworth's activities that afternoon. He was in Vauxhall and Chelsea. A police sergeant, Sergeant Milburn was on duty until 4.30 p.m. at the Vauxhall garage which Mr Acworth visited to return a nondescript van.'

Mr Leary produced two garage books, one concerning nondescript vans, the other a daily record book.

He said the van had been driven forty miles and that the return trip to Kier Park was sixty. The van, he said, had been turned in by 4.30 – so how could I have been at Slough at 4.55?

It was odd, I thought, that he hadn't pounced on the slight and potentially awkward fact that although the duty book said 'To Vauxhall and BD sections' and the diary said '4.30 p.m. to Slough', my statement had said that at 4.55 p.m. I was at Ascot, *not* Slough, and that I didn't get to Slough until about 5.20. It was also odd that he hadn't seized on the fact that the '4' in '4.30 p.m. to Slough' in the diary wasn't the way I wrote a four, and that the original time could have been 5 p.m. – the '5' having since been altered to '3', with a '4' being put in front. That would have bolstered his interpretation of the change of 'BD' to 'Slough'.

I was beginning to think Mr Leary was somewhat less impressive. He hadn't of course been the first choice for this job. Mr John Mathew, who prosecuted at the Rolls-Royce trial – he was also a friend of my father – had turned it down. So had my mother's cousin, Mr John Buzzard, the other top Treasury counsel. Mr Corkery, who was next on the list, couldn't do it because he prosecuted the Salahs. Technically, Mr Leary was fourth choice.

I also wondered why had he made so much of the arguable and even disprovable facts that duty books were totally reliable and that I hadn't claimed petrol expenses.

He then referred to my statement for the Salah trial, and read out the relevant entry, about me and Kelaher observing Kier Park House in the morning and early afternoon before returning to London. The only thing Mr Leary picked out, somewhat half-heartedly, was that at the end of the statement I had written – 'we terminated the observation'.

Why had I written 'we'? he wondered. I was alone, he said, at Slough, if there at all.

I could have told him. It was just a slip, a formula we usually used. Since, in most observations we were never on our own, I and everyone else thought in terms of 'we'.

That turned out to be the gist of the prosecution's case against me on three counts.

I felt rather relieved that that was all it was. It sounded very thin. Even the witness who would be called, Sergeant Milburn, couldn't say I *wasn't* at Slough or Ascot at 4.55 – only that he saw me before 4.30. The alteration of the place and the misleading entries couldn't be definitely said to have any sinister motive.

Viewing the matter as objectively as I could, I felt that my 'Not guilty' would hopefully be echoed by the jury.

But Mr Leary's case against Nobby, Nigel, Nick and Morag, taken on its own, sounded more convincing, and the day ended with the six of us in a depression once again.

The jury were told that a diary entry for 19 January had been altered by Nobby, who changed the time he said he was at Mapledene Road by turning the figure '9' into an '8'. They were told that when Nigel said he saw Mrs Salah in a Mercedes on 19 January he was really at Surbiton, where two customs officials remembered seeing him. They were told that Nick's diary had him dealing with a surety matter at Marlborough Street magistrates court on the afternoon of 13 January when he had sworn on oath at the Salah trial that he had been at Slough. There were witnesses – the sureties, two girls. Nick had also, said Mr Leary, told the Salah trial that he was with me at Ascot on the morning of 18 January, while his diary showed that he had spent most of the morning at the Yard before going on to Inner London Sessions.

Mr Leary told the jury that Morag had said she was at Crevald's boatyard at 9.30 a.m. on 5 January, and that her diary had been altered from: 'On duty 9.30 a.m., engaged office' to 'On duty 8.30 a.m., engaged office and Windsor'. He also said that Morag's pocketbook, which had been produced at this and the Salah trial, was not the same book she had originally been issued with for the relevant period. The issue number on the outside, he said, had deliberately been made unreadable.

Summing up, Mr Leary said that we had 'doctored and monkeyed around with' official police records in an attempt to cover up perjured evidence given at the Salah trial. Original entries in some of our diaries were expanded and times of day were altered to give the impression we were somewhere we could never have been. He said this had been done after we had given false evidence at the Salah trial, and that when suspicion fell on us we claimed the documents had been altered to plug a Scotland Yard security leak.

'That, my Lord, is the case for the prosecution.'

On day 1, we hadn't been allowed to leave the Old Bailey at lunchtime and were put in a cell, a small narrow room, with wooden chairs and a carved-up table, where lunch was brought to us. Morag was taken somewhere else. Nobby refused to eat the lunch, as we all did, as a protest at not being allowed out. We were told the reason for this was that we might interfere with the jury or witnesses. We pointed out that if we wanted to, and we didn't, we could have words with jury or witnesses either *before* the court assembled in the morning or when it adjourned, when we all left the Old Bailey more or less together. All we wanted was a decent lunch.

On the first day at lunchtime we ate nothing, though some of us, being very thirsty, had some of the hot brown water they called tea.

All about us were other cells, on either side of a corridor, most with two or three people in them. It wasn't very pleasant. Some of the inmates, knowing who we were, made remarks.

On day 2, the others brought in sandwiches which their wives had made for them. So did I from then on, though I had to make my sandwiches myself as Sam wasn't with me.

On day 3, after walking down the stairs from Court 8 – our guards used a lift – we were directed into a detention room at the end of the corridor. It was larger than a cell, and equipped with a formica-topped table and slightly more civilized chairs. It had a cell-type door, but this time it was left open. Morag was now allowed to go to Snow Hill police station with a WPC and have her lunch there.

From that day on we five spent our lunchtime hour picnicking in the detention room, sharing our sandwiches, rolls and cigarettes and drinking coffee from thermos flasks. They were fairly lively occasions as someone, mostly Nobby or Nigel, usually had a lot to say about the morning's proceedings, and everyone else either agreed or didn't and raised other points. We all tried to be fairly jokey. But sometimes individuals would seem very tired or depressed. Kelaher was generally quite silent. What with his rank and age and preoccupations he felt rather out of it, and I felt of course that he should never have been there. The only way they could get him had been to get at us.

Since the Salah trial he had grown a dark tea-strainer moustache, and what with his oddly shaped dark hair looking like a wig, all tidy and parted and low on his brow, I couldn't help thinking he looked more like an Edwardian barber than a policeman. In fact the six of us, in my opinion, were the least villainous lot of accused persons to be seen in the dock for some time.

At the end of the lunch break, at five to two, a guard would fetch us, saying: 'Come up now. Let's have you. You're on.'

On Wednesday, the third day of the trial, the witnesses for the prosecution began ostensibly to give evidence against us, though it didn't always turn out that way. Most of them were police officers, uniformed and CID. Most of them we knew and had worked with. Generally they were not at all happy to be there, having to give evidence against fellow officers, having to admit to weaknesses in the system. Nearly all felt sorry for us, I think, and glad it wasn't the other way around.

The first witness to be called into court by an usher – the witnesses waited outside in the hall, sometimes all day – was a customs officer, Mr Newsom. He was sworn in, as everyone was, in the usual way. He took a copy of the New Testament in his right hand, as instructed, and read the printed oath.

Newsom didn't have much to say against us in particular. The main prosecution point seemed to be that Nobby, Nick and Nigel had visited him on 6 August 1970 to ask him if we could borrow one of the intercepts granted to the customs to listen in on the Salahs. We hadn't been able to get permission for an intercept ourselves. We didn't get any joy from the customs either.

Next on was DS Dudley, who joined the Drug Squad after me and was only with us for about six months.

After Mr Leary's examination finished, it was the turn of our QCs to cross-examine, and as there were six of them this took some time, especially as they phrased their questions very carefully and waited after an answer for it to be written down – by the shorthand writer, by the Judge, and by all the other QCs. It was like a school dictation. Everyone made notes.

My QC, Mr Shindler, was absolutely superb. Afterwards, the other defence counsel got up and congratulated him. He asked very few questions, but in doing so killed about fifteen birds with one stone. He was incredible.

Sergeant Dudley admitted to him that an officer at the Yard who was on reserve or night duty, with people phoning him up all evening and asking to be booked off duty, might make a list of the names and then transfer them to the relevant duty books – a fact of some importance in Nigel's defence. He admitted that alterations *were* made in duty books. He said that he met Nobby, Nick and Nigel at Stoke Poges on 27 and 28 July 1970. He didn't mention me, and in fact I didn't remember him being there. This was the occasion when Nick and I visited the Salah flat in The Meads at about 7 p.m. Shindler pointed out to Sergeant Dudley that his duty book entry on that day showed him to be at Loughton in Essex at 7 p.m., where he had phoned in to say he was on the way to Stoke Poges. Shindler then got him to agree that it would have taken him about two hours to get to Stoke Poges from Loughton and therefore he couldn't have got there until 9 p.m.

It wasn't much. But after the prosecution's depressing two-day speech, it was a real tonic. They weren't going to get away with their allegations. We were fighting back, and the prospect that all would be well, as Sam promised, seemed more than likely. I was quite chuffed.

The fly in the ointment was the Judge. He didn't seem to take too kindly to the six defence QCs popping up one after the other and asking similar questions, with particular reference to their own clients.

He said to one QC: 'If you go on with these questions we shall be here until Christmas.'

Sometimes he would sniff and grimace sourly at the jury, as if the defence were wasting his and their time.

Nobby was furious. 'What a way to carry on!' he said.

My father, who is a magistrate, had a lot to say about the Judge when we adjourned, and as time passed his views became more strongly phrased. Basically they were variations of his first and briefest verdict – 'I am not impressed!'

The next day Shindler rose to his feet at one point and said: 'May I ask a question?'

The Judge replied: 'I don't see why you should.'

My father remarked later: 'Discourtesy is unforgivable.'

Kelaher's QC, Mr Oliver Martin, whom the Judge seemed to dislike the most, came in for the roughest treatment. When Mr Martin said on one occasion, trying to ask a question – 'I hope your Lordship will bear with me' – he was growled at by the Judge. Mr Martin continued: 'This is going to be a long trial. Your Lordship will have to bear with me.' And the Judge muttered: 'I shouldn't be so optimistic.'

Later Mr Martin said: 'I shall continue with my questions tomorrow.' To which the Judge replied: 'I was afraid you would!'

It seemed to us that the Judge had much more time for Mr Leary, who was suitably deferential in turn.

Occasionally the Judge repeated points made by prosecution witnesses. This happened while he was taking notes. He would say: 'I didn't quite get that,' then read over what he had written down and ask the witness if that was correct. In this way the point was made twice.

We were somewhat discouraged by the Judge's show of impatience with the defence. It seemed to me, and of course I knew I had to be wrong, that the outcome of the trial had somehow been predetermined.

The witness after Newsom and DS Dudley was DI Peck, who had left us in October 1970. He was a very large and solid man, with a rough voice that over-rode his nervousness. What he said was brief, abrupt, and not very notable.

Detective Chief Inspector Bolton, who had been a DI with us after Peck, didn't get off so lightly. He was next in the box.

Bolton had worked in the same office as us for several months. We had eaten with him, drunk with him, gone on observations with him. Now he was standing where he was and we were where we were. He avoided our eyes. Built like a Welsh prop forward gone a bit to pot, he parried awkward questions with his chin, shifting his hands and feet as he did so.

He agreed with Mr Tudor-Price, the prosecution number 2, that when Nobby was on an investigation in the Cayman Islands (with Commander Barnett) he, Bolton, had inspected the intercept each day. He had also been to Brixton (Wilson's Garage) to observe, and had gone to Bulgaria in April. He said that Kelaher had discussed the need for security with him, mainly because a number of civilians were employed there.

Answering Mr Shields, the QC defending Nobby, he agreed that deceiving entries had been made in diaries and duty books.

He told Nigel's QC, Mr Parker, that the Salah investigation was a very big operation involving about one and a half tons of cannabis worth as much as £1½ million. He said the senior officers connected with the Rolls-Royce case had kept it very close, and that he didn't know about it until the day before the arrests.

He agreed that he had made a statement for the purposes of the Salah trial and believed it contained details of his observations at Brixton. The statement, he later said, was made on the same day he had been questioned by Mr Mees in Paddington Green police station – a week before the rest of us were.

He also said he had appeared in the witness-box at the trial, though later he didn't seem to be certain about this.

Mr Parker said: 'It was accepted that you saw what you said you saw?' He was referring to the Brixton observations.

'Yes, sir,' said Bolton.

'Nobody suggested – did they? – that you had *not* been keeping observation on those two days there?'

'No, sir . . .'

'It was never challenged by either Mr Hudson or Mr Lloyd-Eley that you did not go to that place?'

'No, sir.'

The Judge interrupted.

'That is not the subject of any charge, is it? – the Brixton observation?'

'My Lord,' said Mr Parker, 'it is not suggested that this period of observation –'

'It is not the subject of any of the charges in the indictment. Is it?' the Judge demanded.

'My Lord, it may go to the issue of conspiracy. It is one of the dates –'

'I only want my question answered. It is not the subject of any count?'

'It is not the subject of any count of perjury,' Mr Parker

replied. 'But it may go to the count of conspiracy because of the dates.'

The Judge growled and said nothing further. Mr Parker resumed his cross-examination, turning to another matter.

'There is one thing that baffles me,' he said. 'For the purpose of *this* trial you made a statement, did you not?'

Bolton agreed, and a copy of his statement was handed to him.

Mr Parker read part of it out. ' "I did not work with them operationally until the moment when I had to go to Bulgaria." '

'Them' meant Nobby, Nigel, Nick and me.

Mr Parker said: 'That is wrong, isn't it?'

'That is wrong, sir – yes,' said Bolton, adding later that it was cleared up further on.

Mr Shindler, when it was his turn, began with his customary brisk announcement. 'I appear for Mr Acworth – whom I think you know already,' he added. He went on: 'A very hard-working officer . . . reliable, as far as you were concerned, and trustworthy?'

Bolton paused for a second and then agreed.

Shindler proposed and Bolton seconded the fact that I, as a buyer, had had a dangerous role.

'You have told us,' continued Shindler, 'that your part was confined to Bulgaria . . . the intercept . . . and Brixton.'

Bolton agreed. Shindler swept smoothly on.

'Let me remind you – I know it is a long time ago – but you yourself kept observation, did you not, in August 1970 in Stoke Poges?'

Bolton denied this. The relevant duty book dealing with 17 August was provided and handed to him. He was asked to read out the relevant passage.

' "1 p.m. to Stoke Poges." '

' "1 p.m. to Stoke Poges," ' repeated Shindler.

'I cannot recall going there,' said Bolton.

'Your involvement . . .,' said Shindler sharply, 'began very much earlier than you told us about. Didn't it?'

He also sorted out the fact that Bolton had twice been to Brixton. His diary and the duty book were produced as confirmation.

Bolton explained. 'It was one observation over two days.'

Very clever, I thought.

But he put his foot right in it when he said I was authorized to drive my car.

'He was authorized?' repeated Shindler.

'Yes.'

'Would you be surprised to hear – as we shall hear in due course – that he was *not* authorized to drive his own car until June 14th, 1971?'

'Well,' said Bolton. 'To the best of my knowledge I understood that all Drug Squad officers *were* authorized. To the best of my recollection.'

Shindler then queried the fact that Bolton, one of whose functions had been to check up on official expenses, hadn't thought it extraordinary that I never put in a claim in respect of mileage.

'Wasn't the reality of the situation this?' he asked, clutching the lapels of his gown. 'Nobody knew that Acworth was not authorized to drive his own car; but because of the scarcity of motor cars he was driving his own, and because he was a keen young officer he was paying for it out of his own pocket?'

'Not to my knowledge, sir,' said Bolton.

'Because,' said Shindler accusingly, 'if you admitted that, you yourself would be in breach of one of the regulations.'

'I think this matter is too serious to take that into consideration, sir,' said DCI Bolton.

He answered well – no doubt of that. I wondered how he had answered the questionnaire that Mees had put to him the previous July.

Miss Southworth, Morag's QC, cross-examined him next and was followed by Kelaher's QC, Mr Martin.

Bolton agreed with Mr Martin that Kelaher had had a conversation with him about security. He wasn't sure when it was and couldn't remember any details. However, he agreed that in important inquiries false entries were accepted as a legitimate method of disguise.

The Judge asked him to reaffirm this.

Bolton did, saying that he had not been personally involved in such a practice and wouldn't have done it anyway without being authorized. He would have consulted the Commander of C1.

Mr Justice Melford Stevenson said: 'Do I gather from that, that without such authority you would not dream of doing it?'

'I would ask for authority from somebody far superior to myself,' said Bolton.

'You wouldn't do it without such authority,' repeated the Judge.

'No, sir,' said Bolton.

Later, when he was re-examined by Mr Leary about whether or not he had ever received such an instruction, the Judge again intervened.

'If it was a case in which you personally had any involvement, would it not be difficult to forget?' he asked.

'I would think so, sir,' said Bolton.

'So would I,' said the Judge, and looked at the jury.

Commander Virgo, now retired from the force, with his red face, bald head, white moustache and big eyes, looked like a reincarnation of Colonel Blimp. You wouldn't have thought, just looking at him, that he had had one of the most important jobs at the Yard – the head of C 1.

Tudor-Price examined him in chief.

'Have you heard that instructions were given that duty books and diaries should be falsely –?'

'I haven't heard anything,' Virgo protested.

The QCs smiled. Virgo assumed a very blank expression. It was obvious he wished he wasn't there.

'Did you ever give such an instruction?'

'No, sir.'

Later, he said that although he had discussed the subject of disguising entries in duty books and diaries with Kelaher he didn't remember giving Kelaher his blessing or any backing to take such a step, and that Kelaher, as far as he was concerned, wasn't acting under orders.

'If there was a security leak,' continued Tudor-Price, 'would you expect to be consulted?'

'I would expect to be,' said Virgo, and then added: 'But I might not be.'

'Would you expect a Chief Inspector to give an instruction to falsify a diary?'

'No, sir!' said Virgo definitely.

'Duty books record what people expect to do,' suggested Tudor-Price.

Virgo agreed, and also agreed that they might not be accurate.

Asked about diaries he said: 'I would expect that any diary that *I* kept would be accurate. . . .'

And he complained: 'There's been so much trouble over diaries. . . . There is a saying, "If they want to they can always get you on your diary." '

Commenting on my alteration of my diary for 22 January, making BD into Slough, Virgo said: 'He should have initialled it and crossed it out,' and added tolerantly: 'I can understand him getting in this state.'

He was trying very hard to be fair. It was difficult for him – he wanted to be honest and not to let anyone down.

His loyalty to the police and policemen came over strong when our counsel embarked on a long recital of our excellences and the commendations we'd each received. I'd had 4; Nobby 13; Nigel 4; Nick 5; Morag 8; and Kelaher 23. Virgo wasn't slow in joining in our praises.

Of me he said: 'I regard Mr Acworth as an outstanding officer – for such a young officer.'

He said I had come to his notice 'in a good way'. He said I was the most junior officer for promotion to Sergeant he had put forward.

I may have been put forward, I thought, but I didn't get it.

Virgo was becoming quite confused by now, almost emotional.

He claimed that he had got me into the Drug Squad, when in fact he hadn't. He meant to say the Dirty Squad. Then he totally misunderstood a question about Kelaher, taking it to be a reference to the Basil Sands affair.

'I was very sorry about that,' said Virgo, and had to be rescued by the defence.

But he needed no prompting to extol Kelaher, who was, he concluded, the drug expert of the United Kingdom.

I liked Virgo. I was sorry to see him leave the witness-box.

Detective Chief Superintendent O'Connell, who appeared next, supported Virgo's view of Kelaher as a dedicated and energetic detective.

O'Connell was the most senior DCS in the Yard. He was tall, slim, and very upright, and for some reason had a patch over his left eye, held up by a bandage round his head.

He recalled in detail an occasion when he was a DS on the Flying Squad and engaged on an inquiry concerning a team of pickpockets at Sandown Races. It became evident, he said, that the team had prior information about police movements, as whenever he went to the racecourse, pickpockets were nowhere to be seen. When he failed to go, they were active. To plug the suspected internal leak he one day wrote in his duty book that he was going on special leave and 'put the word around to that effect'. Instead, he went to the racecourse and made many arrests. He suspected a fellow officer was responsible for the leak, but could never prove it.

O'Connell said there was a need for security at the Yard and a need for officers to guard against revealing information in idle gossip.

There had been some rotten apples at the Yard, he said.

How did they *get* rotten? I wanted to ask.

There were many other witnesses, supposedly for the prosecution. But they also made some points for the defence. And at one point, while Mr Leary was questioning ex-DI Bailey, Nick wrote a note for his counsel which said: 'Mr Howard, I am sacking you and leaving Mr Leary to conduct my defence.'

DCS McGowan, a stocky Scot, with greyish, thinning hair and an untidy appearance, said that I was an exceptional officer on the Drug Squad and also while I was under him in the East End.

Commander Barnett was next – a dour Scot with a staccato way of speaking. He spat his replies, with the minimum of words, out of one side of his mouth. It was he who had helped sort out the customs people on the telephone when they were being awkward with Nick and me on the Isle of Wight.

He agreed with the defence that I was probably armed when I went buying LSD up at Muswell Hill.

Looking at his double chins and hearing him speak reminded me of a time when he came to tell some DCs who had taken the Sergeant's exam that they had all failed. He said: 'You know as much about police work as my arsehole knows about steam navigation.'

I never saw him smile. But he was a most respected man and very impressive in the box. His evidence mostly witnessed to Kelaher's excellence in the Drug Squad. He also said it didn't surprise him that Kelaher took it on his own head to make a decision about a security clamp-down. If he had gone to a higher authority, he would almost certainly have got a 'No', said Mr Barnett.

He was the last of the high-ranking CID men to be called to the court.

The rest of Friday, the fifth day of the trial, was taken up with other witnesses.

Teresa Gould gave evidence relating to Nick and her going to Marlborough Street court as a surety.

Barry Cockerell, a youngish customs man, wouldn't move an inch from his statement that Nigel was with him when Nigel had said he was observing the Salahs on 19 January.

Sergeant Milburn, of the uniformed police, stated that on 22 January I took out a nondescript van from the Vauxhall garage at 10.30 a.m. and returned it before 4.30 p.m. when he went off duty.

Inspector Shaw, also uniformed, admitted I was authorized to drive police vehicles from May 1967 and not May 1971, as he'd said in a statement – an error that had misled the prosecution.

Albert Maughan, a police photographer, produced photos of Kier Park House, Mapledene Road, The Meads, and Crevald's boatyard.

Those were some of the witnesses for the prosecution.

At the end of the first week I had stopped worrying. The trial seemed to have little to do with me, or any of us accused. We sat dumbly in the dock watching a legal game.

The jury dutifully looked and listened, listened and looked. What they made of it all I couldn't begin to guess. Perhaps they wondered, as I did, what it was really all about. They had heard senior police officers say that duty books and diaries were not totally accurate and could be and had been fabricated and falsified. Yet this is what we were basically accused of doing.

It was all bloody unnecessary, I thought. The charges made against us should never have gone so far. If anyone needed dealing with, he should have been dealt with internally and dismissed. The trial need never have taken place. As it was, it was damaging to the police force – and in addition costing the country about a quarter of a million pounds.

My father said his views about the lack of leadership in the police force had been borne out to the nth degree.

He said: 'The poor chaps serving under these fellows are left out on a limb. Everyone passes the buck and looks after themselves when the mud begins to fly. How can any policeman possibly hope to be both honest and make truthful reports in his various books? His integrity and security are subtly undermined every day. It's an impossible situation.'

A DS personally known to me told me one lunch break down in the cells that the Met were still losing more men than were joining. They were now nearly 5,000 understrength – despite a massive publicity campaign to recruit more men. Police pay was good, but as TV programmes like *Softly, Softly* showed, it was a fairly thankless job, with long hours and loads of paperwork. Dull it was, more often than not, and duller the prospects seemed when you looked at your senior officers. There were very few leaders. Perhaps my father was right.

One thing I felt was certain – the Commissioner, Sir Robert Mark, wasn't going to right any basic wrongs. Whatever happened to the six of us, it would not be so easy to root out the forty-two senior officers said to be named in the diaries of a certain Soho strip-club owner, who alleged they had all taken bribes of several sorts.

I once read an article about police corruption in New York. It said that a commission set up to investigate this had found that in 1971 well over half the police force in the city had engaged in corrupt activities. It wasn't all that different here, I thought. If Mark was really going to deal with police corruption in London, he would have to get rid of half the CID and uniformed policemen he had. In my opinion, that's how many were bent.

That weekend I ate a lot and drank a lot and slept a lot. I drove about the countryside, seeing and doing as much as possible. I went to Avebury and Oxford. But everyone wanted to know about the trial, and all I wanted to know was what Sam was doing. Everyone also assumed and assured me I would be found not guilty. But I wasn't so sure. Everything in my life told me that something again would go wrong.

23

When I returned to the Old Bailey on Monday morning it was raining. In fact there was a lot of rain that last week in September, and in early October.

Nothing happened that day. One of the jurors was absent – he had a migraine. Mr Leary so informed the Judge, who remarked that in such a serious case as this he thought the whole jury should be present. He hoped that the man would recover soon and, as no one objected, the court was adjourned.

This meant that the court sat for only three days that week. For on the Friday and the following Monday the Old Bailey was on holiday. Many barristers and QCs were Jewish, and that weekend was the Jewish New Year.

Tuesday, day 6, was entirely taken up with *more* prosecution witnesses, including several experts.

There was Mr Timms, Mrs Levington, DS Evans, Mrs Summerskill, DS Gaston, and Mr Fryd. There was also Mr Hansford and Wendy Clark. The experts were mainly on about pocketbooks and diaries. Substitute pages, they said, had been sewn into Nobby's diary – three double pages in fact. Hansford, a customs man was questioned about Nigel being at Surbiton. Wendy Clark, the other surety at Marlborough Street court – this concerned Nick – broke down under some brilliant kid-gloved cross-examination by Mr Howard. She said that Superintendent Faulkner had let her read her statement an hour before she appeared in court. This he should never have done, without the proper authority.

In the dock, we quietly sucked away at Polo mints and Tunes, sometimes grimacing, sometimes smiling at the things witnesses said. Notes were written, mostly by Nigel, Nick and Nobby, and we had whispered consultations over the edge of the dock with our solicitors. Chris Murray, who was looking after three of us, had a busy time in this respect – always on his feet, giving and taking messages and instructions. He was in Court 8 every day. On top of this he was working full time in David Napley's office on other cases. At lunchtime he usually ate with my father. In the evening, after going over what had happened that day in the trial and preparing for the following day's proceedings, he was engaged in laying carpets and painting his new home. He worked like a black, yet in court he was always cool, calm and collected. My father spoke of him in the highest terms, as being one of the most hard-working and efficient young men he'd met and 'extraordinarily wise'. It was reassuring having Chris and Shindler and Anns on my side.

When we got bored, or fed up, or just couldn't think any more, we gazed idly at the jury, and not so idly at the Clerk of the Court. The original fellow had been replaced by a beautiful, dark-haired bird. She sat in front of the Judge's desk facing us, with a little barrister's wig on her head, and a sweet and innocent look on her face. She did nothing, except make a note of new exhibits. She said nothing, though just before we entered the dock each day I was told she read a roll-call of the jury. She could have been Shakespeare's Portia.

'She can have my pound of flesh anytime,' said Nigel somewhat crudely over lunch.

In the Press box after the first week were usually the same two women. The reporters who had thronged the box on the first day had gone elsewhere. All the national newspapers on the second day had carried stories about the charges against us, and *The Times*, the *Guardian*, and the *Daily Telegraph*, who had the best coverage, had continued to report some of the details of the prosecution's case, quoting high-up policemen and experts. But in the second week, when the defence got really going, they stopped writing about us altogether.

'They'll be back for the sentences,' said Nobby. 'Bloody vultures.'

My father wondered whether the Press were in fact boycotting the trial. Chris said he didn't think so.

'It doesn't deal with bombs, riots or police brutality,' he said. 'They probably think the alleged alteration of diaries and charges of perjury are very minor matters. They haven't got onto the issues yet.'

We had a lot of opposition in this respect. The Bomb trial, concerning the car-bombs in London in March, was on at Winchester. The Poulson affair was still developing. In Birmingham, a Catholic priest and six other men were up on bomb-plot charges. In the court next door to us four fellows accused of riotous assembly in Downing Street were being tried. Three eventually got suspended sentences – the fourth was acquitted. In another court George Ince and four other men denied taking part in a silver bullion hijack case. An American business man, accused of firearms offences, slashed his wrists in the dock. He was later jailed for seven years.

What amazed my father – I always met him briefly after the court adjourned – was that nothing had been made by the Press of the fact that a large majority of the jurors assembled for our trial had the same names as people who had records at the Yard.

'It's absolutely fantastic,' he said. 'It beats me how anyone like that can be allowed in a court of law.' And he thought it extraordinary that no newspaper had commented on the fact that for the first time passages from an intercept had been quoted in court.

It was like being at Wimbledon – on No. 8 court. The Press and the crowds were around the Centre and No. 1 courts. No one seemed aware that the match in progress on Court 8 had the widest and most serious implications concerning the Law.

One person had. She was a chubby lady, an American, who sat in the Press box every day, and made pages of notes in long-hand. She was going to write a book about the trial. She talked to just about everyone, mostly when the court adjourned, and was very friendly, and definitely on our side. So, she said, were the jury. She'd noticed their reactions. Actually, and quite innocently, she was the cause of a minor sensation one day after lunch when the Judge remarked that a member of the Press had been observed in conversation with one of the jury. He issued a warning. This mustn't happen, he said, even though the person concerned, an American, might be ignorant of our laws. Of course we all looked at the lady.

'I died,' she said to me the following day. 'I felt so embarrassed. It was really awful.'

She explained that she'd met the lady juror in the loo. They'd exchanged polite pleasantries about the discomfort of sitting so long in court – nothing about the trial itself. They were still chatting when they emerged and walked towards the court and were seen by one of the prosecuting policemen, who apparently told Mr Leary.

'No one wants to talk to me now,' she said. 'They're all afraid.'

The other woman in the Press box was a girl with a stunning figure who wrote everything down in shorthand. I heard she was there on behalf of a solicitor, one of whose clients had been done by us. The solicitor was said to be hoping to get some evidence to support an appeal.

Some others who'd been done by us were in the public gallery. They'd come along to gloat, and would stare down at us with grins of glee, sometimes mouthing various words of foul abuse. One of them was later evicted. Former informants also dropped in now and then to have a look. Two other persons in the gallery, we were told, were from the ITV *World in Action* programme, gathering material. The only people we were pleased to see up there were two middle-aged ladies. One or other, if not both, was always in attendance. They had been in the public gallery throughout the Salah trial. If they caught us looking up at them they would smile and wave – to begin with. As our trial progressed they became less cheerful and demonstrative. Eventually, one stopped coming altogether.

On Wednesday, day 7, Nick had the shits.

His counsel, Mr Howard QC, told the Judge first thing in the morning and asked if it would be okay for Nick to leave the court at times as he had a stomach upset. This he was allowed to do, if he left quietly and if it was really necessary. It was – once.

The main witness on this day was Mr Fryd, from the police laboratory and an expert on handwriting. Strangely, he appeared to have difficulty in reading the original diaries and duty books, even Nigel's, and kept interpreting Nigel's initials as 'RL' not 'NL'.

He was asked about my signatures in the garage books at Vauxhall. They were fairly indecipherable, and might have been, it was claimed, simulated forgeries – whatever that meant. He became rather confused about this. He said the signatures could have been badly made as a joke, or that, as it was January, my fingers may have been frozen with cold.

The Judge said: 'At this rate we will end up with a report from the Meteorological Office.' Everyone laughed.

Another witness, Sergeant Beeken, uniformed and on his toes, said he had made a timed drive in a mini from the Yard to Kier Park, obeying of course the speed limits. It took him fifty-two minutes. We did it of course much faster than that.

The defence soon pointed out that we all had fast cars, were always in a hurry, and very likely didn't observe speed limits or traffic signals. Sergeant Beeken admitted that a Mini-Cooper S could do 100 mph.

Day 8 produced another joke from the Judge. We thought of starting a joke-book.

Mr Shean, a former uniformed Sergeant who became an instructor in dog-handling when his golden labrador, Yogi, died, was being questioned about Morag. At one point the Judge remarked: 'You had the great good fortune to be dealing with dogs, not humans.'

On that day the policemen who had been involved in the inquiry and questionnaire gave their evidence – DS Sullivan, Superintendent Faulkner, Detective Superintendent Gittus and Detective Chief Superintendent Mees.

Basically they described how they had come to get their hands on our diaries and the documents in the case.

Throughout the trial Mees and Sullivan sat at right angles to Mr Leary at a small table piled high with a thousand documents. More were in a filing cabinet beside them, and others were kept in a side room. Though I couldn't really like Mees, I couldn't help feeling sorry for him. Most of the time he looked somewhat miserable, hunched up with his elbows on the table. He can't have liked providing the prosecution with ammunition to shoot down other policemen, and he may not have liked the way the prosecution were going about it. He didn't seem to have thrown himself whole-heartedly into the task of getting evidence to convict us – at least, that was my impression. There were curious holes in the evidence, and nothing was being proved either way except things that didn't do the police force any good. He can't have liked that.

I wondered if his reaction was the same as ours: What a farce.

To my father, sitting against the wall behind Mees, it was the most thrilling thing he'd ever seen. Appalled as he was by some of the goings-on in court he was fascinated by it all and determined to be in court every day, though he hadn't originally intended doing this.

'It's an education to see these great brains fencing with each other – and they *are* great brains. It's better than any theatre,' he said.

The trial went into its third week and resumed on Tuesday after the Jewish New Year. It was day 9 and the great brains now put on a special display.

The jury remained outside the court and were eventually sent home while four of the defending QCs individually made a submission that in seven of the counts of perjury there was no case to answer. This affected Morag, Nigel, Nobby and myself.

They claimed that in order to prove 'perjury', some physical witness had to say that the defendant wasn't where he claimed to be and was somewhere else – also that such a witness was needed to corroborate the documentary evidence. This particularly applied to Morag and me, and with me there *were* no physical witnesses.

There was a very high-powered debate – most of which I didn't understand. Precedents were quoted. Passages were read out from some quite ancient trials.

Mr Leary's interpretation of them was basically that they didn't apply in this case. Some of the evidence couldn't be dissassociated from the conspiracy charge.

The Judge kept saying: 'Yes, yes,' as he checked over and read through the examples that were quoted.

Leary was almost obsequious at times. 'If I can try to assist you . . .' he would say, or – 'My Lord, if I may help you . . .'

The Judge would paraphrase a certain point and then ask: 'Is that right?'

Mr Leary's catchphrase was 'oath against oath'.

He said: 'The Crown says that there is evidence of alteration which provides corroboration as to the falsity of the evidence.'

And so on.

In effect it was a trial within a trial, as most of the perjury counts against us were gone over once again. If the submission succeeded, the first three counts against me would have been dropped. But it didn't, and they weren't.

The Judge at the end of the afternoon said he was not going to withdraw any of the counts and the jury would have to decide for themselves.

I was bitterly disappointed. The thought of sitting through a month and more of accusation, implication, mystification and misinterpretation was very depressing. I wanted to leave. I wanted to go home.

The one thing that I didn't want seemed bound to happen now. I would have to go into the witness-box.

My father was of the opinion that the Judge's decision could provide the basis for an appeal. He thought that the three perjury counts against me and the one against Morag should have been dropped. But if they had been, he said, the prosecution's sandcastle would have started falling apart.

'It's jolly weak as it is,' he said. 'Take away four of the counts and the tide of common sense will soon sweep the rest away.'

The Judge, he thought, had been in a spot – adding that four of the defence QCs were also recorders and judges.

We were standing beside the dock after the adjournment. People were chatting in little groups, discussing the day's speeches. I looked at Mees and Sullivan, who were tidying up their desk. Leary leaned over and said something to Mees, who almost smiled.

The bastards, I said to myself.

I wondered who would report to the Commissioner that night. We had heard that one or other of the senior police officers in the court reported every day to Sir Robert Mark about the case. I thought of him sitting alone at the top of his great glass tower at the Yard, brooding over our destinies like the Dark Lord of Mordor.

Nick went into the witness-box on the next day, Wednesday, 3 October. He was there for two and a half days, until the Friday.

Leary tore into him, demanding answers to all his questions and pouring scorn on most of the answers.

Nick couldn't remember, didn't know, wasn't certain. He wasn't even definite about the order Nobby had given about false entries being made.

Later, my father remarked that Nick, as it seemed to him, had 'dropped quite a few catches'. He added that it was fortunate Nick's counsel had managed to pick several up off the ground and return them to the wicket-keeper.

I watched Nick's awkward, rather abashed performance, and became rather anxious. He hadn't been very convincing. The thought of myself being publicly exposed, being asked endless and difficult questions, being forced to answer, being led into traps which I wasn't clever enough to avoid – all this made me tremble a bit. I would get confused, my mind would go blank, I wouldn't know what to say.

Later that Wednesday, when I got back to the flat, I didn't need to say anything to Sam.

She had at last returned, and was lying in a dopey, drink-happy haze on the sitting-room sofa. Her father was flat out asleep in the spare bedroom. They had both had a very boozey twenty-four hours in Amsterdam before flying back to England.

'Hallo,' said Sam and dreamily smiled as I put my arms around her.

She said nothing more, and neither did I, for at least half an hour.

Sam stayed in London for two nights, and then on Friday evening I drove her to Hertfordshire to stay with Sue and Robert. She was going to look after their children for a while as well as Jane's and Charles's. She would also stay with my parents.

We didn't do anything in particular that weekend. Sam was very good humoured, and told me all about her visits in France and Holland, where most of the time not spent in travelling had been spent with wealthy friends and relations, eating and drinking. I knew already what she'd been doing as she'd written to me every day while she was away. But I wanted to hear her talk. If she'd recited the multiplication table I wouldn't have minded.

Most of the time I sat with her and held her hand. We talked a little about my emigrating to Africa or Australia after the trial – with her of course. But about the trial I didn't have much to say, apart from the fact that it was going very well. My father helped to put her in the picture. He was much better at that.

On the Friday before this, day 12, Nobby had gone into the witness-box, though his examination-in-chief didn't really get going until the afternoon.

In the morning there was a bomb scare, and for an hour everyone who was in the Old Bailey had to leave and gather outside in a courtyard at the back, jurors, defendants, prisoners, policemen, QCs, solicitors and judges.

Nobby's evidence lasted for three days, ending on the afternoon of Wednesday, 10 October.

He stood in the box in his brown suit, with his hands either holding the sides of the box or folded across his chest. He spoke positively and clearly and his replies were brief. My father thought he was 'absolutely first-class'.

He explained how his diary entries came to be made and what he was doing on the disputed days. He also explained that he had substituted three pages in his diary in order to protect an informant.

He was also questioned about the activities of the rest of us, and said with a grin that I was a bit of a wanderer. People smiled, and I looked at the ceiling.

Again there were long pauses as the Judge wrote down some of the answers.

'Just a moment,' he would say as he made his notes. And both prosecution and defence would advise the witness: 'Watch his Lordship's pen.'

The Judge now had a cold, and carefully blew his nose in a handkerchief now and then. He still made the occasional funny remark, though not so often as before.

When Nobby's counsel, Mr Shields, held up a duty book to show him that Nigel had signed out Nobby on 26 February, the Judge peered through his glasses and said: 'Remember I only have human eyesight.'

The jury fell about, as they did on another occasion when Nick's counsel, Mr Howard, asked Nobby: 'A policeman spends weeks and months of fruitless observations and inquiries – This is usual?'

'Yes,' said Nobby.

The Judge commented: 'It's not peculiar to the police force either.'

Nigel's QC, suggesting that Nobby and Nigel argued a bit, and that outside the court Nobby's language was somewhat richer – to which the Judge added: 'I hope so' – suddenly came out with what Nobby was supposed to have actually said.

'Fuck it,' said the QC.

There were subdued reactions in the court. The Judge raised his eyebrows and then slowly smiled. So did the lovely Clerk of the Court. Nobby maintained a serious expression.

It was in fact Nigel's QC, Mr Parker, who first *quoted* from an intercept in court. He was trying to prove that there must have been a security leak, as a man told Kathy after the arrests that her phone was tapped, and because John Salah had spoken so freely to the doctor.

At the end of that particular afternoon, which mainly dealt with matters relating to informants and security, there was a humorous debate between Mr Martin, Mr Leary and the Judge as to who should pay for the copying of civilian witnesses' statements made for the Salah trial. They were to be used by the defence in convincing the jury that there had been sufficient evidence – without ours – to convict the Salahs, and if so, why had we supposedly conspired to manufacture more?

Mr Leary had so far failed to provide a satisfactory answer to this in my opinion.

My father said Leary was 'thrashing around with details, instead of getting down to the things that matter'.

Nobby was back in the box again on Monday, day 13, the start of the fourth week of the trial. Monday was also day 3 of the Middle East war, which had started the previous Saturday, 6 October. Two days later, on Wednesday, when Nobby stood down and Nigel entered the box, the American Vice-President, Spiro Agnew, resigned.

Wednesday was also the ruby anniversary of my parents' wedding. They had been married for forty years. There was no celebration that night. They were saving it for after my appearance in the witness-box.

Nigel's evidence lasted for three days – from late on Wednesday until the following Monday. We were all somewhat apprehensive lest he do himself, and the rest of us, a mischief. He loved an argument and was apt to be a bit cocky. Chris Murray once remarked, to my surprise, that Nigel was very vain. I had never thought of him like that. Chris also said that Nigel was the only defendant he'd ever known who actually looked forward to going into the box. He had however to be told not to wear a different suit each day, as the jury would wonder how he could afford so many. In fact it was his boast he had twenty-seven suits.

My father's opinion was that Nigel was a little too clever in the examination-in-chief, but that when he was cross-examined he did jolly well.

I thought he was fantastic, completely unflappable and polite, and he never raised his voice. Several times he sold Leary a dummy. And he didn't lose his temper, as he might have done. Leary did – twice, and at one point loudly exclaimed: 'What do you mean, sir?'

None of us of course had any witnesses, apart from each other, to back up our disputed observations. No serving police officer, with an eye to his future, would dare to appear as a witness for the defence. But Nick had produced a barrister, Mr Hyams, who remembered seeing Nick in his scruffy buying gear, all bearded and long haired, at Inner London Quarter Sessions on the late morning of 18 January, and he said that Nick had excused his appearance by saying that he had been on an observation. The prosecution had alleged that neither he nor I had been at Kier Park earlier on the 18th. The barrister's evidence suggested that Nick at least may well have been there – and if he had been there, then so had I.

Ten of the counts involved two of us being at the same place at the same time – Morag and me on 5 January at Crevald's boatyard, Nick and Nobby at Mapledene Road on the 13th, Nick and me at Kier Park on the morning of the 18th, Nigel and Nobby on the morning of the 19th at Mapledene Road, and Nigel and Nobby at Heathrow Airport on 26 February.

If the prosecution managed to prove that *one* of us in these pairings was not where he said he was, the other was then discredited as well.

It seemed all of a sudden that this might be going to happen when Mr Leary, after the jury had made their exit at the end of day 17, Friday, 12 October, said he had a new statement which he would like the Judge to see. He apologized for the fact that the statement was in manuscript and hadn't been typed.

The Judge read the statement and Leary said he intended to make an application at the end of Nigel's defence.

Earlier on, Nigel had repeated that when on 19 January he went with the two customs officials on an investigation to a house in Tolworth Rise, Surbiton, he had left them there before 9 a.m. He disputed their statement that they had all arrived there at 9.08, and said it was roughly 8.09. He denied seeing a certain Mrs Oddy, who lived in the house and was said by the customs men to have returned about 9.30 after taking her child to school. Nigel was still there, according to them. According to Nigel he was then at Mapledene Road.

We knew something was up when Superintendent Faulkner, who had suddenly left the court, returned that Friday afternoon with a smile on his face and what must have been a statement from Mrs Oddy in his hand.

On Monday, 15 October, Nigel was still in the box, still being cross-examined by Leary, and then re-examined by his QC, Mr Parker.

I had expected to follow him into the box that day, and all that weekend had been steeling myself against the awesome prospect. I'd been briefed during the week by both Shindler and Anns. I'd had words with Chris Murray, and a long chat with Nigel at his home, and my father had advised me at weekends.

Sam said: 'Try not to worry, love. If you tell the truth, you've got nothing to worry about.'

But on Monday, it was still Nigel, and then his witnesses, two former policemen, an ex-DS and an ex-DI, who confirmed that false entries were made in diaries and duty books and that they had made such entries themselves.

The ex-DI, when questioned by Shindler and Miss Southworth, said that no serving CID officer would or could admit making false entries and appear for the defence, as his career would be ruined.

Nick was coughing noisily on the other side of Nobby, who was looking a lot more cheerful now that he'd said his bit and was ready to joke with anyone. Morag sat upright on the edge of her chair, hopeful and attentive. Her hair was carefully permed and she always wore a tidy suit with the right accessories. Kelaher sat, slightly slumped, hardly moving, watching everything that was going on without showing any reaction.

Half the people in Court 8 now had colds, including our guards. I wasn't feeling too good myself. My throat was sore.

My eye was on the clock in the public gallery. When the ex-policemen had finished speaking, would or would there not be time for me to be called?

Funny thing, I thought – it was 15 October.

Three years ago, on 15 October 1970, Nick and I had watched Palacios load the maroon Rolls-Royce, seen him drive it onto the Isle of Wight ferry to Portsmouth, and later heard of the arrests on the car radio. It had been my finest moment. Nick had said then something about us making the headlines.

We did, I said to myself. We certainly did.

At quarter to four the ex-DI stood down and Leary got to his feet. He wished to speak on the matter he had raised on Friday.

The Judge dismissed the jury. I wouldn't be called that day.

Feeling more relaxed I listened to the polite and legal argument between the Judge and Mr Leary as to whether or not the prosecution should be allowed to enter Mrs Oddy's statement and bring her in as a witness. They debated the niceties of this move. The Judge seemed doubtful of its propriety, for the prosecution's case against Nigel had been concluded. Why, he wanted to know, had Mrs Oddy not been produced by the prosecution earlier? Because, said Mr Leary rather weakly, she hadn't been mentioned by Nigel when he was examined in chief. Oh yes, she had, said Mr Parker, and quoted from his junior counsel's notes.

So it went on until after four o'clock, when the Judge remarked that he had to go to a prior appointment and would continue the debate tomorrow.

It should have been a cliff-hanger. But I felt certain that Mrs Oddy's evidence would be allowed. The dice were loaded. The legal argument was only a game. I had a very nasty feeling that her evidence, when admitted, might somehow and incredibly manage to discredit Nigel – and therefore Nobby, and do the rest of us no good.

But it didn't seem to matter any more. Everything was outside my control, and it was all as I had expected. I didn't care what the outcome was. I didn't care what would happen when I was cross-examined – though I was determined they would get nothing out of me to help them. Not that it really mattered. They were going to put us away for five or ten years – they had seen to that.

I felt fatalistic, yet still somehow optimistic. I had heard that

Ford Open Prison, where convicted policemen were sent, wasn't such a bad place after all.

Yet for a moment there was a sort of rage inside me. I felt very frustrated. It wasn't fair, I wanted to tell these men. It wasn't right!

I went back to the flat, read the newspapers and watched the TV news. I tried to blot my headache out with cigarette smoke and a gin and tonic and ice. I made myself some marmite sandwiches, and later went out and bought some fish and chips. Then I switched the TV on again and settled down to enjoy *Call my Bluff*.

24

'I call Detective Constable Acworth.'

So said Mr Shindler, and accompanied by my prison guard I left the dock, walking around between my father – whom I didn't look at – and Mees and Sullivan who had their backs to me. I entered the witness-box. There I took the New Testament in my right hand and read the oath.

It was just before 2.30 p.m. on day 19 of the trial, Tuesday, 16 October.

Outside, it was cold and wet. Inside, people were looking pale and tired. Two hours earlier, before the lunch break, Nigel had apparently been proved to be lying.

I had to forget about that as I faced my questioners and accusers.

Mr Shindler began the examination-in-chief by getting me to confirm my full name, where I was born and when, and that my father was a naval commander now retired. Shindler said I had been to school in Scotland and though I was 'not brilliant academically' I had won a Duke of Edinburgh's award. He mentioned my VSO spell in Pakistan, that I joined the Police in 1964, that I was in H Division, that I went to the Drug Squad in 1970 and at that time lived in a section house.

Then we got onto details about pocketbooks, duty books and diaries, the rivalry between DS Philips and Nobby in the office, the non-authorization of my car until 14 June 1971, although I'd been authorized to drive official and nondescript police vehicles from 11 May 1967. The point was made that there were only *two* official cars for C 1, that these two served 150 men, and that two weeks' notice of their use was usually required. Shindler established for the jury that an application for me to drive my car had been made on 11 February 1970 and never been dealt with.

'It is still in abeyance,' he said with some scorn, and went on to emphasize that I'd never claimed any mileage expenses.

'It was an unconventional job you had to do,' he said and removing his gold-rimmed glasses stared at the jury.

He was always doing significant things like that – rather like the Judge. In fact everything he did and said in court was done in a very deliberate way. He carefully smoothed papers, grasped his gown, slowly took off and put on his glasses, swayed, leaned, and moved around an arc of 180 degrees, staring at individuals near him as if he were mind-reading. You could almost hear his mind at work. What he said was firmly delivered and full of meaning, and he didn't much relax his style when dealing with me.

To start with I was very nervous, and if I wasn't careful my hands shook. I kept my eyes fixed on Shindler for the first ten minutes or so, and only gradually stole glances at the faces looking my way and at the clock. The last person I looked at was the Judge. Fortunately there were a lot of exhibits to check through and keep me and my hands occupied, though I couldn't help the occasional fidget. My answers I kept very brief, mostly 'Yes, sir' and 'That's correct'. When I was required to say something more I had to think before replying.

It was funny seeing things I had written years ago in duty books and diaries – such piffling things, nothing more than times and dates and places.

What a palaver it all was, and fairly boring for everyone else. Twice the Judge yawned. My guard dozed in a chair behind me. A banging from somewhere in the Old Bailey became a bit distracting.

Shindler went into great detail about the events of 27 and 28 July 1970 – when Nick and I went into the Salahs' flat in The Meads, Stoke Poges. He quoted what had been said about this visit at the Salah trial, to forestall Mr Leary from making any nasty allegations, and he established how the mix-up in dates had arisen.

Nick was coughing again in the dock. I looked at him and thought that if it hadn't been for him, none of this would have happened. If he hadn't got those dates wrong, the 27th and 28th, we would never have been cross-questioned about our diaries at the Salah trial, and then investigated and charged.

I told the court how after leaving the Salahs' flat Nick and I had driven in his car out of the drive, turned right in the road and then left at a junction. Further on we passed a car with Nobby and Nigel in it. We parked beyond them and Nobby came up to have a few words with Nick. We stayed in the car, discussed what happened at the flat, and then Nick wrote it down in a Stationery Office book which he had in the car. I read over what he had written and countersigned it. This happened about ten minutes after we left the Salahs' flat.

Neither of us noticed then that Nick put as the date – not 28 July as it should have been – but 27 July, an error that was repeated in our statements.

What bloody havoc, I thought again, had resulted from that simple, stupid error, and brought us all together in Court 8.

At five past four the court adjourned, and as I was still in the witness-box as it were, my father thought he shouldn't discuss the day's business with me.

He said when we met: 'Well done, son. You're doing fine. Keep it up.'

He looked very tired – he looked his age, with his thin white hair sticking out behind him. He seemed old and anxious. I was sorry for him, but for once I felt more assured than he.

After a cup of coffee in a café opposite the courts with Nobby, Nick and Morag, I went home in the rain, poured myself a gin and tonic and read the papers. This time I didn't have a headache. After watching the TV news I put Tchaikovsky's *Piano Concerto No. 1* on the record-player and looked at a copy of *Private Eye*. But I couldn't help thinking about the trial and especially what happened that morning.

I couldn't give a damn, I told myself. But I remembered my father's sad eyes – and Nigel's.

The inconceivable had happened. Nigel had lost the war.

Mrs Oddy had made her appearance in court about ten to twelve that morning. For over an hour before this the debate about whether or not she should be admitted had swung between Leary, the Judge and Mr Parker, with an impassioned plea from Mr Shields in between. The jury remained outside the court.

The Judge queried the prosecution's plea to re-open their case after it had been closed. He doubted whether the new witness could be classed as in rebuttal and determined it was not *ex improviso*. He wondered whether he should permit the Crown to add to their existing evidence supporting evidence of this nature and how he should exercise his discretion in the matter.

Did the interests of justice require Mrs Oddy to be called? That was the nub, said the Judge – conceding that 'an unfortunate omission has been made in not obtaining this woman's statement earlier on'.

Extracts from red-backed volumes of cases heard in Criminal Appeal Courts were quoted by both Parker and Leary. It was a very civil argument, and though I thought Mr Parker should have won, he lost.

The Judge decided the evidence of Mrs Oddy should be admitted.

The jury were summoned and Mrs Oddy entered the box.

She was a small weary lady in a smart red coat, and didn't look old enough to have a son aged twenty-five. She was plainly nervous, and somewhat embarrassed, though she managed a sweet smile now and then. Everything she said and the way she said it helped to nail Nigel's skin to the door. She contradicted what he had said, namely, that he had never seen her, and that he had left her house and the customs men before 9 a.m.

Leary was practically purring as he asked his questions.

Mrs Oddy stated that on 19 January 1971 she took her little girl to school. They left the house at 8.55. She didn't want the child to hang about, as it was cold, and they had to be there by nine o'clock. The walk took ten minutes.

She came straight home, let herself in and found three men in her hall – two she discovered later were customs men, the other was a policeman. She was very startled. Her eldest son came out of the dining-room and one of the customs men said:

'See your mother in.' She was taken into her sitting-room by the same customs man and questioned for about twenty minutes about a parcel from abroad that had been sent to her student daughter who was no longer living there. The daughter's bedroom and another room were searched by the customs men. This took about half an hour or more. The policeman was in the house all this time.

'Do you remember when he left?' asked Leary.

'I saw him going,' said Mrs Oddy, and added . . . 'It was probably about 11 or 11.30. I can't really say.'

'You've no doubt he left *after* the search?'

'Yes.'

She was then questioned about a note she'd received on 19 May 1973. It asked her to phone Chris Murray about a matter of some importance. She did. An appointment was made. Chris called on her at her home and made notes. She didn't want to get involved, but she agreed to come outside with her husband to identify someone, who might or might not be a customs man. A Volkswagen was parked not far away in a lay-by. They approached the car.

'This gentleman got out of the car,' said Mrs Oddy, 'and the solicitor asked me if we'd met.'

Leary paused before inquiring softly: 'And what did you say?'

'Well, I turned round and said: "Yes, it was the police officer." '

'Did you recognize him?'

'Yes.'

Leary sat down at ten past twelve, triumphant.

Mr Parker, in cross-examining Mrs Oddy and Chris, who was called to the box after making a statement, unavoidably completed the dismal picture.

Mrs Oddy told Parker that the police officer on the morning of the 19th came in to the room where she was before he left and said something to her other son, Peter. He might have said 'Good-bye'. Parker couldn't shake her, and could only suggest she had never seen a police officer that day or even three men. She said she had.

Chris, after taking the New Testament in the wrong hand for the oath, related how after the note was sent, the interview was arranged for 7 September. Nigel picked Chris up and drove him to Surbiton. While Nigel remained in the car, Chris went into the house. He asked Mrs Oddy if she had any objection to seeing a man in a car outside. They went into the street and approached the car in a lay-by and Chris asked Nigel to get out. Mrs Oddy said something that Chris didn't hear and then said: 'That's the policeman.' She had said to him, to the best of his recollection: 'That's the police officer who was there that day.'

I learned later that this visit had been Nigel's idea and that it was carried out on his insistence. Chris had gone along to make sure no legal errors were made.

The result was that the jury would now very likely have some doubts about what Nigel had said in the box. And they would now have doubts about Nobby – who had in effect said that Nigel was with *him* on the morning of the 19th at Mapledene Road.

They would now have doubts about us all.

So it was that when I went into the witness-box myself after lunch, on the heels of Mrs Oddy and Chris, I couldn't have felt in a weaker and more vulnerable position. Fortunately it was Shindler who asked the questions that afternoon.

The next morning – Wednesday, 17 October – I still didn't feel too happy. Mrs Oddy's evidence had been a great surprise to me, really devastating. I wondered why neither the DPP nor the prosecution had thought to call her in the first place. Yet in spite of what she had said I found it difficult to believe that Nigel could or would have lied in such a flagrant way.

Wednesday was a fine day weatherwise – at least what I saw of it – crisp, sunny and cold. Autumn leaves were scattered on pavements. People were wearing coats. At Earls Court, Princess Anne opened the Motor Show.

At the Old Bailey I was in the witness-box all day, day 20, during which Shindler took me through Exhibit 111, the prosecution's schedule (or list) of observations which we had made during the Salah investigation. He and I went through it day by day.

But before going through it in detail, I, via Shindler, made some other general observations.

I said that we normally arrived at the Yard at about 8.30

a.m., but that, as was standard practice, we booked ourselves in officially at 9 a.m. I said I used the other officers' cars as well as my own, or was driven by them, and had made no claim for expenses as I was not authorized to do so. I said that observations made in my spare time weren't shown in duty book or diary. I agreed that the duty book was only a record of expectation not fact – an officer often doing something other than what he'd set out to do. As regards the instruction to make false entries, I said I didn't think it necessary to check this out with Kelaher as what Nobby told me was good enough for me. I said that regulations were broken throughout my service.

I was asked when the instruction to make false entries was given. In the first or second week of November 1970, I replied. DS Pilcher had got some information that Janet was boasting about the fact that she could find out if the customs or Drug Squad were interested in the Salahs. DS Pilcher, I said, went and saw Kelaher, who was on night duty at the time, and told him about Janet's claim. Kelaher said: 'You will have to tell the others to play the inquiry down' – to cut down entries in duty books and diaries and if necessary to make false entries. We were to keep this to ourselves, and use our own discretion in carrying out the instruction. DS Pilcher saw us the following day in the DI's office, I said, and told us what Kelaher had said. Lilley, I said, brought up the question of expenses, and Pilcher said we would have to make them correspond with our diary entries.

We then got down to dates, going from 15 December 1970 to 20 March 1971 when the Salahs were arrested.

Shindler asked me why I had mentioned the Salahs by name on 22 December.

I answered that DI Bailey had told me to show more detail in my diary. When I told DS Pilcher about this he said I should play along with Bailey and show a little more detail to keep him happy.

Shindler covered the three dates referred to in the three counts against me of perjury in great detail – the dates being 5, 18 and 22 January 1971. Basically my evidence about them amounted to an elaboration and confirmation of my evidence given at the Salah trial.

This took the whole of the afternoon, from 2 p.m. to 4 p.m.

The Judge wrote down nearly all my replies, as he had with Nick, Nobby and Nigel, and naturally this doubled the length of the proceedings. There was none of the quickfire question and answer that you see in films. This was useful to me, in that I had time to think before and after I said anything – as had Shindler.

At the end of the afternoon session Mr Shindler asked me if I had deliberately committed perjury at the Salah trial.

'No, sir,' I said.

'And the evidence you gave then and have given today is the truth?'

'Most certainly, sir,' I said.

The next day, Thursday, wasn't so pleasant, in more ways than one. I was dreading the prospect of being cross-examined by Leary, and depressed by what had happened the night before at Wembley Stadium. England had played yet another diabolical game and been knocked out of the World Cup by Poland. It seemed a bad omen.

Day 21 in fact began with some questions from Mr Martin, Kelaher's QC. He asked me about 22 January, with reference to Kelaher, and about Kelaher's wife, who remembered meeting me briefly when, on that day, her husband dropped in with me for a quick coffee. I hadn't seen her before, or since.

Mr Leary's attack, to start with, concentrated on that fatal evening – 28 July 1970. He read the duty book entries referring to that occasion of Nobby, Nigel and Nick, which showed them to have been at Stoke Poges. He then got me to read *my* duty book entry, which said: '4 p.m. to BH. Back later. Here, twelve night, off duty.' There was no mention of me being at Stoke Poges with the others. Mr Leary wanted to know why.

I told him that I had asked Nigel to book me out. 'He obviously forgot,' I said.

'Hmm?' murmured Mr Leary. 'Are you saying that Lilley *omitted* to show the fact that you had been to Slough?'

'I am,' I said.

'Why didn't you show in the duty book where you had been when you discovered the omission?'

'I possibly didn't see it on my return.'

'Didn't see it? But you signed yourself off duty at midnight. Surely you noticed that your previous whereabouts hadn't been recorded?'

'I did not.'

'Didn't you read the previous entry?'

'I may have. I may have looked at it, or I may not have bothered to look at it. I can't remember.'

To my mind, none of this kind of questioning was really relevant to the four counts against me. It made me fidgety and annoyed – especially as my presence at Stoke Poges on 28 July had never been disputed at the Salah trial, not even by the Salahs. But now Leary was trying to suggest that I hadn't been there.

He produced the occurrence book, which showed the names of officers leaving the Metropolitan district. 'Pilcher, Prichard and Lilley' was shown – again no mention of me.

'Your name is not included in the occurrence book,' said Leary painedly. 'Your duty book has not a single entry referring to any observation out there. Can you assist us as to how this comes about?'

I wasn't going to reply to his insinuations, or help him in any way.

I said: 'I've explained how it came about.'

He persisted for a while, then changed tack, seeming to accept the fact that I had been at Stoke Poges, and next implied, as Lloyd-Eley had originally done, that Nick's and my version of what happened when we went to The Meads was a lie.

He asked his questions in a slow, supercilious, suffering way, with his eye on the jury – as if I were mentally deficient. Sometimes he firmed up a bit, saying: 'Come, come!' Or he queried my answers with a long-drawn-out and puzzled 'Hmm?'

'Are you saying that the whole family were so unsuspicious that the first mention of drugs came from a member of the Salah family?'

'Yes.'

'And that John Salah then made an admission implicating everyone there?'

'Yes.'

'Has anything like this happened before or since?'

'Not exactly like that.'

He wanted to know why Nick and I, posing as buyers, hadn't gone in with a flash-roll (a wad of pound notes) to tempt the Salahs. I explained that such a roll wasn't easily got hold of and it hadn't been thought necessary. Then Leary said I'd had one at Muswell Hill. But I wasn't going to explain the difference between the two jobs.

Twice he asked me the reason for my being at The Meads.

'What was the point of you being there?'

'I was there to learn,' I answered.

'Hmm?' said Mr Leary.

Occasionally he flung in direct questions about my veracity.

'Are you telling us the truth about what happened?'

'I most certainly am!' I replied very strongly.

He went on and on about The Meads, going around in small circles.

'Are you seriously suggesting,' he said, 'that this family, seemingly involved in drugs, were disposed to talk in these terms in front of total strangers?'

'Yes.'

'The whole family joined in?'

'Yes.'

'Are you saying that *nobody* wanted to know who you were?'

'Yes.'

'Mr Acworth,' said Leary reprovingly, 'it doesn't happen like that in real life.'

'This is what happened,' I answered.

He then queried the length of time Nick and I were there. In our statements we had said we left at 7.50 p.m. – a clerical error. Nick's notebook had said 7.30.

'Were you there for half an hour, or fifty minutes, or an hour?' asked Mr Leary.

I thought this detail was so petty that I was quite short with him in reply. And when he asked me: 'Were you the time-keeper?' I had to turn to him and say: 'Is that a serious question?'

'It *is* a serious question,' said Mr Leary calmly.

'No,' I answered.

His conclusion at the end of this section of his interrogation about The Meads visit was, I thought, a long way from Counts 1, 6 and 9.

He said: 'So your statement begins with an error, as to date, and ends with an error as to time.'

It was indisputable. I said nothing.

'Is that not true?'

'Yes,' I said.

'What happened to you the rest of the evening?'

'I did these notes with Prichard. I think we went for a drink.'

Mr Leary pursued the matter. He wanted to know what I was doing while Nobby, according to his diary, had a meal – until 7.45 p.m. He wanted to know why we hung around until, apparently, 9.30 p.m.

'We were still trying to find where the first load was,' I answered.

'How did you do that?'

'By making inquiries.'

'What sort of inquiries?'

'Asking people.'

'What sort of people?'

He went on and on. He managed to imply I was lying or looney, pursuing inquiries in the neighbourhood about garages, wandering around ringing doorbells late at night, asking about the Salahs in pubs and nearby houses.

'What *do* you mean?' inquired Mr Leary.

I didn't know. It was all a mess. I really hadn't a clue what happened after Nick and I left The Meads, apart from the fact that we met up with Nobby and Nigel. As I couldn't remember, but was forced into trying to remember – into giving inadequate answers and making up some replies – it seemed as if I was lying, as if I couldn't remember because I hadn't been there at all.

After over an hour of this concentrated niggling and needling over one date – a date six months removed from the dates of the charges – he moved on to the next date in the schedule of observations, 6 August. He clearly intended to cross-examine me in the same way about every single date on which the Salahs were observed.

I glanced at the clock below the gallery – it was midday. It seemed an eternity already. I determined to be as short in my answers as possible, to give nothing away, to say 'I can't remember' and qualify every 'yes' or 'no' with a 'may' or 'might'.

Laboriously, Leary picked away at the few August observations. Having exhausted their possibilities, he moved on.

Between 17 August and 7 October there was a seven-week gap. He wanted to know why. I said I didn't know.

On 7, 9, 11 and 20 October, Nobby, Nigel or Nick went to Stoke Poges. On the 22nd I went to Heathrow Airport.

'What were you doing at London Airport?'

'I really don't know.'

'Look at your diary.'

I had to read out the relevant entry. Still I didn't know.

Then we came to Kelaher's instruction about making false entries. I repeated what everyone already knew, what I'd told Shindler.

Leary queried the fact that I couldn't remember much about such an unusual instruction, that we took it so casually and carried it out so carelessly.

Then the Judge intervened. He had said very little, letting Leary get on with it. But as we were really getting nowhere very slowly, he felt, I suppose, he should clear some matters up. But by this time I was feeling so bolshy and somewhat confused myself, my natural fear of him made me somewhat incoherent.

Mr Justice Melford Stevenson said weightily in his gravel voice: 'Here was this rather dramatic statement that a spy was leaking information to the Salahs. Wasn't this discussed?'

He looked at me and waited. They all looked at me.

'I think we may have said that something should be done.'

He grunted. 'Was anything done to try to discover the source of the leak?'

'I don't specifically know.'

'Did you hear of anybody *else* trying to do anything about it?'

'I don't think I did.'

He paused and said very slowly: 'Did it not occur to you that if it was so important as to excuse the making of false entries in the books you were required to keep, it called for very active measures to discover the source of this leak, if it existed at all?'

My mind had gone blank. I had lost him half way.

'This thing has happened so many times before,' I said.

He repeated the question. 'Did it not occur to you that it was very important to discover *how* it happened, that it called for very active measures?'

'That is why we kept entries down,' I said.

'Well,' said the Judge with a look at the jury, 'if you don't want to answer the question, leave it. . . .'

I couldn't look at anyone – I felt such a bloody fool. But every time the Judge spoke to me, my head emptied, and I couldn't think straight, if at all.

Leary took advantage of my discomfiture and developed the Judge's theme. Then he ended the morning session with a further allegation that I was lying – which I denied.

During the lunch break, down in the cells, the others tried to jolly me up. They told me to relax and cooperate more. But it was useless. As soon as I was back in the witness-box, with everyone looking at me, with my father listening, I became uneasy and embarrassed and my mind just wouldn't work beyond assisting me to make denials of any of Leary's suggestions.

I must have looked and sounded rather guilty. Being aware of this only made it worse.

The two hours passed like a two-hour operation under a local anaesthetic. I kept glancing at the clock, willing the hands to move on and let me escape, while Mr Leary persevered with his probing questions, taking me from 15 December, through Count 1, to 12 January. I answered much as before.

There was another ghastly moment when the Judge interposed again.

Leary had asked whether I had made any false entries before 22 December.

'I don't know,' I replied. 'I may have done.'

'Can you identify any false entries you made?' asked the Judge.

'At this time,' I said, 'three years later, it would be very difficult.'

'Do you think you are likely to have forgotten?' asked the Judge.

'I may have,' I said.

The Judge grunted. Leary took over.

'Have you not thought about it?' he inquired, smoothly.

'I have thought about it,' I said. 'And I'm not sure.'

'How does that come about?' asked Leary.

'I can't remember.'

'Have you tried?' he persisted.

'Those occasions I can,' I said. 'But there were other occasions when I can't.'

When the court adjourned on Thursday at 4 p.m., I had been in the box for ten and a half hours, since Tuesday afternoon. I knew I wasn't being as good under cross-examination as I might have been. But it all seemed beyond my control. In the box I was someone else.

The Judge had another go on Friday morning. It was day 22.

Mr Leary had started off by reading out extracts of the observations on the Salahs on 13, 14 and 15 January. He asked me again why I had written down the name Salah in my diary, if we feared a security risk.

'I thought there was no harm in putting it down occasionally.'

'You're not facing the matter,' the Judge interrupted. 'It is perfectly obvious that any avoidable mention of the name Salahs was to be desired. Wasn't it?'

'I was told to show more detail,' I said, as I'd said before.

The Judge grimaced. 'Why,' he said heavily, 'do you repeatedly mention the name Salah in your diary, and do not disguise it? Could you not have used a code name?'

'I was told to show more detail in my diary,' I repeated.

The Judge sighed and looked about at the court.

'Well, there it is,' he said. 'If you think that's an answer. . . .'

It was a bad and really bumpy trip. It seemed it would never end. My answers became more and more repetitive, as I became more fearful that somehow I would say something stupid or would break down in some way. Afterwards it seemed like a bad dream – only parts of which I remembered.

Mr Leary said, referring to the 13th: 'You're being loyal to Sergeant Pilcher and providing him with an alibi.'

'I am not. I am not,' I said.

He said: 'Two days running you mention in your diary "re Salah"!'

'I was told to show more detail in my diary,' I said.

He said later: 'I am failing to understand this. Mr Acworth, can you help me?'

'What do you want to know, sir?' I asked.

He said, referring to my diary entries about the Muswell Hill affair: 'You put no names, therefore this story that Mr Bailey told you to put more names is nonsense.'

'It is not, sir,' I said.

He said, referring to 18 January: 'John Salah wasn't doing anything. It was evidentially worthless. How were you and DC Prichard making a note that couldn't possibly have any evidential significance?'

'I thought it did, sir,' I said.

He said: 'Mr Acworth, you are not understanding my question.'

'Well, you've been going from one date to the other,' I said. 'I'm not sure which date you're on.'

He said later: 'You were at Scotland Yard, and Sergeant Gillie was phoning in, asking you to book him in at 9 a.m.'

'I was not at the Yard at nine o'clock,' I said.

He said a few minutes later: 'You're taking up too much time making suppositions.'

I heard Shindler laugh. Even the Judge smiled.

The exchanges between Leary and myself became more abrupt.

He said, still on the 18th: 'Your diary shows you were on duty at the same time as Lilley – "11.30 to BH, DP, BD." '

'I copied his diary,' I said.

'Did you tell him?'

'No.'

'What?'

'No.'

'I don't follow,' said Mr Leary.

He said, referring to the 18th: 'Why didn't you show "On duty 8.30, to Kier Park"?'

'I decided not to.'

'Why didn't you show a truthful entry?'

'Because of the instructions.'

'What instructions?'

'The instructions.'

'Why was this day chosen?'

'I just decided.'

'Just a whim. Is that it?'

'Yes.'

'Was it also a whim by Prichard?'

'I don't know.'

He said and got me to agree that Nobby's, Nick's and Morag's duty book entries for the 18th showed, in their own handwriting, that they had been on duty from 9.30 a.m. to 11 a.m. at the Yard and had then gone to Inner London Quarter Sessions.

I disagreed with part of what they showed.

'I was down at Kier Park,' I said. 'And so was Sergeant Prichard.'

'That's not what your diary says,' said Leary. 'Nor your duty book. Nor Prichard's duty book. Nor his diary.'

Eventually we arrived back where we had started.

Mr Leary read from my diary. ' "Then to Ascot, Kier Park, and Slough re Salah family inquiry." Four unnecessary words, which spell out to any spy the object of the observation.'

The Judge joined in. 'You were making a curious rent in the curtain of security and one that was easy to avoid.'

'I was doing what Mr Bailey told me to do,' I said.

The Judge waved a white hand in dismissal and was silent.

'What was that?' asked Mr Leary.

'I was trying to keep the entries down.'

'But what a *ridiculous* answer that is!' said Mr Leary. 'I'm never going to get anywhere on this.'

'Who are you asking?' inquired the Judge.

The jury and some of the others laughed.

But Mr Leary was right. From then on he seemed to resign himself to a more direct cross-examination on the remaining dates. The rest of January, the Salah arrests and the Salah trial were covered in record time.

By 3.30 p.m. it was all over. I had given evidence for over fourteen hours.

I stepped down from the witness-box, and rejoined the others in the dock. They smiled at me encouragingly – except for Morag, whose turn it now was to be grilled. But she wasn't questioned that day.

In what was left of the afternoon, Mr Shindler called three witnesses, character witnesses, who would speak on my behalf. They were my uncle Charles, Rear Admiral Wheen; Mr John Ridgers, a former chairman of Lloyd's Insurance; and my father.

It was almost as bad as the cross-examination, hearing them, one after the other, being questioned by Shindler and singing my praises. I crouched forward on my chair with my head down, so that no one could see my reactions, and stared at the floor of the dock.

They said things in the court they'd never have said to my face – very nice things – and I blushed to hear them. Uncle Charles said he'd played cricket with me and that my integrity had never been in question. He said he was sure I would never take a course I considered to be morally wrong. Mr Ridgers said I was a very honest and decent fellow. My father, trying to control his voice, said that I was loyal and brave as a lion. He said that I had been brought up to serve the community.

I might have been moved by all this if I hadn't been so shattered already. But when I dared to look up again, with my face flushed and my hands sweating, I saw that the two women in the Press box were in tears, and that some of the jury's looks had softened.

As the usher declaimed the formula for the court's adjournment while everyone stood, I glanced across the court at the Judge.

He was looking at me, and to my surprise his expression seemed almost sad.

That evening, in the Guide Club, where Sam had once had tea with my mother and father long ago, my parents held a small party for their Ruby Anniversary. About forty people were invited and I was there as well, without Sam as she was minding some children. My father went around everyone telling them how well I had done in the box. That saddened me a little, as I didn't think I had in fact given a very good account of myself – although I had been myself, for want of anything better. I felt I had let him down. But I'd let him down before and now I no longer felt ashamed. I felt glad really. The ordeal was over. The trial was ending. The verdict was now in the hands of the gods – or rather, in the hands of twelve citizens given the chance to be gods. I hoped they would still be human.

PART SEVEN

Thus can the demi-god Authority
Make us pay down for our offence by weight;
The words of heaven – on whom it will, it will;
On whom it will not, so; yet still 'tis just.

25

'Members of the jury, what you do is vital,' said Mr Shindler, now very near the end of his closing speech. He had been speaking all morning and part of the afternoon, and as he also had a cold, his voice was lower than usual. Occasionally it broke or faded away. The effort required to control his voice as well as his thoughts gave him the jury's undivided and sympathetic attention, which was matched by the personal attention he gave to them, and to my defence.

'Don't make it a memory,' he said very earnestly, swaying and holding his lapels, 'that will haunt your conscience for the rest of your life. You, and you alone, are the judges of fact. I leave young Adam Acworth in your care with confidence. I am sure your verdict will be one of not guilty on all counts of this indictment.'

He bowed, gathering his gown about him and slumped onto his chair below me. The jury transferred their attention from him to me for a moment, and everyone stirred and resettled themselves in the court.

It was Wednesday, 7 November, exactly a year since the summonses were issued. We were now in the eighth week of the trial, which was now in its thirty-third day. The night before, Sir Robert Mark had delivered the Dimbleby lecture on TV, attacking the way policemen in general were regarded and treated by the public and the legal profession.

A fortnight had passed since my appearance in the witness-box, on day 22. In the interim Morag had given evidence for two days and Kelaher for over three. He had also produced several witnesses, ex-policemen, including former Assistant Commissioner Peter Brodie. On two days the court hadn't assembled, as on one day a juryman had had to go to a funeral, and on the other day another juryman had been moving house. On Wednesday, 31 October, half-way through the seventh week, Mr Leary had started his closing speech for the prosecution. He spoke for over two days. Then it was the turn of the individual QCs for the defence – Mr Howard, Mr Shields, Mr Parker, and then Mr Shindler, who was followed by Miss Southworth and Mr Martin.

Kelaher, as a witness, was superb. He dealt with Leary and the Judge very firmly, refusing to be provoked or rattled in any way.

He told the court how he brought an American agent to work in Britain 'off his own bat', as he believed the American methods of drug detection were more efficient and far-reaching than ours. He said he wrote reports to this effect, but they were not accepted.

He was asked by the Judge if he had sought authority to recruit the agent and he replied: 'I did not get any authority from anybody, or ask for it.'

By 1970, he said, there were two Detective Chief Superintendents with the Drug Squad who didn't play any active role in it, and he regarded himself as the senior officer running the squad.

The prime purpose of diaries, he said, was to record and justify expenses.

Then he detailed his involvement in and knowledge of the Salah investigation, and told the court about a conversation he had with Nobby in the Tank (the bar at the Yard) on the subject of security.

He said: 'I weighed up various possibilities in my mind, and my first reaction was to say that *no* entries should be made in diaries or duty books. . . . Realizing that entries had previously been shown with the places involved and the name Salah, and knowing that Pakistanis are cunning and devious people, I tried to put myself in their shoes and see how they would act, and considered that as active criminals they wouldn't be all that surprised at a casual interest in themselves and would expect it. So I told Sergeant Pilcher that under these circumstances the entries in duty books and diaries should be kept to a minimum. . . . This was to be left to the discretion of the officers.'

He said a lot more about the investigation, and was, I thought, rather convincing.

Mr Leary, in cross-examination, raised the matter of Kelaher's whereabouts on 5 March, when Basil Sands was arrested. His diary showed he'd been at Earls Court between 5 p.m. and 7.30 p.m., when he returned to the Yard and met Nigel before proceeding to Mayfair. Kelaher then entered the Adam public house, purchased a meal for himself and an informant and returned to Earls Court.

'I'd left my raincoat there,' he said.

When he returned, as he said, 'some people had been arrested.'

He went to Kensington police station with the customs officers – 'I assisted them,' he said – and was there until 1 a.m.

Leary couldn't really take it any further and didn't manage overall to score many points. The Judge and Kelaher had the occasional battle of stares. Kelaher won one of them on a laugh when, on being asked by the Judge about Niaz Ali's occupation, he was able to reply: 'He's reported to be a high court judge.'

Eventually, after Leary climaxed his cross-examination with the allegation that Kelaher 'had joined with the others to weave a web of deceit to the Salah court,' he stood down at 12.30 on Tuesday, 30 October.

One of the police witnesses who appeared in Kelaher's defence in the afternoon was the balding Mr Peter Brodie, former Assistant Commissioner. He gave evidence on subpoena.

He said that Kelaher played things 'close to his chest' and took decisions with a tendency to interpret regulations without telling his seniors everything.

Mr Martin said: 'Supposing Mr Kelaher decided to go to his superior, Commander Virgo, to seek permission for the men under him to make misleading entries in their books. Would he have got an answer quickly?'

Brodie answered: 'Virgo would say it was a very high policy

matter, which should have been referred up to me, and that would have taken time.'

The Judge intervened. 'What was your view about a person in Kelaher's position taking it on himself without reference to a superior officer to give that sort of instruction?'

Brodie replied: 'My view is that it was a misguided decision on his part.'

He went on to say that if such a matter had come to his notice he would have ordered an inquiry into the source of the suspected leak. And he added that in all his years in the police force he had not come across applications by police officers to make false or misleading entries in their books in order to mask an operation.

Another of Kelaher's witnesses, DS Johns of the Flying Squad, recalled an occasion concerning a jewellery theft when Kelaher had told his men, in the presence of the late DCS Butler, that no one was to show anything in the duty book or diaries about that particular job.

'Mr Butler also told us not to,' said DS Johns.

By the end of that afternoon, on day 28 of the trial, all the evidence, for and against, had been given.

On day 29, Mr Leary began his closing speech, concluding that the false entries Nick, Nobby, Nigel, Morag and I had said we'd made on 5, 13, 18, 19, 22 January, and 26 February 1971, weren't false at all and that we'd lied at the Salah trial about the observations we'd made on those dates.

He said that more lies had been told to this court than at the Salah trial.

He said of Kelaher: 'He knew what was going on. He must have done. . . . If he had been an honest man he would have gone to the court on the Monday morning and said that sadly some of his officers had been lying.'

The fact that he didn't, said Leary, 'smacks of the deepest loyalty. But it condemns him on the count of conspiracy.'

On days 31, 32, 33 and 34, the six defending QCs made their closing speeches.

Mr Shindler, speaking for me, accused the Crown of building their case on theory and speculation. He said they were clutching at straws . . . scraping the barrel.

Of me he said: 'He *kept* those observations. And not a single independent witness has been called to say he didn't! All you've got,' he told the jury, 'are the admittedly inaccurate entries in the diary.'

'It is right,' said Shindler, his voice breaking, 'that you should consider what kind of man he is. . . . All his superior officers have spoken in the highest terms about him. . . .'

He then gave examples and quoted my character witnesses.

He told the jury: 'This does not of course mean that he could *not* have committed certain offences. But you make up your own minds about him. Nowhere was he ever broken. You will remember that my learned friend, Mr Leary, said: "I'm not going to get anywhere, am I?" The reason is, members of the jury, that young Acworth may have been telling the truth!'

Mr Justice Melford Stevenson was late in court on the morning of Friday, 9 November. It was day 35, the last day of the eighth week of the trial, the day on which the Judge would begin his summing-up.

Everyone had assembled in good time outside Court 8, and at 10.30 a.m. we were all in our usual places – defendants, jury, QCs, solicitors, policemen, court officials, members of the Press and of the public. Some of the QCs, like Mr Shindler, were absent as they were now involved in other cases in other courts. So was Mr Leary. Their juniors represented them. My father was as always seated at one side of the court, under the public gallery, where for the first time sat my mother and Sam. People chatted animatedly. It was almost like a speech-day, with everyone waiting in expectation for the head's review of the school's achievements. Only the prizes were different.

Three knocks on the door through which the Judge would enter the court announced his arrival.

We all stood as he walked in carrying his black cap and white gloves. His shoulders were hunched and he walked in a slow, deliberate fashion, like an old man – which of course he was. When he reached his seat he nodded three times – at the prosecution, the defence, and at his clerk, who all bowed in return. He sat and we all did likewise.

He began his speech with a long explanation of perjury and conspiracy and the way they might be proved. He dwelt at length on the burden of proof and the difficulties of the jury's task. Then he asked the jury, in his weighty, well-modulated voice, to consider us.

'You are not dealing here with simple peasants of poor instruction,' he remarked. 'The defendants you see before you are intelligent, highly-trained police officers, each of whom has long experience of the law and legal proceedings. You are dealing here with people quite accustomed to giving evidence themselves. They are not strangers to the witness-box, and are capable of assessing any evidence they choose to give. . . . They are all people of good character. . . . They are people who have earned great credit in their job. If you do find yourselves in any doubt in a question of fact, you are entitled to take that character into consideration in assessing their credibility.'

He talked about 'the police pocketbook' – seemingly unperturbed by the noise of two drills at work for some minutes somewhere in the building and the sound of something being hammered.

'The majority of criminal cases,' he said, 'depend on the evidence of police officers. . . . No human being is capable of retaining in his memory and producing in the witness-box every detail of every case, every word that every witness says. That is why he is expected to make notes in his pocketbook. It becomes a vital component in the machinery of justice. If that pocketbook is distorted or fabricated, the whole machinery goes wrong.'

He described the writing of diaries as 'a rather rigid, carefully factual system of book-keeping,' and read out to the jury the rules and regulations regarding these books, which were, he said, 'part of the machinery which is designed to safeguard criminal justice'.

This system, he said, had been variously attacked by the defence as 'creaking', 'antiquated', 'bureaucratic', and 'rusty'.

'The plethora of adjectives applied to the general regulations,' he continued, 'is wholly unjustified,' and he stressed how important this case was to the general public, as it was to each of the defendants.

'The Crown do not have to prove a motive,' he said. 'We need not speculate what motives may or may not have existed in the minds of these defendants. It may have been an excess of zeal. It may have sprung from a deep conviction that the Salah family were guilty – and I do not hesitate to say it is fairly obvious that they were. The temptation to gild the lily may be – I do not say it is – a temptation that is very difficult to resist. . . . The Crown say here that the first five of the defendants as charged permitted themselves to lie on oath and fabricate records which were designed to support their lies in the witness-box. . . . You may say: "Oh well, the Salahs were as guilty as unpleasant drug-traffickers could be, so what does it matter? Maybe the officers did add bits and pieces to the evidence, but it isn't worth worrying about. If they did gild the lily – who is to blame them?" '

That attitude, said the Judge, would be wholly wrong.

He said we were aware that the intercept could not be quoted in evidence, and that we might have been tempted to embellish our evidence with information gained from a knowledge of what the intercept contained.

He prefaced his remarks about the instruction to make false entries by quoting Mr Brodie, who had said it should go up to an Assistant Commissioner before any question of making false entries was contemplated. The Judge reminded the jury that in Mr Brodie's thirty-seven and a half years of experience as a police officer he had never come across an application to make false entries.

'That leads me,' said the Judge, 'to one, perhaps, of the most important facts in this case . . . the conversation in the Tank.'

He said: 'The Crown say that the instruction can't have been given. It was invented, say the Crown, in order to excuse the practice of making false entries and then lying about them afterwards in the witness-box. What would you think of a bank manager who instructed his subordinates to make false entries in a ledger?'

I didn't think that the analogy was a true one. Curiously, as I heard later, two of the jurymen did in fact work in banks.

The Judge, peering through his glasses, read out the notes he had made of Nobby's evidence about how the order to make false entries had been given. This done, he lowered his papers and regarded the jury.

'That, say the Crown, is quite incredible. No officer of Pilcher's standing could possibly have made such an arrangement.

. . . You may find yourself in the position in which you may say that no such thing could possibly have happened.'

He went on: 'It's not the first time that the excuse of security has been used to cover a multitude of irregularities. And that's what the Crown say in this case. . . . Perhaps even more remarkable, say the Crown – I'm deliberately putting the Crown's case – is the fact that the entries show that the instruction was immediately flouted, because the entries continue to show the Salahs by name.'

He remarked on the 'abstention of taking precautions', and that not the slightest attempt was apparently made to trace how the security leak was occurring.

'It was an invention, say the Crown, to cover up the extreme laxity in the way this case was made up.'

We had, he said, an 'expectation that the Salah ladies were on their way to Dover.' When their cargo failed to arrive in this country, he said – or rather he said that the Crown said – 'use was made of the intercept to build up by false records of observation things that were never seen at all.'

'Use your common sense about this,' the Judge told the jury. 'If, having thought about this, you think that the story about the conversation in the Tank is simply untrue – well then, you will know how to treat the matter.'

He told them: 'The telex, you may think, is the source from which all the other channels of observation sprang.'

He said: 'The informant is a very convenient myth built up by Sergeant Pilcher – the Crown say.'

He talked about 'the entry into The Meads', adding 'if it took place', and said: 'Never mind whether Acworth was there or not.'

The story of what happened there, he said, must be invented – as the prosecution claimed.

He then moved on to the Salah trial.

'Never forget the defendants say the evidence we gave is true, that observations it records are observations we in fact made.'

He told the jury: 'Ask yourselves: Can that statement that all our evidence at the Salah trial was true – can it be right? Can it be right against the background against which the evidence was given?'

Again the Judge quoted Mr Brodie, who although doing his best (said the Judge) to help Kelaher as far as he properly could, had used the adjective 'misguided' to describe the giving of an instruction to make false entries.

'One of the qualities of the CID is loyalty to each other,' declared the Judge.

Commenting again on the instruction, he said that there was a most remarkable silence about it – if it was ever given – and he talked about 'the extraordinary manœuvre of false entries'. He wondered why codewords weren't used.

He concluded this part of his summing-up with: 'So much for the approach to this case, which the prosecution invite you to adopt.'

Then he dealt specifically with each of the twelve counts.

He hardly ever mentioned the defence as such. He practically never said: 'The defence say . . .' The case for the defence was re-presented to the jury by the Judge's reading of extracts from his notes on what we'd said in the witness-box. He did this quite often. He would paraphrase what the prosecution said and contrast it with our actual and sometimes unpolished words of explanation.

He dealt with Counts 1 and 2 – relating to 5 January and involving me and Morag – in this way, and finished with them just before the hour-long adjournment for lunch.

'Well, there it is,' he said. 'I don't think I can help you any more, members of the jury, on those two counts.'

After lunch, he dealt in about half an hour with the detail of Counts 3 and 4, against Nick and Nobby. Counts 5 and 6, against Nick and me, were covered in ten minutes. Counts 7 and 8, against Nobby and Nigel, again took half an hour. Count 9, against me alone, he went through in ten minutes, and ended by saying that this count was 'the least important of the counts in this case'.

What he said about Counts 10 and 11, against Nobby and Nigel, rather passed me by, as I was all of a sudden in a state of some excitement. I was wondering whether what the Judge had said about Count 9 meant that he was suggesting that the jury should find me 'Not guilty' on that one. He had, I thought, given them a fairly clear direction on Count 9, and my mind buzzed with speculation about the other counts against me. I didn't think I was being over-optimistic, but on reflection it seemed to me that my other two counts of perjury hadn't been made so much of by the Judge. He had concentrated more on the counts involving Nobby, Nick and Nigel. I wondered for the first time for ages if I would actually be acquitted.

Then the Judge began to deal with Count 12, the conspiracy charge, which involved us all, and from the remarks he made it now seemed to me that we should *all* go down on that one. It was the only count against Kelaher. And if *he* was found guilty on Count 12, there would very likely be no exceptions for the rest of us, not even for Morag. We would all go down together.

For the last half hour of the afternoon session the Judge dwelt on the seriousness and complexity of the conspiracy charge. Most of his remarks concerned Kelaher.

'I am very anxious,' the Judge told the jury, 'that you should have in your minds the evidence which Kelaher gave.'

'I think the prosecution suggest,' he said, 'that here is Kelaher presented with an empire in which he could do what he liked and get away with anything.'

The Judge then read out a great chunk of his notes about what Kelaher had said in the witness-box with hardly any comment, unless it was to say what the prosecution had said on a certain point.

At four o'clock the court adjourned for the day.

'So this is the way the High Court of British justice conducts its business!' my father said, quietly fuming, and added some remarks about the Judge. Then he went and chatted to my junior counsel, Mr Bryan Anns.

Everyone was milling about in the court room, discussing the Judge's speech. It was like the interval in a theatre.

Father told me later that one counsel had remarked to him that never in his whole career had he heard such an incredible summing-up.

Nobby came to me and said: 'What chance have we got? *Two* closing speeches for the prosecution! That's what we're up against.'

'There's Monday,' I suggested.

'What can he say on Monday? He's been through all the counts – all twelve. What about *our* witnesses – what's been said by others in our defence? There wasn't a flaming mention of Bassett or Hyams.'

Both of them, one a policeman and the other a barrister, had been called to speak on particular and useful points in our defence.

I made a face. I didn't know what to say.

'Looks like you're off Count 9,' said Nobby. 'Lucky sod!'

'You think so?'

'Looks like it. Can't be bad for you anyway. I'm off now. The wife and I are going out tonight. See you.'

'Be good. Bye.'

'I'm sure,' said my father as we left the court, 'if it comes to it, we may well have grounds for appeal – thanks to his ageing Lordship.'

Over the weekend he discussed the matter further with me. I had gone home to Frilford Heath, as Sam and her father had gone to visit friends who'd been evicted from a farm in Tanzania, which wasn't far from the Joubert farm. Mr Joubert was now making plans to return there. His farm was being run in his absence by his wife and second son.

On Saturday I spent a lot of time discussing my future with my brother Bill and my father, who didn't appear to think I'd be convicted. There were suggestions that I might help Bill in his threshing business. My father suggested I might help a fellow he knew who went around the country seeing to the maintenance and construction of golf-courses. I thought myself of going to Australia. It seemed the best way of starting a new life, in a new country, and of course with Sam.

Sunday was a beautiful day, crisp and sunny, with masses of fallen leaves on the ground. With my mother and father and an aunt I went to a Remembrance Day service in the village of Shippon. The vicar there was also the Chaplain for the nearby RAF base at Abingdon, and the church was full of uniformed airmen. Everyone was wearing poppies, and somehow it all seemed specially significant.

I listened with great attention to the service.

There was a reading from II Samuel: 'Saul and Jonathan were lovely and pleasant in their lives, and in their death they were not divided . . . How are the mighty fallen, and the weapons of war perished!'

We sang Psalm 121 – 'I will lift up mine eyes unto the hills from whence cometh my help.'

We sang Hymn 402 – 'He who would valiant be 'gainst all disaster . . .'

Some of the lines of the hymn I sang with much feeling, particularly 'I'll fear not what men say.'

We also sang 'Eternal Father strong to save' – the Sailor's Hymn and one of my father's favourites.

Finally, there was the blessing, which I really took to heart.

'Go forth into the world in peace,' said the vicar. 'Be of good courage; hold fast that which is good; render no man evil for evil . . . honour all men. . . .'

'Amen,' I said, quite loudly.

My mother looked at me and smiled.

I couldn't help thinking it might be the last Sunday I would be free.

26

The death of an Old Bailey judge made Mr Justice Melford Stevenson late on Monday morning. He didn't enter Court 8 until 10.55 a.m., having attended a ceremony in another court with all the other Old Bailey judges and their officials. They had assembled for a special commemorative meeting, which was always held when one of the judges died.

For an hour he addressed the jury about the conspiracy charge, repeating in a different form much of what he had said on Friday afternoon about the instruction to make false entries – 'if the instruction was given', as he said with much emphasis. The rest of us were hardly mentioned. Kelaher was again the main theme of his discourse. Again we heard what the prosecution had said and how the prosecution had put it. Again, what the six QCs who had summed up for the defence had said was all but ignored. Kelaher's answers to Mees's questionnaire were quoted in some detail. Then, as the Judge said it was vital for the jury to have the substance of what Kelaher said, another great wadge of his answers in the witness-box were read out slowly for a solid fifteen minutes. The Judge's way of reading in his best and carefully impersonal manner must in my opinion have bored the pants off everyone. It did me. The reading went on and on. It seemed to me that the Judge was being unnecessarily thorough and perhaps in part just killing time. Anyway, it was really incredible.

At last, at 11.55, he lowed his notes and stopped reading Kelaher's answers.

'What facts,' he asked, 'can we disentangle from all this? . . . It is first apparent that so far as the officers were concerned, the red flag went up when an investigation about the 27th or 28th of July arose at the Salah trial. . . . That is the time when alarm and despondency must have spread among those who knew there were astonishing discrepancies in their diaries. The observations we have had to comb through so laboriously wouldn't have mattered so much if the Salahs had been arrested at Dover. Once the arrest in Bulgaria happened, the officers had to fall back on their observations. The prosecution say that one of the features that really force one's mind to consider that a conspiracy of this sort took place is that so many documents are missing. . . .'

The Judge was probably referring to my diary that covered 28 July 1970, to one of Nobby's and one of Nick's unofficial notebooks, to possibly the odd pocketbook, and to some pages from Nobby's diary that had been substituted by him. We had so many official and unofficial books that it was difficult to keep tabs on them all. And sometimes they got mislaid.

'The prosecution say,' said the Judge, having gone on a bit more, 'that all these matters point conclusively to a plan. . . . They emphasize the concealment from any superior of this astonishing step relating to security.'

It's amazing what a well-placed and well-pronounced adjective can do, I thought. If what we did wasn't 'astonishing' it was 'remarkable'.

The Judge continued. 'Looking at this as a whole,' he told the jury, 'you really can't escape the inference that there was the kind of conspiracy the prosecution suggest.'

He spoke for some more minutes. Then all at once he was making his concluding remarks, about 'this terribly important case', and began to thank the jury for the attention they'd given throughout the trial – which was now in its ninth week and in its thirty-sixth day.

At this point he was interrupted by two of the junior counsel who wished to remind the court, and the Judge, that certain points for the defence hadn't been mentioned. The points were quickly made.

Then, instead of sending the jury out to consider their verdicts straight away, the Judge did what he had indicated on Friday that he would do – he sent them home. The idea was to bring them and everyone else back again on Tuesday morning so that the jury could have a full day for their deliberations.

The court was adjourned half an hour before the usual end of a morning session.

In the long, bare and fairly functional hall outside Court 8 and the other three courts on the second floor, workmen were removing the boards, spars and polythene from the windows. As usual after an adjournment, people came together in the hall in little low-voiced groups to discuss the morning's or the afternoon's events – solicitors, QCs, defendants, relatives and friends. By now we were on first-name terms, which was an unusual situation for defendants and their counsel, and as my father now knew many on the side of the defence he exchanged words with quite a few of them. I mostly listened.

The talk, when it passed from being critical of the Judge's summing-up, was now about mitigation – whether, if the unlikely happened and I was sentenced, further character witnesses might be brought in to speak for me, and whether my QC should make a speech in mitigation. This would be done, if at all, after the jury had returned their verdicts and before the Judge passed sentence.

It was felt that as three character witnesses had already extolled my virtues, it would be laying it on too thick to have any more. Besides, it was doubted whether such a move would have any positive influence on the Judge, perhaps the reverse.

My second counsel, Bryan Anns – Mr Shindler was occupied in another court – said he was one hundred per cent certain that I would get off. Nothing concrete had been proved against me on the perjury charges, he said, and as I was the most junior officer of the six defendants, my part in the alleged conspiracy, if it could be proved, was the least. He was very encouraging and had indeed been very sympathetic to my situation over the last two months. He was a small earnest man, smaller even than Shindler, and had given me a lot of good advice.

I was however somewhat of a spectator in most of this, and was glad to leave with Sam when everything that needed to be said appeared to have been said. My mother – she and Sam had been in the public gallery again – went off with my father to lunch with friends, and Sam and I went to the Magpie and Stump, opposite the Old Bailey, for a quick half and a sandwich.

The pub was crowded. Nobby, Nick and Morag were there and several of Morag's friends, policewomen in their civvies, all looking like social welfare ladies or schoolteachers. One or other or several of them had kept her company at lunch throughout the trial, and on one or two occasions (after she had given evidence) Morag had sat in the dock in the afternoon in a dreamy haze of gin and tonic. The strain of the trial was particularly hard on a gentle girl like her. However, when Sam and I left the pub, Morag and her mates, aided by Nick – Nobby had gone home – were being as merry as they could in the circumstances.

Though Morag, of the six of us, really had the least to worry about, she in fact worried the most. Accordingly, the rest of us were always very cheerful and reassuring about our prospects when she was around, and joined together in tearing strips off the prosecution and the prosecuting policemen, especially Faulkner whom Morag disliked the most. Shindler, in his closing speech, had referred obliquely to Mees's associates when he talked of 'those little ferrets who tried to build up their case on speculation'. Since when, Morag would refer to Faulkner in her strongest Lanarkshire accent as – 'That ferret!'

Sam and I went Christmas shopping as she wanted to buy presents to take back home to Africa. For she had now booked a one-way flight to Nairobi that left on the following Sunday. Her father was returning to Tanzania on the Wednesday, as he'd heard that several farms near his had been taken over by the government. Sam felt she ought to be with her family, especially at Christmas, as it might not be long before they themselves were evicted from their farm – with twelve hours' notice and without being able to take anything with them other than what they could carry.

I didn't think about her leaving England. At the moment I

wasn't thinking ahead at all. It was very pleasant that Monday afternoon just walking about in and out of shops and buying things. In the evening we had dinner with friends of hers in Blackheath, and she spent the night with me in my flat.

I held her as if it were our last night together, sadly aware that my next night might be spent in prison in Wormwood Scrubs.

As it happened it *was* spent in jail – in Brixton Prison.

All those concerned in the trial *Regina* v. *Kelaher and Others* reassembled at 10.30 a.m. on Tuesday, 13 November, in Court 8 as usual. But this time so did a lot of other QCs and solicitors. Once Mr Justice Melford Stevenson had sent our jury out he was going to preside briefly over another hearing in which the singer Janie Jones was the main defendant. So the court that morning looked rather like Waterloo Station in the rush-hour.

Before the Judge could address himself to our jury, Nigel's junior counsel, Mr Graham Boal, stood up and made some points about what two witnesses had said in Nigel's favour, which the Judge had omitted to draw to the jury's attention.

Mr Melford Stevenson thanked the junior counsel for his remarks and turning to the jury addressed them in a jovial, even lighthearted fashion to begin with. Then, becoming more serious, he said: 'All I want to do is to remind you that some eight weeks ago you took an oath to return verdicts in accordance with the evidence.'

Another defending counsel, Mr Julian Bevan, then spoke up, wishing, with all respect, to remind the court that Nobby had offered to pay his fare home from Australia.

The Judge thanked the counsel and readdressed the jury, again in a heavily humorous, almost benevolent, way.

He said: 'If the worst comes to the worst, overnight accommodation has been arranged for you.' He added in a more solemn manner: 'It only remains for you to choose a foreman, or indeed a forewoman, from one of your number. You may now go out and consider your verdicts.'

One of the ushers stepped forward, and holding a New Testament in his right hand, faced the Judge and the Clerk of the Court.

'Silence!' said the usher to the restless and noisy court, and rattled through his oath of obligation. 'I swear by Almighty God that I will well and truly keep this jury in some convenient and private place, with such accommodation as the court shall direct. I will not suffer any person to speak to them, neither will I speak to them myself touching the trial had here this day, without leave of the court, unless it be to ask them if they are agreed on their verdict.'

The Judge smiled at the jury and nodded.

The Clerk of the Court – our lovely lady had been replaced by a stern and middle-aged male – said as the jury rose to their feet: 'Will you follow the usher?'

This they did, going one by one out by the Judge's door.

We six in the dock watched them go until all twelve had disappeared. Then the court was adjourned once more and we were taken below.

While the jury deliberated in their specially secluded room at the top of the building, we five male defendants played cards in our detention room on the ground floor. Morag was in a cell on her own in the women's section with female warders for company.

We played most of the morning and all the afternoon. After several rounds of Chase-the-Lady, paying five pence a head to the winner, we moved on to Nine-Card-Brag, at two pence a win. We smoked a lot of cigarettes, drank a lot of coffee and didn't eat much of our picnic lunch. We had several visitors, legal ones, as friends and relatives weren't allowed near us – nor were their bits of home comfort like flasks of tea and half bottles of scotch. But Sam was able to get a friendly policeman to give us six Crunchie bars she had bought.

Chris Murray came down to see us twice. Bryan Anns called to tell me his thoughts about an appeal, should the worst happen. We also discussed the possibility of there having to be a re-trial in the event of the jury not reaching a majority decision on all twelve counts.

This seemed quite likely after the Judge's summing-up. The jury must have had the impression that they should find us *all* guilty of conspiracy, and *some* of us guilty of perjury. But if they found any of us guilty of perjury it seemed, even to us, that the conspiracy count must also go against us. It depended how far they had followed, or wanted to follow, the Judge's line of thought. On the other hand, we were all fairly convinced that he had overplayed his hand and that they would probably have to work things out for themselves.

We heard that the previous night the Judge had attended the Lord Mayor's Banquet. We wondered if this had something to do with his decision to send the jury out on Tuesday morning rather than before lunch on Monday when he'd virtually finished his summing-up. If he had hoped to avoid putting them in a hotel on Monday night and imagined they'd reach a decision on Tuesday, he was wrong. In the event he didn't even wait all day on Tuesday for a decision or even all night, as he was quite entitled to do.

After five o'clock he sent a messenger to the jury to inquire how they were getting along. Apparently they had come to no decision whatsoever. So at 5.25 p.m. the court was recalled.

From the dock we watched the jury emerge from the Judge's door and take their seats. Their faces were sombre, their expressions set. They anwered their names brusquely as the Clerk read them out from a list. After the customary loud treble knock on the door the Judge made his entrance.

Knowing the jury's undecided state, he told them that transport had been provided to take them to a hotel where they would stay overnight. They were not to discuss the case, either with each other or with anyone else. They could resume their deliberations together in court the following morning.

The Judge genially wished them goodnight.

A male and a female usher were then sworn in, promising 'not to suffer any person to speak to them', and they and the jury left the court. Their destination was Berners Hotel near Oxford Circus, as I discovered later.

I looked up at Sam and my mother in the gallery as the court stood for the Judge's departure. None of us in the dock would go home that evening. We would also be put in a safe place overnight. As expected, and as with any other defendant in this situation, we would spend the night under lock and key.

Morag was taken to Holloway; we five to Brixton Prison.

In the basement of the Old Bailey we were searched, 'frisked', by prison warders who masked their feelings by being ultra-brisk and efficient. Everything we were wearing was itemized and described, down to the make of my wrist-watch and the colour of my socks. My address-book, wallet, keys, cash, comb and a two-bladed pen-knife I always carried were taken off me, itemized and put in a large brown envelope. It was a procedure I had witnessed many times before when arrested persons were charged with their offences. Now it was happening to me, and to the others, including Morag who had as usual been taken to the separate women's section.

I signed the formal acknowledgement of the removal of my belongings in the place indicated, but not in the place I had always signed before.

Then I was returned to the cell where the five of us were kept, locked in, until transport arrived to take us to our accommodation for the night.

It was not until about 7.30 p.m. that we were released from the cell – only to be handcuffed to each other.

The feel of the handcuff around my right wrist, the sound of it locking, put my heart in my boots.

No one was joking now. I was handcuffed to Vic, Nobby to Nick, and Nigel's hands, crossed in front of him, were handcuffed together.

Why some exception couldn't have been made in our case, I don't know. But there we were, five innocent-until-proved-guilty policemen, prisoners of the system.

We were taken out to a small mini-bus with barred windows, attended by two prison warders, and were driven first to Holloway prison in North London, where some papers about the Janie Jones case were handed in, before journeying south through the West End of London, across the River, and down through Stockwell and Clapham to Brixton.

The great gates of the prison opened to let us in and the mini-bus, after winding past faceless walls and barred windows, came to a halt in a featureless well-lit courtyard.

We entered reception and were given practically the full treatment of any convicted person entering the prison.

First our particulars were taken down in detail: married or single, date of birth, next-of-kin, religion, physical description, colour of clothes, even of our underwear. We were spared having to have a bath and being given prison clothes. But after being weighed we saw a doctor, who wanted to know if we had any broken limbs or suffered from any ailments. We weren't actually examined.

The warders and the doctor were really rather sympathetic to our situation. One of the warders, who made out our entry forms, was an ex-PC. He said: 'I don't like having to do this to you, mate. I want you to know that.' The doctor, who was called Bligh, asked if there was anything he could do.

'Get me out of this hole,' I said. 'Or give me the key to the front door.'

By now we were more ourselves again. Being where we were had a certain novelty and interest – and it was, after all, only for a night.

We had had a laugh as soon as we arrived, for when a warder came to unlock our handcuffs, Nick said: 'Do you want mine?' and was able to hand his half to the man, having slipped out of it already in the mini-bus. He had very supple and narrow hands.

The whole procedure of being received took some time. We were dealt with one by one and taken from room to room. The warders all had great bunches of keys, and a sound of clanking keys and the banging of doors accompanied us wherever we went. In between we waited on uncomfortable slatted seats and at one point were offered some supper. Nobby, Nigel and Vic refused. But Nick and I, being somewhat peckish, accepted the offer. Prisoners in denims brought our supper to us on a tray – a slice of dried bread, spaghetti rings and corned beef, and a cup of tea, all cold as hell.

'Serve you right,' said Nobby.

'I'll never trust these holiday brochures again,' said Nick.

The last part of the receiving procedure was the issue to each of us of a pillow-case, two sheets, a toothbrush, toothpaste, a comb, a towel, and a clean shirt. Thus equipped we were escorted to our quarters.

Our cells were in the segregation unit. They had orange doors, with wire-meshed panels above for ventilation and the usual peep-holes.

The warder said good night as I went inside my cell and banged and locked the door behind me.

It was about 9.30 p.m.

The cell had a high barred window, grey and cream walls and a single ceiling light. It smelled of disinfectant and urine. On a low and narrow bed was a mattress, three blankets and a pillow. On a table were some books and a knife, fork, spoon and a mug. There was also a chair, and in a corner was a wash-stand, on which were a jug and a basin, a small mirror, soap, shaving-soap, and a nailbrush. Underneath was a plastic chamber-pot with a cover and some bog-roll.

I made up my bed, looked at the books, which were war and adventure stories, and after lights-out at 10 p.m. listened for a while to the obscene shouts and yells of men in the main prison. They were calling to each other like animals, in a wild variety of accents, Irish, Scottish and West Indian, and the noise was worse than any jungle at night.

Then I went to sleep.

I woke at 5 a.m. and lay in the cold cell thinking dully and disjointedly about many things and not liking most of my thoughts.

At 7 a.m. a warder let me out to fetch some hot water in my jug and to go to the loo. I was then locked up in my cell again and washed myself in the basin. I didn't shave, although a razor was provided. Soon afterwards breakfast was brought on a trolley and a prisoner dished out to me a plate of bacon and fried bread, a slice of bread and margarine, and a cup of tea.

At 8 a.m. we were taken out of our cells and back to the reception area to the sound of a terrible yelling from another cell.

'One of our coloured brothers doesn't want to go to court,' remarked a warder.

We handed back all the gear we'd been given and were again handcuffed together – Nobby to Vic, me to Nigel, and Nick to a prison officer. Then we were led outside, where Nick gave another demonstration of how to slip out of a handcuff.

'Excuse me,' he said to the guard to whom he'd been chained. 'I think you've forgotten me.' And he gave the guard his handcuff.

After a short delay a green single-decker arrived. It was already full of prison officers. We boarded it and were driven out of Brixton Prison about 9 a.m.

It was a very fine morning, cold and mistily sunny. I looked at what I could see of the streets and the citizens going to work through the barred windows of the bus, but everything I saw seemed very far away. It was like looking at old pictures of another time and place. I felt very remote from everything, even from the others, and only really aware of my immediate surroundings: the hard seat on which I sat, the walls of the vehicle, and the dark uniforms of the guards.

As we crossed the River by Waterloo Bridge I noticed that all the buildings were flying flags.

It was Wednesday, 14 November, day 38 of the trial. It was also the birthday of Prince Charles, who was twenty-five.

It was also a very special day for another reason. Later that morning the wedding would take place in Westminster Abbey of Captain Mark Phillips and Princess Anne.

27

'Have you reached a verdict on any count?' asked the Clerk of the Court.

'We have,' said the jury's foreman.

'Are you all agreed?'

'We are.'

'Do you find Adam Buzzard Acworth guilty or not guilty on Count 9 of perjury?'

'Not guilty.'

I looked up, my heart pounding, first at the jury, then at the Judge. I was conscious again of where I was and of who I was, and of the other five defendants in the dock. Everyone seemed to be looking at me. I looked down again. Morag reached out and patted my arm.

The Judge was speaking. He said: 'I can now accept a majority decision on any of the remaining counts, if not less than ten of you are agreed. . . . Will you try again, please?'

It was 10.40 a.m., and a kind of miracle had happened. The jury had returned to the court at the usual time that morning, and easily, almost casually it seemed, decided that I was not guilty on Count 9. It was the only decision they had made so far and they had been allowed to declare it – to get it out of the way. Now they were retiring to go over again the other eleven counts.

I watched them leave the courtroom with a silly smile on my face.

The Judge stood – we all stood – and as the six of us turned to leave the dock I looked back up at the gallery. Sam was there. She raised her hand and smiled. She was sitting with two friends of Nick Prichard. My mother was now downstairs in the court with my father. We had tried to persuade her not to come today, but she had insisted on being present when the verdict was announced. I glanced down at her and saw she was holding onto my father's arm and looking as worried as ever. My father nodded at me in approval.

Down in the detention room the five of us began playing cards again. But as our money which had been taken off us hadn't been returned, no one made a profit this time. We sat around the scarred table with our jackets off, surrounding ourselves with a fug of cigarette smoke. Only Vic had shaved in Brixton. The rest of us hadn't bothered and were beginning to look like gangsters. Nobby hadn't eaten since lunch the previous day and was looking rather drawn and shadowed about the eyes. Nigel, who had never really recovered his composure after the shock of Mrs Oddy's evidence, hadn't slept very well in his cell and was pale and quiet. Nick was paler than ever, and his walrus moustache was drooping and lank. We were still however fairly cheerful and talkative.

The other four thought that the decision of 'Not guilty' on Count 9 was a step in the right direction. They were pleased for me, but naturally more concerned with the counts that involved them. Besides, there were still three other charges levelled against me, and we all expected the conspiracy charge to be the big decider. I was however secretly pleased to think that I'd got off Count 9, as it was the only charge against me alleging that I'd not just made but fabricated a false entry. It also seemed to indicate to all of us that the jury were divided on the other eleven counts and strengthened the idea that there might have to be a retrial. Not that we wanted this particularly – not after two months of being at the Old Bailey. But retrials on average were known to favour defendants. So generally we were feeling more optimistic, and got rid of our various frustrations by angry and aggrieved criticisms of our night in Brixton jail.

By lunchtime the jury were still out and had given no sign of returning. By this time games of Chase-the-Lady and Nine-Card-Brag had become somewhat uninteresting and we were all feeling and showing the strain.

Also by then, a mile or two away, Princess Anne had become Mrs Phillips.

'Some of the jury must be mad at missing the wedding on TV,' said Nick, stubbing out his hundredth cigarette.

'At this rate they'll miss the repeats,' murmured Nigel.

'No, they won't,' said Nobby. 'They'll bring in a verdict this afternoon and be home in time for tea.'

'So will we,' said Vic.

We nodded and agreed with this, though I suspect that each of us rather doubted him. Some of us wouldn't be home for many months – let alone for tea that day.

For once, no one had brought any lunch, and any food in the way of sandwiches or such wasn't allowed to be sent down to us by relatives or friends. Mrs Prichard, who had come to court that morning, was able to get a friendly policeman to deliver a thermos of coffee. But that was all that got through the blockade.

Nick shared it out, and he, Vic and I accepted what the Old Bailey canteen had to offer as lunch. It wasn't that bad: hamburgers, potatoes, carrots and onion sauce, followed by blancmange. Nobby and Nigel refused to eat anything. By now, Nobby hadn't eaten for twenty-four hours.

We were going over again the possibilities of a retrial and had got out the cards for another game of Nine-Card-Brag when we were suddenly summoned to go upstairs. It was just after 2.15 p.m. The court were reassembling.

Mr Justice Melford Stevenson consulted a scrap of paper in his hands. He gave a long sniff, breathing in through his nose, then looked up and gazed at the crowded assembly. The Press box and the gallery were filled. Every available seat was taken, and standing under the gallery were assorted CID and uniformed policemen, friends and pressmen who couldn't find anywhere to sit.

I couldn't find anywhere to look, except at my hands clasped between my knees. I fiddled with the family signet ring on my little finger.

The Judge said: 'I have received a note, which says that the jury have arrived at a further three unanimous verdicts and seven majority verdicts. But they are apparently having some difficulty over Count 12, the conspiracy charge. There's some trouble about the interpretation of the last two lines of the indictment as written. That's right, isn't it?'

The foreman of the jury nodded.

'Well, let's see. I thought it was clear enough. But perhaps we ought to have a look at it.'

He read out the two relevant lines – 'namely, that false entries had been made in the said diaries for security reasons on the instructions of Victor Richard Kelaher and Norman Clemence Pilcher', and he said that: 'So far as instructions by Pilcher and Kelaher are concerned, they agreed about the conversation in the Tank. That is common between them. The prosecution's case is that no such instructions were given . . . I don't think that the last two lines complicate the situation. . . . The real question is whether there was a conspiracy.'

He said not much more before sending the jury out again. Again the court was adjourned. It was now 2.40 p.m.

I didn't look at the gallery. I didn't look at anyone. Everyone was looking at the six of us as we left the dock, wondering which of the three unanimous decisions and the seven majority ones applied to us individually – and what the decision would be on the twelfth count.

Down below, Nobby and Nick were worriedly trying to work out on which three counts the jury had come to their unanimous verdict. We were all sitting around the table. Vic made the occasional comment. He was looking anxious for the first time in weeks. He and the other two seemed to think that if any of us had been found guilty of perjury there shouldn't have been a doubt about the conspiracy charge. Nigel said hardly anything. The previous day he had written letters to his wife and some friends – he seemed to have accepted the fact that things could go badly for him. Now the others seemed to have the same opinion about themselves. Nick, who was a freemason, still had a spark of optimism. But of the five of us, I was now perhaps the most confident.

I didn't really know why. But, as I had already been found 'Not guilty' on one count, I reckoned hopefully that of the three latest unanimous verdicts two might apply to me and the other to Morag. It didn't seem unreasonable.

Then I remembered the conspiracy charge and all that the Judge had said about it in his summing-up. My hopes faded and I became as anxious and despondent as the others.

We couldn't settle anywhere. It was very tense. We chain-smoked, and fiddled about. Every now and then someone would go on a talking jag, trying to sort out something logical and reassuring from the turmoil in his head.

'Won't be long now,' said Nobby.

At that moment a prison warder opened the door.

'You're wanted upstairs again,' he said. 'Let's have you.'

We stopped what we were doing and stood or sat where we were for a dreadful moment. We looked at each other as if we were seeing each other for the last time.

'Oh, God,' said Nigel.

'It'll be all right,' said Vic.

'Soon be over,' said Nobby. 'Come on. Let's face the music.'

'Good luck,' said Nick to no one in particular.

'All the breast,' I murmured, and thought of Sam and my parents. I had to put on a brave show for them and take what was coming like a man, as I'd been taught. I lifted my chin and straightened my back and went upstairs with the others.

But when I got into the dock my resolve weakened and I flopped in my chair feeling very tired and weak at the knees. I leant forward and examined my hands. To my right, Nigel shifted his chair to the back of the dock and sat looking at the ceiling. On my left, Morag sat as she had always done, upright and holding onto her handbag in her lap.

I was aware that the court was even more crowded. Faces were turned in our direction, wondering, tense and expectant. People spoke in whispers, if they spoke at all.

The jury returned. I stole a quick glance at them. They looked more relaxed, now that their work was ended, their decisions all made. The Judge came straight in after them. We all stood. The Judge sat down and we followed suit – except for the Clerk of the Court who remained on his feet.

Nothing I could say or do now would cancel anything I had said or done before. Nothing would stop what was going to happen from taking place. I never felt so helpless and hopeless in my life.

'Mr foreman,' said the Clerk of the Court.

The foreman of the jury, a very large and red-faced man called Cyril Barnes, laboured to his feet.

'Mr foreman, have you reached verdicts on all counts on which at least ten of you are agreed?'

'We have,' said Cyril Barnes.

The Clerk then told the court that the jury, who had retired to consider their verdicts the previous day, had deliberated for a total of eleven hours and fifty-five minutes.

Then he turned again to Mr Barnes.

'Will you answer as I put the charges to you?'

In the dock I bowed my head to my knees, resting my forehead on my hands. I could hardly breathe – I kept having to swallow. My mind was saying over and over: 'Oh, please, not me.'

I heard the Clerk speak.

'Do you find Adam Buzzard Acworth guilty or not guilty on Count 1?'

'Not guilty.'

'Do you find Morag McGibbon guilty or not guilty on Count 2?'

'Not guilty.'

'Do you find George Nicholas Prichard guilty or not guilty on Count 3?'

'Guilty. By a majority of ten to two.'

'Do you find Norman Clemence Pilcher guilty or not guilty on Count 4?'

'Guilty. By a majority of ten to two.'

'Do you find George Nicholas Prichard guilty or not guilty on Count 5?'

'Not guilty.'

'Do you find Adam Buzzard Acworth guilty or not guilty on Count 6?'

'Not guilty.'

'Do you find Norman Clemence Pilcher guilty or not guilty on Count 7?'

'Guilty. By a majority of eleven to one.'

'Do you find Nigel Patrick Lilley guilty or not guilty on Count 8?'

'Guilty. A majority of eleven to one.'

I was not guilty on Count 9. So were Nobby and Nigel on Counts 10 and 11.

'On Count 12, do you find the following guilty or not guilty? George Nicholas Prichard?' 'Not guilty.' 'Norman Clemence Pilcher?' 'Not guilty.' 'Nigel Patrick Lilley?' 'Not guilty.' 'Adam Buzzard Acworth?' 'Not guilty.' 'Morag McGibbon?' 'Not guilty.' 'Victor Richard Kelaher?' 'Not guilty.'

Someone in the court gave a faint scream. People exclaimed, gasped, said indistinguishable things. Someone was crying.

Slowly I raised my head.

Mr Cyril Barnes was talking. He was asking the Judge if the jury could add a rider to their verdicts. He was saying that as far as the three who'd been found guilty were concerned, the jury took the view that the offences were of a minor nature and not undertaken in any spirit of malice. 'In view of the past records of the accused,' said Mr Barnes, 'we ask you to deal with them with the utmost leniency.'

He sat down. Below me Bryan Anns was on his feet. He said something to the Judge about my being discharged. Miss Southworth spoke for Morag. Mr Martin spoke for Vic. Bryan looked up at me and smiled. I was amazed to see tears in his eyes.

'Very well,' said the Judge.

I stood up, holding onto the edge of the dock, and in a daze followed Morag and Vic and one of the guards out of the dock.

Outside the court, Morag turned to me at the top of the stairs beside the lift and I saw that her eyes were red and that the tears were running down her face.

'Congratulations, Adam,' she said in between sniffs. 'I'm so glad for you. For us.' She blew her nose. 'But . . . It's terrible . . .'

She got into the lift to go down to the women's section and gave a little wave as the door closed.

I looked at Vic, and his eyes were sad and serious. And I realized with an awful shock that no one had followed me out of the court. Half our number had been left behind.

On the other side of the green door were Nobby, Nick and Nigel, on their feet to hear the sentence of the court.

Vic and I went downstairs in silence. The guard who was with us offered his congratulations.

'Thank you,' I said.

In the hall below, the prison officers who were on duty there came up to us wanting to know what had happened. Vic told them. We were asked to go into the detention room and wait until the others came down.

'What will they get?' I asked, not looking at Vic.

'Don't know,' he said, pacing about. 'Three to four years. I'd have got seven.'

'Seven!'

'If I'd been found guilty.'

'We're *not* guilty,' I murmured.

'No,' he said. 'We're not. We're free. It's all over.'

I looked up at him. His eyes were sparkling.

'Do you know,' he said, 'it's the third time an inquiry has acquitted me? The *third* time.'

Upstairs in Court 8, as I heard later, the Judge addressed each of the convicted persons in turn before passing sentence. The three stood facing him: Nick with his head up, his eyes wide and staring; Nobby with his mouth clamped tight and his face scarlet; Nigel with his shoulders braced, his face white and his eyes bright with shame.

The Judge told Nick and Nigel that he noted their records and what the jury had said and that it was his view that they were to some extent the victims of dishonest superiors.

He sentenced each of them to eighteen months in prison, and said it was a very lenient sentence.

To Nobby he said: 'You poisoned the wells of criminal justice and set about it deliberately. What is equally bad is that you have betrayed your comrades in the Metropolitan police force, which enjoys the respect of the civilized world – what remains of it – and not the least grave aspect of what you have done is to provide material for the crooks, cranks, and do-gooders who unite to attack the police whenever opportunity occurs. You will go to prison for four years.'

Nobby opened his mouth and said in a choked voice: 'Thank you.'

When they came downstairs, Vic and I came out of the detention room to meet them. They looked sick and shattered and avoided our eyes if they could.

There wasn't much that could be said. They told us what the sentences were and managed in spite of everything to congratulate Vic and me on getting off. We huddled together briefly, shook hands, clasped each other's arms or shoulders, and all I could say was: 'I'm sorry . . . sorry . . . sorry.'

Then the prison officers led Nobby, Nick and Nigel away from us and put them in the detention room which Vic and I had just vacated. The door was closed on them, and the key was turned in the lock.

We two were taken down another flight of stairs to the basement where our property that had been removed the day before was handed back. There were further congratulations from the warders and discussions about the sentences and the Judge. Then a senior officer arrived with our release papers and told us we could go.

We thanked the people who were there and they wished us all the best. We walked along a corridor to our freedom. A warder opened a door for us and let us out into another corridor beneath the Old Bailey courtrooms.

Sam was waiting beside the door for me. She flung her arms around me and burst into tears.

Somehow I never cried at all that day, although I might have many times. I was stunned by the turn of events, and went through the rest of that afternoon and evening in a dream.

My mother and father met me on the stairs leading up to Court 8. Sam stood aside as my mother embraced me, her head close to mine.

'Thank God, thank God,' she whispered and kissed my cheek. 'Oh, thank God it's finished.'

My father gripped my arm. 'Well done, son,' he said. 'I knew you'd make it.'

Sam started to cry again. My mother put her arms around her.

My father, who still had the light of battle in his eyes, was already formulating plans to take what to him were unsatisfactory aspects of the trial to higher levels. He also thought that Nobby and the other two must appeal. My mother said very little, but she had lost her wan expression.

We were all rather subdued, for our thoughts were still in part with Nobby, Nick and Nigel. Nick's little wife, Rita, who had been in court, was very upset and had to be looked after. The other two wives had stayed away as instructed. But friends of Nobby and Nigel were there, sorrowfully waiting in the halls for news of what was happening below and whether they could see the prisoners. I went and spoke to them, and people in turn came to me, saying how glad they were for me and sad about the others.

I spoke to many people in the Old Bailey before I left – among them Shindler, Bryan Anns, Chris Murray and some of the other QCs, barristers and solicitors. The two women in the Press box and some members of the Press also exchanged a few words, as did one of the ushers and a couple of the court policemen who had been on duty throughout the trial. Of the prosecuting policemen, Clarkson, Faulkner and Sullivan didn't come near me. Gittus I approached myself and asked him about the disciplinary charges still pending against me. He said he would probably see me about them in a week or so. It seemed likely that until they had been dealt with, I wouldn't be able to resign from the police. At one point Mees came up to me and said that if anyone had had to get off, he had wanted it to be me. Thinking of the three who hadn't got off, I felt I wanted to hit him.

I wondered if Sir Robert Mark would be satisfied with the jury's verdict.

Eventually it was time to go.

About the time that Nobby, Nick and Nigel were taken in handcuffs to prison in Wormwood Scrubs, I stood in the gathering dusk of the street outside the Old Bailey, saying good-bye to my mother and father. They were going home to Frilford Heath.

Sam and I picked up my car and we drove to Battersea in

time to collect her father and his luggage and take him to Heathrow Airport. There he got a plane to Nairobi – something that Sam would be doing on Sunday.

I bought an *Evening Standard*. On the front of it was a picture of Princess Anne and Captain Phillips and the headline – MAN AND WIFE. Inside, among all the pictures and stories about the wedding, were two small paragraphs on page 7 about me being acquitted on a count of perjury, Count 9. The other verdicts and the sentences would be in the next edition.

We drove back to London and to my flat, where Sam's brother, Christian, and one of her girlfriends called Deezy produced a bottle of champagne to celebrate my acquittal. Then we went out, just the two of us, and had dinner at Spot 3.

During the meal we went over the details of the trial. I still couldn't really believe it was all over and that I could start again. Nor did I know in fact where to start. It seemed to depend on Sam. And what she decided depended on what happened in Tanzania. My main thought was still to get away and make a fresh start in Australia. But no move could be properly made until the disciplinary charges against me – such as going outside the Metropolitan area without permission and failing to initial and date mistakes in my diary – had been made and heard. Then, unless I was dismissed, I would resign.

Whatever happened, I felt sure that my luck had changed and that everything would turn out now for the best.

When we returned to the flat about 11 p.m., we were in time to watch an edited repeat of the Royal Wedding on TV, on BBC 2. There was still some champagne left and we sat side by side on the sofa, sipping our drinks, and watching the splendid sights and colour of the morning's ceremony in Westminster Abbey. Then there were the scenes at Buckingham Palace, the departure of the bride and groom, a bonfire at the village of Great Somerford, the bridegroom's home, and a fire-works display at the end.

It couldn't have been more appropriate.

We didn't talk very much. The fact that we were watching a wedding made me conscious of our own situation. I was also very aware of the three who wouldn't have seen or heard anything of the wedding that day or night and were now alone in their cells in Wormwood Scrubs.

For a moment a shot of Prince Charles in the Abbey reminded me of our meeting three years ago at the time of the Salah investigation.

I wondered what *they* were doing now.

It was when the Princess and the Captain reappeared after signing the marriage register and started the long walk down the aisle to the great west door of the Abbey, with the organ playing a triumphant, magnificent cascade of music – it was then that it suddenly hit me that I was *free*.

I turned to Sam and said, raising my glass: 'To us!'

She smiled back at me and raised her glass.

'Here's to a happy ending,' she said.

I leant over and kissed her and said: 'And may there be many more!'

POSTSCRIPT

by Gordon Honeycombe

That wasn't the end of it all. Months before the trial started, about the time that Adam and the other five were publicly summonsed, suspended and committed for trial at the Old Bailey, several persons whom they had earlier arrested on drugs charges and then helped to convict appealed against their sentences and at the same time made certain serious allegations against the arresting officers. These allegations included perjury, theft, the receiving of bribes, the planting of evidence and the misappropriation of drugs. The sentences of several of those who had made the complaints were thereafter quashed on appeal, and eventually six of the complaints came to be fully investigated by the police.

These investigations, which started before the Perjury trial, continued during and after it. The six police defendants in the trial were not of course all involved in all six sets of complaints, some of which also named officers currently serving with the Drug Squad, but the six were aware throughout their trial that these investigations were being made. They were questioned by the investigating policemen before and after the trial and submitted in some cases to questionnaires as lengthy as that put to them in July 1972 by DCS Mees. Papers on each complaint were then sent to the DPP.

One by one the complaints were either dropped by the police themselves or dismissed by the DPP. But two involving Adam were still unresolved in March 1974, four months after the end of the trial.

It was now three years since the arrest of the Salahs, and by this time Adam, who had been prevented from earning a living since his suspension in November 1972 and had been forced to exist on a DC's basic pay for eighteen months, was in a very depressed state. He had passed the time, when not being questioned by fellow officers, barristers and solicitors, by helping his brother Bill on the latter's farm-estates, and when the trial was over, he refused to resign from the police force until he had been entirely cleared of *all* allegations and until the forty or so police disciplinary charges which had been levelled against him had been dropped. He wanted his good name and reputation to be fully restored before he left the police. But the continuing anxiety and uncertainties, and the absence of Sam, who had returned to her home in Tanzania soon after the trial, got him down. He was also worried by the problem of what to do with his life once he was out of the police force. He had been a policeman for nearly ten years and was qualified for nothing else.

On 13 March 1974 matters came to a head. Adam reported to the Yard at 3 p.m. and went up to the offices of A10 where he saw DCS Atkins, the senior officer who was carrying out investigations into complaints made by one of the men arrested in connection with the Rolls-Royce affair in October 1970. Before Adam was officially questioned about the details of certain observations which had taken place years before, DCS Peter Gittus entered the room and informed him that no action would be taken against him in the other case in which he was still involved. So there was now only one outstanding case in which he was concerned. In the presence of a solicitor he was asked 135 questions in all about this case, to which he made no reply. At their conclusion, he announced that he intended to emigrate to Australia at the end of May and wished both Atkins and the DPP to know this. The following morning he returned to the Yard and made out an application for annual leave. He was told it would probably not be approved. None the less he went out and reserved a seat on a charter flight to Nairobi which was leaving four days later. He then drove back to his brother's farm. In the afternoon he telephoned the Yard and was told that he could go on holiday – if he sent in his resignation. He was told that the disciplinary board which would hear the disciplinary charges against him had been fixed for 6 May, and that if he gave the required month's notice and dated his resignation 6 April, he could be out of the police force at midnight on 5 May.

He returned to London on Friday, visited the Yard, and wrote out his resignation. He then bought his plane ticket to Africa, where he would join Sam.

He flew there on the night of Sunday, 17 March. On that day, the *Sunday Telegraph* announced that DCI Victor Kelaher had been given a medical discharge from the police and would receive an ill-health pension. The paper said he was suffering from nervous strain and had been under treatment at St Thomas's Hospital for over a year. A senior consultant to the police had recommended that Kelaher should be discharged on medical grounds, and the recommendation had been accepted by Sir Robert Mark. The discharge would take effect on 10 April 1974.

Morag came up before a disciplinary board in May. She was found guilty on eight charges, reprimanded and transferred from the CID to the uniformed branch. She appealed against this, and before long she returned to the Yard as a WDC. On 13 June, Nobby, Nick and Nigel, who had been sent to Ford Open Prison, near Arundel in Sussex – a prison with a reputation for comfort and good food – appealed against their convictions and sentences. Their appeals were heard before the Lord Chief Justice, Lord Widgery, Mr Justice Park and Mr Justice Forbes, and were all dismissed. The sentences were not reduced. In relation to Nobby and Nigel the court held that the evidence of Mrs Oddy was inadmissible and that the Judge had been wrong in admitting it. But under a certain proviso of the Criminal Appeal Act 1968 they held that there was no miscarriage of justice.

Nick and Nigel served a year of their sentences, and were released on 11 November 1974. During their stay at Ford, Nick did a good deal of reading; Nigel worked in the kitchens. Nobby may be released on parole in the summer of 1975. In the meantime he is employing his time and energies in looking after the welfare of the other prisoners.

A week after this book was published on 23 September 1974, Francis Morland, who had jumped bail after the arrest of Palacios and the others concerned in the Rolls Royce affair back in October 1970, appeared in court at the Old Bailey. The prosecutor was Mr John Mathew, who had had the same task in March 1971 at the trial of Palacios. Morland, who had been paroled after serving three years of his eight-year sentence for drug-smuggling in America and then deported to Britain where he was arrested on his arrival, pleaded guilty to conspiring to import cannabis into Britain between August and October 1970. He was sent to prison for eighteen months. The wheel had again come full circle.

Adam was by this time in Australia. In March 1974, soon after he resigned from the Police and flew out to Tanzania, he and Sam became engaged. They celebrated by hitch-hiking all over Kenya, covering 1500 miles in a fortnight. They eventually returned to England on 22 May to a loving welcome from Adam's parents. At the end of June, Adam and Sam said their goodbyes and flew to Singapore, where they got on a boat bound for Western Australia. There they soon found themselves jobs and a home, and six months later, when they heard that the Joubert farm in Tanzania was about to be nationalized and taken over they decided to return there for the last time before settling permanently in Australia. This they did, and on 3 January 1975, at the Joubert Farm, Adam and Sam were married.

On the following pages are details of some Arrow books that will be of interest.

R. C. SHERRIFF

The Fortnight in September

Mr and Mrs Stevens have visited Bognor for their summer holidays every year since their honeymoon and their children – Mary, now grown-up and eager for experience, Dick, in the difficult stage between boy and manhood, and young Ernie, happiest playing cricket on the beach – love the place and its familiar attractions as much as their parents do.

All our own memories of long summer days by the sea, of sandcastles and peppermint rock and strolls along the prom are evoked in R. C. Sherriff's classic novel of English family life.

JOHN HARRIS

Covenant With Death

The Epic Novel of the 'War to end wars'

'Your generation was born to suffer in this war, but it's got to be won whoever falls, and we rely on you. Never mind your pals. Just keep going.' Fine words – and for a few hours the men believed them.

Next day they were dead, torn to pieces by the machine guns in the first few minutes of the Battle of the Somme. This is the story of those men. The story of their courage, their trust and their final betrayal.

FRANCIS KING

A Domestic Animal

'Italians are not really domestic animals . . .'
Antonio Valli, a brilliant Italian philosopher in his thirties, comes to a red-brick university for a year of research.
Handsome, impulsive and with an insatiable need for admiration and affection, Antonio captivates all who come into contact with him – including Dick Thompson, the successful middle-aged novelist in whose house he goes to live.
Soon Dick has fallen completely – and disastrously – in love with his flamboyantly heterosexual lodger. Out of this ill-fated relationship, Francis King has created a novel of bitter and painful complexities.

PAUL HENISSART

Narrow Exit

Tunis. Shortly after a shaky government welcomes Arab terrorist Salah Al Houranni, Israeli counter-intelligence pulls off one of its most spectacular *coups*: the guerrilla leader is kidnapped from under the noses of his own guards. Then Alex Gauthier, head of the Israeli espionage network in Tunisia, misses a vital transmission. And within hours *Operation Flood* is in ruins.

The three commandos and their prisoner wait on a lonely beach for a submarine that never appears – and Gauthier must risk breaking his cover to prevent their capture . . .

GORDON HONEYCOMBE

Dragon Under the Hill

To Edmund Laidlaw, the holy island of Lindisfarne is an enchanted place – beautiful, full of legend.

But it has a terrible and bloody history, as Laidlaw discovers when he takes a holiday there with his wife, Runa, and their young son Erik.

Caught between past and present, Laidlaw watches horrified and helpless as a dark remorseless power reaches out from the grave to overwhelm his son and exact a terrifying vengeance.

'An impeccable formula; a niceley-balanced mixture of detection, slow but startling revelation and ultimate horror.' *Times Literary Supplement*

JONATHAN GATHORNE-HARDY

The Rise and Fall of the British Nanny

Marvellously researched and beautifully written

W. H. Auden, Observer

The reader will find most of the relevant facts and most of the points worth making about the British nanny. Mr Gathorne-Hardy is certainly right in insisting on the importance of her role.

Richard Crossman, Sunday Times

This excellent book . . . brings into a single volume a wealth of scholarly and curious material.

Ronald Blyth, Washington Post

A treasure-house for social historians, anthropologists concerned with interacting culture patterns, and students of oral traditions.

Times Literary Supplement

RUTH RENDELL

The Face of Trespass

'A really major Detective-story writer' *Edmund Crispin, Sunday Times*

Two years ago he had been a promising young novelist. Now he survived – you could hardly call it living – in a near derelict cottage with only an unhooked telephone and his own obsessive thoughts for company.

Two years of loving Drusilla. The bored, rich, unstable girl with everything she needed – and a husband she wanted dead.

The affair was over. But the long slide towards deceit and violence was just beginning . . .